AUTUMN FIRES
by Lydia Browne

Praise for Lydia Browne's previous novels:

Wedding Bells: "This story is painted in vivid color. . . . ingenious plotting stirs the emotions." — *Rendezvous*

Heart Strings: "A lovely romance . . . a slice of sunshine. You won't want to miss it!" — *Romantic Times*

Passing Fancy: "Delightful . . . witty dialogue and teasing sensuality . . . heartwarming." — *Romantic Times*

Summer Lightning: "Filled with charming characters, a unique twist to an intriguing plot and lots of romance."

— *Affaire de* (

Titles by Lydia Browne

WEDDING BELLS
HEART STRINGS
PASSING FANCY
HONEYSUCKLE SONG
SUMMER LIGHTNING

AUTUMN FIRES

Lydia Browne

JOVE BOOKS, NEW YORK

AUTUMN FIRES

A Jove Book / published by arrangement with
the author

PRINTING HISTORY
Jove edition / August 1996

The Putnam Berkley World Wide Web site address is
http://www.berkley.com

ISBN: 0-515-11928-8

A JOVE BOOK®
Jove Books are published by The Berkley Publishing Group,
200 Madison Avenue, New York, New York 10016.
JOVE and the "J" design are trademarks
belonging to Jove Publications, Inc.

PRINTED IN THE UNITED STATES OF AMERICA

10 9 8 7 6 5 4 3 2 1

AUTUMN FIRES

One

"'Where the wicked cease from troubling,'" Bethany murmured.

From beneath the cloth dampened with eau de cologne that lay over her eyes, her sister said, "I beg your pardon?"

"Nothing, dear. Only I think we're almost there."

The big wooden sign appeared to drift slowly past the train window as the locomotive pulled the cars alongside the depot platform. The words on the white sign were deeply carved and painted a rich green. "Welcome to Cedar Groves. Pop. 725 (In Winter)."

Bethany wondered if her sister and herself were included in that number. They had been once, before going away to live with their father's sister in New York. She could only hope they'd find a place here again.

Charlene, realizing they really were at the end of their journey, threw off the queasiness that had plagued her from the start. "Oh, my, where's the basket?"

Bringing out the wickerwork basket and the small leather traveling case from under the seat, Bethany began to help her sister pack up their belongings. Somehow they'd managed to scatter things all over their two seats. A magazine had fallen to the floor, a few candy wrappers were crammed between two cushions, and the bottle of cologne rattled on the narrow windowsill. Bethany grabbed it just as the locomotive stopped, sending all the passengers rocking. Those who had stood up too soon sat down again, hard.

A spout of steam flew past the window as the locomotive

sighed, as if glad of a pause on its long journey west. The gray-haired conductor walked through the long coach, announcing the station. He paused by the Forsythe girls' seat.

"This is it, ladies," he said, hauling his big gold watch out of a tight waistcoat pocket by the chain. "Make sure you've got all your belongings together."

"Thank you, Mr. Patterson," Bethany said, smiling up at the man. "It's hard to believe we managed to pack so much into one little basket and one little bag."

He chuckled and walked on, calling, "Cedar Groves. Five-minute stop only!"

"We'd better hurry, Bethany," Charlene said. "We only have five minutes!"

"That's plenty of time. Did you eat that other orange or did it roll away?"

"No, I didn't eat it."

"I wonder . . ." Bethany said. Her stays wouldn't let her bend over to look for it, even if she wanted to. "Oh, well."

She put the last few things into the bag and closed it with a firm hand. "There, that should be . . . oh, bother. Where did that blanket come from? However did we get all this in there? It won't fit now."

"I'll carry it over my arm," Charlene said. "Can you manage the picnic basket?"

"It'll balance the case nicely. Here, you carry the fruit basket. Why that beau of yours had to . . . never mind. It was a kind thought."

And the hothouse grapes had been the only thing Charlene had been able to worry down on the trip. Bethany thanked heaven again for a stomach that never knew qualms.

Bethany hurried forward, one arm in front of her holding the basket, the other behind her carrying the case. She had to flatten herself sideways to sidle past the people stretching their legs and chatting in the aisle.

As she reached the open door to the platform, she glanced

back to see if Charlene was making progress. Her sister couldn't leave their seat for the moment, as a man blocked the aisle. Charlene hadn't the assurance to poke him sharply in the back, as Bethany would have done.

"Watch it, miss!" A man's voice, sharp with alarm, called out to her.

Bethany stopped, aghast. She'd nearly run down a girl, a highly pregnant girl, who had just entered from the platform. "Oh, I'm sorry," she said.

The girl, pretty in her face, though tired-looking and pale, gave her a trembling smile. "I'm all right."

"You'd better hurry and find a seat, Amalie."

Bethany had dimly noted the presence of a man next to the girl. Now she glanced at him, something vaguely wrong in his tone attracting the attention. Surely a man with his wife in a delicate situation wouldn't use a tone of such impatience, of such terseness.

He was very good-looking to begin with. A square, solid jaw, dark brows and hair, and deep-set eyes. His shoulders were broad in their black coat, his shirt dazzlingly white by contrast. A prosperous businessman . . . perhaps. But his cream-colored waistcoat was embroidered with ruby thread, very flashy.

Bethany said to the girl, "Go along to our seat. That's my sister back there. No one else has taken it yet."

She gave the man a *look*, as though to say, "See, *that* is the proper tone of voice."

He had transferred his scowl from his wife to Bethany. She met his stormy eyes straight on. "Come along; I'll show you," she said, pricked by that scowl.

Fortunately, the poter came by and politely asked the man blockading the aisle to move out of Charlene's way. She smiled at the porter. As Bethany came up, leading the others, she heard her sister say, "Mr. Wilson, I hoped we'd see you again. Thank you for your many attentions during this trip."

Charlene glanced at Bethany, who fished a few dollars

from her pocket. The porter smiled, his teeth a gleaming flash of white in his smooth black face.

"No, thank you, ma'am," Mr. Wilson said. "No tipping on this train. 'Gainst regulations."

Bethany said, "This is Mrs. . . . Mrs. . . ."

The girl mumbled, "Mrs. Robbins."

"Friends of yours?" the porter asked, taking the answer for granted. "How far are we to have the pleasure?"

"Pansy Spring," her husband said, still gruff.

Mr. Wilson said, "Well, set down and make yourselves comfortable. If you need anything now, you just pass me the word. We've got footstools and blankets and it won't be a lick of trouble for me to bring 'em."

Bethany took the fruit basket from Charlene. "Here. You might want an orange. The air on this train gets awfully dry." She gave the man another *look*. He might have had the common sense to realize they were going to need some food and water if they were going all the way to Pansy Spring.

The pregnant girl's eyes began to tear. "Th-thank . . ."

Mr. Wilson peered out the window. "Say, weren't you ladies going to Cedar Groves? Y'all better get off the train!"

Charlene squeaked in alarm. "It's moving! Oh, hurry!"

The train had indeed begun rolling forward, seeming to gather itself together like a snake before once more making the effort to pull its body behind it. As Bethany hurried down the aisle, her sister following closely, the rude man pushed roughly past them, reaching the platform first. "Well!" Bethany huffed.

The metal platform between the cars magnified every sound, the clanking of the couplings echoing and bouncing. Though the train still went slowly, soon it would gather speed. This was the moment to step off safely. But that man stood on the steps.

"Excuse me," Bethany said loudly. Really, if he was too frightened to . . .

He looked up and she found herself scrutinized by eyes of such a pure green that she let out a little cry at their unexpectedness. A sudden fancy told her she was looking into the eyes of some pagan deity, the spirit of the woods perhaps. But she had no patience with such nonsense.

"Come on," he said, holding out his hand.

She couldn't take his hand. Couldn't he see she had luggage?

"All right then."

He shot his arm around her waist and lifted her, dragging her across his body. For a moment she was suspended, held above the flying ground below solely by the strength of his left arm. The green eyes were much too close. They filled her world.

His firm lips twisted. Suddenly his arm tightened even more around her. He kissed her, hard. Bethany forgot her precarious position, forgot that the wind played havoc with her skirt, forgot that the whole world could see her ankles. A thrill shot through her, swift and emphatic, as though this stranger had sealed some bargain with her she couldn't recall making.

Then he set her down, so gently that she didn't even fall, though she tottered. Not from the sudden contact with the cinder-strewn sideyard, but from the feeling that his warm mouth still toyed with her own. Dropping her luggage, she pressed both hands against her lips as she watched the stranger deposit Charlene in the same manner. But he had not kissed *her*.

As she helped Charlene up, brushing off her skirts, Bethany wondered why he hadn't. After all, the sort of man who could kiss another woman while his pregnant wife sat only a few yards away would hardly care who . . .

"What a nice man," Charlene said. "I never would have been brave enough to jump off by myself."

Bethany realized Charlene hadn't seen the outrage committed upon herself. "We'd better hurry," she said. "Grandfather Ames will be wondering why we didn't get off the train."

"Wait. We have to thank him," Charlene whispered.

"Who?"

"Him!" Hiding her hand in front of her body, Charlene pointed her forefinger at the man coming up behind them.

Bethany was appalled to find her cheeks pink. All the more so, since it was with anger. But he wouldn't know that. He would think this blush was for him, a response to his outrageous actions.

The last clacking, rattling car went by, followed by the square caboose, as the stranger reached them. "You dropped your things," he said.

"Yes, I . . ." Was that her voice? That high and squeaky sound never came from her throat, unless by some mischance she'd swallowed a mouse.

"Let me." He stooped and picked up both pieces. "Did you come a long way?"

Charlene answered when the silence stretched a little too long for politeness. "Yes, all the way from New York City."

"That's quite a distance to come all by yourselves. Somebody *is* meeting you?"

"Yes," Charlene said. "Our . . ."

"Here they are!" someone called gladly.

"Oh, my goodness," Charlene said, her voice surprised. "The whole town's turned out."

Bethany reacted slowly. She'd been so busy concentrating on *not* watching this overbearing male that she hadn't looked at anything but the uneven ground. Nevertheless, she caught more than a glimpse of his strong hands and well-proportioned body. Her blush seemed to have set like a permanent stain.

Then a band began to play with a rolling drum and braying trombone. As Bethany topped the short rise that separated depot from sideyard, she saw that every face turned in their direction. Most of the people were women, many of whom she recognized.

As soon as the two sisters stood on the wooden planks of the platform, they were surrounded by smiling faces and found themselves shaking many hands. Bethany noticed, for it was hard to miss, that most of the women wore white satin sashes, crossing their bodies from right shoulder to left hip.

As she smiled and nodded, she tried to read what the hand-lettered sashes said on them. "Spiritual Clean?" she asked, but everyone was making so much noise she couldn't be answered.

Bethany found herself facing a tall, queenly woman with a bust that would do justice to a battleship. Her large hat, burgeoning with silk flowers, sat on her pompadour of richly tinted brown hair above a face that, if no longer young, was remarkably handsome. Bethany remembered her name—Mrs. Tubbs—and her position as wife of the many-times elected mayor. She remembered just in time to use the woman's name naturally when they exchanged near-miss kisses of greeting.

"This is quite a reception, Mrs. Tubbs," she said as loudly as she could.

The lady only smiled and bowed. Then she held up her hands in a commanding gesture. At once, both the band and the crowd went silent.

"Friends," Mrs. Tubbs said in a strong, carrying voice. "Today we not only rid ourselves of a menace to the continued harmony and morals of our town, but we are pleased to welcome two new members of our league. I've known them both since they were little girls and they will serve as shining beacons of glorious womanhood. My friends, let me be the first to welcome Bethany and Charlene Forsythe back to their home!"

A cheer arose from the crowd, the women wearing the sashes the most enthusiastic. Mrs. Tubbs held out her hand. As if conjured out of thin air, two sashes appeared. Bethany saw plump little Miss Ivey still stood two steps behind Mrs. Tubbs, helping out as she always had and always would.

Before Bethany could speak, she and Charlene found

themselves decorated with the sashes. Glancing down, she saw that whoever had lettered the words hadn't left quite enough room. Though it read Spiritual Cleanliness, the last two syllables were considerably smaller than the rest.

Bethany wasn't sure she wanted to join anything at the moment. She had too much else on her mind. Besides, what if there was some sort of membership fee? If her grandfather's circumstances were as dire as he had written, they might not have the money to waste.

Before she could decline with regrets, however, Mrs. Tubbs signaled the band to start up again. As the musicians raised their instruments, Bethany saw Charlene press two fingers to one of her temples in a gesture Bethany knew well. All this noise and confusion on top of a long and arduous train journey was too much for her gentle sister.

As the trombonist gave the downbeat, Bethany spoke up quickly and loudly. "My sister and I are overwhelmed by your kind reception!"

The trombonist, whom she recognized as the town schoolmaster, unchanged since her girlhood, dropped his hand. Except for one beat on the drum by the inattentive percussionist, everyone turned to listen.

Bethany smiled to fill in the awkward moment. She hadn't really any idea what else to say but everyone was waiting for her to make a speech. It seemed to be an eternity before she spoke, though she knew it was only a few seconds.

"We . . . uh . . . are looking forward eagerly to taking up our place in the community. Our one hope is to find here in Cedar Groves the kind of friendship and . . . uh . . . camaraderie impossible to find in a large city like New York. And your welcome here today gives us every hope that we will find it. Thank you."

There was a smattering of applause, led, after a moment, by Mrs. Tubbs. She gave Bethany an arch little glance and then said, "I see that city life has improved our friends out of all recognition. It wasn't so long ago that Miss Bethany bolted from the stage at the class presentation, too shy to recite."

The applause was mixed now with laughter. It all stopped abruptly, however, when a deep masculine voice said, "What do you want me to do with this stuff?"

Strange to feel that she knew that voice already better than that of any of the people standing here, people she'd known all her life. Stranger still to feel a sudden lightening of her heart.

Bethany turned to him and said what she should have said before, "Thank you for your help, Mr. . . . ?"

"I'm Brent Houston." He gave the be-sashed ladies a hard stare, then turned his green gaze to Bethany. "They'll tell you all about me. I'm the man who ruined your grandfather."

Brent hustled in through the swinging doorway of his saloon, the Golden Lady. Behind the gently curving oaken bar, Nolan the barkeep glanced up. His greeting died on his lips. Quickly he returned to polishing his beer mugs.

Though he noticed Nolan's reaction to his scowl, Brent didn't relax his frown. His boot heels made little noise over the sawdust-sprinkled floor as he headed for the stairs at the rear of the saloon. Perversely, the silence only made Brent angrier. He wanted to stomp and stamp, and make certain everybody heard it.

He didn't vary his course, though Jerry, the kid who pushed a broom around the saloon, had to shrink back against the wall to keep from being run down. As he entered his apartment, Brent slammed the door. He knew Jerry and Nolan were probably discussing the boss's bad temper. Let 'em.

The decanter of amber liquid on his sideboard invited him. His mouth twisting, Brent worked the stopper free. Then he banged the bottle back down on the tray. He didn't want a drink, though it might cut through the fog he was in.

"What a terrible day," he said aloud. He wrenched at his tie and left it hanging but he still felt strangled.

Nothing so awful had ever happened to him before. He prided himself on being a man of the world, cool-headed and clear-eyed. His business helped to inspire his picture of himself; he saw so much unrestrained emotion, so many people drowning sorrows in drink when a little common sense would have saved them. His common sense had pulled him through more than one tight spot and with any luck always would.

And yet . . .

Brent sank into the sprung wooden chair in front of his opened rolltop desk. All the cubbyholes were tidy, all the papers filed and controlled. That was the way he imagined his brain to look, until this folly had overtaken him. He hadn't been sleeping well lately. That was probably the real problem; it had nothing to do with the girl.

Closing his eyes, he clutched his hair, his elbows on the desk. At once, a face filled his inner vision. Radiantly pretty skin, smooth pink lips, her rich brown hair caught under a demure bonnet, and looking at him with those thickly fringed eyes. . . .

Shaking his head to clear it, Brent sat up and reached for a thin stack of unanswered letters. But for the first time in his life, he couldn't concentrate on business.

Brent pushed back his chair and kicked his heels up onto the desk. If he couldn't think about business, let him at least take a businesslike attitude to the problem that plagued him.

He had to admire the efficiency of it. One instant, one turn of a neat little head, and his whole universe had shivered into a million pieces, as though a mirror had smashed.

Then there was the cleverness of it. He'd fallen for the one girl he couldn't possibly have. Brent knew from his own experience that the harder something was to obtain, the more passionately men longed for it and the higher the price they'd pay for it.

She had turned when he'd warned her to watch out. Then she'd looked straight at him. Brent relived the spark that had shot through him at the sight of her dark blue eyes. It had rocked him, stealing both thought and speech away. She must have thought him as heavy-brained as an old bull. She'd definitely assumed a love affair between Amalie Robbins and himself, a notion that was totally false.

They were lovely eyes, with a shimmering blue in their depths like the mysterious heart of a sapphire. When he'd looked deeply into them, he'd forgotten the rules he lived by. The funny thing was that her sister wasn't that much different in looks, but he'd felt nothing when he'd helped Charlene Forsythe from the train. Yet something had compelled him to kiss Bethany.

If she wasn't calling him a heartless brute at this moment, it wouldn't be his fault. But she'd weighed nothing while nestled in his arm, and more than that, she'd given him such a look of fearlessness that he couldn't help himself. Bethany Forsythe was as defenseless as a kitten with the pride of a tiger. He found the combination completely endearing. Brent realized he was grinning like a fool at the remembrance.

A knock at his door made him sit up and pretend to be absorbed in his work. "Yes, come in," he called.

"Busy, cowboy?" Dina's voice had the sensual weight of silk. The slight southern drag of her words added to her charm.

"Paperwork. Bills, mostly."

"Poor sweetie. Can I help?"

Brent shook his head. Sure he had himself under control, he glanced up and blinked. "A little early for spangles, isn't it?"

"It's not bad, huh?" Dina swayed into the room, her round and womanly figure encased in a dress of wine-colored velvet. The shoulders and bust of the dress were spangled over with gold flecks that caught the light.

"The men'll like it."

She hitched her hip onto the edge of his desk and gazed down at him. "What about you?"

Even fully dressed, Dina always seemed to have just risen from a humid bed of love. Brent hadn't always been immune to her effect, but long acquaintance had removed much of the temptation. Besides, he never was one to wait in line.

Now he gave her a glimpse of his old devil-may-care smile. "You're a picture."

"They say downstairs the boss is in a foul mood. Putting that girl on the train get you down?"

"Guess it must have been that. Those old biddies were waiting for us at the depot. With a band, even. I think they would have been just as glad to ride me out of town too."

"You and me both. You know, Brent, I been thinking . . ." She traced a light pattern on the back of his hand with a careless forefinger. "They say there's big money to be made in San Francisco. Why don't we head out there? Start a bigger and better joint than we've got in this one-horse town."

"I hadn't heard all the saloons out West had packed up." Unobtrusively, Brent moved his hand out of range of Dina's touch.

"Course they haven't—what do you mean?"

"Out there we'd just be another saloon; we'd be lost in the crowd. Here, on the other hand . . ."

"Yeah, here! Look Brent, I've been meaning to talk to you 'bout that." Visibly, Dina got herself under control. In a calculatedly erotic gesture, she put up one hand to pat her hair, thrusting her breasts forward. After she could be sure he'd gotten a good look, she relaxed, saying, "I don't have anything against Cedar Groves; it's been good to me. But, Brent, we gotta face facts."

"Which facts?"

"Why, you know as good as me that the cattle ain't comin' back. No cattle, no cowboys, or buyers. Without them, what happens to the Golden Lady? You gonna make money from the farmers and their one glass of beer a night?"

"Probably not." Brent took up his pen and a sheet of paper. After writing quickly, he blotted the page. "Here," he said, handing it to her.

"'Pay to the order of . . .' say, what's the idea?"

"I've always thought of you as my partner, Dina. Now I'm buying you out."

"I don't want to . . ." Then the full-breasted, lovely blonde glanced again at the paper. "Say, how many zeros is that?"

"Lots," Brent said. "Enough to start a nice place in 'Frisco. If you'll take my advice, you'll get yourself a place on the water. . . ." He patted her velvet-covered knee.

"It wouldn't be any fun without you."

He knew she didn't mean it. "There are other fish and it's a great big ocean. Maybe you should get married."

Dina gave him another little flash of skin. "This is so sudden," she purred.

"Not to me," Brent said, a little faster than was strictly complimentary.

"I didn't guess it would be. 'Sides, I've been married."

"This time, try sticking with it."

"I may still be married, come to think of it." Dina eased off his desk. She folded the paper and tucked it away in the hollow between her breasts. "Maybe in 'Frisco I can catch myself a millionaire. If I do, you'll get this back."

As she sashayed slowly out, Brent found himself feeling a little sorry for the millionaires of San Francisco. They wouldn't know what had hit them.

He'd been meaning to buy Dina off for some time. Brent wondered why he'd chosen today to do it. It had to be that girl.

Brent got up and poured himself a drink. The lukewarm tea refreshed his mouth but did nothing for his mood. Love doesn't happen like that, he told himself. Her eyes were just eyes, bluer than most, prettier than some, but not magical. Most likely, by tomorrow he wouldn't be able to remember her name.

Two

Bethany sat next to Mr. Bigelow as he drove her, Charlene, and the mountains of luggage from the baggage car, to her grandfather's house. Though she felt sorry for the horse, neither she nor Charlene had wanted to leave anything behind in New York, despite the lip service they'd given to a speedy return. At least the road to Upper Grove had been laid with gravel since they'd gone away, which made for quite an improvement in the ride.

"Yep," Mr. Bigelow said when she commented on the change. "Now that we ain't got cattle churnin' up the roads, we can go for paving."

Charlene, on Bethany's other side, said, "They'll be putting down macadam next." She looked much brighter now that she was in the open air, a little pink flushing her too-pale cheeks. The train ride had been exhausting even to Bethany. Poor Charlene's hands shook with weariness.

Every minute, Bethany expected Mr. Bigelow to turn off the main road. But he kept on a steady course, driving his horses up to the hill that separated one half of Cedar Groves from the other. Surely her grandfather wasn't still living in Marmion House, that grand mansion he'd built for his bride, not in his reduced circumstances?

Mr. Bigelow drove down Ames Street, the discreetly shaded boulevard where Bethany and Charlene had spent their childhoods. The houses were set back from the street, their broad green lawns as forbidding as moats. Gingerbread trim curled in profusion over stately windows and doors yet lent no giddiness to the architecture. One did not laugh simply because a matron wore lace. Most of the houses were aproned with large porches, some curving around to the back, supporting roofs with columns better suited to the Parthenon.

Bethany smiled at the sight of her favorite house. "There's the Trumbull place," she commented to her sister.

"Your particular dream house," Charlene said. "Most girls dream of marble palaces and you moon over that clapboard farmhouse."

Bethany loved it because it had no air of having grown too big for its britches like so many of the houses on Ames Street, her grandfather's among them. Even with broken windows and a sagging porch, the Trumbull place, abandoned to mice and the four winds, had a quiet dignity all its own. She'd always admired the strange little balcony that jutted out from the steeply sloping roof at the level of the attic, sheltering the front door far below. Bethany turned around on the wagon's hard seat to catch a last glimpse of a house that would never be hers, but that kept a certain part of her heart.

"There's Mrs. Messenger," Charlene said, lifting her white-gloved hand in a polite wave to the woman sitting in a rocking chair on the semicircular porch of her *very* grand house.

"A lot of people seem to be outside today," Bethany said in a dry undertone. "Do you suppose it's in our honor?"

Then the wagon pulled up before what they still thought of as their house. A white bedsheet hung from the tower window and flapped in the mild breeze of the early autumn afternoon. "Look," Charlene said, drawing her sister's attention upward. "Manny's glad we're home."

"Either that or she's surrendering."

The house sat on its corner as if it had been there from time immemorial. A four-section tower, each section ornamented with a window of a different shape, rose above the baronial oaken door. Of pale gray stone, topped by a sloped-shoulder mansard roof, no two levels the same height, the house looked as though it had developed naturally, a piece at a time. Actually, Mr. Ames had built it for his wife's wedding present, forty-five years before.

Yet, despite its grandiose air, despite the envy it conjured in the hearts of the women of Cedar Groves, today Marmion House wore a welcoming air. Perhaps it was the golden and amethyst chrysanthemums that lined the narrow walk, contrasting with the cool gray stone and the green grass. Perhaps it was the sheer white curtains billowing out from all the opened windows. Most likely, however, the feeling came from Bethany's knowledge that two people who loved her lived there.

The wagon had no sooner stopped than both the big oaken doors were flung open and her grandfather hurried down the steps. She could see his mouth moving as he came on, though he was still too far away to be heard. As always he wore faultless gray checked trousers and a cutaway coat. Bethany couldn't recall ever seeing him in any other garb.

"My girls! My girls!" he called, clasping his hands over his heart, not minding the walking stick he still held. He stopped at the end of the walk, his gaze flickering between Charlene and Bethany. His deep blue eyes, which he'd passed along to them, showed a glitter of tears.

Mr. Bigelow helped Charlene down and she flew at once into Mr. Ames's arms. Bethany, putting her hand into Mr. Bigelow's rough grasp, had a sudden image of a pair of startlingly green eyes and a wryly twisted mouth, those of the last man who'd taken her hand in his. Mr. Bigelow didn't know why Miss Bethany suddenly glared at him. He hurried to unload their baggage.

"I can't believe you're really here," Mr. Ames said as Charlene stepped out of his embrace. At once, he threw his arms around Bethany. He still smelled of bay rum and his large pepper-and-salt mustache still tickled her ear. She leaned her cheek tenderly against his hair. "It's good to see you. We've missed you."

They smiled at each other. Then Mr. Ames put his arms around their two waists and turned them toward the house. Though his head hardly topped their shoulders, he was so excited that he seemed much taller than five feet two. He seemed to bounce between them like a poorly tethered balloon.

"We're going to have a lot of fun now that you're home, my chickabiddies! I've bought one of those newfangled badminton sets and had the piano tuned. Maybe we'll give a party."

The girls exchanged a look over his bald spot. Bethany shook her head when Charlene would have spoken. As they walked up the four stone steps to the front door, Bethany said to her sister, "You still look a trifle peaky. Maybe you should lie down for a bit before supper?"

"Oh, yes, my dear," Mr. Ames said, a shadow of concern crossing his high forehead. "There's your own little room all ready. I've made just a few improvements here and there, just to improve your pleasure. Are you sure you wouldn't like to lie down, too, Bethany? Mrs. Manning will call you in plenty of time. Or a bath, now? We've an abundance of hot water, you know."

"Do you have gas laid on all the way out here?" Bethany asked in wonder.

"I insisted they bring gas out to our house the first minute they could. Just in your ears, my sweet ones, Marmion House still leads the fashion in Upper Grove. Everyone was afraid of being blown to Kingdom Come if they had gas laid in their houses. Then I have it here and suddenly every house on Ames Street is lit by gas."

The hall was no longer as shadowy as Bethany had remembered. A semidraped figure of Greek legend stood poised on the newel post of the stairs, lifting aloft a wavering flame. Charlene exclaimed, "Isn't it lovely! Much nicer than the one at Aunt Poste's home."

"I forgot that you girls are used to gas—no need to warn *you* not to blow out your light!"

It seemed to Bethany that her grandfather was just the slightest bit unwilling to meet her eyes. He fussed a little too breathlessly around Charlene, insisting on showing her the way to her room, despite announcing that it was the same one she'd slept in since her girlhood. Despite his age, Bethany was reminded of a puppy who'd done wrong and frisked about in the hope of not being found out.

"Now you have to tell me what's different?" he demanded, heading under the archway at the beginning of the tiny hall, three paces in length that led nowhere but to Charlene's small, white room.

Charlene looked about her with fond eyes while Bethany stood in the hall behind her grandfather. "Nothing," Charlene said, giving a contented sigh. "It's exactly as I remembered it, in every detail."

"No, no," Mr. Ames began. Bethany put her hand on his well-padded shoulder and squeezed a tiny bit. He looked up at her, blinked his eyes in a wise-owl way, and said, "You're right. I haven't changed it a hair! Just a jolly joke to say I had."

While removing her bonnet, Charlene sat on the bed. "That's better than having things all fancy and new. It's so good to be home at last."

Bethany said, "Let me help you off with your boots."

"No need. Elastic-sided, remember?" Yawning, Charlene stretched her arms out in front of her like a cat. "I'll just lie down on top of the counterpane for a little while. Please wake me with enough time to wash my hands and face, will you, Bethany?"

"Certainly! I'll be glad to change out of these sooty things myself. Trains are so dirty these days."

Bethany closed the door noiselessly. She stood for a moment with her ear pressed against the panel. Glancing at her grandfather, she nodded with satisfaction.

In unspoken agreement, she and Mr. Ames started down the well of steps silently. In the snug library, Bethany untied the broad ribbons on her bonnet and tossed it onto her grandfather's ornate desk. After tugging off her gloves, she gave an absentminded pat to her coils of brown hair and walked over to inspect the books behind the glassed doors. Here were her old favorites and quite a few new treasures to be explored.

"How is Charlene?" Grandfather Ames asked.

Bethany faced him squarely. There was no point in wrapping things up in clean linen. "Not well. Rheumatic fever is nothing to take lightly."

"*Does* she take it lightly?"

She couldn't keep a smile of pride from appearing as she said, "I dare swear she would if she had the strength. But she tires easily, and can become very downhearted. She can't do half the things she used to do. The doctors have forbidden her so much that was entertaining. Traveling especially wears her down."

"If I had known she'd been so sick, I never would have called you girls home." His voice dropped low with guilt.

"She didn't want me to tell you for fear you'd worry too much." Bethany came to his side and pressed a kiss to his cheek, as smoothly hairless as a baby's. "It was Charlene who insisted we come home in answer to your letter. She was never really happy in New York, only sometimes, when Aunt would take us to the country in the summer."

"But what about her fiancé? Surely, she was happy with him."

"Oh, Mr. Diccers? I don't know what she saw in him. Well, he is a handsome fellow, if you like that type."

"What type?"

"Tall, very blond, and with no conversation beyond the America's Cup Races."

Mr. Ames chuckled. But Bethany wasn't thinking about what she'd just said. Once again, she saw the sharp angles and planes of Brent Houston's face, dominated by a pair of brilliant green eyes. Though not strictly handsome, he had rough good looks that would make any breathing woman look twice. No doubt that was why her thoughts kept dwelling on him. And of course, the man did not resemble her own fiancé in the slightest.

"What about this fellow you're going to marry?"

Her grandfather's words were so in tune with her thoughts that for a moment she didn't realize he'd spoken. "Gerrald is very nice. He's rather quiet, actually. He likes birds."

"I believe his father manufactured sewing machines?"

"That's right." She looked down at the small aquamarine ring that decorated the third finger of her left hand. The gold filigree of the ring, set with a very fine, though pale, stone, hardly showed up against the slight golden tint of her skin. Her aunt, she recalled, had been sharp with dissatisfaction over Mr. Stowe's lack of ostentation. She'd made snide comparisons between Bethany's ring and Charlene's, a ruby the size of the fingernail of the finger the ring adorned.

"I was surprised," Mr. Ames said, "that neither young man made the trip out West with you. I would have thought . . ."

"Mr. Diccers is having a yacht built and felt he needed to go and be nursemaid. As for Gerrald, I'm sure he very much wanted to come. But his mother felt such a trip without any chaperon but Charlene would be too damaging to my reputation."

"Oh, your Gerrald has a mother?"

Bethany caught her grandfather's eye and gave a furtive gurgle of laughter.

"Is she a harridan?"

"No, entirely the reverse. More of a clinging vine than a martinet. And his sisters are just as bad. Three of them, if you please, all unmarried and likely to stay so. They cling to him as if he were the sole prop of their lives."

"He sounds bedeviled, poor chap."

"Actually, you know, I think he likes it that they need him so much. Sometimes, I feel that he . . ."

Bethany closed her lips firmly over what she was about to say. Yes, sometimes she felt that Gerrald was a little worried by her strong-mindedness. Occasionally she'd wake up late at night, wondering if she really could marry him and live with all four of his closest female relatives in one house. But she remembered the sewing machine money. Under the circumstances, she'd be a fool to turn down a man with that kind of money.

"Grandfather," she began, facing him squarely. "In your letter, you weren't very clear as to how bad things actually are . . ."

A slight expression of unease passed over his face. He tugged at the hairs of his mustache. "Speaking with absolute frankness, my dear, I feel I must tell you that, so far as our wealth is concerned, things haven't . . ."

A noise made them both look toward the library door, a sound more like a kick than a knock. Before Mr. Ames could call permission, the door swung open and Mrs. Manning, the housekeeper, bustled in, carrying a loaded tea tray.

As Bethany bent to kiss the woman's cheek, she thought how horrified her aunt would have been by the familiarity. Servants knew their place in her great, cold house on the corner of Fifth Avenue, and they had better keep to it!

But it would have been impossible to treat Mrs. Manning with distant courtesy. They'd begun calling her Manny when they were babies. Not only had she taught them their letters by making alphabets out of pastry as well as nursed them through everything from measles to their first menses, but also she was in love with their grandfather.

"There you are, Miss Bethany. My, but you've grown fine!"

Obligingly, Bethany turned around so Manny could see all her fine feathers. Though her dress was made of a heavy black cloth, suitable for train travel, it had the long tight bodice and ruffled skirts so popular in New York but not yet seen farther west. Only Mrs. Tubbs had worn anything close to the fashion; the other women preferring perhaps to be practical.

"How many yards in that skirt, Miss Bethany? Enough to make two waists for me, I'll guess."

Considering that she was built along the lines of a mourning dove, Bethany thought she guessed correctly. Like Mr. Ames, Manny's graying head came scarcely to Bethany's shoulder. For all that, she scolded her kindly, as though Bethany were still a little girl.

"Now you sit down and eat up every bite. I know what it's like on those trains. And don't trouble yourself about Miss Charlene. I peeped in on her and she's sleeping like a baby."

All the while she was speaking, Manny laid out two cups of tea and whisked the covers off the food. She wrestled a chair to the side of Mr. Ames's desk and then pointed him into the other one with a commanding forefinger.

"We'll get your strength up with good, plain cooking," Manny said to Bethany. "I can see that living in that sinful city pulled you both down. When I think what blooming children you were when you left here . . ."

"I think they're still blooming," Mr. Ames said stoutly.

Manny took no notice. "All those nasty trams and underground railroads . . . it stands to reason you couldn't very well stay healthy there. And poor Miss Charlene . . ."

Bethany said, "The doctors say she'll be fully recovered soon, Manny. There's no need to worry as long as she's careful not to overdo."

"Oh, doctors," the housekeeper replied with a gesture that condemned the whole medical profession to insignificance. She glanced at the tea tray. "Lands, if I haven't been and forgotten the milk!"

As the door closed behind her, Bethany shared her smile with her grandfather. He looked up from the small cake he was attempting to gnaw and said, "She's delighted to have you girls home again."

"She still can't cook though, can she?"

Mr. Ames put his cake down gently so not to break the

plate. "No. But I try to look on the bright side. Most men my age have lost all their teeth. Mine get so much exercise they're like a man of twenty's."

"I noticed she wasn't speaking to you. Have you done something to make her angry?"

Mr. Ames studied his clean fingernails. "Delia hasn't spoken to me since the morning I put you two girls on the train."

At first, Bethany thought she hadn't heard right. "You mean, since *this* morning?" When he shook his head, she said in amazement, "You mean, she hasn't spoken to you for five and a half *years*?"

"Not a word."

Bethany put her hand to her lips. "My goodness," she mumbled inadequately.

"She is . . . ah . . . a stubborn woman."

Hiding her smile in her hand, Bethany said, "I should say so." But she couldn't quite hide the laughter that trembled in her voice.

Mr. Ames's mustache twitched too, but he said sternly, "You find it amusing, heh?"

"How do you manage?"

"Well, she's been my housekeeper for twelve years. She knows what I like and what I don't, and I haven't changed very much since you girls were little. And as Delia only knows eight dishes, plus poached eggs . . . she does make delicious poached eggs though I don't know how they escape . . . there aren't that many instructions I need give her. It isn't as though I'm suddenly going to take a fancy for pheasant under glass, you know."

Bethany said, "I hope you are going to take a fancy for that, Grandfather. I hope everyone in town is going to be positively *lusting* after things like that."

"Bethany!" Mr. Ames said, shocked.

"I should wait to tell you after Charlene wakes up, but I just can't wait. While we were in New York, the very day we received your letter asking us to come home, we made up our minds what to do."

"What to do?"

"We're going to save the family fortunes!"

Three

They were still discussing the matter over dinner, two hours later. The wax candles flickering in the fine silver candelabras sent a glow as of hope over Charlene's face, and lessened the years their grandfather wore. For a man whose pink scalp showed through his white hair, Peregrine Ames had the tenor voice of a much younger man. As they discussed the girls' plan, it went higher still.

Charlene said, cutting across her sister's eloquence, "Perhaps Grandfather is afraid we'll appear fast, Bethany. Aunt certainly thought we were risking our reputations by opening a common eating house."

"And as I told her, it won't be common. It will be very uncommon."

Mr. Ames said, "I'm not concerned that much with your good names. Young girls do all sorts of things now that they never did in my day. Progress is a wonderful thing. Besides, it isn't as though you'd be serving liquor."

"Thank you, Grandfather," Bethany said, reaching over to pat his dry hand. "I never knew you were such a supporter of women's rights. Next thing you know, you'll be suggesting we should get the vote."

"I'm no radical," he said with a smile. "I am simply of the opinion that a woman should be able to earn her own living." A shadow fell across his beaming countenance. "Though I hate to see any female member of my family slaving away for a lot of anonymous strangers."

Charlene said, "It could be worse, Grandfather. We might have decided to open a saloon."

At once, Bethany held up her napkin to shield her face from her grandfather's view while she swiftly poked her tongue out at Charlene. Her sister giggled.

Mrs. Tubbs had wearied both sisters' ears while pouring out a vast number of words on the subject of Brent Houston. "A gambler, a consorter with low persons of the female kind, a wrecker of decent homes! That saloon of his is the center of all that is wicked in our town. We ladies are circulating a petition to have him closed down!"

Despite Bethany's protestations that she really wasn't remotely interested in Mr. Houston or his works, Mrs. Tubbs had gone on. "If he's not in league with the devil, he's next door to being one himself. Most of the other saloons and houses of ill repute have closed, driven out of their foul business now that the cattle have stopped coming. But it will take the concerted efforts of our league to drive Mr. Houston out."

Miss Ivey whispered, "He *is* handsome, though," and received a quelling look for daring to speak up with an unofficial opinion of her own.

"Bethany! Bethany!" her grandfather's voice summoned her back to the present.

She wrenched her attention away from the flame of a candle that had held her spellbound. "I'm sorry, Grandfather. I . . . I must be more tired than I knew. What did you say?"

"Pass the salt and pepper, if you please."

"Certainly." She picked up the tiny silver basket that held the two spices and passed it down to him. "Grandfather, I am very surprised to find you still living here at Marmion House."

"And where else should he live?" Manny said, returning to the dining room with a tureen of soup. She began ladling the clear broth into the white Wedgwood bowl before Mr. Ames. "Mr. Ames has always lived here."

"I mean, with things being the way they are. The money . . ."

"Ah, yes," Mr. Ames said, staring into the depths of the soup as though expecting to see a prophecy. "I confess it never occurred to me that you girls would believe it necessary to recoup the family fortunes. When I wrote to you, I hoped you'd come home, that's true, but I never expected . . ."

"Well, we can't run around playing badminton and croquet while we wait to starve."

Manny said with an aggrieved sniff, "You're in no danger of that, Miss Bethany!"

"No, of course not. I didn't mean it literally." She got up to hold open the door for Mrs. Manning as she carried out the heavy tureen. Charlene was drinking her soup with every sign of contentment, though the first taste reminded Bethany of why her grandfather had asked for the seasonings before being served. Without a word but giving her a wink, he pushed the little silver basket back to her.

The soup was closer to that served in purgatory rather than in paradise. Bethany realized the best way to gain Mr. Ames's support was to make him a customer. With a smile, she excused herself and stood up. Her grandfather rose to his feet, his napkin in his hand and a look of inquiry on his mild face.

"I'll just go have a word with Manny."

The aprons were still in the long drawer by the washtub. Bethany withdrew the top one to tie over her silk dress. The smooth white cotton crackled with starch as she tied the bow behind. She was willing to swear it would stand by itself, given half a chance.

Entering the kitchen through the waiter's pantry, she smiled at Manny and went over to the big black-iron stove against the wall. Every surface from the burners to the bread-warmer had some pot or pan on it. Manny, flushed and panting with the heat, put down on the kitchen dresser the water she'd been sipping.

"Now, Miss Bethany, what are you doing?"

"Isn't there a prayer meeting tonight? There used to be one."

"No, it was changed to Thursdays when they started holding these Spiritual Cleanliness get-togethers. They claim Saturday nights are best 'cause that's when most men go down to the saloons. Plus, of course, it gets everybody in the right frame of mind for Sunday. More praying goes on at one of their meetings than in a month of Sundays."

"Aren't you a member?"

"Lands, no! A housekeeper isn't hoity-toity enough for Mrs. Tubbs and her crew."

As if she weren't really thinking of what she was doing, Bethany crossed to the dark blue dresser and took this spice and that from the shelf. Absently, she added flour to the drippings in the bottom of the roasting pan that still sat on the stove.

"Now what are you doing, Miss Bethany?"

"Oh!" Bethany said, looking down at the thickening gravy in mock surprise. "Force of habit, I suppose. Uncle Poste always said I made a better gravy than his French cook. I, of course, told him I learned everything I know from you."

Manny preened. "I have heard folks talk about my gravy."

"I'm sure they do. Didn't Grandfather used to have some burgundy in the cellar?"

"I wouldn't know."

"Just a thought. Nothing like a splash of wine to help a sauce along." Bethany went on stirring the gravy, adjusting the stove lid so that just enough heat emerged from the body of the stove to keep the sauce warmed but in no danger of scorching. She made a long reach for the bottle of milk on the counter and poured in a few drops while still stirring, stirring, stirring.

Manny asked, "What's this I hear about you and Brent Houston?"

Jerking around in surprise to stare at the housekeeper, Bethany nearly spilled the gravy. She lifted her dripping spoon up high. "What have you heard? There's nothing to hear!"

"I heard he carried your bags off the train today. Don't look so surprised, honey. News travels pretty quick around here, or did you forget?"

"I suppose I've grown used to the slower pace of New York City." Recovering her senses, Bethany continued to stir the gravy, though her hand trembled a little. Thank goodness no one had seen him . . . misuse her.

Gerrald had kissed her once, a clumsy, mismanaged affair. There'd been no pulse-quickened trembling with the insane desire to throw her arms about his neck and caution to the winds. But then, Bethany reminded herself, they'd been at a lawn-bowling tournament at the time, not dangling above a rushing train track in danger of their lives.

"So," she said with pretended casualness, "who is Brent Houston? We weren't exactly introduced."

"And Eugenia Tubbs didn't cram your ears with his evil ways? That gal must be slipping. Personally, I think she's been comparing Mr. Houston—who is a handsome feller no matter what else he might be—to that lard bucket she married. Tubbs is as Tubbs does, I suppose, though I'm not one who should talk." She put her hands on either side of her ample waist as though measuring the width.

"I didn't think Mr. Houston was so very handsome." Despite her care, Bethany spilled some gravy as she poured it into the crystal sauce boat that stood ready on the much-scarred kitchen table.

"Then you must need glasses. Or maybe you're comparing Mr. Houston to this feller you're engaged to? Is he handsome, Miss Bethany? A pair of pretty things like you and Miss Charlene should marry handsome men."

"Next time we'll let you pick them out," Bethany said merrily as she picked up the carving knife and fork and laid them beside the platter where the roast reposed. As she feared, the roast had a dry, unappetizing look. Bethany didn't remember Manny being *this* poor a cook. Perhaps she was punishing her grandfather in more ways than with her silence.

With any luck at all, the potatoes in their jackets would still be edible, though the vegetables were a sorry slimy mess in the bottom of the pot. Judging by color alone, the only clue left, they might have once been self-respecting peas or green beans.

After gnawing his way through the entree, Mr. Ames scraped up the rest of the gravy with the side of his fork and sucked it off. "Really good," he whispered to Bethany. "First time it hasn't been lumpy or gritty that I can remember. But one batch of gravy doesn't make a restaurant."

After dinner, Bethany helped Manny with the dishes while Charlene set up a game of chess with her grandfather. The contemplative nature of the game appealed to both of them.

Charlene said, "I haven't had a really good match since I went away, Grandfather. Aunt Poste didn't think chess was ladylike, and Ronald doesn't play."

"I've hardly played at all myself, though I confess I got the pieces out and dusted them in hopes you would want a game."

Manny refused to allow Bethany to wash while she wore a silk dress. "One spot of grease and it'd be ruined! And it's so pretty too. I've always admired you in pale pink. Whatever else that aunt of yours might be, she wasn't stingy in the way she dressed you girls."

"It would be false economy to be stingy while dressing a turkey too."

Manny chuckled. "Well, this much I will say for her. By what your grandfather tells me, she found you a pair of fine young men to marry."

"By what he tells you? But I thought . . ." Bethany blushed a little as she realized she might be thought nosy.

"Oh, he talks to *me*," Manny said. "I just don't talk to him. I was mad clear through when he knuckled under and sent you off to live with your aunt. Why, even when she came out for your ma's wedding, I thought she was a snippy little piece of goods! Didn't think an Ames was good enough for her brother, and purely hated the fact that your ma and pa wanted to keep on living here in Cedar Groves."

"Yes," Bethany said quietly. "That's still a grievance. I think she loved Pa more than she loved anybody else. He was her only brother."

"I just didn't want you girls turning out like her. But I should have trusted you more."

"Are you still mad at Grandfather?"

"Mercy, no! I got over being mad last year." She shook her head sadly. "The trouble is I hold a grudge. It's not Christian and I've prayed for help but there's no doubt I can hold a grudge. My whole family was that way. My pa didn't talk to his cousin Earl for sixteen years over a matter of some stolen eggs. And we won't even mention the War Between the States for fear of fighting it all over again!"

Bethany rubbed her neck. Bed was starting to call to her, but she wanted to have one question answered before she retired. "How long do you think it will be before you start talking to Grandfather again?"

"I wish I knew. I purely hate to be in the wrong."

"I suppose you could start tomorrow. At breakfast. Ask him if he'd like more coffee or something."

"You know I want to, Miss Bethany. I would too, if I could get the words out. If I could just say one word to him! But I can't get it out. I'm afraid the habit of not speaking has gotten to be too strong. It's a terrible thing to hold on to a grudge so long it becomes dearer than kith or kin. Don't you do it, you hear me?"

Bethany smiled. "I never hold a grudge. I just explode like a firecracker and then I'm always sorry afterward."

"Your grandfather's like that. When I started this nonsense, sometimes he'd just get purely furious. He'd yell and jump up and down. That only made me madder. If only I could get one single solitary word out . . ." she said again.

"I'll try to think of something," Bethany promised. She looked around the kitchen. "Is that all the dishes? Goodness, that hardly took any time at all."

"The harder you gab, the faster the work goes," Manny said complacently. "That's what my ma used to say."

She untied Bethany's apron strings. "You two girls should sleep in tomorrow. There's nothing to do that won't keep till the afternoon. Nobody'll expect you to go to church your first day back."

"Charlene's bound to insist on going," Bethany said. "She never misses."

"You leave Miss Charlene to me. I saw those shadows under her eyes. We've got to build her strength up."

"If you can keep her in bed on a Sunday, you're better than I am. I practically had to sit on her when she was sick. Whenever the church bells rang, she'd try to get dressed."

The housekeeper looked at her shrewdly. "At least you're right as rain."

"Of course I am. Chipper as a cricket."

"Except you've got shadows under your eyes too."

Self-consciously, Bethany touched her face. "It was a long trip."

"You can't fool me, child. Your aunt wrote about how you never left Charlene's side, how she wouldn't have any other nurse but you."

"That was . . ." Bethany began, waving her self-sacrifices away as unimportant. The first major disagreement she'd had with Gerrald was over her refusal to leave her dangerously ill sister to attend a cotillion with him. He hadn't seemed to understand that she simply wasn't able to go nor would she enjoy herself if she had gone.

"That's why you're going to sleep late tomorrow too."

Bethany sketched a salute. "Aye, aye, Mrs. Manning, ma'am."

She hurried up the back stairs, the fifth riser squealing as usual. Her room, painted the gentle pink she adored, commanded a view of the street through the organdy curtains. It looked out on the half-round roof of the bay window in the drawing room, the window that added a touch of wedding cake to the otherwise Italian style of the house. A strong breeze, the harbinger of fall, rattled the panes of glass in the center of the three windows in her room.

As she looked around for a bit of paper to wedge in the sash, she heard her sister call. Bethany stepped out into the hall. "Yes," she half whispered, "I'm here. Do you need me?"

Charlene stood beneath the archway of her little lobby, her bare toes showing beneath the hem of her padded silk dressing gown. "Come and sit with me for a minute. I want to talk to you."

The little room at the rear of the house wasn't half the size of Bethany's. But just as Bethany loved the view from her windows, Charlene loved being above the garden, even when the flowers were gone to seed. A tall maple tree shaded her window and the squirrels kept her company.

"Hop into bed, Charlene," Bethany said. "Have you got a hot water bottle?"

With her delightful giggle, like a breeze sweeping across an aeolian harp, Charlene said, "Manny put in three of them!"

Bethany saw two of the ceramic bottles stacked on the dressing table. "You don't mind if I take an extra one back to bed with me, do you?"

"Take all three if you want. I'm always warm enough in this bedroom, not like that marble mausoleum I had to sleep in at Aunt Poste's house. Five radiators and not one of them near enough to the bed to do any good!"

Looking at her sister as she sat up with the pillows behind her, Bethany felt relieved. Yes, there were dark circles under her eyes, but the eyes themselves were bright and sparkling. The old enthusiasm had come again into her light voice while her lips were pink, not pale. Coming home had been the right thing to do, even if they had to become poor as church mice to convince Aunt Poste to let them do it.

Charlene said, "I think Grandfather will see how good our idea is as soon as he's had a chance to think it over. When I told him about my pastries, I swear he had tears in his eyes!" She leaned forward, her elbows on her knees. "If that pie we had tonight was an example of what he's had for dessert for the last five years, I wouldn't be surprised if he *was* crying!"

"I'm afraid Manny hasn't improved her skills much since we left."

"It's worse than that. I think her cooking has actually gone downhill! If only there was some way *we* could take over for a while . . . then we could prove to Grandfather that the restaurant is a good idea."

No longer surprised that her twin sister and she frequently came up with similar ideas, Bethany said, "Maybe we could persuade her to take a short holiday. After all, it has been five years."

Charlene shook her head, the curl papers dancing. "That won't work; you know she'll never leave Grandfather. No matter how furious she is with him."

"Why should she leave?" Bethany said quickly as an idea occurred to her. "She could have a vacation right here. We'd wait on her hand and foot, and she could do whatever she pleases!"

"It might work . . . but she'd never let us, unless we put it to her just right. Let me think about it. You know I've always been better at wheedling her than you are."

That was perfectly true. "We'll talk about it more in the morning. It's so late."

"It's only eleven o'clock. We stayed up much later in New York. Besides . . ." Charlene gave her sister a sideways glance. "I wanted to ask you. What was it like?"

"What was what like?" Bethany said, still thinking about cooking.

"You know. What was it like when Mr. Houston kissed you?"

For a moment Bethany just stared at Charlene, her mouth hanging open. Then she asked, with surprise and horror, "You saw him do it?"

"Of course I did. I was standing right there on the platform. I thought my heart would stop! He certainly is strong!"

"Too strong." Bethany seemed to feel his powerful clasp once more as he took her whole weight and brought her body close to his. She closed her eyes and passed her hand over her forehead, suddenly feeling as though a hot water bottle was the last thing she needed. A distressing thought came into her head. Her eyes snapped open.

"He didn't . . . that is . . . he didn't mistreat you too, did he?"

Charlene grinned, showing her straight white teeth. "Why would he?"

"Well, a man like that . . ."

"Bethany! Don't try to make me believe you couldn't tell!"

"Tell what?"

Rolling her eyes at her sister's thickheadedness, Charlene said, "Why, he couldn't take his eyes off you! He watched every move you made the whole time. I wouldn't be surprised a hair if he was already in love with you. Love at first sight."

"That's ridiculous," Bethany said flatly.

"Why is it ridiculous? In that play we saw last year . . ."

"Life isn't a play."

"Isn't it a pity!" Charlene said with a giggle.

"Besides, a man like that . . . Well, you heard what Mrs. Tubbs had to say about him. A common gambler. A saloon keeper."

"Don't gamblers and saloon keepers fall in love too?"

Charlene's ingenuousness didn't fool Bethany. It was an act Charlene had found very useful in New York, especially as her fiancé had a preference for empty-headed girls. Being so fatuous himself, he liked girls who made him look intelligent by comparison.

"I'm sure they must," she replied, "but not with me. I'm not that kind of man's type of woman." She remembered the pretty, if tired, face of the girl he'd been putting on the train. The pinch of jealousy she felt surprised her. What was that girl to Mr. Houston? And what difference did it make to her?

"Besides," she said abruptly, "Mr. Houston's feelings don't enter into the matter. I'll never see him again. That's for certain."

Four

"Let's go over it again," Charlene said, drawing the collar of her long coat closer to her throat. Though the sun was shining, a frisky breeze brought a taste of autumn to the air.

"It's very simple. We'll just go in. We'll ask for Mr. Houston to come down and then we'll make our proposal."

Bethany started forward to cross the unpaved street. Lower Grove hadn't yet received the improvements of Upper Grove. She found Charlene dragging on her arm. Stepping back onto the narrow boardwalk that hugged the base of the buildings, Bethany asked, "What's wrong?"

"I don't know if I can," Charlene said in a small voice. "It looks so . . . so ugly."

Looking across the street, Bethany considered the building. Someone had lavished the big glass window with gold leaf, spelling out the name of the saloon in curling letters. The double front doors under the portico shone in a shiny Chinese red paint, lending a cheerful air to the white building. If it had housed any other kind of business, she would have thought it charming. As it was . . .

"It's just tawdry, Charlene. Cheap and flashy like an imitation diamond ring. We'll be all right. We're not staying to have drinks, you know."

"All the same. I'd rather wait here."

"Here? In the street?" And in this wind? Bethany thought, but didn't say.

"I'll wait in that doorway. It's sheltered enough and nobody will see me. And if you'll be quick . . ."

Charlene looked physically ill at the thought of entering the Golden Lady. For herself, Bethany felt nothing more than a little shameful excitement. Not at the thought of seeing Brent Houston again—that thought, she convinced herself, only filled her with dread—but at the idea of stepping foot into the kind of a place she'd heard so many warnings against. Curiosity might have killed the cat, but she had always heard that satisfaction had brought the poor puss back to life.

"All right," she said after inspecting the doorway. "I'll try to keep an eye on you from the window. Promise me you won't talk to strange men."

"I'd be too frightened to speak to anyone," Charlene said.

Bethany took off the bright blue silk scarf that draped over her shoulders and tucked it around her sister's. "You'd better have this if you're going to stand around in the fresh air. Wrap it around your throat to keep the cold out."

"It's not that cold!" Charlene protested with a flash of spirit.

"Please?"

After seeing Charlene safely into the doorway, where she stood like a saint in a church niche, Bethany once again headed for the Golden Lady. *Just let me carry things off with a good style,* she prayed silently. *Don't let him see how frightened he makes me.*

It was cleaner inside than she expected. The long walnut bar fairly shone with elbow grease and beeswax. The furniture at home, subject to Mrs. Manning's hatred of dust, didn't shine so brightly. Even the few brass cuspidors scattered around gleamed. Even the sawdust around their bulbous bases that collected near-misses seemed fresh.

In addition to being clean, the saloon was empty. The gangs of good husbands and fathers driven to degradation by drink must have taken their custom elsewhere this afternoon.

She saw herself in the big gold-framed mirror behind the bar. Her dove-gray suit with black braiding had always seemed ladylike while leaving visiting cards on society ladies or while running errands to the shops for her aunt. It didn't fail her now. She took courage from the sight. No one looking at her would guess her knees had suddenly begun to tremble.

Reflected in the mirror, the bartender's eyes grew big at the sight of a well-dressed young lady. He smoothed the thin strands of hair that covered his all-but-bald head as he turned around. "What kin I do for you, girlie?" he asked with a smile that was gap-toothed but kindly.

"I'm looking for the proprietor. Mr. Houston?"

Though the bartender had been surprised to see her, he didn't seem to be stunned by her request. Bethany wondered how many women came looking for Mr. Houston. Her hot cheeks grew pinker still.

"I'll trot along an' see if he's free. D'ya keer for anything? A swig o' somethin' now?"

Bethany wasn't a teetotaler. Her aunt had served liqueurs and wines at her frequent dinner parties. She said, "Would you have a small sherry?"

The barkeep shook his head. "We got beer, Monongahela whiskey, blackstrap, and Martinez what's made with gin and this vermouth stuff. Don't sell many of that there drink, but I'll slam you one together iff'n you want. Just right for a lady, don'tcha know?"

Bethany smiled at the man's evident desire to please her, a stranger in this world of strong drink. "No, thank you. I'm not really thirsty. But I would like to see Mr. Houston, please."

The barkeep slapped his hands together. "I forgot. Be right back." He hurried toward the stairs at the back of the large room that obviously led to the upper floor.

Alone, Bethany indulged herself by gazing around. The brass sconces on the walls as well as the lamps over the tables were fed by kerosene oil. A leather-topped table drew her attention and she went toward it. This must be the kind of place where hard-bitten men played cards for high stakes.

Perhaps at some other time it was. For now, however, someone had laid out a complicated game of solitaire on the brown surface. Bethany squinted at the cards, which were perfectly clean and new, trying to figure out the game. She thought that the red nine on the turned-up pile probably belonged on either the black eight or ten.

She'd just begun to reach for the card when someone said, "Miss!" Bethany jumped, feeling as guilty as though she'd been caught with her hand in the till.

But it was only a boy, perhaps sixteen years old, though his sharp-featured face made him look older. Shockingly towheaded, his hair seemed almost white, though his brows and lashes were brown. A white apron falling from around his waist like a stiff cone, he came out into the room, leaving a red-painted door swinging behind him.

"Listen, there's some coffee going in the back if you want it. Mr. Nolan musta forgot to mention it."

"I honestly don't care for anything. But thank you," Bethany said, smiling. He ducked his head and seemed to regret having spoken. Unable to resist asking an obvious question, she hoped her smile would make up for the impertinence. "You shouldn't be in here, should you?"

He stood straighter with pride, though it showed that his pants were too short. "I *work* here! Mr. Houston pays me to sweep up."

Bethany looked around again. The gaudy roulette wheel caught her eye as did a copy of the pink *Police Gazette* left on a chair, the pages spread open to a picture of a coy girl holding a pistol. A sour odor she hadn't noticed before seemed to worm its way up through the piney fragrance of the sawdust.

"Have you worked here long, er . . . ?"

"The name's Jerry. Jerry Windom. Mr. Houston's let me work here for the better part of a year."

Every time Jerry had cause to speak Brent Houston's

name, he seemed almost to catch his breath as though pausing in worshipful respect. Bethany looked at the boy's patched trousers and badly darned shirt. She saw that a sharp elbow had worked its way nearly through the darn on the right side. The wonderful Mr. Houston must be paying this boy a pittance.

"You like working here, then, Jerry?"

"Oh, yeah. The customers are real friendly, though kinda scarce now that the cattlemen aren't coming around. But the girls still give me tips, 'specially if I help 'em with the drunks. I'm stronger'n I look."

"I'm sure you are." The life he described in these few simple words shocked Bethany. This saloon might look harmless in the afternoon light but evidently things were vastly different when the lamps were lit. For a moment she seemed to hear a vulgar tune from the red-painted piano, the shrieks of tainted laughter, the grunts of men plunged in bestial pleasures. And this boy, leaning on his broom, taking it all in, blinded to its evil by his admiration for Brent Houston.

She reached for her purse. "I'll take some coffee, please, Jerry. Will this pay for it?"

He looked at the eagle on the half-dollar she pressed into his hand. "Gosh, miss. I don't have no change."

"That's all right. Take it home to your mother."

She glanced at him as he sucked in his breath. Suddenly his face had turned as pale as his hair. He stammered something indistinct and backed away from her as rapidly as though she'd sprouted a second head.

"Jerry?" she asked, wondering and surprised. A low cough from the direction of the stairs made her look up. A spasm jolted her heart as she saw Brent Houston scowling down at her.

He didn't speak a word or move. Then with great casualness, he leaned his elbow on the banister and stared down at her. His expression did not lighten.

Bethany straightened her shoulders. Let him glower!

After coming this far, she wouldn't be unnerved by black looks. And if he wouldn't speak first, then she would.

"Good afternoon, Mr. Houston. My name is Bethany Forsythe. I have come to see if the property you own on Isabella Street is available for rental."

"I see." His green eyes flicked up and down over her gray suit. "Come on up. I never discuss business down here."

"Well, really, I . . ."

Standing upright, he brought his gold watch out of his waistcoat pocket, his vest today decorated like a medieval tapestry with green and gold vines. Mr. Houston didn't say another word, merely glanced at his watch.

Bethany thought of her sister, who must be wondering by now if she'd been kidnapped. But she couldn't ask Mr. Houston to excuse her while she went out to reassure Charlene. "Very well," she said.

As she came up to the stairs, she expected him to withdraw, to give her room to pass. Instead, he stood there, watching her come on. Her cheeks burning now like two hot coals, Bethany lifted the hem of her heavy skirt the least amount that would allow her to climb stairs without tripping.

Though she knew he could see only an inch or so of white petticoat, her act seemed all too intimately inviting under those appraising eyes. She hadn't been able to forget the hardness of his lips on hers. The last three nights, she'd awakened in the darkness to that touch in her dreams.

One step below him, she said, "If you please."

He moved over just enough for her to pass. The trail of her skirt passed over his shoes, and the feathers on her small round hat must have waved beneath his nose. He came up the stairs directly behind her and pointed over her shoulder when she hesitated on the landing, unsure of which way to go.

"Along there. Should I send for a chaperone?"

"I doubt that will be necessary," Bethany said, though his breath brushed her ear, causing a strange tingling there.

This was more than his office, though a large desk stood in the first room. This was an apartment, neat as a new pin, pleasantly, even elegantly decorated. The nice taste that had eliminated vulgar paintings from downstairs, which she always believed to be part and parcel of any saloon, was at work in this room too.

The decorating scheme mixed masculine colors with artistic techniques. Small pictures in gold gesso frames, tasteful dark mahogany furniture, warm reds. Through the open door that led to the room beyond, she saw a corner of a coverlet in the same Chinese red as the front door. Bethany realized it must be Mr. Houston's favorite color at the same moment she realized she was looking at the man's very large bed.

Instantly she averted her eyes. No nice girl ever saw a man's bedroom before she married him. Looking at the carpet, swirled with gold dragons, she reminded herself that she was now a businesswoman. He couldn't frighten her with a bed. Her chin came up and with it her spirits.

"Care for a drink?" he said, stepping over to the sideboard.

"No, thank you. About this property, Mr. Houston . . ."

He poured out a healthy helping of amber liquid from a lovely decanter. Bethany wondered with exasperation whether the men here ever thought about anything but drinking. Mr. Houston certainly seemed well used to spirits. He tossed off the liquid without a cough or a splutter.

"You were looking at a property down on Taylor," he said without turning around. "Why'd you change your mind?"

"How did you know . . ."

"I have ways."

Something about the way he said that chilled her. She suddenly felt that she'd stepped into another world entirely when she entered the Golden Lady. There were mysteries here and she lacked the keys to understanding. Well, she could be just as cryptic as he was, if it came to that.

She asked, "Do you mind if I look out your window?"

"I beg your pardon?" Now he turned to face her, but she'd already walked away toward the three long, narrow windows that she judged would look out on the building where she'd left Charlene. She dropped her bag on a low table as she passed and pulled off her gloves.

"Oh, good, she's all right." With the velvet drapes pulled aside, she could see just the tip of Charlene's boot where a shaft of sunlight cut down between the buildings.

Stepping back, she found Mr. Houston at her shoulder. "My sister's there," she explained. He wasn't that much taller than she was, but those inches were allied to a broad chest and a strong arm—and she had occasion to remember his strength.

"Why didn't she come in with you?" he asked.

"She didn't think it was quite proper. Now about this property . . ."

"She was too scared, you mean." He reached out and touched her chin with just the tips of his fingers, raising her face so he could see into her eyes. Bethany only bore his touch an instant before tossing her chin free.

"You're not scared at all, are you?" he asked, a flicker of respect coming into his green eyes.

"Certainly not! After all, we're simply discussing business. That is, I keep *trying* to discuss business."

His lips twitched as though he were on the point of breaking into a smile. Bethany found herself holding her breath. What would he look like if he let real emotion warm his face? But he controlled himself, and she felt an oddly strong sense of disappointment. "All right," he said. "Let's talk things over. Have a seat."

Bethany paused for a moment. Though his words were perfectly American, had she heard the faintest, merest trace of a British accent underneath the words? That was an accent she'd always found particularly appealing, although she'd never gone mad for it the way some of the other debutantes had done.

She sat on the edge of an armchair's plush cushion. "My

sister and I intend to open a restaurant. The property you hold on Isabella Street would be, we feel, all but ideal."

"All but ideal? It's perfect for it. I think it's even got a stove already on the premises. What kind of restaurant?" He continued to stand, his back to the sunny window. Bethany couldn't see his face to read his expression. His voice gave nothing away. She knew by now that his face wouldn't reveal much either, but it was disconcerting not to see his eyes. She realized that she could read them, sometimes.

"My sister and I learned to cook many fine dishes while we were living in New York with our aunt. Her cook was famous, and he let us learn from him. We want to re-create some of those dishes here. I will be the chef while Charlene will create the desserts."

"Fancy cooking?"

"Naturally we would provide some plain dishes. But for the most part, yes, we would offer gourmet fare."

He said, "Seems kind of funny to me. I mean, two pretty girls wasting their time learning to cook so elegantly. Weren't you on the catch for some husbands?"

"Really . . ."

"What's the matter? Couldn't you find one?"

She sighed and decided that she'd rather answer his impertinent questions than go on dodging them. "My sister and I felt that we had a fine opportunity to better ourselves by learning to cook well. My aunt thought that we should know these things so that when we had homes and husbands of our own, we would be better prepared for the life we were to lead."

"But no men came along to make this life possible?"

"Really, Mr. Houston," she said condescendingly. "A woman doesn't need a man to have a good life. If you'll rent us the Isabella Street property, I'll try to prove it to you."

"You can try. But I doubt I'll come around to your opinion." He crossed one long leg over the other and leaned back against the window frame. "Do you two think there's enough money in it for you to pay rent? Regularly, I mean."

"That would depend on the rent." She leaned forward. They'd attempted, with their grandfather's help, to work out a budget but Mr. Ames had no idea what Mr. Houston would ask for his property.

"What I don't understand," Mr. Houston said, "is why a couple of nicely bred Upper Grove girls want to start working for a living. Had a falling out with your grandfather?"

Bethany was listening so intently to his voice to decide whether he really had a British accent or not that for a moment she missed the import of his question. Then she got angry. He was too impertinent!

"I don't see how that's any of your business, Mr. Houston. If you'll kindly state the rent, I will be able to determine . . ."

"You ought to learn to control your temper if you're going to succeed in business," he said calmly.

He crossed the room to sit on the second armchair. Leaning back, he rested his elbows on the arms and steepled his fingers. Bethany noticed again the length of his legs in their checkered trousers, but it was the concentrated focus of those rich green eyes that troubled her nerves.

He said, "But it's okay with me. I flare up like that when I get angry too. But I never stay mad very long."

"I assure you I'm not the least bit angry. However, my sister is waiting. If you will just let me know . . ."

"What was wrong with the one on Taylor Street? I'd like to know your opinion so I can fix the problem for the next person who might look at it."

Now Bethany didn't know which way to look. There had been nothing wrong with the property on Taylor. Nor had there been anything amiss with a similar location on Ramsden. The only drawback to these properties was the problem with the space on Isabella Street. Namely, they were all owned by Brent Houston.

Her grandfather must have thought she'd lost her mind when she refused both of these desirable locations. When he'd found the corner store on Isabella and Madison streets, she'd asked first who the landlord was. He'd wanted to know why she cared. At that question, she'd been just as tongue-tied as she was now.

"There . . . there was nothing really *wrong*," she stammered. "It simply wasn't right."

He nodded as if he understood. "I've almost completely redone this place, because it wasn't the way I wanted it when I got it."

"It's very nice," she said, feeling obliged to say something.

"It's the best." His flat tone admitted no doubts. "What about your restaurant? Are you interested in being the best?"

"If I can be."

"Why do you want to open a restaurant?" he asked again.

She said levelly, "Because we *have* to work for a living, Mr. Houston. My grandfather's wealth has evaporated."

"That's what I heard."

She met his gaze straight on, her curiosity overwhelming her desire to be businesslike. "However, he tells me that you, in point of fact, had nothing to do with his losses. Why did you say that you'd ruined him?"

"I didn't. I said that everybody at the station would tell you that I had ruined him." Bethany seemed to see a sudden hot light leap into his eyes. She looked away, embarrassed and uneasy.

As though he'd spoken his thought, Bethany understood he was thinking of what else had happened the day she arrived in Cedar Groves. How she longed to ask why he'd kissed her! That of course was impossible. Plain speaking had its limits. Much better, much more civilized to pretend she'd never given the matter a second thought.

"About the rent . . ." she prompted.

"I make it a hard and fast rule, Miss Forsythe, never to rent to anybody without being sure I have a stake in their business. You're going to have to take me on as a one-third partner."

"That's impossible," she said flatly and rose to her feet. He stayed lolling in his chair. "Why?"

"Because I already have two partners." That was the sound, logical, no-nonsense part of her speaking. The flighty, sensitive, emotional part acknowledged that to see this man more than once in a great while would be dangerous to her sound, logical, no-nonsense part.

She hadn't put forward half the reasons she had for wanting the Isabella Street property, nor brought up her arguments in favor of a low rent. Instead, she'd said things she hadn't meant to, behaved in a way she hadn't intended, and she greatly feared had made a fool of herself into the bargain. The only thing that could have been worse would be to give in to this unsettling urge to ask him why he'd kissed her and not Charlene.

Brent asked, "Who are your partners? Your sister and your grandfather?"

"That's right. I couldn't possibly take on another partner."

"Sure you can. This partner's holding cash."

"Cash?" she asked, ceasing to back up. Cash was interesting.

"You're going to need cash to start. There are suppliers to pay, wages to pay, furnishings to purchase. A partner with deep pockets could come in handy."

These were all items her grandfather had put down on that half-reasoned, half-dreamed budget. "That's true," Bethany said. "But why . . . ?"

He shrugged. "I think you've got a hold of a good idea. I want a piece of it. I'll write up a nice contract and we'll sign it. You can tell your sister and grandfather about it when you get home. If you'll let me, I'd . . ."

"I couldn't sign anything," Bethany said. She felt as though she'd been rudely awakened from some trance. The warm sound of his voice had lulled her into giving him a certain amount of trust. She'd spoken honestly and clearly. But now he'd unsheathed his claws and she saw the tiger in him.

"Sure you can. It's just a formality," he said, rising and crossing to the desk.

"You are perhaps unaware of the fact that I cannot sign any binding contract?"

"Why not?" He ceased to turn over papers in search of a pen.

"Because I'm a woman and the law doesn't hold me competent to sign anything. Of course, I'd be happy to take the contract to my grandfather. He is in charge of the business, at least on paper. As a matter of fact," she said, unstringing the mouth of her small bag, "here is a note from him to you, expressing his interest in the property."

"Why didn't you give me this right away?" Brent Houston asked, tapping the heavy cream envelope against his thumb.

"I wanted to see what your response would be to our proposal first." She couldn't hide a slight smile, certain it wasn't every day a woman could be clever in his distressing presence.

"That was very cautious of you, Miss Forsythe. I'll keep that approach in mind the next time I have a proposal to make."

She left with a return letter to Mr. Ames and a feeling that she'd escaped the first visit to this tiger's cage with her skin intact. By the expression on his face, Mr. Houston had been startled and almost amused by her knowledge of the law. She would have liked, however, to have seen the contract he had been intending to draw up. Would she have found herself all but enslaved to Mr. Houston?

Charlene waved and called to Bethany before she could examine herself to find out why that thought did not appall her as much as it should have done.

Her sister stood beside a tall young man with wavy blond hair falling a little into his calm gray eyes. "Bethany, may I present Mr. Emmett? Do you remember him, Bethany?"

She squinted up at the man, realizing for all his imposing height he couldn't be more than five years older than herself. However, he must be nearly six and a half feet tall. He seemed rough-hewn compared with the man whom she'd just spent a confusing half hour.

"No, I don't believe I . . ." Then she looked more closely. He had a slight triangular scar on his temple that pulled at the skin around his right eye. "My goodness," she said with pleasure, "Virgil?"

He looked older than twenty-four when he took her hand in a firm clasp. "It's good to see you again, Bethany. It's been a long time since I dipped your pigtails in the inkwell."

"And got well belted for it, as I remember."

"Yes, you fetched me a blow on the ear I can still feel sometimes when the weather turns cold." He rubbed his ear through his slightly long hair, giving her a wry smile.

"You deserved all you got," Bethany said with a determined nod. "But how . . ." She glanced between Charlene and Virgil.

"Oh, he was so brave. There were these three men—they looked so rough—I was scared. Then Mr. Emmett . . . what took you so long, Bethany?"

Virgil lifted one shoulder as though in half protest against being cast as the hero. "I don't think she was in any danger," he said when Bethany pressed her hand to her heart. "They were just some drifters."

"Oh, he came up and asked me if I needed any help. They took one look at him and scattered like chickens in a thunderstorm. But what took you so long, Bethany?"

"Mr. Houston was busy when I first went in; I had to wait."

Virgil Emmett had a soft, sympathetic voice. "You went to see Houston?"

"That's right."

"Friend of yours maybe?"

"No," she said emphatically. "I'm merely trying to rent one of his buildings. Nothing else."

"It's just I see he's still looking after you from his window."

Bethany turned. Across the street, she could see a dark figure standing in the center of the triple windows. As she looked, the curtains fell together, swinging as Mr. Houston stepped away.

Five

Naturally, Charlene pressed Mr. Emmett to come home to supper with them. But he said, touching his soft flannel shirt apologetically, "I just came downtown for a beer after work. I'm not dressed for visiting."

"But you look fine," Charlene said, her cheeks pink. "Doesn't he, Bethany?"

"We don't dress, Mr. Emmett. Grandfather usually has dinner in an old smoking jacket and bedroom slippers. And as Charlene and I are doing the cooking, we won't be fancy either." She hoped she'd be forgiven for maligning her grandfather, who always dressed with great propriety, but the part about Charlene and herself was true as Gospel. Virgil Emmett could count himself fortunate if he didn't sit down with three women still wearing stained aprons.

"Well, I'd like to . . ." he said, hesitating, shifting his booted feet as though embarrassed.

Perhaps he thought they were being too forward, Bethany thought. She said quickly, "Of course, we'd like to have your wife and family come too."

His slow grin held great charm. *He* wasn't afraid of showing his feelings. "Oh, I'm not married, Miss Forsythe. Never managed to find a girl brave enough to take me on." His warm gray eyes fell on Charlene. "Just didn't seem to be anyone in Cedar Groves to interest me."

"I'm sure lots of pretty girls live here," Charlene said brightly. "We went to school with some real beauties. Don't you remember Ida Parks?"

"Sure, Ida's a great gal. I see her and her five little ones all the time 'round town."

"Five?" the girls said together in amazement.

Charlene said, "But surely, she's not that much older than . . ."

"She married a widower. Got a head start as you might say. Only the littlest is hers completely."

"What about Melody Dalrymple? Now I remember her as being really lovely. She had those golden red ringlets that I always envied; they were so bright and pretty, just like a new penny. Don't you remember her, Bethany? She wouldn't give you a peppermint stick that year they were all the rage, although you'd given her one the week before."

"Of course I remember." Charlene had never forgotten a moment of their school days. Bethany could hardly recall the faces of those who'd declared themselves her "bosom friends" either here or in New York. But she agreed to remember Ann Davies; anything to keep those roses blooming in Charlene's cheeks. When had she last seen her sister this talkative and lively? Was it before her illness, or before her engagement to Ronald Diccers?

"She's married to a farmer now," Virgil said. "Put on a few pounds since school, but her hair's just as red. Nope, I've looked around, Miss Charlene, and all the best girls either married early or left town. Some of them went as far as New York City. Come to think of it, the very best ones went that far."

Charlene gave a little feminine giggle while Bethany rolled her eyes. Though she'd been included in the compliment, she had an idea that was just camouflage. Did Virgil Emmett remember his school days as vividly as Charlene did?

A sudden rootle-toot on a wind instrument and a rattle-bang on a drum made all three turn around. They'd been talking so intently that they hadn't noticed the collection of women behind them. Though there were only about half a dozen, they were a mixed bag so far as age and looks were concerned. The only thing they had in common were the white stripes of their sashes.

"Oops," Virgil said. "No beer for me, I guess. Not unless I want to be hearing about it for the next two weeks."

The women arranged themselves in short rows outside the Golden Lady. Bethany recognized Mrs. Tubbs in the forefront, with Miss Ivey, as always dressed in a near-imitation of Mrs. Tubbs, standing slightly behind and to the right. The mayor's wife gave the downbeat and the women broke into wavering song.

> "Oh, don't drink that evil brew,
> Your wives and children depend on you.
> For the family home is best of all,
> And drink will lead you to a fall.
> Abstain, abstain! Oh, please refrain.
> Through strength of will, Heav'n you'll gain."

As they continued with the next verse, the dreary tune rising and falling as monotonously as a boat on mild ocean, the front door of the Golden Lady opened. Brent Houston appeared in the doorway and lounged against the jamb. Bethany saw him grimace at the sight or the sound of the assembled singers. He seemed to be torn between amusement and cynicism.

"He's got guts," Virgil said. "But he's fighting a losing battle. Women always win this kind of war. They've got all the weapons on their side."

"Why do you say that? They can't drive him out of business, can they?" Charlene asked.

"Maybe not directly. But their men won't hold out against a real effort by their wives to keep 'em from going to a bar. 'Specially since they've turned drinking into a sin. Even the ol' reverend came out against it before he died, and he used to like a slug of whiskey better than anybody. This new feller that got the call last spring lives in Mrs. Tubbs's pocket, you might say. He can preach a sermon on the evils of drink at the drop of a hat, and she drops a lot of hats."

Bethany watched Brent, listening to Virgil with only half her attention. The gambler, neat in his dark suit, had brought out a pack of cards from his pocket. With nimble, skilled hands, he proceeded to do card tricks.

He shuffled and stacked the cards, making them arch into parabolas and fall in elegant cascades. They seemed to march like soldiers over the backs of his hands and tumble like acrobats into stacks and fans.

"Isn't he wonderful!" Charlene said, dancing a little jig on the pavement in glee. "Look how fast he goes!"

They had seen magicians in New York, entertaining at parties and on the stage. Some had performed all over Europe or had come from mysterious China. But Bethany knew Brent Houston left the professionals looking like awkward schoolchildren, learning simple tricks from a book of parlor games.

One by one the singers broke off, fascinated by the effortlessness of the tricks. Bethany realized they watched the result of thousands of hours of practice. When he reassembled the pack and seemed to make it disappear in thin air, even Miss Ivey neglected to copy Mrs. Tubbs, still singing resolutely, and joined in the general applause.

Brent bowed elaborately. As he stood straight again, he glanced directly at Bethany. The sardonic smile faded from his lips. For a moment he looked stern.

Though she felt certain his performance had been motivated by nothing but contempt for his critics, Bethany applauded too, the sharp claps picking up where the others left off. Heads jerked in her direction and she stopped, but not before she'd seen a new smile awaken Brent Houston's face.

The smile, pleasantly warm, faintly fugitive, above all *human*, took her by surprise. The man she glimpsed behind that smile could be more dangerous than the one she'd seen in the saloon. Even more frightening, she felt as if he guessed how he affected her, as if he read not only her mind but her heart.

Before he went in, he bowed like a cavalier, hand on his heart, to the ladies in front of the saloon. His smile, however, had been reserved for Bethany alone.

Virgil Emmett walked the girls home. He didn't ask them why they were walking, instead of riding in a buggy, though Bethany knew he had to be wondering. She could be grateful he was so gentlemanly as to accompany them. Charlene could talk to him about the difficulties of farming while she took time to sort out her thoughts before discussion muddled them further.

Charlene, walking with her hand hooked lightly in the crook of his elbow, kept sneaking peeks at her around his stocky body. There was no time to tell her privately what Brent Houston had said about the rent. Mr. Emmett had to be invited in to meet Grandfather Ames, whom he hadn't ever formally met, though they knew many of the same people.

"Pardon me for not rising," Mr. Ames said, sitting in his comfortable wicker rocking chair on the front piazza. The sun made a warm pool around him and the kitchen cat had leaped upon his gray-striped knee. With his paws tucked beneath him on supple wrists and an expression of pure bliss on his face, the cat had gone to sleep under Mr. Ames's stroking hand.

"Would hate to disturb that cat," Virgil said.

Charlene corrected him. "Grandfather's rheumatism is acting up." She dropped a light kiss on the older man's head and asked, "I hope you're feeling better now."

"I can manage to hobble along," Mr. Ames said in a weakened voice. Bethany, however, noticed that his voice was perfectly strong whenever the conversation turned on some other subject than his health.

Now he peered up at Bethany, his eyes as bright and interested as a leprechaun's. "Did you see Houston? What did he say? Speak up, child."

"Mr. Houston sent a letter to you by me." She pulled it out and gave it to Mr. Ames.

Virgil cleared his throat. "Well, I better be gettin' along now . . ."

"Don't be ridiculous," Mr. Ames said. "Stay to dinner. That is, if there's enough to feed a man with meat on his bones, not an old picked-over skeleton like myself."

Bethany had to chuckle at her grandfather's forlorn tone. "There's more than enough if you'd like to stay, Mr. Emmett."

"Please stay," Charlene asked, looking up at him through her surprisingly thick lashes.

"I'll go get it started," Bethany said, taking his answer for granted. "If you're not feeling too feeble, Grandfather, perhaps you can go down to the cellar and bring up some wine. Oh, Charlene, tell him about the rally we saw."

Bethany escaped to the kitchen. There she found Manny peeling potatoes. The older woman looked up guiltily as soon as Bethany entered.

"You're supposed to be taking a vacation," Bethany said, taking away bowl, spud, and peeler.

"Oh, now, Miss Bethany, you'll ruin your hands! Let me at least . . ."

"Now, no. We agreed you were to have a whole week to just be lazy, and you're not living up to your end of the bargain!"

"My goodness, one short talk with Mr. Houston and you come back wheelin' and dealin'! What next?"

Bethany ignored the comment about Brent Houston. "What's next is you're going to go out there and have a nice conversation with Grandfather, Charlene, and Mr. Emmett."

"Who?"

"Virgil Emmett. We went to school with him."

"Oh, that'll be the one Charlene took such a fancy to."

"What? When? I never heard . . ."

"When she was a young'un. She'd come home from school every day and sit down here to tell me how wonderful this boy was. Nigh talked my ear off. I remember how she cried and cried when he graduated and she still had four years to go. She thought she'd never see him again, but I told her in a town this size they were bound to meet up. And seems I was right, though it took a mite longer than I reckoned."

Until that moment, Bethany would have been willing to take her oath that Charlene told her everything. She certainly had few secrets from her sister. Oh, one or two things perhaps. For instance, she'd never mentioned the fact that she disliked anything with coffee or coffee flavoring. She hadn't ever expressed her doubts about the Republican party or the wisdom of tight-lacing. Nor had Bethany ever admitted the number of times she'd considered breaking her engagement, but that was just a silly, girlish fancy. Of course, she wanted to marry Gerrald, even if his eyes weren't green! Besides, she knew no green-eyed men who were the marrying kind.

"And there's something else you should know, Miss Bethany," Manny said as she took off her apron.

"What's that?"

"Your grandfather has never had rheumatism a day in his life!"

While bending over the basin in her bedroom, her face running with water, Bethany heard footsteps coming quickly down the hall. She groped for the fine linen towel hanging over the bar. Her door opened hard upon a brief knock.

"Is there enough dinner for one more person?" Charlene asked.

"You mean, for Mr. Emmett? I already said . . ."

"No, one more in addition."

"Yes, there should be . . ."

"That's good."

"Why? Who is coming?" As Bethany raised her face from the towel she saw she was alone. Though she had on only her white lace corset cover and petticoats, she stepped out into the hall to ask Charlene again who was coming. But her sister only waved as though she hadn't time to stop.

Bethany buttoned on a fresh shirtwaist. She inspected her skirt for the white dust of the flour she'd spilled while preparing Chicken Cockaigne. Most of it had brushed off. She dampened her fingers and removed the rest before putting it back on. After correcting the flyaway hair that sprang from her smoothly bulging chignon, she decided she looked presentable enough to go down and serve dinner. The heat of the kitchen would add a hint of color to her cheeks, which she felt were always too pale.

Manny took the lid off the large pot simmering on the stove. She had the air of a fastidious archaeologist uncovering the tomb of a mummy. "Is it supposed to be pink? I've never hard of pink soup."

"Yes, it's supposed to be pink. And you're supposed to be in the dining room. Wait, come here."

Bethany had picked almost all the white roses from the garden to complement the white linen and crystal on the dining-room table. She'd placed a few of the smaller blossoms in a simple glass vase she'd put on the kitchen windowsill. Now she cut the stem of one in half with a quick stroke of a hastily snatched-up knife. "We'll tuck it in like so," she said, thrusting the dethorned stem into Manny's upswept graying hair.

"No, now. Flowers and such, that's for you young girls. It looks—oh, I don't know—funny on me."

Bethany took the older woman by the shoulders and turned her to face the black glass that was the night-backed window. "You see? You're as young as anybody here. You're certainly younger than me."

Manny put her arm about Bethany's waist and leaned back to see up into her face. "Troubled, dearest?"

"Just a long day. Now, scoot along to the dining room. I've got to start pulling things out of the oven. Has Charlene put out the hors d'oeuvres? Yes," she answered herself, seeing that the big silver tray was gone from the kitchen table.

Alone, she took a deep breath and let it out in a gusty sigh. Protecting her hands with a towel, she tugged open the largest oven door. A wave of heat as though from a forge blew wisps of hair about her face—so much for her neat hairstyle! She had had to improvise cooking her roast, as she had no spit.

"First serve the soup," she said to herself. "While they're eating that, glaze the onions."

She backed out through the butler's pantry, carrying the heavy tureen. The swinging door squeaked as it moved and she sighed silently, remembering too late that she'd meant to grease the hinge.

As she went around the glittering table, she bestowed on each person—her grandfather at the head, Charlene, Mr. Emmett, Manny at the foot—a sweet if mechanical smile. Her mind was busy with times and temperatures, while at the same time concentrating on holding the heavy tureen. She only dimly realized that the other side of the table had someone sitting at it. This must be the extra guest.

She stopped, bent her knees slightly to bring the soup into range for the guest to serve himself, and looked full into the serious green eyes of Brent Houston.

Suddenly the soup tureen seemed as heavy as a boulder. Her arms began to shake. He served himself with what seemed deliberate sluggishness.

"And what is this?" he asked.

For a moment Bethany stared stupidly at the pink puree of pearl barley and carrots. She seemed to hear in his tone a reflection of Manny's doubt. Straightening, she said crisply, *"Le potage d'orge perlée à la Crecy."*

"Of course. I should have guessed."

Safe in the kitchen, Bethany pressed her hands to cheeks far warmer than the heat of the room merited. What on earth is he doing here? Now she understood why Charlene's smile at the table had been more amused than supportive. Bethany could only assume that her grandfather's note must have contained an invitation to dinner as well as a discussion of business.

A shameful little thought skittered through her mind. Had any of the neighbors seen Mr. Houston come into Marmion House? She dismissed the thought as unworthy of her. She had a dinner to serve. Mr. Houston was a guest and the laws of hospitality were strict. She couldn't expect to pick and choose among the persons who came to her restaurant, and she might as well begin practicing at home.

Picking up the tray that carried the curried trout, Bethany hoped this would be the best dinner Mr. Houston had ever eaten.

That charitable thought lasted until the fish course was actually on the table.

She couldn't have said when she first became aware that people were laughing at her. Charlene couldn't seem to meet her eyes. Virgil Emmett did meet them, but only to grin and chuckle, though he tried politely to turn the laugh into a cough. And her grandfather had that roguish smile that she instantly recognized as boding no good.

As she served Manny, she heard a whispered, "Never mind, dear," that did nothing to sooth her.

Only Brent kept a straight face. At first she was mollified. If there was some joke at her expense, at least he remained unaware of it. But no sooner had she gone out than she heard guffaws behind her. Though she'd never heard him laugh, somehow she recognized the sound.

She pushed open the swinging door between the pantry and the dining room, as though to check for something she'd forgotten. Covertly, she glanced at Brent. His face was instantly as composed as a statue. She remembered he was a gambler, and thus used to keeping a poker face.

Going back into the kitchen, she twisted around to try to see her back. Had her bustle slipped? No, the very modest-sized swag across her hips remained in place. Perhaps she had something on her nose. Glancing in the window, nearly as good as a mirror, she saw her face was clean, but gave it a quick swipe with a tea towel just in case.

Perhaps she shouldn't be so suspicious. Probably they were laughing at some joke. But why, in that case, did she feel it was her presence that set off the hilarity?

She removed the pot with the onions from the stove top and put it on the sideboard. A familiar squeak behind her made her say impetuously, "I wish someone would tell *me* what's so exceptionally funny."

"We're just having a good time," Brent said. "Isn't that what you want?"

He didn't wait for her to answer. With the soft-footed inquisitiveness of a cat, he walked around the large rectangular room. Though he didn't actually lift pot lids and taste the contents, he seemed to be thoroughly examining every inch of the large kitchen.

"It must be a hundred and two in here," he said at last. "Why don't you open these windows? Get some ventilation going. At least a cross-breeze would cool you off."

"And bring in every fly for five miles. No, thank you." She was dying to know what he thought of the food so far, but was too proud to ask him. Instead, she said with a forced smile, "You should go back in and sit down. The main course is coming up. A special fillet of beef with glazed onions."

"Another course? I'm about ready for dessert myself. Not that I'm criticizing . . ."

"Oh, thank you for telling me. Otherwise I might have been confused." She stood there, holding a dripping spoon over the pot, trying to think of a polite way to tell him to leave. She hated to cook with someone standing over her. And was she imagining things, or had the temperature in here risen noticeably since he'd come in?

He gave her that heart-stopping smile she'd only glimpsed before. The spoon fell out of her suddenly nerveless fingers. Quickly she groped for it, turning away from the effect of his smile. It didn't mean anything more than his seriousness had.

He could probably come up with a million expressions, mournful, solemn, or ecstatic, each one as meaningless as the one before. Any expression, any promise, to get what he wanted.

Brent said, "If I were you, I'd step outside for a minute. Get a breath of air."

"If you were me, you'd realize you had too much to do to go anywhere." There, that was a hint and a half!

For answer, he came nearer and took the spoon out of her hand. "Come on. I'll go with you, if you're scared of the dark."

"Mr. Houston . . ."

"Call me Brent. We're partners now. Your grandfather just agreed to it."

Her lips tightened at the mention of her grandfather. She hadn't had time before dinner to take him aside and ask him if it was true that he'd faked rheumatism. She couldn't imagine why he'd been reluctant to see Mr. Houston in the afternoon if he'd intended all along asking him to the house for dinner.

"Mr. Houston, I can't just go off and leave dinner to burn . . ."

"I'm sure Mrs. Manning will be happy to watch over . . ."

"It's my responsibility."

"What good is a responsibility if you can't shirk it every now and then?"

His eyes had a bad effect on her. He focused them on hers and she could almost feel her will draining away. She blinked and straightened. "No, thank you. If you want air, there's plenty of it in the dining room."

She started to step away. The roast must be done by now. He caught her forearm. She paused. Despite the heat of the room, his hand was warmer than her skin. He slid his fingers lightly, almost caressingly, down to her hand.

Bethany felt a thud in the pit of her stomach that was all but audible. His fingers were ever so slightly rough from the manipulation of countless decks of cards. Yet his hands were not delicate or fine. They were blunt-tipped. When they laced through hers, she felt as if she'd never been touched before.

"Mr. Houston . . ." she sighed between lips suddenly gone dry.

"Come on," he said softly. "It's a fine night."

Bethany went outside with him, apron and all. As she went out, she heard, ever so faintly, the squeak of the pantry door.

Six

The air lifted the damp hair at the back of her neck, deliciously cool on her skin after the heat of the kitchen. Though she'd cut most of the white roses, the fragrance of the dusky reds and merry yellows still perfumed the air. A festival of dancing stars spangled the perfectly black sky above the verandah roof.

"Like I said, it's a fine night," Brent said, his voice quietly thrilling.

"Yes," she sighed. Then with a shake of her head, she tried to dispel the romantic atmosphere that lived beyond the kitchen. "It isn't too cold yet. A few more weeks though, and the frost will certainly be on the pumpkin."

"You ought to see the moon too," he said, still in that caressing voice. "Just a thumbnail, really, but bright enough to read by. It's on the other side of the house."

He settled himself on the verandah railing, looking out into the evening. Bethany could have reached out to trace his profile like a silhouette against the blue-black velvet of the night. Curling her fingers into her palms to keep them still, she stood beside him, not touching him at any point.

In the darkness the garden had a mysterious quality that beckoned to her. Even though every brick-lined path was as familiar to her as her own bedroom, it held a secret quality under the moon that promised wonders both new and strange.

But she had no time to explore. She had to be hardheaded, a businesswoman. And so what if her fiancé hadn't written a line in a week? She hadn't written him either, beyond a civil note to let him know they'd arrived safely. Probably he'd been too busy. His eldest sister, Prissy, was preparing for college and had thrown the family into a tizzy, her mother being certain her precious child's female organs would shrivel up under the pressure of university life.

She sighed again, a pragmatic, unromantic sigh, thinking of her fiancé. Before the breath had left her lips, Brent also took a deep breath and let it out slowly. Bethany turned her head to glance at him. He stared out into the night. What thoughts prompted that sigh? She felt certain his thoughts would have nothing in common with hers.

"Your grandfather tells me you're engaged to get married," Brent said.

"Why, yes," Bethany answered, not pleased to learn she'd been discussed in her absence. Plus, the aptness of his comment unnerved her. Before, she'd been glad at least that he couldn't read her mind. With a superstitious chill, she wondered if he could.

"I'm surprised that you came back to Cedar Groves instead of marrying him right away. If he's as wealthy as your grandfather said . . ."

"He mentioned Gerrald's fortune?"

"Not in so many words." He faced her. "He just said that the boy's father had been in manufacturing. Now, I may be just a saloon keeper but I know that means money."

"Gerrald is the son of J. Raingerford Stowe."

"Stowe's Sewing Machines?" Brent whistled. "That makes my curiosity even worse. As a matter of fact, unbearable. You could have been on your honeymoon by now, if you'd shown a little more initiative. I'm going to be up nights wondering why you aren't Mrs. Stowe at this very minute."

Bethany decided Mr. Houston must be a very good gambler. He could say a thing like that and make it sound as if he really would be up all night. "I don't see that that is anyone's business but my own. And I include my grandfather in that."

"Family aside, we have a right to know if you're going to cut and run back to New York and what's-his-name. If you leave, we won't have a business."

"His name is Gerrald Stowe." Bethany tapped her toe on the flagstones. "And if you must know, we decided on a long engagement soon after he proposed. It wouldn't be seemly to jump into matrimony because my grandfather lost his money, though it might be sensible."

"How long an engagement?"

"Well, of all the . . . Two years. Now, if you're done prying into my personal affairs . . ."

"Just business, Miss Forsythe. I only gamble at my own establishment, never at other people's places of business. I'm a very prudent man."

He was also a very attractive man. Somehow the darkness emphasized his nearness. She'd heard of someone being too close for comfort, but she'd never known what it meant before now. More than that, being alone with him, listening to his voice without distractions, his faint trace of British accent was clearer than before.

"You don't have to worry," she said, a bit breathlessly. "Your investment will be perfectly safe. I'm not going anywhere for quite some time."

"You relieve my mind. I think you and your sister have a good idea with this restaurant. But please, no pink soup. There aren't many men in the world brave enough to eat a thing like that, and I can't think of any man who'd order it."

"They won't have to order it. We're not going to offer a choice of items, not right away. We'll post the menu in the window and if customers are interested in what is being served they will come in."

"That's a strange way of doing business."

"It's the French way. If you don't like it, Mr. Houston, you're not obligated to be a partner. That was your idea."

"Well, however you plan to serve things, I don't think you should serve pink soup."

Bethany put her hands on her hips and said firmly, "That

happens to be a very fine French recipe. One of the greatest chefs who ever lived, Careme, invented it."

"French, hey? That explains it. Anything else French on the menu tonight?"

"Just pastry." His mention of the dinner made Bethany walk absentmindedly off the verandah. Lifting her skirt above the dew-damp grass, she went around the corner to peek in the kitchen window. She didn't see Manny. What she saw was smoke.

"Oh, merciful heavens!" Turning on her heel, Betany brushed past Brent who stood close behind her.

She rushed into the kitchen. A towel plucked from the edge of the sink served to protect her hands as she snatched open the oven door. Acrid smoke billowed and rolled from the opening. The chokingly corrosive odor set her coughing, yet she fanned the smoke away enough to glimpse with burning eyes the charred ruin of a once-fine roast beef.

The ebony crust gleaming like obsidian, the meat looked as if it had been flung from an erupting volcano. Her eyes streaming as much from disappointment as from the thick air, Bethany said, "Damn!"

Then she glanced guiltily around for Brent. He unlatched the windows and tossed them open. The smoke swirled and thinned in the cross-breeze. With luck, he hadn't heard her lapse from good taste.

A moment later Grandfather Ames walked in. "Do I smell something burning?" he asked innocently.

Perhaps the look Bethany threw him was a trifle savage for he took a step back. "Where's Manny?" she demanded.

"Um, Mrs. Manning has retired for the evening," he answered, digging one polished shoe tip into the flagstoned floor.

"Retired? But she was supposed to be watching the dinner!"

"Oh, was there more dinner, my dear? I confess I thought we were finished. Very good and filling I found it too. Mr.

Emmett was most impressed, especially by Charlene's Charlotte Russe."

"You had dessert?" Bethany looked at the ruin of her pièce de résistance and had to master an unseemly urge to break out into howls of mourning. Though she supposed this was a small disaster compared to some in the annals of history, still she couldn't help feeling betrayed by those she trusted. First Manny "retired," then Charlene served dessert.

Wanting to ask the two some pointed questions, Bethany asked, "Where is Charlene now?"

Grandfather Ames tore his gaze away from the smoldering roast; it seemed to fascinate him. "She is showing Mr. Emmett the yard, as I believe you were showing it to Mr. Houston?"

Bethany ignored that. "When she returns, please ask her to see me. At once."

"Certainly, my dear. Certainly. And now, perhaps Mr. Houston would care for a drop of brandy as a digestive?"

"No, thanks. I'll help Miss Forsythe with the dishes."

Bethany looked at him with narrowed eyes. Was he joking, finding humor in her distress? He seemed perfectly serious, but she'd already learned that she could tell little from his expression. He could probably vow undying fidelity and not mean a word of it. Only his eyes sometimes gave away his true feelings, but they were hooded beneath his heavy eyelids.

"Thank you, Mr. Houston, but I can manage."

"Then I'll just have a seat and talk to you." He pulled out the Windsor chair from the kitchen table and sat down, crossing his legs as though he meant to stay awhile. Turning toward Mr. Ames, he asked, "I hope Mrs. Manning feels better tomorrow."

Bethany very much wanted to ask her grandfather why Mrs. Manning had left so abruptly, but didn't feel she should in front of a stranger. The woman she knew would never suddenly abandon her responsibilities. With a pang of guilt, Bethany realized none of this would have happened if she'd stuck to her guns when Mr. Houston had asked her to go outside. Let it be a lesson to her to resist temptation, especially good-looking temptations in fancy waistcoats.

Her grandfather left to slip his brandy in solitude, though he didn't seem particularly depressed. She could have sworn she saw the beginnings of a delighted smile on his face as he left. Bethany said to Brent, "You don't really have to stay, Mr. Houston. As a matter of fact . . ."

"You'd prefer my room to my company?"

"Not that," she said hastily, appalled by such plain speaking.

His grin spread slowly from one side of his face to the other, playing up the deep lines in his cheeks. Bethany couldn't tell if those lines had been carved by happiness or sorrow. However, his smile lightened the studied blankness of his face.

"You've got to make up your mind," he said.

She vowed she wouldn't ask him what he meant. "I'm just thinking that it's late . . . I'm sure you have a lot to do in the morning . . ."

"Not much. Most of my business takes place at night."

With a trace of acid in her tone, she said, "Then I'm sure you'd like to see how business is faring this evening."

"No, I'd rather sit here." He leaned his elbow on the table and watched her, a golden sparkle of laughter glinting in his eyes like sunlight on deep water.

Bethany plucked an apron off a hook and tied the bow behind with firm tugs. Then she began to pump up water in the sink.

Abruptly she said, "Make up my mind about what?"

"About whether you're a nicely brought up girl or a businesswoman. A businesswoman would have found some way of getting rid of me by now."

"I don't want to get rid of you," Bethany said, concentrating on the water springing from the pump. "But I can't entertain you properly at the moment."

He stood up and crossed the room to where she stood.

Closing his hand over hers on the pump handle, he said, "Let me help you."

"I don't . . ."

He sent the handle down and water gushed out.

His other hand rested on the curve of her waist. Though she wore several layers of clothing, including a spring-boned corset, his touch seemed to burn right through her. His breath stirred the hair beside her ear. The warm scent of clean male filled every breath she took, defeating the lingering smell of burned roast beef. The temptation to lean against his strong chest nearly overpowered her.

Bethany wondered if she should have eaten something before serving dinner. She felt dizzy. Yet she had to be honest with herself. Her head only revolved in this distracting whirl when Brent Houston stood close to her. Remembering the touch of his lips, she shivered.

Brent stepped back suddenly. "That's enough . . . enough water to do dishes, isn't it?"

"Oh, yes," Bethany said, recollection herself. "More than enough. Thank you."

She glanced at him discreetly. She caught him in the act of running his hand back through his hair, a confused look on his face. His breath seemed to be coming a little more quickly. He met her gaze, and instantly his face seemed a pleasant, if blank, expression.

Bethany said, "I don't think we'll need to bother you much about the building. If you'll just make arrangements to give me the keys . . ."

"I have them here, Miss Forsythe." He dropped his hand into his coat pocket.

Wiping her hand on her apron, she held it out. He cupped the back of it in his own and stood looking down into the palm a moment. "You have soft hands," he said. "Lady's hands."

"They won't stay like that for long," she said cheerfully. "I'm one of the world's workers, now."

"I shouldn't give you these keys," he said, his eyes solemn.

"Yes, you should." She made a grab for them.

Quick as a whip stroke, he jerked his hand back, carrying the jingling silver keys out of her reach. Bethany made a second, abortive snatch for them, jumping up an inch or so. Realizing she was in danger of losing her precious dignity, she crossed her arms lightly and said, "Would you rather give them to my grandfather? Not that it matters; I'll get them sooner or later. And my hands will just have to become rough."

With something like a bow, Brent handed her the keys. "If you need anything—new paint or paper, say—you know where I'll be."

"At the saloon?"

"At the saloon. But you don't have to come down there if you'd rather not. Just find some kid to bring me a message."

That reminded Bethany of something that had bothered her all day. "Mr. Houston, that boy who works for you . . ."

"Jerry?"

"Yes, Jerry. I wonder if you'd let him come work for me."

Brent no longer looked as though he were on the point of leaving. He sat down on the edge of the kitchen table, his long legs dangling. "Well, he's a good kid. Does what he's told and doesn't take all day about it. But there's lots of good kids in town, most of whom need money about as badly as he does. So why do you want him particularly to work for you?"

"I don't know any other young men, and he seemed to be bright and hardworking."

Those green eyes had narrowed, dulling their light. "What are you going to pay him?"

"Whatever you do, I suppose."

"I mean, what are you going to pay him with? I can't be expected to stump up money for him. I get all of his labor now. I don't want to pay him the same wage if I'm only getting one-fourth the good of him."

"He's not a slave," she said. "I hope?"

He chuckled and said, "No, he's not. But you have to see my point of view. What's the real reason, Bethany?"

She overlooked his use of her first name, though an inward pang told her she'd wanted him to call her that. "It's a little presumptuous of me, Mr. Houston, but I don't think a boy of that age should be working in a place where they serve distilled liquor."

"Whereas someone who serves wine at dinner is all right? You women have funny logic. Tell me, are you going to stay a member of the Spiritual Cleanliness gang?"

Bethany looked him in the eyes. "That's none of your business, Mr. Houston."

"Yes, it is. Considering that we're partners."

"It seems to me that all the benefits of this 'partnering' go to you."

He stood up. He was taller than she was, putting her at a distinct disadvantage. She didn't back away, however. She went toe-to-toe with him and his striking green eyes.

With a feather-light touch, he swiped her chin with his knuckle. It was a patronizing gesture, such as a man might make to a boisterous child. Bethany tightened her lips and stared him down. He only grinned. "Yes, I get more benefits than you know. But maybe you'll wind up with a few too, in the long run."

He walked out the back door. Bethany watched him go, her lips tight. "Irritating man!" she said and hoped he heard.

As she began to set about the dishes, she reviewed their conversation. " 'We're partners, you know,' " she said under her breath, mimicking him. "I have the right to poke and pry, Miss Forsythe, but I don't answer any of *your* questions." She snorted in a most unladylike fashion. "You keep me so far off balance, Mr. Houston, that I can't even *think* of any questions. Well, that's going to change, sir, just you wait and see. I don't care to be interrogated at your whim. Just you wait until we meet again!"

"Who are you talking to?" her sister said.

Bethany plunged a plate into the rinse water. "The most annoying man I've ever met."

Charlene came a step farther into the kitchen. "Mr. Houston, eh?"

"No one else but!"

"Never mind," Charlene said, slipping into another apron and reaching for a dish towel. "When our restaurant is a success, you'll be able to buy his property from underneath him and then you won't be bothered by him ever again."

"It had better be more of a success than this evening's dinner or we'll wind up in the poorhouse."

She saw a guilty shade slide across Charlene's face. "Oh, I forgot about your roast!" She glanced pityingly toward the still smoldering hulk.

"Yes, Grandfather told me that you served dessert." Bethany shut her mouth tight over the recriminations that boiled up inside her. The ruination of the dinner was really no one's fault but her own, though she was willing to share some of that blame with Mr. Brent Houston. What had she been thinking with?

"I'm sorry. I should have remembered that we discussed the menu. It just flew right out of my head." Her tone was one of genuine wonderment.

"You don't think Mr. Emmett had anything to do with your absentmindedness, do you?" Bethany teased.

Her sister's forget-me-not blue eyes went round with shock. "Certainly not!" she said. "I'm engaged to Ronald, and very happily so. Mr. Emmett . . . yes, he's very nice, but he is no more to me than any other old school fellow, and that's all."

"Yet he's grown up to be a very attractive man."

"Has he? I . . . hadn't noticed." Though her color didn't change, Charlene seemed to be focusing more concentration on drying the pudding mold than the little ridges really merited.

Bethany wondered again if she had as deep an understanding of her twin sister as she had always believed.

Slowly, fishing around in the bottom of the sink for a lurking dish, she said, "Manny told me . . ."

"Oh, that's right! You weren't there!"

"Wasn't where?"

"At the table. It turns out that Grandfather used to be sweet on Mr. Emmett's Aunt Celia. He went on asking about her and asking about her, raving about how beautiful she was and how they'd come within inches of getting married before he married Grandmother. And poor Manny kept getting paler and paler. Finally, she tried to change the subject by asking Grandfather a direction question."

Breathlessly, Bethany asked, "What was it?"

"She said 'Mr. Ames, do you think it will rain tomorrow? I wanted to set out some bulbs.'"

"And what did he say?"

"Nothing!"

"Nothing?"

"Not a syllable. I confess I was holding my breath. He just quoted some piece of poetry about daffodils—'lonely as a cloud'—I think. A few minutes later, after he'd asked Vir . . . Mr. Emmett where his aunt lived now, Manny excused herself and left the table. I think we should talk to her."

Bethany shook her head. "I'm surprised at him. You'd think after five years he would have had enough silence." She untied her sister's apron, then turned to let Charlene untie hers. "I think we should have a talk with Grandfather first, though. I have some questions for him, like why he pretended to have rheumatism this morning."

Mrs. Manning said, "I wouldn't waste another breath on that old rascal!"

Bethany and Charlene saw that the housekeeper had taken off her best black satin dress and was once more wearing the neat, hard-wearing clothes they were accustomed to seeing her in. But what made them more curious was the wickerwork suitcase she'd put down on the floor while she drew on her gloves.

"Where are you going, Manny?" Charlene asked, fluttering like a startled bird to the woman's side.

"I don't know. But I'm done with this house and that old reprobate for good! Celia Emmett, indeed! And after all I've done for him!"

"But, Manny, what shall we do without you? Oh, you must stay!"

"You girls will get along fine without me; you've proved that the last couple days. You're fine cooks, the pair of you, better than I'll ever be. And I hope he gets a bellyache from eatin' too much rich food," she added with something like a snarl.

Charlene's eyes overflowed with tears. "Don't . . . don't go," she sniffed. "At least wait till morning. Think it over. This has been your home for so long and . . . and we just came back!"

Mrs. Manning patted Charlene's shoulder and looked toward Bethany. "What do you think, Bethany? Should I go, or stay?"

"Go," Bethany said. "By all means."

Seven

Early the next morning, before Bethany's morning tea had even come to a boil, Mrs. Tubbs came to call. Her shadow, Miss Ivey, scurried in behind her just as the big front door started to close. Bethany had no choice but to be civil, especially when Mrs. Tubbs said in a low, stressed voice, "May I have a word with you, Miss Forsythe? I have something of a private nature to discuss."

Bethany wished Mrs. Tubbs had saved her confidences for a time when she wasn't wearing her oldest dress. Nevertheless, she showed them through the vestibule and hall into the sunshine-filled breakfast room.

Her grandfather was in the library, having left a firm request tacked to the door that he be left undisturbed, and Charlene was occupied in polishing the mahogany legs of the dining-room table. Fortunately, Bethany had already cleared the breakfast dishes from the smaller table.

"Won't you sit down?" she asked, indicating the plush chairs set in the corner where the windows looked out onto the garden.

"Thank you." Mrs. Tubbs sat in the low chair, her back perfectly straight, kept so as much by self-discipline as by her corset. She ran her fingers over the crisply slick surface of the glazed sateen of her dress.

"You too, Miss Ivey?"

The plump girl only shook her head and simpered, preferring to stand a few feet behind her adored idol. Bethany took the other chair, though the consciousness of work undone nagged at her. Determined to be pleasant if it killed her, Bethany asked, "Would you care for refreshment? Some tea?"

"No, we can't stay long." Mrs. Tubbs opened her fussy little bag and withdrew a pristine handkerchief. Briefly she wiped her lips, as though debating with herself how best to broach a difficult subject. "I have heard something, Miss Forsythe, something shocking. Though I do not care to repeat such vile slander, I feel it my bound duty to inform you of what is being said. After all, forewarned is forearmed, is it not?"

"I suppose so. What have you heard, Mrs. Tubbs?"

"There is a rumor being circulated—ridiculous, of course. Your friends don't believe a word of it, naturally. However, there are others, my dear, even in our own Cedar Groves, who rejoice in the downfall of the righteous."

Mrs. Tubbs took a firmer grip on the tortoiseshell edge of her bag. She tried to bend her lips into a merry smile. "You'll undoubtedly laugh when you hear. Some ignorant people are actually suggesting that Brent Houston had dinner here last night." She chuckled most unconvincingly, her eyes as shiny and black as the shoe buttons they sew on stuffed dogs.

Bethany looked down into her hands. She recalled wondering whether anyone had seen Brent enter Marmion House. Obviously, her fears had been justified. She wondered how many busy tongues had speculated and were speculating still on this gossip.

Longing to tell a lie, Bethany held back the sinful urge. "Yes," she said at last. "He did eat with us."

"My dear!" Mrs. Tubbs exclaimed, letting her bag fall. "Not really! Tell me you are joking."

"No indeed. I am entirely serious. Mr. Houston seemed to enjoy his meal very much."

Mrs. Tubbs clicked her tongue. A belated echo came from behind her. Bethany glanced up, aware of two bright brown eyes gazing at her speculatively from over the back of the chair. Then one eye closed in a lightning flash wink.

Bethany stared blankly at Miss Ivey, then closed her eyes and gave her head a shake to clear it. She glanced again at the round face and smoothly controlled hair of the "shadow" and knew her mind must be playing tricks on her.

Miss Ivey looked just as she always did; a few pounds overweight, a placid face, and an absolute genius for choosing the wrong clothing for her plump figure. Right now, she dripped with military braid, in blatant imitation of Mrs. Tubbs's elegant gown. But Mrs. Tubbs's clothes were sent to her specially from Jordan Marsh in Boston, whereas Miss Ivey made her own dresses and could never contrive to sew a straight seam.

Mrs. Tubbs leaned forward and put her warm, dry hand over Bethany's. "My good girl, you must listen to wiser heads. Though this man may have some superficial charm, reflect! He is a rum seller, a man of the lowest character and morals. By the use of the evil glass, he leads good men to perdition. And if you only knew what blandishments such a man uses on innocent girls! What life can he offer . . ."

Bethany slipped her hand free and held them both up to stop the flow of words. "Goodness, he only *dined* here. It's not as if he admires me, or my sister."

"Who knows what such a creature might admire? If you allow him the freedom of your table, who can say what liberties he'll try next? I'm only thinking of your good. Having no one to 'mother' you, that is."

"You're very kind." Willing to believe the mayor's wife meant well, Bethany didn't want to snub her. She also had in mind the obvious fact that Mrs. Tubbs's patronage might very well mean the difference between success and failure for their new restaurant.

"However," Bethany continued, knowing she took the coward's way out, "you'd have to speak to Grandfather about whether Mr. Houston comes here again or not. It is his house, you know. He can invite whoever he wants to."

"Surely you have influence with him?"

"I don't know anyone who has influence with him," Bethany said, a tinge of bitterness on her tongue.

"I'd very much like to see him," Mrs. Tubbs said, rising. She stood looking down her rather bumpy nose at Bethany until she scrambled up from the chair. The dark brown, hard-wearing Mother Hubbard she wore looked twice as dowdy beside Mrs. Tubbs's bandbox freshness as it had when she'd put it on.

"He did request not to be disturbed this morning. He's doing research." Bethany glanced through the hall to the closed six-paneled door of the library. Maybe Mrs. Tubbs's early visit was a blessing in disguise. He'd have to come out to speak with her, which would suit Bethany's purposes perfectly. She couldn't implement the second half of the marvelous plan she, Charlene, and Manny had devised last night if Grandfather never emerged from his dusty lair.

Bethany nodded abruptly. "All right. But I warn you, he's a great believer in the Rational Dress Movement." She let her gaze touch the gold braid on Mrs. Tubb's gown, taking note of the hanging swags across the skirts and bustle. The white satin ribbon of her league crossed her chest as her sole ornament, except for dangling jet earrings.

Mrs. Tubbs tossed her head defiantly, the plumes and bows on her flowerpot-shaped hat nodding and bending like rushes at the water's edge. "I'm not afraid. He must hear what danger to which he is exposing you sweet girls. Smallpox would be preferable to the insidiousness of the Demon Rum. And he should know that man's ill qualities better than anyone."

"Why do you say that?" Bethany asked.

"With all the time he spends at that low saloon?" Mrs. Tubbs asked incredulously. "He's there most days gambling, though I hope he'll see the error of his ways now that he has his lovely granddaughters to keep him home."

Bethany felt if she hadn't been so quick on her feet, Mrs. Tubbs would have surely patted her cheek. As she led her visitors to her grandfather's door, she reflected on the difference between "mothering" and "patronizing." Mrs. Tubbs certainly seemed to have the two confused.

Rapping quietly at the heavy panels of the library door, Bethany called softly, "Grandfather? Someone's here to see you."

A chair creaked and she heard the double thud of feet hitting the floor. When the door opened, Mr. Ames's eyes looked a little bit bleary. Bethany wondered if the allure of the midmorning nap was the reason her grandfather's monumental history of the county hadn't yet been finished.

He looked from one female face to the next and said, "My goodness, if it isn't Mrs. Tubbs. To what do I owe the pleasure?"

"I have a serious matter to discuss with you, Mr. Ames. Are you aware . . . ?"

At that moment his eyes took on a fixed and glassy look. His chin trembled as he strove to hold in a colossal yawn. It defeated his attempts to bury it. His mouth opened. Though his hand flew up at once to cover it, Bethany could have sworn for a moment she glimpsed his shoe leather, so far did his mouth open.

"I beg your pardon. I don't . . . I don't know what's come over me."

"You've been working too hard, Grandfather, obviously."

"Yes, yes, that's it. Overwork. The history you know. Well, a cup of coffee will soon set me to rights. Would you care for any, Mrs. Tubbs?"

"No, thank you. Coffee is a stimulant and I never touch them." Her eyes narrowed as she looked Mr. Ames up and down. She seemed to sniff the air, her flared nostrils twitching.

"Ah, but there are some stimulants suited to the morning. Bethany, dear, would you ask Mrs. Manning for a pot of coffee? Oh, and some of those little cakes she keeps for company."

Bethany took considerable pleasure in saying, in a meek,

subservient way, "I'm afraid Mrs. Manning isn't here, Grandfather."

"Ah, yes, today is marketing day. Or was it yesterday? Well, perhaps you'd oblige?"

Bethany wanted to say more, but recollected in time that she didn't want her grandfather's personal affairs spread all over Cedar Groves. At least, not any more than they were already.

She hurried first into the dining room. Her sister's bustle bobbed and dodged under the table as she worked, the scent of lemon oil wafting around her. A dreamy little tune came buzzing up from the depths. Bethany went down on one knee and peeked into the dim recesses of the massive table.

"Mrs. Tubbs has called, Charlene. She wants to warn us against Mr. Houston."

"Well, she doesn't need to warn you, does she? And she certainly doesn't need to warn me. The man has never looked at me twice."

She came out from beneath the table, a damp, dirt-streaked rag in her hand. Sitting back on her heels, she asked, "Have you had a chance to talk to Grandfather?"

"Not yet. Listen, go into the library and sit in on what they're saying. Mrs. Tubbs seems to think Grandfather has spent a lot of time at the Golden Lady."

"But you said Mr. Houston denied . . ." She stood up and tossed the oil-soaked rag onto the table. "Yes, I'll hurry." Sniffing her fingers, she said, "If only I didn't reek of lemon!"

"Here, you've got a cobweb in your hair." Bethany plucked it off and gave a smoothing pat to Charlene's light brown waves. Considering that they'd both had about the same amount of sleep, which wasn't much, her sister looked almost indecently pretty. Her cheeks were pink and her eyes bright. They had been so since she'd became reacquainted with Mr. Emmett.

On the way to the kitchen, Bethany resolved to find out all she could about what Virgil had been doing since their school days. Having little liking for Mr. Ronald Diccers, of the vacant eye and inane laugh, Bethany thought a strong, healthy man of Virgil Emmett's stamp might be just the one for Charlene. And as for the Diccers's fortune, what of it? So long as one of them married money, the other one might as well marry for love.

With that determination clear in her mind, there should have been no reason for her to stare out at the verandah off the kitchen. It wasn't as if Brent had seized her in his arms and kissed her until she was breathless. For a moment Bethany dwelled on that picture, feeling a half-frightening, half-delightful shiver.

Then she shook herself and took herself strictly to task. If she wanted to go all moony, she should go stand around the depot, breathing romantic sighs. That at least would make some kind of sense.

With a firm tread, she carried the massive silver coffee service into the library. A discreet cup at the side held her tea. As she set it down on the table topped with a thick slab of green marble, Mrs. Tubbs was saying, "If you would just look over these pamphlets . . ."

Mr. Ames hailed the appearance of the tray with more than ordinary delight. "Do try some of these little cakes, Mrs. Tubbs. Come now, do. Sugar isn't a stimulant, you know." He chuckled at his little joke as he poured out coffee for his other guest.

Though Mrs. Tubbs might refuse and go on talking temperance, Miss Ivey was not so slow. With her head to one side like a bird considering a bug, she looked the tray over. Then with a quick darting hand, she plucked a cake frosted with pink sugar and set it on her plate. At the first bite, her eyes went wide. After that, the only appreciable sounds were Mrs. Tubbs arguing the evils of even one drink, Mr. Ames civilly humming something that might be mistaken for assent, and Miss Ivey snapping up cakes like a frog catching flies in a swamp.

"That's one who'll visit our restaurant," Charlene said when the door closed behind them.

"If we offer tea. Say, there's an idea. Afternoon tea. Even if the women won't come to breakfast, lunch, or dinner, they might come to tea."

"Are we going to offer breakfast and lunch? I thought . . ."

Bethany smiled. "Is my ambition overreaching itself again? No, we won't offer anything but dinner. At least, not at first."

Mr. Ames poked his head out of the doorway. "I don't mind that you showed the ladies in, Bethany, but please try to remember that I don't wish to be disturbed in the mornings. Mrs. Manning never . . . by the way, you didn't say where she went."

"Oh, she's gone," Bethany said lightly. She didn't dare look at Charlene for fear she'd lose her straight face.

"Gone? Gone where? When will she be back?"

"She didn't say. Did she say, Charlene?"

"No, she didn't say."

Mr. Ames came out into the hall. "When did she leave?"

"Last night. She just packed her bags and went."

Bethany glanced at her grandfather, hoping that the shock would bring him to his senses. If he couldn't see that Mrs. Manning would make him a perfect second wife, then he needed far thicker glasses than he used for reading.

The problem, as she'd pointed out to Manny and Charlene last night, was that Grandfather was too comfortable. He was used to having all his needs met without having to ask for a thing. With Manny anticipating his every want, without a word passing between them for five years, he had little reason to want to make their employee/employer relationship warmer and more binding.

Mr. Ames put his hands in his pockets and then took them out. He crossed his arms, first one way and then the other. It was as if he literally did not know what to do with himself.

"Well," he said at last. "Well, I . . . I definitely wish her every . . . that is, I'm surprised she left without her back wages. And she'll need a good reference. She never could cook, you know. I suppose I'm well rid . . . this is certainly all very sudden."

He tugged at his mustache and frowned down at the floor, deep in thought. Bethany said, "Grandfather, I'm wondering why . . ."

As though she'd broken the spell he was under, Mr. Ames suddenly said, "That reminds me. I had better . . ." He sidled over to the large hall tree and took his hat and stick off the antler hooks. "You girls will be going downtown later, I believe. I shall meet you at the corner of Isabella and Madison at two-thirty. I hope to have hired a painter by that time. You'll be able to show him what you want done."

With that, he left the house. He closed the door very quietly as though not to wake a sleeping guest.

Frustrated, Bethany said, "I don't remember Grandfather being quite such a slippery character, do you? It seems every time I try to ask him a question, he changes the subject or leaves. Maybe there is something more wrong than we know."

"What could be more wrong than losing every cent?" Charlene asked.

"All I can say is that he lives very well for a pauper. Nothing seems to be missing."

"Why would anything be missing?"

"I thought he must have sold something to keep going. But all the furniture seems to be here and all the furnishings too. That silver coffee service for instance. It's the same one we've always had and yet surely he could have sold it if he really needed money."

"Perhaps he sold Grandmother's jewelry. That might have brought in enough."

"No, don't you remember? *We* have Grandmother's jewelry already. He gave it to us so our come-outs would be dazzling."

"That's right. Only aunt would never let us use them, though I've always thought those old-fashioned settings were prettier than the modern stuff."

Bethany nodded and agreed, though privately she thought she liked the new platinum better than the old rose-gold. Her engagement ring was gold.

"If we're going to meet Grandfather downtown at two-thirty, we'd better hurry and take baths."

"Oh, yes. I can't wait to get this lemon oil off my hands. Did you see Mrs. Tubbs sniffing?"

"She wasn't sniffing for lemon oil, Charlene," Bethany said. "She was trying to tell whether or not Grandfather had been drinking. She was smelling us too for the same reason, I imagine."

Charlene tossed her head. "Remind me to gargle with champagne the next time she comes to call."

Bethany knew it was not for the painters that she put on her nicest walking dress, in navy-blue flannel decorated with tiny silver beads. The man-tailored jacket with the open lapels contrasted with the point at the waistline that lent her body an illusion of otherworldly slenderness.

Even while she put on the absurd little hat, set very square over her brows, she scolded herself for her folly. This was not a costume to wear to visit an uninhabited, rather dirty storefront. It would show every speck of dust. Nor, if she cherished any hope of seeing Brent again, were her chances very high. No doubt he'd been up later even than she herself, as he had a busy saloon to supervise.

She felt much more confident once she had it on though. Her last lingering doubts about its suitability vanished when she met Charlene coming out of her private lobby. Her sister had put on a silk dress, showing brocade between her chin and her waist and another panel between the folds of the silken skirt. The velvet reverse of her lapels and sleeves only served to dazzle the viewer further.

The girls looked at one another and broke into laughter. Without a word being spoken, Bethany knew why Charlene had emerged in her finest feathers. At the same moment she realized how transparent she was being herself. If she ever doubted that she and Charlene shared more than they concealed, that mutual laughter healed her.

"Do you think I should change?" Charlene asked when they'd caught their breath.

Proudly, Bethany said, "No. If nothing else, we shall at least *look* prosperous. Let Mrs. Tubbs and her kind stare. At least we aren't dripping with gold braid like a couple of female Napoleons."

"She was a little overpowering, wasn't she?"

"More than a little. And I wonder why she lets Miss Ivey copy her clothes. It wouldn't be so bad if they wouldn't wear the same thing on the same day." Bethany debated telling Charlene her odd fancy about Miss Ivey's wink. She decided against it. If she was having hallucinations, why worry Charlene with them? The two sisters went out arm in arm, locking the big front door behind them.

Bethany liked the painter the moment she met him. "Tully O'Dell, at your service, ma'am," he said with a slight bow. About fifty, he didn't have to give his name to proclaim his nationality. It was in his voice, his ruddy cheeks, and the twinkle in his sky-blue eyes.

"A new coat o' distemper on the walls to give 'em a bit of a shine and some of this here heavy stock paper on the ceiling to cover over the cracks in that plaster, and sure you'll have a grand-lookin' place. A restaurong, your grandda's sayin' it'll be now?"

"That's right, Mr. O'Dell. We'll hope to see you here after we open."

His round cheeks became a little pinker. "There's no doubt a man gets terrible tired of his own cookin', Miss Forsythe. When would you like me to start with the paintin'?"

Bethany looked at her grandfather. He nodded and tapped his pocket significantly. Bethany took this gesture to mean that he could afford to pay Mr. O'Dell. "As soon as possible, if you please."

Mr. O'Dell looked up at the ceiling and rubbed the fingers of his right hand against the palm of his left. "Let me see, now. I must finish painting Mrs. Shay's shed, and then there's the schoolhouse cloakrooms. . . . Will Tuesday morning suit you, Miss Forsythe?"

"Excellent," Bethany said with a smile. "We'll plan on opening two weeks from this Friday, then."

"So soon?" Charlene asked. "What about . . . ?"

"The sooner the better."

Bethany glanced around the big square room. The front door was flanked by windows on each side that made the dining room sunny and bright in the daylight. The pine floors would shine well with the addition of some wax aided by elbow grease, a substance she possessed in abundance. With an assortment of tables and chairs, flowers and gay tablecloths, the customers would swear they were in New York's chicest café. She'd put candles on the tables instead of lamps so the women's faces would take on a glow. Not to mention that the men might be more willing to eat strange things if they couldn't quite see them, even pink soup!

The splendor of her vision dimmed a little when they went into the kitchen. If she'd thought it really could be as bad as the first time she'd seen it, this second visit confirmed her poor impression. The stove was of the old Franklin variety, crotchety and temperamental. The water that trickled from the pump had a definite brown cast. The windows were tiny, smeary squares. The curtains were those spun by lean spiders in the corners. Charlene and Mr. Ames would only go as far as the doorway, while Bethany raised her skirt and trod the dirty floor.

"Are you sure this will be all right?" Mr. Ames asked. "I know the location's good, but can you really work with this kitchen?"

"Some things that require steady heat we can do at home

and then rewarm them here. But many fine dinners have been cooked on a stove just like this one."

Charlene added bravely, "As for the rest, hot water and soap will work wonders."

"That's the spirit!" Mr. Ames said, though his eyes still looked doubtful.

"We'll get an early start first thing tomorrow, Charlene."

Mr. Ames said, "It's a pity Mrs. Manning isn't here. She would have been such a help. You're entirely sure she never said where she was going?"

"No," Charlene said. Bethany shook her head.

"Curious woman. I do hope she's all right."

Bethany locked the door after everyone. She looked up at the storefront and turned to the painter. "We'll need a sign too, Mr. O'Dell."

"Why, naturally. What'd you want it to say?"

Bethany tucked her arm about her sister's waist. "We'll call it *Chez Charlene*."

"Oh, no," Charlene protested. "We should call it *The Two Sisters*."

"If an old man may make a suggestion," said Mr. Ames. "Why not call it *The Isabella Café*? For the street and, may I say, for your beauty." He bowed with a flourish, smiling, when they clapped their hands in approval.

Eight

The first task Bethany undertook the next day was to wash the small windows in the kitchen. She dragged a wooden stepladder borrowed from Mr. O'Dell out into the dirty alley behind the building and hung a pail of soapy water on a nail driven into the side.

Holding her plain skirt in one clenched fist, she climbed up. Though heights always made her dizzy, she would have climbed an Alp to wash a window in this kitchen. She set to work as though the success or failure of her restaurant depended on having streak-free glass.

While climbing down to move the ladder, Bethany heard the first chittering squeak. A rattle sounded as an empty tin can fell over in the pile of trash at the end of the alley. With a queasy feeling in the pit of her stomach, Bethany climbed up quickly before turning her head to peek in that direction. She saw a squat brown body disappear in the shadows, following by a skinny, nakedly pink tail.

In a tone of fierce determination, she said, "I'm giving fair warning. Any rat found on the premises of The Isabella Café will be cat's meat by morning!"

"We'll be careful, ma'am."

Bethany was startled. Only by a sudden grab at the ladder did she keep from falling. Her face burned. How she hated to be caught looking foolish, and the shame was all the keener because it was Brent who'd caught her.

He walked over to the bottom of the ladder and stood looking up at her from beneath the brim of a rakish hat. "It's sporting of you to give all the rats a warning. But aren't you afraid of scaring off customers that way?"

She said crisply, "The two-legged variety is welcome . . . so long as they pay their bill."

"I'll keep it in mind." His smile was slightly more open today than the last time she'd seen it. He didn't instantly hide it beneath an assumed mask of blankness either. "I'm very impressed with the work you've already done on this place, Miss Forsythe. After hardly a day, it looks almost as good as new."

Bethany realized she'd been half hoping he'd call her by her given name, as he had when they'd been alone. That worried her. She had no business daydreaming about Brent Houston. It came as a shock to realize how much time she'd spent doing just that.

"It just needs to be cleaned up and painted. The last tenants left it in a state." She scrubbed the small square window before her. If he was impressed now, just wait until she'd had a chance to really roll her sleeves up to do battle. "Who was here before us, anyway, Mr. Houston?"

"Some photographers. They used the kitchen as their darkroom."

"Darkroom?" Bethany asked.

"Where they developed their plates."

"Oh, yes. I remember from the last photograph I had taken." Bethany went up on precarious tiptoe to reach the farthest corner of the window. A lunging swipe with sponge and . . . "Got it!"

Her sponge was black with dirt. She plunged it into the bucket and swirled it around vigorously. A strange strangled sound from Mr. Houston made her look down. "Did I splash you?"

She saw that a few threads of her skirt had caught on a splinter on the ladder. The material had dragged upward, showing Mr. Houston her ankle as far as the outward curve of her calf. Though his face was averted, it was as if his sideways glancing eyes had the power to burn her. Her calf tingled above the leather of her high-button boot.

Even as she wondered if the revealed limb met his no-doubt high standards, Bethany made an aborted attempt to free the snagged cloth. She only succeeded in hiking her skirt up another quarter inch. If she tried to climb down, the snagged skirt would reveal her bloomers as far as her waist. She was forced to ask him for help. *Remain calm,* she counseled herself. *This was embarrassing, but not a disaster.*

"Would you mind freeing my skirt, Mr. Houston?"

His voice came out deep. "Not at all, Miss Forsythe. Please hold still."

His fingers brushed the smooth-spun cotton of her hosiery as he reached up. Just that fingertip touch sent the blood to Bethany's head. She clutched the rough wood of the ladder and felt it shake.

Somewhere she found words. "Thank you. It's an old skirt but I'd hate to have it rip."

"It must be old. I noticed it has no bustle."

Bethany retreated a step farther up the ladder. What was he doing, noticing whether she wore a bustle or not? Was his gaze riveted to her bustle area? That odd burning sensation started again, all the more appallingly because it had moved away from something fairly innocent, like an ankle. This was a deeper fire.

"You're very knowledgeable about women's clothing," she said, to say something.

"Part of the business, you know. We used to put on floor shows down at the Golden Lady and I had to approve the costumes."

"The skimpier the better, no doubt."

"Well, the girls weren't exactly singing hymns. Or militant anti-rum chanteys." His tone was humorously rueful. Obviously, he'd felt nothing. Her leg was just another feminine limb to him, no more, no less. Bethany tried to feel glad about that. She found it more difficult than she would have believed possible.

"Mrs. Tubbs has warned me about you," she said suddenly.

"That was kind of her. Has she any reason in particular, or just general apprehension?"

"I'm not sure. She doesn't like to come right out and tell anybody anything."

Looking down on him from atop the ladder only made Mrs. Tubbs's half-veiled warnings seem more realistic. She realized this was the first time she'd seen him in the sunlight. It made his eyes crinkle at the corners as he looked up at her and brought out the amber glints in his green eyes.

Furthermore, she found herself liking him. He didn't take himself so seriously that he was outraged by the very existence of the Spiritual Cleanliness movement. Nor did he act as though what he did for a living made him more moral or more sinful than the next man.

"But you think Mrs. Tubbs has reason for warning you against me?" he asked.

"Well, you are in the saloon business."

"Yes, I am."

"On the other hand, you also own this building as well as the one on Taylor and the one on Ramsden."

"That's right. I also own a property in Upper Grove. I hadn't realized you'd looked at the Ramsden place. My information methods must be breaking down."

"Do you know everything that goes on in Cedar Groves?"

"It's my business to know things about people, Bethany. If I were a woman, I'd be called a nosy-parker. Since I'm a man, I get away with things by calling it business."

There were things she'd like to know. As Bethany climbed down the ladder, she wondered if he knew the real state of her grandfather's bank account. If she asked Brent, would he tell her? But she couldn't ask a stranger about such a private matter, even if, at the moment, he seemed more like a friend.

He held the ladder steady for her. When she reached the ground, she stood between his arms. Very slowly, a quiver awakening within her, Bethany turned.

She hadn't been this close to him since the first time they'd met, the first time he'd kissed her. She kept her eyes cast down, for fear he'd look right into her soul and know how much she wanted him to kiss her again. With all the other responsibilities she had, with all the other things she had to think of, that first kiss had troubled her concentration on those other matters. Maybe if he did it again, that first kiss would retreat to the level of unimportance it deserved.

He said, "Bethany," no laughter in his tone now.

Slowly, as though each weighed a thousand pounds, Bethany lifted her eyes. She saw the pulse beating in his throat above the hard wing collar. His mouth was set in lines of determination and his eyes dwelt on her lips. For a moment their breath mingled. She knew that she wanted him to kiss her and not to wipe out the memory of that other kiss, but to reassure her that this attraction was indeed mutual.

Not a sound disturbed the alley until someone nearby called Bethany's name on a note of distress.

Brent stepped back instantly and seemed to draw away to an even greater distance emotionally than physically. Bethany put out her hand as though to bring him back, but curled her nails inward instead. "Yes," she said, her voice louder than she would have wished. "Yes, Charlene, what is it?"

The window above them flew up and Charlene put her head out. "Oh, hello, Mr. Houston. Bethany, they're making a delivery from the train. It's the supplies we ordered from Chicago. I've told them and told them we don't have any place to put this stuff, but they won't take it back, even though they must have plenty of room at the depot." She dropped her voice to a carrying whisper. "Besides, we can't possibly pay for it yet."

"I'll come in," Bethany promised.

"Hurry. I can't believe how many boxes there are." Satisfied, Charlene shut the window.

Bethany started away for the open end of the alley. She heard him say her name and felt, rather than saw, him reach for her arm. All she knew was that she wanted to get away from him. Not because he frightened or disgusted her, but because she couldn't trust herself another moment.

"Bethany," he said from behind her.

"I can't stay."

His hand closed on her shoulder and she paused, his touch stealing her will. He asked in a low voice, "When can I see you alone?"

"What . . . what for?"

"You know." He slid his hand across her from one shoulder to the other and, trapping her with his broad-cloth-clad arm, pulled her gently against his body. Bethany could hardly breathe. His warmth, his strength, surrounded her and she wanted nothing more than to fall back into it. But she had to be strong herself or nothing would be right.

"Charlene's waiting for me."

"I'm waiting too. Let me know when I can meet you somewhere, alone." He brushed her cheek with his lips. Bethany knew he must feel the tremors that shook her at that touch.

"I . . . I've got to go. Please."

He opened his arms and let her fly.

To add to Bethany's confusion, there were mounds of boxes in the dining room. Small ones that held fish, and big ones that held beef. Square ones filled with linen, and octagonal ones protecting wheels of cheese. Two bags of oranges leaned against the wall. A large bag of the especially fine flour Charlene liked to use for her cakes stood sifting its contents in a delicate white dust.

"Did we really order all this?" Bethany asked her sister in an undertone.

"They have the invoice."

They were the two Garden brothers who ran the freight part of the train depot. Burly, grizzled men who wore their caps on the extreme back of their heads, they were famous in Cedar Groves for their C.O.D. collection tactics. They'd been known to camp on a deadbeat's doorway in shifts to collect the merest nickel owed to Montgomery Ward's or the Bloomingdale Brothers.

"What . . . what do we owe you?" Bethany asked.

One of the brothers (no one could tell them apart anymore behind their huge mustaches) held out a clipboard with a yellow invoice attached. Bethany glanced down over the list and came to a screeching halt at the total line.

"Fifty dollars?" Her voice went up in a batlike squeak. "We can't possibly . . ."

Mr. Garden took the pencil from behind his ear. "This here a temperance dining room?"

"I . . . yes, I suppose . . ." She was so appalled by the want of thrift she and Charlene had shown in ordering their supplies that she hardly knew what she was saying. How had a slightly better quality cheese, added to a few extra oranges, come to this formidable total?

"That's right," Brent answered for her. "Despite the fact that I'm here."

"Yes, sir, Mr. Houston. We got a delivery for you out on the wagon too. Some fine-looking bottles."

Bethany asked, "What does temperance have to do with anything?"

"New rule of the railroad, ma'am," the other Garden brother said. "Fifty percent reduction for temperance hotels, dining rooms, and entertainment halls."

"That's very good of the railroad," Bethany said. "That reduces our shipping costs from one dollar to fifty cents. However, I'm afraid the total sum is still . . ."

"That's what they're trying to tell you," Brent said. "The invoice will only be twenty-five dollars because you're running a dry place."

Charlene gave a glad cry and clapped her hands. "That's wonderful!"

Bethany, on the other hand, frowned as she thought it over. "That makes no sense," she said. "Dawson's Meats would lose money. So would Harvey's Cheeses and the fishmongers. No, I don't think that can be right."

The two Garden brothers glanced at Brent. He said, "They pass the burden along to the rum sellers, Miss Forsythe. We end up paying for your fish when we buy our whiskey."

"That isn't right either."

"Maybe not. But I suggest you leave the worrying about it to the railroad. It's their headache."

"That's right, miss," the brother with the clipboard said. "Twenty-five dollars."

Twenty-five was definitely preferable to fifty. However, the difficulty remained. Not expecting her supplies so soon, Bethany hadn't asked her grandfather for money to pay for them. If she couldn't pay, the Garden brothers would take everything back all right, but it wouldn't sit in the depot freight office until called for. All these things would be shipped back to their sources. Even with fast train service, very little of it could be reordered and reshipped in time for their opening.

Bethany hated the very thought of turning to Brent. Even more, however, did she hate the idea of putting back the opening and of having people say "I told you so." She'd made more than one foolish decision in her life because she wanted to avoid that horrible phrase.

Before she could ask Brent, he said, "Come down to my place, boys, and I'll settle Miss Forsythe's bill along with my own. We're partners, you know."

As he left with the carters, she said, "Grandfather will repay you as soon as he can get to his bank."

He tipped his hat. "Not a problem. Partner." Glancing around at the piles everywhere, he said, "I'll send Jerry over to give you a hand with all this."

She called after him quickly, "Thank you, Mr. Houston."

"Brent," he said, giving her a look that brought the color surging up into her cheeks. Then he said, "Good afternoon, Miss Charlene. Now don't work too hard. Your sister worries, you know. Sometimes needlessly, but she does worry." He winked at Bethany and walked away from the entrance.

Bethany let out her breath in a shuddering sigh. What was it about this man that made her lose her senses? If anyone had seen them in the alley, they would have thought her the most abandoned creature in existence! And yet, Brent's arms had felt so right around her that she could feel them even now. She wished she had the courage to tell him that she would meet him alone, but at the same time knew she'd never bring herself to sneak away to a secret rendezvous.

Charlene danced forward. "How wonderful! You know, I feel as if we really can open next week. But aren't men funny?"

"Funny? How?"

"Didn't you see all that winking and waving they were doing?"

"Who was?"

"All three of them," Charlene said with a nod toward the door. "They were busier than those Navy semaphore signalers that Ronald showed me at a regatta." She began to perform oddly disjointed motions of her hands and arms.

"They did?" Bethany watched Charlene for a moment, her eyebrows puckering. What had it all been about? She glanced out the window. He was standing in the sunny street, talking to the Garden brothers.

Filled with curiosity, she stepped outside just in time to hear him say, "Now, you've got that clear?"

"Yes, sir. We charge Miss Forsythe half price and get the rest from you." The Garden brother who wasn't speaking gave a sudden tug to the other one's arm. He fell silent.

Brent's back suddenly went stiff. He didn't change his easy attitude, only it became ossified. Bethany realized he knew she was there. He said, "Drive on to my place, boys. I'll meet you in a little while."

The Garden brothers left, urging their mules to greater speed than a mule was usually willing to touch. Bethany was reminded of boys fleeing a stirred-up hornet's nest. Perhaps her tapping toe gave them the clue.

She managed somehow to keep a lid on her temper, though little puffs of steam did keep escaping, bubbling and whistling through the gaps. Keeping her voice down, she said, "I suppose you're responsible for the low price my sister and I were quoted on a new stove, as well."

"I do a lot of business with the general store."

"And do you do a lot of business with Mr. Radowitz? That price he's asking to make our new tables seemed absurdly low at the time."

"You know how it is," he said. At last he turned to face her, his expression cool, "In my line of work, I lose a lot of tables to fights. Radowitz is just including yours in with mine. The more you order, the bigger the discount."

"You'll be repaid, Mr. Houston. You can count on it."

"You don't have to repay me anything. These are risks I take as a partner in this business."

"I'll discuss it with my grandfather," she said firmly. "I'm sure he'll be happy to rework the percentages so you receive a larger share."

When he looked up and down the boardwalk where they stood, she glanced both ways as well, to see what he was looking at. No one was in sight. Brent stepped up out of the street to stand toe to toe with her. Before she could back up, he'd taken her hand. His skin was warm and rough.

"I don't want a bigger percentage," he said. "I just want . . ."

His other hand came up. With the lightest of touches, he skimmed her cheek with his thumb. Bethany shivered and he smiled. "So soft," he whispered as he lowered his head.

This kiss was different from before. It was just as strong, just as explosive, but longer, much longer. And warmer. Despite the fact they stood on the street, Bethany seemed to feel again the swirling rush of the air as the train hurled her along, safe from destruction only by Brent's strength. Only this time she didn't have any idea where she was going.

Somehow her hands wound up on his shoulders. The moment they tightened, she recalled her straying senses. Her eyes flew open and she pushed her arms straight, forcing space between them.

Shaken, she said furiously, "Do you treat all your partners this way?"

He only grinned at her, a silly, victorious grin, that had the effect of making Bethany madder still. Her heart beat almost painfully fast, and though she tried to tell herself it was from anger, it had started beating that way before she got mad.

"If I had known I was to be . . . be mistreated in this way, I never would have come to you to rent this place. I've never been so . . ."

"You're not insulted, Bethany."

"I'll be the judge of that, thank you! And if my grandfather knew . . ."

"He'd horsewhip me. Well, I'm not saying it wouldn't be worth it."

He still looked so indecently pleased with himself that Bethany longed to slap him. But she refused to lower herself to his barbaric level.

"Good-bye, Mr. Houston," she said and spun around to go in. The first thing she saw was Charlene staring out at them through the oval glass in the front door, her hands pressed against her lips, her eyes round with shock. Bethany realized Charlene had seen everything. She could almost hear the gabble of questions tumbling from her sister's lips.

Trapped between two difficulties, Bethany glanced at Brent. "Please go away," she said. Though she spoke with all the cold pride she could summon, a pleading tear came shyly into her eyes. "Please."

The cocky look faded from his handsome face. "All right. But don't take on so, sweetheart. It was just a kiss, you know. I liked it. I'd like to do it again."

"I'm sure to you . . ." She changed her mind about what she wanted to say, fearful, always fearful of giving too much away. "I'm afraid you don't understand, Mr. Houston. I'm engaged to be married and . . . and I love my fiancé. Very much."

Brent supposed he should have been in the dumps. After all, Bethany had just told him she was in love with the other man in her life, a man moreover who could offer her a fortune, a good life, and the highest tone of respectability. Yet he walked along Madison Street whistling.

He'd never meant to get his feelings mixed up in business. The paths he'd trod before coming to Cedar Groves, when his heart had been broken so thoroughly that it still missed pieces, had taught him to stay cool no matter what the provocation. He'd grown used to looking at every situation from all possible sides to see what was in it for him.

Now he'd broken every rule of his life. He let the girl he had fallen for do a business deal with him. Brent had no regrets about getting the rawest deal he'd ever put his name to. He had a quarter of the responsibility, a half of the debt if the business failed, no guarantee of profits, and he didn't care a snap of his fingers. If he didn't feel so darn good, he'd see a doctor for he'd undoubtedly gone totally insane.

Take today for instance. A prudent man would have

jollied Bethany along. He would have taken off his coat, rolled up his sleeves, and pitched in with the heavy work. He would have wormed his way into her heart by inches.

But every time he gazed into those richly blue eyes, his hard-won prudence flew out the window. The kiss he'd stolen had been proof of his madness. And yet . . .

He couldn't regret it. Not when he remembered the way her lips had seemed to melt under his. Not when he thought of the soft yielding of her body against him. He had to stop walking for a moment and catch his breath. In love with another man? He'd bet the house that she'd never kissed her fiancé like that!

Approaching the Golden Lady, he touched his hat to the two women standing outside the door. They wore white sashes across their bodies and gasped in horror at his audacity. He stopped and said, "It's rather warm today, ladies. May I offer you some refreshment? A glass of lemonade sounds good, doesn't it?"

Though the younger of the two looked at him as though he'd crawled out from beneath a rock, the older lady said, "No thank you, Mr. Houston. May I offer you this pamphlet?"

He glanced at the neatly bound blue booklet. "*Pits of Horror*? Sounds interesting. Thank you, ma'am."

He touched the brim of his hat again and entered his place. As he passed the bar, he said, "Nolan? A couple of glasses of lemonade for the ladies out front—and don't take no for an answer."

"Sure, boss. I reckon we got a doily fer the tray 'round here someplace."

The place was reasonably busy for the afternoon. A few men drinking on their own, and a couple of businessmen sitting at the far table, their hats pulled down low over their brows. "Hey, Houston," one of them called, waving him over. He changed course to sit with them.

Without being told, Nolan brought Brent a glass when the men asked if they could buy him a drink. As an artistic touch, the barkeep had stuck a sprig of fresh mint in the amber tea.

After some desultory talk about the weather keeping fine for September, Milner, who owned the local millwork, said, "You gotta do something 'bout these women, Houston."

"Yeah," his friend Trask said. "You ain't gonna believe what they're a-doing now."

"What's that, gentlemen?"

"Didn't ya see 'em? Takin' down our names as we come in."

The third man sad, "My wife won't like it."

Trask said, "How d'you think my sister's gonna act? She's already at me, day and night. You drink too much. You smoke too much. You should be livin' a cleaner life."

"Cleaner?" Mr. Milner asked. "She wants you to take more baths?"

Trask said, "That's what I asked her and she got all sniffylike. Seems Miz Tubbs done give her these books and such trash. All 'bout deep breathing, pure thoughts, and athletic stuff. I says I already know how to breathe just fine. It's the principle of the thing, she says." He shrugged elaborately. "Whaddya do with a woman who's got principles?"

Brent said, "I'm afraid the ladies have every right to stand outside my door and write down your names."

"What about the law?" Mr. Milner asked, giving the table a thump with a meaty fist.

"I talked to the town constable about it just last week. There's not a thing he can do unless they damage my property. Let's hope there are no Carry Nations in Cedar Groves. I don't want to send any woman to jail."

"Do 'em all a world of good," the third man said grumpily. "'Specially my wife."

Brent finished his tea. "The only thing I can recommend, gentlemen, is that you enter and leave through the back door. It won't keep them off for long, as I have great respect for Mrs. Tubbs's generalship. But it might serve for a time." He crooked his finger for Nolan to return. "Please have a round on me."

"Thanks, Houston," they said, Mr. Milner adding, "You're all right."

Mr. Trask said, "And hey, Nolan, put some of that there mint in my whiskey. If it's good enough for Mr. Houston . . ."

Brent walked behind the bar to check on the levels of the bottles. He noticed that the cigars were looking a little battered and made a mental note to have Nolan put out a fresh box. When the barkeep came back, he said, "Hand out a few of these cigars to the regular customers. They've about had it anyway."

"'Sright. Listen, boss," Nolan said out of the corner of his wry mouth. "Take a gander at a couple o' fellers, will ya?"

"Sure. Who?"

"The skinny one wearing the darby, and t'other one's wearing ankle jacks."

Brent turned to face the mirror behind the bar and put his hands up to adjust the thin black tie he wore. Though he seemed to be looking at nothing but himself, his finely honed peripheral vision allowed him to focus instantly on the two characters Nolan had pointed out.

The first one was about thirty, rail-thin, with a mean slope to his mouth behind a three-day growth of beard. His battered black hat looked odd on his square head, his ears and cheekbones seeming to stick out farther than the brim. He sat behind a mug of beer as though lying in wait.

The second man wore noticeable black half boots, the tight lace winding through ten holes on either side, giving them their uncomfortable name of "ankle jacks." For the rest, he was neither handsome nor ugly. Clean-shaven, he sat and smiled to himself in a way that gave Brent a creepy, familiar feeling. He'd been in holdups before and had no wish to repeat the experience. He knew, however, that as long as he was running a saloon, the danger came with the territory.

He turned around again and said to Nolan in a carrying voice, "We'll have to stay late tonight and do a stock count."

"Gosh, Mr. H, I wanted to . . ."

"Sorry, tell her she'll have to wait." That got a laugh. Under its cover, Brent said, "You better bring down the shotgun and hide it behind the bar."

"Okay, boss," Nolan said, shamming disappointment. "I guess it won't do her no harm to be waitin' fer me, fer a change."

Brent winked as he clapped the bartender on the shoulder. "I'll ask the constable to keep an eye on the place too."

He didn't look at the two suspicious characters as he headed up the stairs. But he wouldn't forget them either. He knew their kind. They didn't have the guts for a daytime raid, or the nerve to attack more than one man. Nolan alone they might tackle but if they thought two would be here they might leave the Golden Lady for easier prey.

Upstairs, Brent ignored the piles of work waiting for him on his desk. Instead, he lay down on his red coverlet, his hands behind his head. He couldn't even make the attempt to keep Bethany out of his thoughts. She just turned the key and came in. He smiled at the idea of her at home with him.

But how was he to woo and win her? What had he to offer against what the competition could hand out? A heart so full of love that it was a wonder it hadn't burst yet? What good was that compared with the flowing wealth of a tycoon's son? He'd seen enough of the world to know what unlimited money could buy. Bethany deserved flawless jewels, fine houses, elegant gowns, and perfect security. He couldn't offer her any of that.

Long past the point of wondering whether she was the right woman, Brent thought only of how to make her his own. He liked how she flared up over the little scam he'd run, trying to save her money and her face. Though the matter had been delayed by their kiss—for a moment Brent's whole body tightened—he had no doubt she'd make her grandfather hatch a whole new deal to pay him back.

What had Trask said? Principles. What *do* you do with a woman who had principles?

Nine

"Bethany!" Charlene exclaimed the moment her sister's neat shoe lifted over the threshold.

Bethany closed the door softly. She expected a barrage of questions and hardly knew how to answer a one of them. Turning, she said, "I know what you're going to say, Charlene. I . . ."

A sharp knock interrupted her. Her heart sank when she realized the most likely person to be knocking was Brent. She shuddered to contemplate what he must be thinking of her at this moment. There was a lot of hard words a man could call a woman.

But a woman stood on the stoop outside, her head and shoulders muffled in a black silk veil so heavy it did not even flutter with her breathing. Bethany opened the door an inch and said, "I'm sorry, ma'am. We're not open yet."

"Out of the way, quick!"

The woman pushed in, Bethany retreating as she recognized that voice. Mrs. Manning threw back her veil, revealing her hot, red face.

"I been hanging around outside all this time waiting for the men to clear out. Mercy, you girls do collect 'em!"

Mrs. Manning unpinned her close-fitting hat and took it off, shaking out the veil. Bethany took the hat from her hand and laid it on a packing crate. She asked, "How are you liking the Station Hotel?"

"Not bad. But kind of lonesome. Folks come and go so fast there's hardly time to talk to 'em. Luckily, it turns out

I know the mother of one of the maids and we've been having some nice chats. Lands, the stories she can tell . . . !"

Catching her breath, she glanced around. "This place is coming along right smart. I got so much time on my hands now that if you were wanting some curtains stitched up, or some tablecloths hemmed . . ."

"Thank you, Manny," Charlene said, coming forward to kiss the woman's cheek. "How we do miss you! Grandfather too."

"That's right," Bethany said. "He was saying only today that nobody makes coffee the way you do."

Charlene coughed and Bethany gave her a hard, steady look. They'd both heard what Mr. Ames had actually said, but there was nothing wrong with making him sound more complimentary than he had meant to be.

Mrs. Manning preened herself a trifle. "It's the eggshells," she admitted coyly. "You should use that trick here."

"I'll keep it in mind," Bethany said tactfully. "And we'd be thrilled to have you help us decorate the café. I thought red curtains perhaps. Is all that orange muslin still in the attic?"

"That stuff we dyed that year and it came out such a funny color? Yes, I never could bring myself to do anything with it. Are you sure you want *that* color for your curtains?"

"Charlene thought if we gave it a bath of brown dye, it might come out a nice deep red."

Mrs. Manning looked doubtful. "It couldn't hardly be worse. I've thought about making it into garments for the heathens but I don't think it would be Christian charity to make clothes for them out of something I can't abide myself."

A voice, with a touch of the old blarney about it, said, "A foine noble-hearted lady, to be sure."

Mr. O'Dell stood in the doorway, bringing with him a slight smell of linseed oil. "Good afternoon, Miss Forsythe,

Miss Charlene. I brought the paint colors you were wishful to see."

His bright eyes dwelled on Mrs. Manning with an expression of unusual warmth for one stranger meeting another. Bethany hastily introduced them to each other.

"Mrs. Manning?" he said half to himself. "I'm wondering if you ever met my good wife. Dead now, poor thing. Alanna O'Dell."

"Of course, I remember her very well. She used to sell me eggs and chickens. Didn't I . . . ?" She broke off and colored, the pink in her cheeks contradicting the meaning of the gray cast of her hair.

"Yes, ma'am. You came to her funeral, a thing many a good woman didn't do, us being Catholic and all. You'll forgive me for not answering your message o'condolence."

"Of course I will, Mr. O'Dell. Alanna was a fine woman. And an honest one. She never cheated me, which is more than I can say for Mr. Walsh. I know I've paid ten cents a pound for his thumb more than once."

"Indeed, ma'am, there's many a great rascal goes unhung. May I be gettin' you a chair, now?"

Bethany noted how Mr. O'Dell deferred to Mrs. Manning's opinion when he showed them the sanded pine stick with a selection of colors painted on it. "All my own recipes," he said, his voice deep with pride. "My father, now, was a great hand with mixing shades. Never wrote down a one and yet could match a color to the life after ten or even twenty years."

"I'm partial to that creamy white," Mrs. Manning said, holding her hand next to the shades to see how they brought out her skin tones.

"Not as white or creamy as that hand," Mr. O'Dell said quickly and gallantly, though to tell the truth Mrs. Manning's hands were rather red.

Bethany recalled how much Brent regretted the inevitable coarsening of *her* hands, but remembered even more vividly the way her hands had tightened on his shoulders. Broad shoulders, hard with muscles, no need for extra padding under his black coat. She found herself wondering, with a shocking lack of modesty, what he'd look like without it on.

With an effort, Bethany reined in her stampeding thoughts and turned her attention to the pressing issue of paint. "That ivory will do nicely, Mr. O'Dell. We want something light and cheerful, but not white."

Mrs. Manning said, "True, white's best, but not if you're going to be cooking and serving food. You'd have to be scrubbing down the walls once a day. And your fancy new paint'll soon wind up down the waste pipe."

"Very fine," Mr. O'Dell concurred. "Very true. The ivory it is, Miss Forsythe. Me and the boys will be here bright and early tomorrow morning."

"Boys?" Mrs. Manning asked, with her head tilted, as inquisitive as a sparrow.

"Yes, two strappin' lads. Tremendous workers. Not the kind to sit on their hands and let the hours slip away."

"I hate to think how they must be missing their mother," Mrs. Manning said.

Bethany could have sworn she saw just a flicker of a smile pass over Mr. O'Dell's mobile face. Instantly, however, he assumed a melancholy twist of his mouth. "Something dreadful. And then there's my good girls. I wonder if . . . you being so kindhearted an' all . . . but no! 'Twould be a terrible charge on your time. Forget I said a word."

"But you haven't said a word!" Mrs. Manning protested.

"Nor have I. Well, I was just wondering . . ."

"Yes?"

"Though I find the boys to be easy enough, it's my girls that have me be-boggled. If I could talk over their difficulties with a warmhearted woman such as your good self . . ."

Mrs. Manning chuckled comfortably and put her arms around Bethany's and Charlene's waists. "I daresay there's not much I don't know about young girls. You can be sure my advice is worth more than a plugged nickel too. Here are my references."

Charlene put her soft-petal cheek next to Mrs. Manning's. After an instant, so did Bethany. Mrs. Manning smiled and gave them each a squeeze. She said, "I thought when they went away, they'd never come back. Though I missed them something terrible, I can't complain about the way they've grown. They're sweet, good girls and I'll never be ashamed of them."

Bethany straightened. Many warnings about the questionable goals of men had come from Mrs. Manning when they were growing up. She'd warned them about strange men who spoke to you on the street, suggested that a girl should always find a female friend to walk home with, and not to ask directions of anyone but a policeman, a minister, or a professional man. However, Bethany could not recall a warning against kissing gamblers on street corners. That danger should definitely have been described.

Mr. O'Dell said, "I'll be needing the key, Miss Forsythe. Unless you were planning to be here to let us in? Six o'clock in the morning, we'll be starting."

"I don't think I will be awake then." She detached the brass key from the ring Brent had given to her.

As he tucked the key into the pocket of his loose-fitting jacket, Mr. O'Dell glanced at Mrs. Manning. "May I beg the pleasure of seein' you home, ma'am? It's at Mr. Ames's house, you'll be livin'?"

"No, Mr. O'Dell. For the time being, I'm laying my head at the Station Hotel."

"All the better. I walk by there every day that heaven sends. If I may see you so far . . ."

Mrs. Manning graciously inclined her head, like a noble lady recognizing her champion in the lists. She said to Bethany, "You let me know about them curtains. There's a sewing machine at the hotel they use to mend the sheets. Don't see how they can mind my using it, seeing what they charge a night. It's a scandal, that's what. Right with you,

Mr. O'Dell." She skewered her hat to her coils of hair with a long hat pin and threw the veil over the top.

Charlene said, "Wait! Grandfather will want to see you. He's supposed to be here by now."

"Give him my love, if he asks, which he won't. The old goat." Mrs. Manning sashayed out of the restaurant on the painter's arm.

"She can't still be mad at Grandfather," Charlene said. "Maybe she's trying to make him jealous."

"That's probably it," Bethany said cheerfully. "After all, you wouldn't go on not speaking to someone for five years unless you really cared very deeply, wouldn't you?"

Charlene turned large, uncomprehending eyes on her sister. "What was that?"

Bethany only smiled, not sure herself now whether she was making sense or not.

"You know, Bethany, I'm worried about you. I think you're working too hard. Maybe we should wait another week before we open. After all, there's not much point in opening on time, if you're going to break down under the strain."

Laughing a little at the turnabout in her sister's attitude, Bethany said, "You've got better things to do than to worry about me. I'm strong as a mountain. You're the one who's supposed to be resting every afternoon."

"I get too restless to rest."

"Dr. Oppenheim was very emphatic about . . ."

"Oh, all those doctors were old maids, making faces to amuse the child. I'm fine. I can work like a dog if I have to. Of course it depends on what I'm working for." For a moment Charlene seemed to be thinking of something else; she had a faraway look in her eyes. Then they came back to the present, all their old snap and sparkle vivid and alive.

"It's funny. When Mrs. Tubbs asked us to work on the tableau they're giving for Temperance, I felt so exhausted I could scarcely keep my eyes open. But after all this work for the restaurant, I feel fresh as paint."

"I know exactly how you feel," Bethany said, a giggle escaping her lips.

"But we shouldn't be talking about *me*," Charlene said. "You're the one with the interesting things to talk about."

"Me? Oh, you mean, the new recipe I'm going to try out on Grandfather. Since the oranges came today, all I need is some grated cheese for the . . ."

"No, no," Charlene said with a little, humorous stamp of her foot. "Don't be so provoking! What about Mr. Houston?"

"It's starting to get dark earlier and earlier," Bethany said. "We'd better make sure those windows are all locked now that we have our supplies. It would be terrible if . . ."

"Don't change the subject, if you please! What happened? What did he say? Did he kiss you or did you kiss him?"

"Certainly not!" Bethany protested.

"Then he kissed you."

"I suppose he did . . . I mean, of course he did. And I'm furious! Simply . . ." She couldn't maintain her highly outraged frown in the face of such blatant glee.

"That makes twice. Once on the train, once outside the store. Unless . . . did he kiss you on the verandah?"

"No, on the lips. Now stop that!" Bethany said as Charlene giggled behind her hand. "I wouldn't ask you to tell me everything if you kissed Mr. Emmett, would I?"

"Why do you mention Mr. Emmett?" Charlene's somewhat pale cheeks were suffused with an enchanting blossom pink. "I'm sure he never . . . Oh, Bethany, if he ever kissed me, I should just fall down and die!"

Bethany had never seen such shy rapture on her sister's face before. She looked as if she'd been given a holy vision of paradise, making Bethany feel a little forsaken. She said slowly, "Mrs. Manning seems to think you were awfully fond of Virgil Emmett when we were all in school together."

Charlene's blush intensified. "That . . . that was a long time ago. I've grown up a lot since then."

Bethany said, "Besides, there's Ronald to consider."

"Oh, yes. Ronald." Charlene toyed with the bright ring on her finger. "I never asked why you didn't like him, Bethany. He's really very nice, once you get to know him."

"You mean once he stops sneering at people and telling them what perfect fools they are?"

Charlene did not leap to her fiancé's defense. Rather, she sat down on a low stool and interlaced her fingers around one upraised knee. It was as if she were deeply interested in Bethany's opinion, though she must have known it would be unflattering.

As though she were thinking it through for the first time, Charlene said, "Yes, he can be a little . . . But I'm sure he doesn't *mean* to sneer. He just has a sneering kind of face. I saw this painting his mother has in her bedroom, done when he was about seven. Though she said he'd been a sweet little boy, there was something condescending about him even then. I'm sure it's just his face. Long noses can look very haughty even when the person doesn't mean to be."

"I'll admit he can't help his face. Though he could try not flatly contradicting everything someone says and then say he doesn't expect you to know any better, being just an ignorant female."

"Did he say that to you?" Charlene asked in wonder.

"No, he wouldn't dare," Bethany said, remembering the times she'd given him a very straight stare and forced him to change the subject, if not retreat from his dogmatic heights. "However, he frequently said it to you."

"No, he hasn't ever. I . . . I would have remembered."

"Perhaps he didn't come right out and say it like that, but he implied it often enough. Maybe you should write Mr. Diccers a little note, thanking him for his interest and telling him you'll return his ring by Wells Fargo Express."

Rather than getting angry at this plain speaking, Charlene smiled merrily. "I will if you promise to return Mr. Stowe's ring in the same wagonload."

Though she'd removed the small ring this morning,

Bethany instinctively glanced down at her bare hand. "My ring?"

"You can't really mean to marry Gerrald Stowe? Old Mr. Two Rs?"

"A man has the right to spell his name however he wishes."

"Yes, but if it's so queer, he shouldn't get huffy and write nasty letters if someone makes a natural mistake! And I don't know why his family makes such a point out of repeating some illiterate ancestor's spelling errors. How many times did he tell you about that business in the French and Indian War?"

"More than once, certainly. So you don't like Gerrald?"

"I'd like him better if he were a somewhat less dutiful son and brother. Were you even alone with him when he proposed?" Bethany tried to control her expression, but Charlene saw through her. "Who was there? His mother? Did she propose for him? Or did he actually say the words himself?"

"He's not henpecked, Charlene," Bethany said, in all fairness. "Quite the opposite. They absolutely encourage him to lay down the law for them. As they are very nearly . . ." Bethany closed her eyes tightly. She'd been uncharitable enough for one day.

"Yes, they are very nearly brainless, aren't they? Mrs. Stowe dithers and Marcia takes after her. Prissy might be all right if she ever stopped reading and daydreaming but half the time she doesn't hear a word you say. And as for Geneva . . . well, she'd make a perfect wife for Ronald because she defers so beautifully to male opinion. The only words I've ever heard from her are 'Well, Gerrald says . . .'"

"I've seen you at that trick," Bethany said, forced to smile by the accuracy of Charlene's observation. "You managed to convince Mr. Diccers there were very few brains in your oh-so-fluffy little head."

Charlene admitted it. "Yes, it wasn't very difficult. You're right, of course. He is happy to think I am nothing but a mere doll." Her deep blue eyes became calculating. "It really was the best way to handle him. I wonder if Mr. Emmett likes fluffy-headed women."

"He always seemed very sensible, from what I remember of him at school."

Charlene shrugged and said, "Now that we've accounted for the characters of our fiancés—I suppose we can call them our *former* fiancés after all this plain-speaking—I've only the one question."

"What is it?"

Charlene leaned forward. "What do you think of . . ."

"Mr. Emmett? Oh, I think he's . . ."

"No!" Charlene said impatiently. "What do you think of Mr. Houston? After all, you did kiss him."

"He kissed . . ." Bethany put out her hands in front of her as though she were signaling to stop a runaway train. "No, you don't. We're not going to discuss that again. I haven't got a word to say about Mr. Houston. Not one."

"Come now," Charlene said coaxingly. "There must be something you can say. Just say the first thing that comes into your head."

"I couldn't use language like that! I'm a nice girl."

Charlene gave her enchanting giggle, like champagne pouring out of a bottle. Then she tapped her cheek with her forefinger, a habit when thinking. She said, "Mr. Houston is very good-looking. Though I don't know if he's what I should call handsome. But still, there's something about him that makes it hard for a girl to look away. Maybe it's the way his eyes stay so hidden. Makes me wonder what he's thinking."

Bethany could hardly believe the feeling that leaped up in her at this brief word of praise from her sister. She'd been mildly, foolishly jealous before, over dolls when she was a child, or of some other girl's new hat now she was grown, but she'd never felt a white flame of jealousy before. It swept through her heart, burning out every other liking.

For a moment she would have liked to have slapped Charlene. In an instant, however, she'd locked that emotion away in a little box. After all, Brent Houston meant nothing to her. It wasn't as though she were in love with him, or anything remotely approaching that divine and tender passion. Just because he kissed her didn't mean she had to be in love with him.

Consequently, therefore, every woman in the world could praise him if they had nothing better to do with their time. It would be a matter of utter indifference to her. If Charlene wanted to set her cap for Brent Houston, Bethany would do more than only wish her well. She would do everything in her power to see Charlene happy, even if her eventual choice turned out to be a gambler who could make Bethany herself lose her senses of purpose, direction, and responsibility.

The next morning, Bethany went down to Isabella Street to see how Mr. O'Dell and his sons were coming along. As she approached the corner, she saw a boy sitting on the front steps, spitting meditatively into the street. His chin rested heavily in his hands, propped up as they were on his knees. Bethany recognized the nearly white shock of hair as belonging to the boy at the saloon. His name rose to her lips easily.

"Jerry?" she said in surprise.

The boy scrambled to his feet, his fair-skinned face flushing. "Mr. Houston sent me over. He said I'm supposed to work for you now."

"That was very good of Mr. Houston."

In response, Jerry made a wry face and shrugged.

"You don't think so?"

"I kinda liked working at the Golden Lady. There was always somebody around, you know?" The cool morning breeze, delightful to Bethany in her long tweed coat, made Jerry turn his second shrug into a shiver.

He dug his fists into his pants pockets and said, "An' sometimes I'd find a couple of quarters on the floor. No penny-ante games at Mr. Houston's." He peered in the window beside them before saying, "No, ma'am. Everything's first-rate at the Golden Lady."

Bethany didn't let his reluctance ruffle her. Of course any normal boy would rather work at a gaudy and gay saloon than for a couple of women. It was perfectly understandable—all the difference between Sunday School and a circus.

"Please come in, Jerry, before you make up your mind." She opened the door and motioned for him to pass inside first. Glancing over him as he walked in, Bethany was shocked and had to restrain a gasp.

He'd been thin when she'd seen him last week as though he'd outgrown his strength, the way teenaged boys sometimes did. But now he looked drawn and almost skeletal. The boy hadn't an ounce of superfluous fat on him, nor even any necessary fat. His elbows were as sharp as stones where they stuck out of his ragged shirt. In addition, his pants were about an inch and a half too short, showing off knobby ankles. His thin shoulder blades looked as though they were about to slice through his shirt like arrowheads. If he wasn't precisely a walking skeleton, he might have been in training to become one.

The air was thick with the smell of the egg-blended distemper that Mr. O'Dell and his sons slathered onto the walls. Though it made Jerry cough, to Bethany it was as sweet a scent as fine French perfume. She'd be open in no time, if it killed her.

Mr. O'Dell introduced her to his sons. When he'd claimed them to be strapping lads, he hadn't exaggerated. Whether from swinging paintbrushes or lifting livestock, the O'Dell brothers had developed amazing chest and arm muscles.

They professed themselves delighted, then blushed and wriggled like schoolgirls whenever she spoke to them from then on. She never had the chance to judge, from their smiling "go on with you, miss" and reassuring "won't be long now, miss," whether they'd inherited their father's charming accent and winning ways. They also made Jerry look more than ever like a walking stick beside their rude good health.

"Nothing amiss with Miss Charlene this day, I hope, Miss Forsythe?" their far from reticent father said, loading his brush with paint.

"Not in the least," Bethany said, silently thanking God for sparing her sister. "She's making a little something to keep you gentlemen's strength up."

"Oh, now, you shouldn't be wasting your talents on us," Mr. O'Dell said.

"We're not," Bethany said quickly. "You're helping us test the recipes. We want to please our customers and we can't do that by only serving the things we like."

"Ah, now. If we're helping you, that puts a different face on things."

Jerry had seated himself on the stool Charlene had used yesterday. His hands hung limply between his bony knees and he blinked stupidly when she spoke to him. "Oh, I'm all right. Mr. Houston wasn't too sure what you want me to do around here."

A wealth of hero worship filled his voice when he mentioned Brent's name. Bethany looked at the boy with exasperation, though she was more vexed with the man who sent him than with the boy himself. Hadn't Brent eyes to see that this boy was practically starving to death? Apparently, he couldn't see past the end of his nose, any more than her grandfather could see that Mrs. Manning was in love with him. Were all men essentially blind?

Ten

"It was the incident with the cream cakes that convinced me something was seriously wrong," Bethany said, standing in Brent's living room/office.

"What did he do? Steal them?" He leaned back at his leisure in the spring-back chair, his hands behind his head.

"No. Not a single one. What he stole was half a chicken."

"So the boy likes chicken." He shrugged.

Bethany tried to keep a lid on the bubbling pot of her temper. "Likes it so much he filled his pants pockets with it?"

"I don't understand why you're so annoyed. So the boy hooked a few chicken legs. Most kids do that kind of thing; I did it myself."

"I can believe that."

His green eyes flicked up at her as she muttered the comment. His lips twitched but he went on. "I've always found Jerry to be honest enough. Maybe he didn't feel he knew you well enough to ask for a second helping. Are you going to call the constable on him just for that?"

Bethany gave him a *look*. Why did he have to be so provoking? "I have no intention of informing Constable Richardson about this minor loss. I don't feel it's his business. Yet."

"You think Jerry will steal from you again?"

She lustily exhaled in an aggravated sigh. "Will you kindly get it out of your head that I'm angry because he stole food?" she said, holding on to her calm but feeling as though she were about to shriek like a teakettle. "That's not what I've come to see you about."

He looked her up and down, a warm light in his eyes. "I'll entertain any ideas you want me to, Miss Forsythe. I did want to see you alone. But not to talk about Jerry."

Bethany was determined not to let this conversation stray from the main point. When she'd knocked on his door and he'd opened it, she'd seen both surprise and delight on his face. He'd taken her by the hand to bring her into his apartment. Nerves jumping in the pit of her stomach, she hurried to explain her appearance here. Though Brent gave every evidence of listening with interest, she couldn't help but be aware that he was ever so slightly disappointed.

"Nevertheless," she said, "I feel we must discuss him."

"Very well. But maybe you could manage to be a little clearer?"

She had already explained how Charlene had brought a large picnic hamper with her to work to feed the painters. They'd naturally invited Jerry to partake. After a momentary hesitation, which they'd put down to shyness, he'd eaten with enormous eagerness.

Neither girl could understand how a chicken had vanished so quickly, though they knew how men, especially young men, could eat. It was only when Jerry had risen to his feet, a drumstick tumbling from his pocket onto the floor, that they'd realized where it had gone. The boy had turned red, swayed as though he were about to faint, and bolted from the restaurant.

"I think," Bethany said, "that you should go to his house and talk to him."

"About your chicken? It's probably long gone by this time."

Bethany's temper bubbled more turbulently. It might only be that he was glad she was here, but he was finding her just a little bit too amusing. "I want you to talk to him about what he does when he isn't working here. Why is he so thin?"

"He's growing, that's all. Boys get skinny at about that age. I did myself."

"All right then. Why are his clothes in such bad repair?"

"He's poor, Bethany. Not just without funds, as you and your family seem to be, but poor. The poor don't buy new clothes."

"I'm aware of that. Very well. Why did he change the subject when Charlene said something about our mother? That first day I was here, he nearly ran away when I made some comment about his mother. Why?"

"I don't know. Maybe he's shy. Maybe he's ashamed of his parents and doesn't want anyone to know. That makes more sense than whatever it is you're suggesting."

"You don't even know what I am suggesting."

"Well, what are you suggesting?"

Bethany didn't want to say it, but it was forced out of her. "I don't know. All I know is that there's something wrong."

"Female intuition?"

She met his eyes with cool haughtiness. "Why not?"

He shook his head. "Ever since that girl in Santa Fe told me she had a feeling I'd be facing bullets if I played one more hand of poker, I've had a lot of respect for female intuition."

"You avoided the trouble?"

"No, I played the hand, and sure enough . . ." He rubbed his arm as though it ached.

"Then you'll talk to Jerry. Just a friendly chat. Find out if he needs help."

"In other words, Miss Forsythe," Brent said, sitting up straight, "you want me to go to Jerry's home and pry into his private life."

"Yes, I do." Bethany poked her chin out as she said it.

"Why not go yourself?"

"Do you think he'd talk to me, a stranger? He thinks you're wonderful, for whatever reason. If you bothered to take an interest . . ."

The mention of the boy's hero worship seemed to shame Brent. He stood up, the humor fading. His black brows twitched together, giving him a formidable frown.

Though glad he seemed at last willing to be serious, Bethany could have wished he had remained seated. As he lolled in his chair, she almost despised him for his unwillingness to bestir himself on another's behalf. On his feet, all the power of his personality seemed to come to the fore. She remembered just how dangerous to her peace of mind he could be. She backed up a step or two.

"You're right," he said. "He'd never talk to you. But even a boy of sixteen has a right not to have strangers come poking and prying into his life. If he comes to me with a problem, that's one thing. But I can't . . ."

"Then it will have to be the constable."

He looked at her, one of his eyebrows going up. She hadn't known he could do that, and it subdued her for the moment. "Extortion, Miss Forsythe?"

"If you want to call it that. I should call it being concerned and acting on my concern."

"Good Lord, you're a cool hand. But have you asked yourself whether you're wrong? What if I go to him and ask him a lot of questions and it turns out there's nothing in the world wrong with him or with his mother? Then I've stolen his privacy for no good reason and I look like a fool into the bargain."

"Oh, well, we mustn't have that!" she said sarcastically. He colored. She could see he was starting to get angry too, which pleased her perversely. Being angry alone is very frustrating. And some wickedly feminine part of herself wanted to know just how much emotion this man kept hidden in his soul.

She said, "All your talk about privacy is just an attempt to avoid responsibility, Mr. Houston, and nothing you can say will convince me otherwise."

"I'm not responsible for Jerry."

"Everyone's responsible for everyone," she said hotly. "Just because you're a bachelor doesn't mean you can evade taking care of other people."

"No one ever took care of me, Miss Forsythe. And I . . ."

"Yes?" She hadn't realized until that moment how much curiosity burned in her heart. How had he come to be living in Cedar Groves? Had he always been a saloon keeper and a gambler? Where was his family? Had he ever been married or even in love? Where had that trace of England in his speech come from? He gave so little of himself away that she couldn't even begin to guess the answers.

Brent didn't finish what he'd been saying. He walked past her to look out into the street. Bethany wondered if he often stood there like that, his powerful yet sensitive hands clasped in the small of his back, his head lowered in deep thought.

Bethany decided she'd said all she could. If she stayed any longer she'd either wind up screaming at him or kissing him. A delicious thrill shot through her at the remembrance of his kiss, both surprising and appalling her. A thrill was the last thing that thought should give her.

She looked around to see if she'd left anything. Her gloves, too heavy for the weather, lay on top of his desk. As she picked them up, he turned around. She saw at once that he'd mastered his anger. She wished she had his self-control.

"Are you going?" he asked.

"Yes, I promised to meet Charlene at the café to help her finish blacking the stove."

"I hope you'll forgive me if I don't appear when you open."

She glanced at him in considerable surprise. Of course he was going to be there. "Why wouldn't you?"

He spread his hands apologetically. "You want people—the right people—to go there. If they think they'll meet me there, they'll never come near the place. To the women of Upper Grove, I'm just a rum seller, you know."

"But . . ." She knew he was right. Yet how flat all her excitement became when she realized Brent would not be at the grand opening. Somehow she'd been dreaming an image of him standing at her side when she welcomed her first guests. "You *should* come. You're . . . you're our partner."

"But nobody knows that except the people who were at your grandfather's house for dinner that night. Emmett won't tell anyone; he's famous in town for his closed mouth. As for Mrs. Manning . . ."

Bethany heard a laugh come into his voice. She realized he was perfectly aware of Mrs. Manning's whereabouts. His information methods worked well some of the time.

"I suppose you own the Station Hotel too," she said archly, drawing on her gloves. She flexed her fingers and smoothed the brown leather over her hands. There was permanent bulge over her left ring finger where her missing engagement ring had stretched the leather out of shape.

"No, but I know the owner well. He's one of my regular customers."

Though she could have sworn she was thinking only of the tiny shell buttons on her gloves, Bethany said suddenly, "You've decided what to do about Jerry."

"Just how do you guess that, Miss Forsythe?" The humor had definitely returned to his tone, but he still sounded like the King of England whenever he said her name.

"I don't know. I . . . I think I'm getting to know you a little."

"Maybe you are. Maybe I like it."

Bethany closed one more loop around a little button. Then what he said struck her. She wanted very much to turn his words away with a light answer. Then she realized that her hands were trembling. She stared at them in worried surprise.

Very slowly, as if her movements were not entirely under her control, Bethany turned her head to look at Brent. The day was growing old. The sun did not dazzle her eyes through the window at his back. She could see him very clearly. The thing that Charlene had said was true; the unthinkable thing was fact.

"I should go," she said quickly. "It's late."

"I'll walk you to Isabella Street."

"No! I mean, no thank you. I'm sure it must be out of your way."

"Not too far. Jerry lives in Bacon Lane, a couple of blocks from your café. Besides, you shouldn't be walking by yourself through the bar. It doesn't look right. Somebody down there might get the wrong idea about you."

"Really, Mr. Houston, that's hardly . . ."

"Don't you think you can call me Brent now?"

"I couldn't." Her back was literally against the wall. He'd put on his hat, cocking it over his eyes. Now he faced her.

"Are you all right? You look a little flushed." He peered under the brim of her hat. She kept her head down but could still sense the smile he gave her.

He took her hand. Bethany felt her heartbeats come more quickly. All he did, however, was close up the last button on her glove. "Missed one," he said and patted her hand before he released it.

Bethany realized that she'd known what she was doing when she'd refused to let Charlene come with her. She wanted to be alone with Brent. She'd come here with a hidden hope that he would take the opportunity she offered to kiss her again. This time she'd meant to kiss him back, to enjoy once in her life the pleasures she'd heard nice girls never knew. She sneaked a glance toward the red bedspread in the room beyond and discovered she had no idea how far she would have been willing to go.

She had little to say as he walked her back to the café. He didn't seem to notice her silence, chatting as he did of how the town had changed since he'd come to it six years before. Here was her chance to find out everything she wanted to know about him, and she failed to take it. The two things she'd discovered in his apartment so amazed her that she could hardly think. Bethany couldn't even tell if she was happy or horror-struck.

He left her at the door, passing a few words of greeting with Charlene. She was waiting on the doorstep, unable to abide the smell inside any longer. "I'm going straight home and take a scented bath," Charlene confided as soon as Brent had walked on. "Anything besides the smell of paint!"

"Yes, dear. Whatever you like."

"Then I think I'll teach my pet elephant, Accordion, how to leap through burning hoops."

"That will be nice." Bethany watched Brent walk away. He held his shoulders straight and his steps were firm and unhesitating. But he hadn't made her trot to keep up or slowed down so much to protect her feminine weaknesses that she'd been outpacing him either. He had a nice, steady walk, a man's walk.

"Bethany!" her sister cried. "Have you listened to a word I said?"

"Certainly. Warm bath, scent, elephant, hoops. But I told you Accordion was a silly name for an elephant. Obelisk is so much more elephant."

"Well, I was starting to wonder whether Mr. Houston had hypnotized you. You had the strangest look on your face."

"Did I? It must be the heat. This dress is really too thick for this time of year. Do you think we'll have an Indian summer?"

Charlene picked up the basket at her feet. "Don't change the subject. Is Mr. Houston going to see what's wrong with that boy?"

"Yes."

"Did he kiss you again?"

"No," Bethany said, embarrassed by how forlorn that

single syllable sounded. "No, he didn't kiss me. He buttoned my glove."

"That's the strangest way to go about courting a girl that I've ever heard of. *Giving* her gloves is a well-known token of affection but buttoning gloves is something new to me."

Brent had turned the corner. Bethany made her decision. "Would you mind very much walking home by yourself? I feel I ought . . . that is, Jerry is working for us now. That makes us responsible, doesn't it?"

"I suppose so. No, I don't mind if you don't come right now. As a matter of fact . . ." Bethany heard Charlene's hesitation and saw her blush. "As a matter of fact, Mr. Emmett did say he might be coming by here on his way home."

"Shall I wait with you until he comes?"

"No, you might lose Mr. Houston. Besides, here he comes now." Charlene nodded over Bethany's shoulder and she spun about, almost expecting to see Brent, though he'd gone off in the other direction.

Instead, she saw Mr. Emmett. Though he greeted her, he had eyes only for Charlene. Realizing that not only did she leave Charlene in very capable hands but that her sister actually wished for her absence, Bethany hurried off after Brent.

At Christmastime in New York, Aunt Poste did her Christian duty like so many fashionable ladies by leaving hampers for the poor. Bethany and Charlene had often helped her, tying the big bows on the handles and by adding one or two little treats of their own. Then they'd all bundle up in the sleigh, if there was enough snow on the streets, and go off on their errand of charity.

The slums and tenements looked like friendly giants under their snug hats of snow. A mound of trash might be noxious in the summer but in winter a gleaming white shell turned it into a fairy castle. The snow altered all the filth and offensiveness into a pristine and even romantic landscape that might have been anywhere in the world except for New York's Lower East Side.

But this was autumn, bleak and naked. There was no gentle, concealing snow. Nothing disguised the ragged paint, the sagging roof, the pitiful plain despair of poverty. Bethany could only stare about her in appalled silence. In New York, she'd learned to expect a certain amount of squalor. It shocked her to the core to realize that Cedar Groves also had a slum.

She reached the unsheltered doorway just as Brent raised his hand to knock on the warped and twisted boards of the front door. "I'm responsible too," she said.

Brent looked at her then with the same half-angry, half-wondering expression he'd had the first day they'd met, when she'd helped the pregnant girl he had escorted to the train. Bethany now had the knowledge to interpret that look. He'd given himself away in his office. Brent Houston was in love with her.

He knocked at the door. As though in answer, they heard a baby crying, a kind of choked squall. The thin sound suddenly cut off to be replaced with a rasping sound that raised all the hairs on Bethany's neck.

She didn't wait for Brent to knock a second time. When she turned the doorknob, it came off in her hand. She dropped it. Pushing open the door, she went rudely in.

A baby, about five months old, lay on its back in a carved wooden cradle. There didn't seem to be another soul in the squalid two-room house. Bethany snatched up the choking child, turned it over her arm, and gave it a quick, sharp blow on the back.

Something small and dark shot out of the child's mouth to spin away rattling into a corner of the room.

At once, the baby began to cry lustily. Bethany turned it right side up and held it against her shoulder. "There, now. All better," she said firmly.

The child might no longer be choking but it certainly

wasn't all better. For one thing, she'd be very surprised if
the diaper now pressed against her wool dress had been
changed since morning. For another, the child's pale hair
was all matted and stuck to the pinkly gray skull. He or she
smelled of many a day passed without washing.

"Do you see a change of diapers anywhere?" she said to
Brent over the sounds of the now hiccuping baby.

He stood a few feet inside the room, staring at her. "I
wouldn't have known what to do," he said. "You . . .
you're amazing, Bethany."

The baby had stopped crying and was trying to grab the
feathers in her hat. She smiled at the baby, taking one of its
wrists in her hand and waving the tiny limp hand. "Say,
'Hello, Mr. Houston.' Say, 'Where's that diaper?'"

When he came back to report that the only diapers he
found lay in an unwashed pile in the backyard, Bethany
went to see. Though the diapers were as bad as he said, there
was at least a pump. She set Brent to working it, determined
to bathe this baby before another moment passed, even if
she had to settle for a sponge bath. One glance showed the
baby to be a girl.

"There's no food in the house either," she said as Brent
stood beside her making faces at the baby. "I checked all the
cupboards while you were pumping. And I can't find
anything for the child to wear, except for one slip and it's in
no condition to be worn either."

Brent reached inside his coat and brought out with a
flourish his shining red handkerchief. "If I may donate
this?"

"Thank you. That will do nicely." She dried the baby off
on what Brent recognized as a very finely embroidered
ladies petticoat. He shot a glance at Bethany and wondered
how she'd managed to slip it off without disturbing any of
her clothing.

She wrapped the handkerchief around the child's loins,
tying off the corners. "Now, you're dressed better than a
princess. I bet not even Indian princesses wear *silk* diapers."

The baby smiled with an open toothless mouth. Her hair now stood straight up. Though damp, it showed signs of becoming a fluffy golden crown.

Brent looked at the little girl peering at him from over Bethany's shoulder. "Her eyes certainly are blue," he said. "They're almost the same color as yours."

"Whose baby is this?" she asked. "You don't suppose . . . no, he's too young."

"You mean is it Jerry's? He's not too young, Bethany."

She didn't want to hear that. Walking away, she bent awkwardly to pick up the thing from the corner that the baby had had in her mouth. "It's a wooden bead from her cradle," she said. "That's so dangerous. She's lucky she didn't choke to death before we got here."

"Now you really are responsible," Brent said.

"Yes." Bethany looked around the tiny house. The second room held only two piles of straw covered by dirty mattress ticking. The far end of the main room was lined with cupboards, empty except for a strong smell of mice. For the rest, it was dark, cheerless, and filthy.

"This is dreadful," she said. "Are you sure Jerry lives here?"

"That's what he said when I hired him."

"How long has he worked for you?"

"Eight months, give or take a little. Believe me, Bethany, if I'd known he was living like this, I would have done something about it sooner."

Bethany nodded. "I do believe you. I don't think you're the kind of man who would turn a blind eye once you saw something was wrong."

"But you're a little disappointed in me because I didn't go out of my way to see what was wrong? I don't know that I blame you. But it will be all right now. I'll see to it personally. For instance . . ."

From another pocket he brought out a memorandum book with a small gold pen attached. Unkinking the silken cord that kept the pen with the book, he said, "Now you tell me what a baby needs, and I'll go at once down to Brooke's general store and buy it. Milk, to begin with."

"That's right. And some of that new Nestlé lactated food. I've heard it's very good."

"Nest. Lac. Food," he repeated, writing. "And . . ."

Even Bethany was surprised by the number of things a baby needed, especially when it had nothing at all. Brent smiled as he wrote in his book. "Washing soda, soap, scissors . . . Should a baby have scissors, Bethany?"

"We need them to cut the diaper cloth, you . . . man. They don't come in nice little squares straight from the store, you know."

"I don't know the first thing about children. Why do you?"

"I used to love to watch all the neighborhood babies at church or during the day. I've always liked the littlest ones best of all."

Though Brent watched, Bethany looked into the baby's eyes and made gushing, gooing noises with a complete lack of self-consciousness. The little one laughed noiselessly and waved her tiny but perfect fingers. She had long golden lashes fringing her remarkably blue eyes. Her nose was just a baby blob, slightly moist, and her lips should have been a wee rosebud, but weren't. Bethany thought her the most delightful baby she'd ever seen, though somewhat thin.

"Well, she'll soon fatten up with all this food on the menu," Brent said when Bethany voiced her opinion.

He came closer and put out his finger. The infant caught it at once and tugged, trying to convey this strange object to her mouth. He chuckled and said, "A born charmer, that's you. Ol' Uncle Brent will hurry along with the goodies, kid. I wish we knew your name."

Above the baby's head, Bethany met his smiling look with a tender smile of her own. All at once, Brent's face changed, become serious, almost fierce. Up until now, Bethany had acted on maternal instinct alone. Now she wondered how all her actions had appeared to him. He had said he thought she was "amazing." But was that good or bad? And why did his opinion of her suddenly matter so much?

"I'll hurry back as quickly as I can," he said, freeing his hand. For an instant, his crooked forefinger brushed her cheek. "Will you be all right here alone?"

"Of course. Besides, I'm not alone."

The air in the little house was damp and cool. Bethany put the baby down in her cradle. At once the child began to cry. Talking to her, reassuring her that this was only temporary, Bethany wriggled and writhed out of another of her petticoats. Fortunately she'd been taught from earliest childhood to always wear at least three.

This one was red flannel. It made an admirable baby shawl. Wrapped up in its warmth, still lingering from Bethany's body, the little one's blinks became longer and longer. Though she'd snap herself awake with a shake of her head, in a few moments, however, her head had fallen like a drifting leaf onto Bethany's shoulder. A bubble came and went between her slack lips with a whiff of sweet baby breath. Bethany found herself grinning like a fond fool.

There was really no place to sit down. So Bethany paced back and forth across the floor, though she yearned to take a broom to it. She had a strong suspicion the broom had gone the way of the furniture—sold for a few mouthfuls of food.

Her shoulder became quite numb. The one time she tried to put the child in her cradle, the blue eyes had opened in an accusatory stare while the child caught her breath to yell. Bethany managed to shift the baby to the other shoulder and she went back to sleep at once. Bethany continued to pace. With any luck at all, Brent would be back very soon.

She'd gone into the wretched backyard of hard-packed dirt and shattered glass for a breath of reasonably fresh air when she heard a voice cry, "Dory? Dory, where are you?"

The female voice sounded far too young to be the child's mother. At once, Bethany went back into the house. Though the sun had left only golden and pink streaks in the sky, she could still see.

"Who are you? What are you doing with my sister?"

The girl who flew at her and all but snatched the baby from Bethany's arms could not have been older than seven.

Eleven

"My momma's gonna be back in a minute, so you better get outta here!" the little girl said loudly, stomping her feet on the dirty floor. The baby startled awake and began to scream like a steam whistle at the surprise and suddenness of her sister's shout.

"Where is your mother?" Bethany demanded, though she had a dreadful suspicion that she already knew.

The little girl began jostling her sister in an impatient attempt to quiet her. "She . . . she's just around the corner. Be quiet, Dory! Be quiet!"

Not surprisingly, the baby did not quiet down. Her screams became too piercing to bear. Bethany had had no idea that such a small being could produce such an enormity of sound.

Taking charge, Bethany lifted the baby firmly out of the little girl's arms. Dory ceased screaming at once, though she went on whimpering. Brent's silk handkerchief was soaked.

"Give me back my sister!" the little girl yelled and charged forward. "You got no right . . ."

Carefully embracing Dory, Bethany held the baby up out of the child's reach. "I don't mean her any harm. She seems to like me, that's all."

"I can take care of her myself." Her eyes, more gray than blue, grew sulky under her lowering brows. She too had blond hair, peeking out in wisps from under a dirty kerchief. The skirt of her print dress gaped in a large rip, showing her mud-splashed bare legs underneath.

"Obviously you've been doing just that for some time now." Determined to win the girl over, Bethany added, "And doing a fine job, I'm sure. She seems a very healthy baby."

"Course she is. Why wouldn't she be? Really, lady, Momma'll be back in a minute. You don't gotta stay."

Bethany nodded. "I'll wait for her. Tell me, do you have any *clean* diapers? I couldn't find any before."

"I was gonna wash 'em," the girl admitted. Then she flared up again. "You got no right to be askin' me questions. Give me back my sister."

Once again, Bethany had to lift the baby out of range of her sister's grasping hands. "She's fine where she is. How old is Dory?"

"Be six months old next week. And like I say, she's plenty healthy so you got no cause . . ."

"What's your name?" Almost against her will, Bethany was fascinated by this tiny virago. Though she hardly reached Bethany's elbow and with a mouth full of missing teeth, she argued her points like a Philadelphia lawyer.

"Faye Windom. What's it to you?"

"I'm Bethany Forsythe. Your brother works for me."

"Jerry?"

"How many brothers have you?"

"Just Jerry. But he works down at the Golden Lady. He never said nothing about no woman. Unless . . . are you Mr. Brent's fancy piece?" Her eyes, though they had little of the child about them, were still frank enough to look her up and down with open curiosity. "I guess not," she said.

"Definitely not," Bethany confirmed. Had Brent a "fancy piece" at the saloon? Was he merely toying with her affections? And since when did she have any affections that he could possibly toy with?

Baby Dory had taken to gumming Bethany's collar. Realizing the baby was hungry, Bethany wished Brent would hurry back. "Is there anything for the baby to eat?" she asked.

"Not till Je . . . Momma comes back. And she'll be here soon; so you might as well get going. She won't want to talk to you." This was said all in a rush.

"All the same, I think I'd like to speak with her. Also, Mr. . . . Mr. Brent is going to meet me here." As Faye thought this over, Bethany wondered what further stratagem the girl would try to get rid of her.

"Well, if it's Mr. Brent . . ." Faye said grudgingly. "He's a straight shooter. Jerry tells me all about him and the saloon. One day, he says he'll take me down to see it. Mr. Brent's okay. He wouldn't never rat anybody out."

Bethany understood that Jerry's working at the saloon was bad not just for him, but for his sister too. A girl of this age should know nothing of the seamy underside of life. Yet she seemed to have picked up some phrases that horrified Bethany who could only snatch a glimpse of their meaning.

Nor should she be the sole caretaker of a baby. A child of this age should have nothing to care for except dolls, kittens, and a patch of flower garden. That had been Bethany's and Charlene's childhood. Looking into these gray, already hardened eyes, she realized just how protected and sheltered a childhood they had been given.

Faye said grudgingly, "All right, stay if you want. Jerry'll be here soon. He'll tell you everything's on the level. You won't need to talk to the judge."

"What judge?"

The little girl's thin shoulders lifted in a shrug. "You know, the judge. Jerry says he wears a black cape and has a hammer made of gold."

Bethany wondered if the "judge" was some character out of a folktale, dreamed up to frighten small children into being good.

Faye went to sit down on the straw that served as a mattress. She said nothing further, but kept shooting dark glances at Bethany.

Bethany paced, humming a snatch of "I'll Take You Home Again, Kathleen" to quiet Dory. She'd begun to whimper again, as she sought, as blindly as a puppy, for something to eat. "It won't be long now," she said. "Mr. Brent will come back with an armload of tasty yummies for Dory."

It kept getting darker. Bethany knew there wasn't a lamp in the house. She wondered if these children simply went to bed as soon as it was dark, like savages. With any luck, Brent would remember to buy candles.

As soon as the sun was gone, Bethany became aware also of the cold draft that blew across the floor. The door, warped and gaping, did little to keep out the chill. Though it was only early autumn, each night became a little colder than the one before. What would this little shanty be like in another month?

When Brent came back, he was not alone. But Bethany had no leisure to talk to Jerry now. She only took the lighted lantern from his hand so she could rummage through the box of goods Brent set on the floor. However, she did glance at Faye just in time to see her thrust something under the dirty straw.

Then she ran over to her brother and began pouring out her grievances. "She got no right to come barging in here. Like I told her, Momma'll be back in a minute. She don't need to stay. She's bossy."

Her brother put his hands on the little girl's shoulders, holding her still. "Faye, it's all right. I told Mr. Brent everything. He knows Momma's gone."

A silence fell. Even the baby stopped whimpering. "You . . . you told?" Faye whispered. "But we swore we'd never let on. You said you'd die first."

Unable to meet her accusing eyes, Jerry said, "I had to tell. I didn't want to. I had to. We can't keep going by ourselves, Faye. We've tried. For three months, we've tried. I'm awful tired. I know you are too."

"We were doing fine till she showed up," Faye said, stabbing her thumb toward Bethany.

"But I don't know if we would of made it through the

winter, Faye. You don't have any shoes, and we sold the blanket. I just don't know what else we can do."

Crouched down to search the groceries, Bethany continued to paw among the boxes and cans. Though her heart twisted at the sadness of the children's situation, she had a hungry baby to feed. She stood upright, the beige and brown can of lactated food in her hand. Ignoring everything but the task in hand, she asked Brent, "Did you remember to buy a bottle?"

Brent reached into his pocket for the teardrop-shaped glass bottle, liquid measurements marked off in red numbers down the side. "I didn't want it to break. The nipples are in the little bag."

He colored at using that word and Bethany smiled at him. "Was it very embarrassing?"

When his grin broke through, Bethany thought she'd lose her breath. If she'd ever thought him less than handsome, she took it back now. "As I walked out the door, Mrs. Watson ran into the back and put on her hat and coat. I swear she's telling everyone in town I have a secret baby hidden away somewhere."

"Don't worry about it," Bethany said, walking into the back. "By tomorrow all the gossip will be about me. When I show up at home with three children in tow . . ."

Brent shook his head. "No, Bethany. They'll be living with me. Jerry and I talked it over on our way here."

"But . . ." Bethany began. Then she said, "We'll discuss it after I feed the baby."

Then all three followed her into the back. The space was so tiny, Bethany kept stepping on other people's feet. Not all the exasperated glances she had in her arsenal could make them move. The children especially watched her every move, as though they were afraid she'd snatch the baby and run out into the night with her under her arm.

Bethany filled the bottle with the water from an extra pailful she'd drawn for the baby's bath. She added the food, ignoring everything and everyone else. She mixed it well, all while balancing a squirming baby on one hip. However, in order to stretch the rubber nipple over the bottle, she needed both hands.

Wordlessly, she handed Dory to Brent who, after juggling her for a moment as though she were a too-hot water bottle, passed her on to her big brother. Jerry handled his tiny sister like a mother, one hand under the bottom, the other soothing the back.

"Everything really should be boiled first," Bethany said, taking the baby back, "but I think it's more important to feed you right away."

"You don't need all that stuff," Faye said scornfully.

"How do you feed her?" Bethany asked, tickling the corner of Dory's mouth to get her to open it.

"You just dip a corner of cloth in some milk and let her suck. It's easy."

It also explained why little Dory was so much thinner than she needed to be. But Bethany kept silent, knowing Faye had done the best she could. At her age, Bethany knew she would have been incapable of caring for an infant for an hour, let alone for endless months.

It took Dory a few tries to manage the rubber nipple. In a very little while, however, she was guzzling the slightly sweet liquid like a suction pump. Even Faye laughed at the baby's round eyes of delight.

When she held out her arms for her sister, Bethany gave Dory to her at once. The little girl sat down cross-legged on the dirt-marked floor, cradling the baby in her arms. "Is that good?" she asked, tipping the bottle up for Dory.

Bethany's eyes were a little misty. She watched the two girls and only heard that Jerry was speaking to her after a moment. "I'm sorry; what did you say?"

"I said, thank you, Miss Forsythe. We sure value all you've done. Mr. Brent . . . he told me how you saved Dory's life and I want you to know we're grateful."

This had the sound of a good-bye speech. "And now you'd like for me to go? I'm afraid I can't do that, Jerry."

"But we'll be all right. We're going to go stay with Mr. Brent. Isn't that right, Mr. Brent?"

"That's right," he said over his shoulder. He went back to watching Dory eat, a sloppy sentimental smile making him look more like a fond father than a gambler. Only his waistcoat, gray with brocaded mourning doves, showed him to be something more.

"I can't let you do that," Bethany said.

Now Brent tore his fascinated gaze away. He frowned, the lantern at his feet casting strange shadows into his face. "What do you mean, you can't let me do that?"

"Just what I said. You can't take these children to a saloon, not even for a single night. It's bad enough that Jerry was working there. Now you want to expose two more innocent children to that place of yours?"

"I never come to no harm, Miss Forsythe. . . ." Jerry protested, but the adults paid no attention.

"So we're back to that, are we? What's wrong with my place? It's clean and it's warm, which is more than you can say for here."

"Yes, I agree. But Marmion House is clean, warm, and a home, not a gambling den."

"That gambling den *is* my home, as you ought to know by now."

"That may be true, but it cannot be a good home, not even for you, so long as you have drinking going on downstairs. Just how is a baby supposed to sleep there, with a lot of raucous men kicking up their heels till all hours? And as for Faye, how is she supposed to learn to be a nice young lady with all those . . ." She couldn't think of a polite word.

"You read too many lurid books, Miss Forsythe. And as for those . . ." He imitated her hesitation, "They'll at least teach her to be a real woman, not a stuck-up prig!"

"Meaning me? Thank you very much, Mr. Houston. I'm so glad to know your opinion of me. I had thought . . . but there, it just shows how wrong I can be. Nevertheless, I stick to my position that a low rum-selling house of shame cannot be a proper environment for children!"

They faced each other like fighting cocks, hands on hips and faces thrust forward. Though Jerry had followed every word of their argument, Bethany saw that none of the children had so much as batted an eye in alarm over their loud voices and angry faces. What kind of home life had they had before their mother had passed away?

Ashamed of herself, Bethany turned away from Brent. "I'm sorry," she said to the toes of her shoes. "I know you have a decent place. I've heard that you never sell to someone who's a known drunkard and you won't serve anyone who seems to have had too much already."

"I'm sorry too, Bethany," he said, brushing the tips of his fingers down her arm. "I know you're not . . . what I said you were."

"But I am." She glanced up into his face. "I can't just let you take these children to a place I know would be bad for them. I certainly can't let you take the girls there. You must see how terrible that would be."

Brent lifted his hands helplessly. "But I gave my word. I promised Jerry I'd look out for them."

Though Bethany hadn't known Brent a long time at all, she knew him well enough to understand how highly he valued his word of honor. She stared at him helplessly, knowing they'd reached an unbreachable impasse.

From the floor, Faye said, "Yuck!"

Bethany glanced at her while Faye stared in disgust at the ruin of a red silk handkerchief. "The diapers!" Bethany said and rushed into the other room to open out the soft roll of cloth. A quick run with the sharp scissors and she had a large rectangle.

The men had gone out into the backyard. "Cowards," she called after them as she and Faye changed Dory. With a full tummy and a clean backside, the baby dozed off before they had finished. Asleep, she looked like a hand-tinted drawing on the cover of the *Ladies' Home Journal*.

Bethany yearned to take a brush to the hair that Faye had pushed out of sight beneath that spotted handkerchief and see if she was as pretty as her infant sister. As Bethany had already noticed, her brows were strongly marked, showing determination, and she had a stubborn chin. As these were features she had herself, Bethany felt that she'd met a kindred spirit. If only they hadn't gotten off to a bad start!

"Wrap her up in this," Bethany said, giving Dory the red flannel petticoat she'd taken off earlier.

"I'll put her in her cradle," Dory answered, taking the petticoat.

"Then you'd better get ready to leave. We'll be going up to my house in a little while."

"We're leaving here?" Faye looked around the dirty rooms. "That's okay by me. Is your house nice?"

"Yes, it's very nice."

"With . . . ?" Faye changed her mind visibly and shrugged her thin shoulders. "It don't matter to me."

"What did you want to ask? It's all right. I won't laugh."

Faye looked at her out of the corner of her eye. "Has it got a marble bathtub?"

"No," Bethany said, having trouble keeping her promise. "Just cast iron, with lion's feet."

"Oh."

"Have you ever seen a marble bathtub?"

"Oh, no. But Momma used to tell me this story about Cinderella, and how the first thing she did when she got to the palace was to take a bath in a marble bathtub. But I guess there ain't no such thing." For a moment Bethany knew Faye imagined herself as the loveliest girl in the world, sinking down into the delights of luxury. She wondered if hardship and drudgery were easier to bear with a dream like that, or if the dream only made the reality more bitter.

Bethany said, "I do have some scented soap, however. If you'd like to borrow some . . ."

For a moment Faye's eyes shone. Bethany saw that she was indeed a pretty child, when the pink was in her cheeks, even if those cheeks were not as plump as they should be. Then, once again, the light went out of her, leaving her drab and drawn. Bethany realized sadly that Faye had remembered that she did not like her.

"No thanks."

Brent and Jerry came back, the boy first as though to scout whether it was safe. Jerry seemed calmer, as though Brent had repeated his assurances of his responsibility for the children. But Bethany was determined not to give in.

"You'd better get your things together," she said. Faye obeyed, carrying Dory into the "bedroom." Bethany spoke to Jerry. "It's getting late, and I'm sure you'll want some dinner when we get home."

"Bethany," Brent said in a low voice, "he doesn't want to go with you."

"Why not, Jerry?"

The red blood ran under the boy's face, making his pale hair stand out even whiter by comparison. "I just met you today, ma'am. I've known Mr. Brent for a while."

"That's true. Though I don't know why we couldn't be friends who simply haven't known each other very long."

"And then . . . well, you got family, ma'am. How's it goin' to look to them, you comin' back with a bunch of shirttail kids to your fancy house."

Bethany smiled. The genuineness of her smile took Jerry aback. He glanced at Brent as though for support. She said, "Jerry, which member of my family are you worried about? Charlene would love to have you three stay. She's as soft as a marshmallow where children are concerned. And as for my grandfather, the only danger you might face from him is the danger of being taught to play chess."

Brent took her by the arm. "Come out back with me for a moment, Bethany."

She went, understanding the need for a private conference, saying over her shoulder, "Get your things together, Jerry."

The moon had risen, a golden rind of a celestial melon. A nightjar sang somewhere beyond the alley. If it weren't for a strong odor of cat mingled with the pile of dirty diapers, the cool evening could have been quite romantic. Bethany looked at Brent, little more than a broad-shouldered shadow beside her. She could see his white collar gleaming. Was she right? Was he in love with her?

"He's afraid, Bethany. You've got to stop pushing him."

"Afraid? Of me?"

"Of your kind of person."

"What kind of person am I? Am I an ogress?"

She could feel his difficulty in trying to explain another person's feelings. "No, of course not. But you are an Upper Grove woman."

Bethany knew what that meant. She'd met enough women who typified what an "Upper Grove woman" was. "You mean, an interfering busybody with too much time on her hands. Nothing to do but pry into the affairs of her neighbors."

"Yes," he said with no politeness to soften the blow. "He's afraid if they go with you, they'll wind up in the hands of the county law. There's not a judge in the state who wouldn't send these kids to the orphanage."

Now she understood why Faye was so terrified of the "judge." She asked, "Has Jerry done something against the law? Or are you still thinking about that chicken today?"

"No. But he's seen orphaned children wind up being sent away by the courts before. I've tried to explain the system to him, but he isn't listening. He's too afraid."

"Yet I think he's very brave. Keeping them together, keeping this house going. Where's their father, by the way?"

"He left last year to follow some gold strike in Colorado. Swore to come back with a fortune and they haven't heard from him since."

"That's horrible. And poor Mrs. Windom! It was when she had the baby, I take it?"

"That's what he says. She lasted the first three months, getting weaker and weaker. Then she died. They only had enough money to bury her 'proper' as Jerry says. They've been living on scrapings and tips ever since."

Bethany felt the cool sting of tears on her cheeks. "To think what they've been through. . . ." She sniffed and he took her hand in the near-darkness. Needing the touch of another human being, she left her hand in his and said with a throb in her voice, "Let me take them home with me, Brent. Let me take care of them."

"I promised the boy, Bethany. I promised him."

She slipped her hand free. "Yes, I know. But there's got to be some way. . . ."

"Well," Brent said, musing. His voice hardened. "What if I take the boy to my place and you take the girls to your house? He's used to the saloon. That way, the girls won't be exposed to the contamination you think I breed."

"Brent, I don't mean . . ."

"No," Jerry said from the back porch. The grown-ups turned around, surprised to be overheard. "We don't split up. Not ever."

Brent said, "It'd only be for a while, son. Until we can figure out something better."

"No."

"Jerry," Bethany began.

"No."

"I think he means it." Brent walked back toward the house. "We'll just have to think of something else right away."

Twelve

Approaching Marmion House, Bethany felt as though she were leading a parade. She carried the baby in the lead. Behind her, Faye had slung over her shoulder a bag containing their few belongings that hadn't gone to the pawnbroker. Following Faye came her brother, looking like a strange animal with Dory's cradle upside down on his head. As the finish to this line, Brent walked along, trundling a wheelbarrow.

When Charlene opened the door, a flood of gaslight illuminated the strange procession. "Bethany?" she asked, peering out into the darkness. "What on earth . . . ?"

"These are the Windoms," Bethany said. "You know Jerry. This is Faye and Dory. They're going to be staying with us for a little while. You've already met Mr. Houston."

"Yes, of course." She glanced at the wheelbarrow, which he'd pushed right into the foyer. Never had Bethany appreciated her sister's worth more when she merely said, "Good evening, Mr. Houston."

"Good evening, Miss Charlene." Bethany could tell from the thick sound of his voice that he was having difficulty keeping his laughter inside.

Giving the others her warm, completely genuine smile, Charlene said, "Hello, children. I'm Charlene. I'm so pleased to meet you. What an adorable baby!"

Dory had managed to sleep through the commotion attendant on getting everyone and everything together. Now she continued to rest as limply as a sack of potatoes on Bethany's shoulder.

Bethany said, "I think the first thing to do, Charlene, is get the cradle set up. In my room, I think, so I can take care of her if she wakes in the night."

"She don't never," said Faye. Her fists had ground into her eyes more than once in the last half hour. Now, however, as she stood at the foot of the stairs, her eyes were wide with wonder. "Is that a wool carpet?" she asked, bending down to brush her fingers reverently over the stair runner.

Jerry stood in the hall, close by Brent's side. He seemed stupefied by the speed with which his circumstances had changed.

"We'll have to make up extra beds," Bethany said. "And I'll have to talk to Grandfather."

Charlene put her hand to her lips. "He's a little upset right now. The Tubbses called on him earlier this evening." She dropped her voice to a breath. "I heard him swearing awfully after they'd gone."

Not hearing any of this except for one word, Bethany snapped her fingers. "Tubs! I'll fire up the stove. We'll need lots of hot water for baths."

Brent touched Jerry on the elbow. "Come on. I'll introduce you to your host. You'll like him, I'm sure. He's a scoundrel but an amusing one. Besides, it'll be safer in the library." Though Brent didn't flick so much as an eyelash in Bethany's direction, she knew those last words were aimed at her.

"Yes," Bethany said ungraciously. "Get out from underfoot. If you can."

Though it hadn't been used since her own babyhood, the nursery next to her room had been cleaned regularly by Mrs. Manning. While her talent did not lie in the kitchen, she had a genius for cleanliness that shone in the spotless floor and fresh curtains. Nevertheless, it lacked the warmth of a room where children played every day.

Bethany found herself apologizing for it when she showed

it to Faye. Washed and dried, fed, all but lost in one of Bethany's nightgowns, the girl looked like another child entirely. But her attitude remained the same. "It's all right," she said grudgingly. "Someplace to put my head."

Yet Bethany noticed how her eyes lingered on the ornate plastic ceiling medallion. Her grandmother had felt that a child's room deserved as much beauty as one of the public rooms. She'd had the master plasterer who'd decorated the ceiling in the dining room work here as well, decorating not only the ceiling but the four corners. Here his fat, naked cherubs held up slingshots and dolls, instead of fruits and vegetables.

"I always thought of them as angels watching over us while we slept."

"Kinda fat for angels, ain't they? How do they fly?"

Charlene had made the bed while Bethany had shown Faye where to bathe. She'd waited outside the door for the little girl to finish, and had made certain there was a bar of her very best scented soap in the dish. Though Faye had pretended to ignore it, Bethany had noticed a definite scent of lilacs in the air when she let the water drain out.

Now the girl turned back the coverlet and climbed in between the soft, cool sheets. She lay down and immediately closed her eyes, less to invite sleep, Bethany thought, than to shut out the sight of the bossy adult.

"Don't you say prayers?"

"No. Why should I?"

Bethany realized Faye had a point. There would be little this child would be thankful for. Her father gone, her mother dead, nothing in her life but poverty and overwork. Bethany wanted to say something kind and Christian, but all she could think of were dreadful platitudes about being thankful no matter what. She knew from her own experience how hard it was sometimes to be thankful for what she had, when there were so many things she wanted. It had been a long time since she had knelt in prayer before sleep.

She stood hesitating by the small white bed. Then she

knelt down herself, looking at the blond hair spread out on the pillow, Faye's face turned away from her.

"Heavenly Father," she said slowly, "I ask that you bless and keep all those I love. I ask for the wisdom to do as you would have me do in all things, both great and small. Amen."

She let her hand rest on the blond head for an instant and the little girl did not jerk away. "Good night. Pleasant dreams." A suppressed sniffle was the only reply. "There's a handkerchief under your pillow, dear."

Bethany turned down the lamp and left the room through the connecting door. A tiny flame from the gas jet gave enough light for her to see that Dory continued to sleep, her little bottom in rubber pants hoisted in the air. Bethany drew a warm blanket embroidered with flowers that she'd used in her own childhood over Dory.

She caught a glimpse of herself in her dressing-table mirror. A strange, tender smile curved her lips. Instantly she made a horrible face and poked her tongue out at herself. She wasn't an old maid, turning drippy over a bunch of orphans. She was simply doing her duty as a good person, even if of the Upper Grove variety.

Looking at herself more closely in the dim light, she saw a smear of dirt on her cheek. Her dress had a large ring on the front from baby-created dampness and a series of spots across both shoulders where Dory had dribbled and burped. Though she told herself she was changing clothes merely to be presentable, she knew in her heart the real reason she took the time to change. She was delaying for as long as possible the moment when she'd have to tell Charlene that they needed to make up a room for one more guest in addition to the children.

Bethany entered the kitchen hard upon her knock. "Oh!" she said in surprise and tried to back up. The swinging door batted her on the bustle, driving her forward a few tottering steps.

Charlene, in the act of retreating from Virgil Emmett's

arms, stared at her sister. A slow blush suffused her glowing skin. "Bethany, I . . ."

Virgil's hands tightened on Charlene's slim waist. "Miss Bethany, I . . ."

Bethany glanced at their faces. They seemed dazed, like a pair of train-wreck survivors. She saw no suppressed giddiness, no joy, only two people stunned and amazed. Whatever had happened between them must have been as big a surprise to them as it was to her.

Charlene glanced up at Virgil. "Maybe you'd better go."

He seemed to have trouble prying open his fingers. But at last he and Charlene stood apart. "Maybe I'd better. I'll call on you tomorrow, Charlene."

He plucked his wideawake hat from the top peg of a chair, setting it at an angle on his slightly long blond hair. He turned his straight gray glance on Bethany. "I hope you'll prove to be my friend, Miss Bethany."

"I hope so too," she said, disturbed by this cryptic wish.

He didn't say a word more to either girl, only staring for a long moment into Charlene's eyes. A hint of a smile moved his lips, just enough to renew Charlene's fading blush. Then he went out, letting the door bang softly shut behind him. A whistle floated back to their ears.

Charlene seemed to drift toward the door in her long skirt. She leaned against the frame to watch his shadowy form walk away. "He's asked me to marry him, Bethany."

"What did you say?"

"I . . . I told him I didn't know him well enough to marry him. But I wasn't telling the truth." She gave a deep, unhappy sigh.

"What did he say?"

"He said he'd give me as much time as he could, but that he's leaving Cedar Groves soon and wants to take me with him. Of course, that's impossible. There are too many problems, too many things in our way."

"Yes, like Ronald Diccers. He's definitely in the way."

Charlene didn't seem to hear this reference to her fiancé.

"I could never leave you and Grandfather. Not when we're about to open our new business. That has to come first."

"It didn't seem to come first a moment ago," Bethany said, feeling like a cad for mentioning it.

"I shouldn't have let him kiss me. I . . . I just felt so sorry for him." Charlene closed the door as though shutting her dreams outside in the darkness. More briskly, she stopped leaning against the wall and said, "What about these children, Bethany?"

Though Bethany wanted to talk about Virgil Emmett, wondering where he was going that he wanted to take Charlene along, she respected the fact that her sister had closed the subject as firmly as she'd closed the door. She told Charlene the Windoms' sad story.

"So, I had to bring them here."

"Absolutely. What else could you have done?"

"That's what I thought. The only difficulty was that Mr. Houston had given his word to Jerry that *he'd* watch over them. He was the only one Jerry wanted too. I couldn't convince either of them to relax their position. So . . ."

Charlene interrupted. "Grandfather seemed very pleased to have the children stay. So you don't have to worry about that. I think he took to Jerry right away. Said he has 'pluck to the backbone.'"

"That's for certain. Can you imagine trying to keep that secret and carry such a burden alone? I couldn't do it now, let alone at sixteen."

"I think it would make a difference," Charlene said half to herself, "if the children were one's own."

Bethany could only recall seeing such a look in her sister's eyes once before. The memory of that rainy night when the doctor had told Charlene that all the things she loved best—horse racing, waltzing, sailing and long walks— were now forbidden to her remained with Bethany as one of the most bitter moments she'd ever known. There'd been a remote look in Charlene's eyes then too—the look of someone who hears their own death knell sounding. Bethany could still feel the force of Charlene's sobs, shaking them both, as they held on to each other throughout that dark night.

Foolishly wise, Bethany started the one topic that could have brought her sister back. "We'll have to make up a room for him, of course."

"For Jerry? I've already done that."

"No, for Mr. Houston."

"Mr. Houston!" Charlene stared at her in disbelief. "Why on earth . . . ?"

"Because he's moving in."

The clock in the hall bonged twelve times, each chime more dismal than the last. Bethany, crouched by the hearth, aimlessly feeding twigs to a dying fire, counted each one and asked herself why in heaven's name she was still awake.

Her mind was too active to let her sleep, though she felt the drag of exhaustion in every limb. But as she lay awake in her four-poster bed, listening to the sighs and whispers of a sleeping infant, her mind paced like a panther in a cage. A hundred topics awaited her. Paint and paper, beef or lamb, the fiancé she could hardly picture anymore or Brent Houston. . . .

She shied away from that subject now as she had before. That name had driven her out of bed. She thought a good novel would keep it at bay. Yet once again, his name presented itself between her eyes and the printed word. She'd tossed the book aside to kneel by the fire, twitching twigs into the red heart, seeking pictures in the remains of the crumbling logs.

"Still awake?" he said from the doorway.

Bethany stood up with more quickness than grace, not wanting to be crouching at his feet like a savage over her cooking pot. She was glad of the high collar of her blue gingham wrapper, "I couldn't sleep," she said.

"Neither could I. It's exciting, rescuing people from penury. I don't think I've ever had the experience before."

For the first time, she saw him without his black coat,

though he'd kept on the fancy waistcoat he'd changed into before supper, flame-stitched in red and gold. It hung open, emphasizing his lean body. Bethany looked from it to the fire. Which one was more likely to burn her hands?

He asked, "Are you going to say I usually deliver people into penury?"

"No, I'm not going to say that. I'm just going to say good night."

"Stay awhile?" he asked, without touching her. Yet Bethany felt as though he had caressed her cheek again, as he'd done before. She could almost feel the slight drag of his fingertips and the brushing of his thumb over her sensitive lower lip. She paused in the very act of walking out.

Her breath came raggedly. "Why . . . why should I stay?"

"Because I'm lonely and I think . . . maybe . . . you are too."

That had to be refuted instantly, lest it prove to be true. "No, I'm not lonely. Not in the least. But . . . I'll stay if you want me to."

"Thank you." He gazed into the fire, his hands resting on the marble mantel just at the level of his chest. His foot lifted onto the brass fender. A lock of his smooth dark hair fell across his brow and Bethany had to curl her fingernails into her palms to keep from brushing it back.

"This is a good house," he said suddenly. "People have been happy here."

"I always miss it when I'm away." She knew she should move away from him, not stand here feeling the heat of the fire through her wrapper and nightdress. But he spoke so quietly that she had to stand near to hear. And more than that . . . the conventions by which she lived her life seemed unimportant at this hour. Midnight in New York meant supper at a sparkling dinner party; in Cedar Groves it meant warm whispers and dangerous nearness.

"You and your sister were gone a long time. Five years, your grandfather said?"

"Yes. When our parents died, everyone decided the best thing for us would be for Charlene and I to see a little more of the world than Cedar Groves."

"And did you?"

"Our aunt Poste is very fashionable and leads a busy life in New York society." She spoke softly too, though there was no real reason to. She wanted to keep him by her.

"This fellow you're engaged to . . . he's part of that world?"

"Very much so." With an effort, she conjured up Gerrald's slightly plump face from among the flickering heart of the ashes. She remembered how she saw him last—rigidly, even painfully correct, in his evening dress, with the too-tight tie and too-starched ruffle.

He'd never pulled his tie off and unbuttoned the top three buttons of his shirt, letting the tempting fragrance of his warm body escape. Gerrald never made her feel that a moment without his touch was an agony of wasted time, while the merest brush of his finger absolutely had never sent her tumbling into the madness of unquenchable desire.

"Do you love him very much?"

For a moment she broke free from the spell of intimacy that had been cast over her. "Really, what an improper . . ."

"Are you in love with him?"

He reached out and seized her waist. Whether he pulled her to him or she moved sideways didn't matter. In an instant he'd wrapped his arms around her. His face wore its hardest look as his mouth twisted and came down over hers.

Bethany felt her heartbeats shake her body. Or were they his? Always, he'd kissed her quickly, before she could prevent him, like a conquest. Now, it was as if he'd set himself the task of inciting her total participation.

His mouth moved like a slow prairie blaze, spreading flame everywhere it touched, hotter than the charcoal behind them. Bethany's hands tightened on the open edges of his waistcoat to keep from falling. She was drowning in a sea of fire as he kissed her.

She felt the nudge of his tongue against her lips. Gerrald had never kissed her like this! The very idea would have disgusted her beyond words.

But when Brent tasted the smoothness of her teeth and explored the liquid softness of her mouth, she only let her head drop back, reveling in new sensations.

Tiny sounds broke from her throat. His hands moved on her back, urging her closer still. She was free to break away. Instead, she moved against him, mindlessly, shamelessly.

"Oh, sweetheart," he said thickly. He lifted his hands to her unbound hair, tangling his fingers in the strands. Breaking their kiss, he brushed his lips over her face. She felt his breath sigh in her ear and she shivered, startled by the fever such a simple act could create.

"Brent," she sighed. She said his name again in a husky, questioning voice that sounded nothing like her usual forthright tones.

"Hush, my darling. Just let it happen."

Opening her heavy eyelids, she saw his frowning concentration as he returned again to her mouth. His thick hair invited her hands. She realized she'd been dying to run her fingers through the smooth darkness from the day they'd met.

This time, she was the first to open, the first to take. Through the linen bosom of his shirt, she could feel all the solidity of his body. It would have been impossible to slip so much as a playing card between them, so closely did they stand together.

Yet, Bethany felt somehow that they were still too far apart. Scandalous to think how much more comfortable they'd be with less on.

As soon as that thought occurred to her, it was as if she could suddenly see how they might look to anyone who came downstairs. She would hate to be caught in mid-kiss as she'd caught Charlene. At least Charlene had the justification of knowing that the man she'd kissed was someone she'd known a long time and admired. But to be found closely and passionately embracing a man who she professed to abhor would be ten times more embarrassing.

"Brent," she said again. "I don't think . . ."

"That's right. Don't think."

At some point he'd unbuttoned the high collar of her wrapper. She'd seen the look of disbelief on his face when his hard work netted him only the view of another garment, though this one had a low square neck and was made of thin lawn. His eyes took in the view and she saw them begin to burn.

Now he kissed the side of her throat, then nipped it, there where reaction was strongest. Bethany sobbed aloud as pleasure invaded her whole body. Had she really objected to his kisses? What a fool she was.

Once again he tasted her lips. If only he didn't feel so good! She'd never known anything so heavenly as his slightly rough fingers stroking the sensitive skin of her throat. It seemed the ultimate in sensations until he slipped one finger between the tiny buttons at the lace-trimmed edge of her nightgown.

He moved only the tip of his finger over the smooth roundness at the inside of her cleavage. Bethany held perfectly still, her eyes closed, her whole attention concentrated on his finger, there where no one had ever touched her before. She wanted to be sure he too felt these things.

Though some vestige of maidenliness whispered that she should not, Bethany's bold entrepreneurial spirit encouraged her to explore him. She ran her hands inside the open waistcoat. His body heat seared her hands.

"Pull out my shirt," he murmured against her throat, his voice hardly a breath. "Touch me. Touch me like I want to touch you."

His body was hard. No flabby roll around the waist that came from sitting over sewing machine profit and loss ledgers. Brent's skin was lightly furred with black hair that spread out over his pectoral muscles. This hair was slightly coarse, catching at her fingers. Which of them had unbuttoned his shirt? Was it the same hands that had undone the first five buttons on her nightgown?

She could glance down and see the soft white mounds of her own breasts there. Though she'd been more uncovered in a fashionable ball dress, there was a world of difference between that and a nightgown.

He didn't touch her there again. He only brought her once more into the closest possible contact with his body while he kissed her open mouth. His shirt hung free. The abrasive touch of his crinkly chest hair against her tenderest places drove her quite insane.

"Brent," she cried on a whisper. "Oh, God. Is this wanting you? I don't know . . . I've never wanted anyone before."

He pushed her away, his hands at her elbows. Bethany nearly stumbled into the fire, but he steadied her. His hair was thoroughly mussed by her fingertips and his eyes had a glitter that almost frightened her.

"That's what I wanted to hear," he said in a tone of complete satisfaction. "That's what I needed to know."

"What?" she asked, not even certain herself what she'd said. She felt limp and tired, while at the same time eager with an unnameable hunger.

"That you've never wanted anyone before. But, my God, what the poor bastard missed!"

"What? Who?"

"Your fiancé. I could almost feel sorry for him. But maybe he's such a fool he'll never guess what he missed by not marrying you. If he'd known, he never would have let you stir an inch out of New York without him."

"Brent," she said, pushing her heavy hair back from her face. "What are you talking about?"

She shrugged her wrapper back on and clutched it closed over the gaping placket of her nightgown. In about fifteen minutes a flood of shame and remorse would undoubtedly sweep over her. Her cheeks were already pink with the first wave. In the meantime, however, she wanted to know what he was being so indecently triumphant about.

"You and me, Bethany. And how good it's going to be." Victory rang in his every word.

That she could not stand. With an impatient wriggle, she freed herself from his touch. "Really, Mr. Houston . . ."

"No." He caught at her hand and held it tightly between his own. "No more Mr. Houston. Never again. Don't you realize it yet, Bethany?"

She turned her head and body away, leaving him only her hand. "I only realize that it's very late. Strange things can happen at night. Things people would never think of doing in the daytime."

But there was no evading him by merely turning away. He stepped in front of her with that masculine grace that seemed to be his alone. A hint of laughter came into his voice now, laughter directed at her simplicity. Yet, for all that, Bethany knew he meant every word he said.

"Don't you realize that I could have taken you right here and now? And you wouldn't have lifted a finger to stop me? As a matter of cold fact, you would have been helping me."

There was no point in lying about something so obvious. "Yes, I do realize it."

"What do you think it means?"

"I can't say. Oh, I don't know!" she said in sudden exasperation. "I don't know what you want me to say. I am . . . attracted to you. You're very appealing when you're not being maddeningly irritating."

"I want you," he said softly, his green eyes as soft as spring grass.

Amazing how such a simple three-word phrase could stop her heart from beating, stop her breath from working. And what it could do to her brain! Not even the right three-word phrase—hackneyed and trite on the wrong lips—fresh and outrageous on the right ones. Yet Bethany acknowledged that at this moment she would have given anything to hear three different words from Brent. It would make what just happened between them more understandable if not precisely respectable.

"Now you say it to me, Bethany. Look me right in the eye and tell me the cold-blooded truth." When she only averted her eyes, he challenged, "Scared?"

"Yes!" she shot at him. "Terrified!"

He stood back, releasing her both physically and emotionally. "I would never guess you were a coward, Bethany." But the smile of triumph on his lips was not lessened by this defeat, if it was his defeat and not hers.

Bethany longed to wipe it off with a slap. His caresses she could bear; not his arrogance. But she was afraid that if she struck him, he'd take his revenge in kisses. She'd already proven she had no defenses against that weapon. Though she hadn't his vast knowledge of matters carnal, she knew herself well enough to know that if he had asked, she would have let him do whatever he wanted. More than that, in another moment she would have insisted on it.

"Good night. *Mr. Houston*," she said from the doorway.

As he started after her, undoubtedly with the object of enforcing his desire to be called by his first name, she hurried up the stairs. Though he was only a step behind her as she opened the door to her room, she turned and whispered, "Don't you dare wake the baby!"

That stopped him in his tracks. The sight of his baffled face in the dim glow of a low gas-jet was the only satisfaction Bethany could carry with her as she closed the door.

Thirteen

In Bethany's dream, the music that the dancers revolved to changed to the sound of a baby's delighted laughter. She came to consciousness with the laughter still in her ears, for it seemed Dory had just discovered her toes.

Though the sound made Bethany smile and turn over, she found it extraordinarily difficult to open her eyes. It was as if the sandman, going about his duties very carelessly, had dumped about half a pound in each eye. She hadn't found sleep until long after two A.M. Now, judging by the beams of light dancing in around the blinds, it was about seven.

As she struggled to lift her head from the soft seduction of her pillow, her door creaked a little. There came the sound of stealthy footsteps. Propping herself up on her elbow, Bethany peered blearily through the one eye she'd managed to open. A dim shape materialized beside the cradle.

"Oh, I'm sorry," whispered Charlene, looking toward her sister. "I didn't mean to wake you. I just came in to pick up the baby."

"Be my guest."

Charlene scooped Dory up from her cradle, lifting her high into the air. "Hel-lo, cuddly kittens! I'm your Aunt Charlene. What a *good* baby you are, yessums you are!"

"Please," Bethany said, rubbing her hand over her face. "Not before breakfast."

"Oh, don't you pay attention to grumpy ol' Aunt Bethany," Charlene said in a mock grumble to the baby. "Auntie

Charlene will give you your bathie and your breakie, and then we'll just play-ums and play-ums all day!" Her voice went high as a bat's, which Dory seemed to appreciate. She squealed and the peculiar charm of a toothless grin seemed to bring out the worst in Charlene.

"What a pretty wuzzums! Pretty, pretty baby!" She joggled her up and down in her arms. "Can you say 'pretty baby.' Oh, yes. Oh, yes!"

Bethany said austerely, "All the authorities say babies should be spoken to in a normal tone and that baby talk should be avoided at all costs. They universally are of the opinion that it makes a child slow."

"Oh, nasty ol' authorities. Yes!" Charlene rested the baby on her hip. "We'll go and leave grumpy Aunt Bethany to her sleepy-weepy."

"Thanky-wanky," Bethany said, collapsing back into the warmth of her bed.

What she wanted most was to laze in bed until she could be absolutely and perfectly certain that Brent had gone downtown. With any luck at all, she wouldn't see him for the entire day. That would give her a chance to arrange in her mind both her demeanor and words for when they met again.

But, try as she might, sleep evaded recapture. The questions that had kept her awake last night revived in the sunshine, though once again they'd come out without any answers. One truth, however, stared her rudely in the face and refused to go away.

She swung her feet out of bed sooner than stay there and face facts. But the horrible fact followed her as relentlessly as a vengeful ghost.

She had thrown away her self-respect and her good name in exchange for a few impassioned moments in Brent Houston's arms. How could she have been such a brainless idiot?

Bethany poured water into the basin and wrung out a handcloth. She scrubbed her face, as though that would remove the memory of his kiss. But all she had to do was think about him and her heart sped up, her hands started to tremble, and that strange liquid fire sloshed about in her insides.

She plunged her face into the water and poured it down the back of her neck for good measure. Cold water worked wonders, so she had heard. Whole schools of medical thought were devoted to the benefits of hydrotherapy. Perhaps it would help her regain her sanity.

When she came up for air, the nasty fact was still there. Not sleep, not cold water, not even breakfast could make her lose this horrible feeling. She felt exposed to a cold and searching wind, with nowhere to conceal herself. The thought of facing a smugly smiling Brent Houston across the breakfast table gave her the collywobbles. But he *must* have left the house by now; he was a busy man with a saloon to run.

She slipped down the hall to the farthest point away from her bedroom. The simple pine door of Mrs. Manning's former room was closed. Bethany pressed her ear to the panel but heard nothing, not even the splash of water or—horrors!—a snore. Charlene would know if Brent had left already or not. She'd sneak down the backstairs to ask her for there was less risk of meeting Brent that way, if he was still here.

"Are Jerry and Faye still sleeping? And have you seen Mr. Houston?" she asked Charlene as she chose her breakfast from a plate of warm sweet rolls on the kitchen table.

"I know Faye's still asleep because I peeped in at her," her sister said. "I heard Jerry moving around and I don't know about Mr. Houston. He might have left early."

Charlene had Dory wrapped in a clean diaper. They were on the floor. To Dory's great delight, Charlene blew bubbles through an empty thread spool, dipping it repeatedly into the pan of soapy water between them.

Though there were a hundred things awaiting her attention, Bethany dawdled to watch as she nibbled her roll and sipped her tea. Dory lifted up on her forearms and made a good effort to grab one of the iridescent spheres. Her remaining support trembled and collapsed. But she bobbed up again, hopeful and eager for another go.

"She seems like a very good-natured baby," Bethany said. "I was surprised she slept through the night. I thought they didn't do that until they were much, much older."

Charlene blew another flotilla of bubbles into the air. "It must be because she's bottle-fed. By the way, she had a good breakfast—yes, yes, you ate it all up like a big girl!"

Though Charlene would undoubtedly disregard the necessity, Bethany felt compelled to make things clear. She said, "I don't want the children to be a burden on your shoulders, Charlene. They're my responsibility. I didn't ask you before I brought them home, so don't . . ."

"Oh, no," Charlene said, looking up with such a happy face that Bethany wondered if babies were a good cure for a weakened heart. "I love having them here. This house needs children. It's much too quiet."

Too quiet? Bethany could have argued that point. What with Charlene kissing Virgil Emmett in the kitchen, she herself doing more than mere kissing with Brent in the library, Grandfather keeping his secrets in the library, three children under the roof, of whom two had been entirely unknown to them yesterday, plus Brent sleeping nights in one of the servants' rooms at the back of the house. . . .

Suddenly a scream shattered the morning peace. It seemed to come from upstairs. A moment later Dory went from being a happy baby to one shrieking herself red in the face, frightened by the sudden, nerve-ripping noise. The sisters exchanged a look of utter befuddlement as yet another scream slashed through the air, followed instantly by the gunshot bang of a door. Charlene snatched up the little girl and raced after her sister, already halfway up the backstairs.

Mrs. Manning stood pressed against the wall in the narrow hallway at the rear of the house. One hand patted the double-folded bodice over her heart while the other fanned her face. "There's . . . there's a man in there," she panted. "Naked as the day he was born!"

Bethany saw Charlene's face as she rubbed Dory's back to quiet her. The suppressed laughter in her sparkling eyes and tightly compressed lips was almost enough to set her off, which wouldn't have been very tactful. But Bethany managed to say, "That . . . that's only Brent, Manny. Don't worry. He's . . . he's . . . " A giggle escaped her like a bubble.

"Don't worry? What is Brent Houston doing in *my* bed?"

"Well, you weren't using it."

"That's no reason to put a naked man in it!"

The door at the end of the hall opened. Instantly, Mrs. Manning stepped forward to put one hand each over the girls' eyes. Turned from a lump of jelly into a tigress defending her young, she said sharply, "Don't you dare come out of there until you've got your pants on!"

Of course, it was extremely difficult to completely block the sight of two persons using just one pair of hands. Bethany easily twitched off Manny's restraining hand and took a good look. But Brent, disappointingly, had taken the time to pull on a pair of undyed jeans. They rode low and snugly around his hips, accenting the smooth flatness of his hard stomach.

His leaf-green eyes sought out Bethany. He caught her staring, the edge of her lower lip caught in her teeth.

Last night, she'd seen him, the fire's glow dancing on his body as though he were a hard-muscled savage. In the light of day, he had the finely modeled body of a Renaissance statue. The black hair across his chest that had caught at her fingers when she'd explored glinted with reddish gleams. And it was quite impossible to miss the effect her interest had on him.

She wasn't a total innocent. The girls she'd known in New York had very little bloom left by the time they'd been through a season or two. Sometimes they'd talked freely, when mothers and chaperones were absent or deep in gossip. Bethany, once she'd gotten used to gilding her ignorance with silence, had listened with all her senses.

She knew why Brent suddenly stopped smiling, while the look in his eyes changed from inviting her to share his humor to a sensual challenge. The knowledge started that strange liquid fire spilling over inside her once again. Mrs. Manning's outrage and her sister's laughter seemed very far away. More than anything, Bethany wanted to step into Brent's room and close the door. Her eyes, she knew, gave her away.

By this time, Mr. Ames had appeared at the other end of the house, gorgeous in a richly embroidered robe. Jerry, yawning and running his hands through his nearly white hair, turned up at Mr. Ames's back while Faye, the too-big nightgown pouring over her thin body, jumped up and down to see past the men.

"What in the name of Beelzebub is going on?" Mr. Ames demanded.

"There's no need whatever to swear," Mrs. Manning snapped back. "The devil has more'n enough to do without being dragged into this!"

"Regina! You spoke to me!"

"And why not?" She ignored him and gave Brent the sort of look that made strong men climb trees and try to pull them up after themselves. Brusquely, she gave him an order. "Go put some clothes on. There are impressionable young girls here."

"You're not so old yourself," he said impudently, adding a wink for good measure. He paused, his gaze returning to Bethany. She bore it a moment more, then dropped her eyes, the slow heat of shame rolling into her cheeks. He stepped back into his room.

Charlene was asking the question Bethany hadn't enough sense left to ask. "Manny, what are you doing here?"

Mrs. Manning drew herself up to her full height of five feet three inches. "If you girls had a grain of smarts between you, you would've sent for me last night. Do you think you can collect a crowd of orphans and not have the whole world jabberin' about it by morning? I found out about it about ten o'clock last night and sat up till all hours waiting to hear from you."

"Who told you?" Bethany asked.

"It don't matter. Here I am. These won't be the first children I've watched out for, and I'm hoping they won't be the last. Give me that baby, Miss Charlene."

Dory seemed to realize instinctively that this deep bosom was a safe haven. She stopped whimpering and wriggling to nestle at once against Mrs. Manning. The housekeeper turned toward the still fascinated trio at the other end of the hall and began issuing orders.

"Don't stand about with your feet bare, missy. And as for you, young man, did you brush your hair with the rake? Peregrine, go and shave. You look like a porcupine. And, Bethany . . ."

With a comfortable feeling, such as a soldier once again under orders might have, Bethany said, "Yes, ma'am!"

"Your hair's coming down in the back. Get along to your room and I'll come up in a minute to fix it for you. Charlene . . ."

"Yes, ma'am!" Charlene said, going so far as to snap a salute.

"You're perfect, as always."

Bethany all but skipped as she hurried back to her room. "The lark's on the wing; The snail's on the thorn; Manny's in her kitchen—All's right with the world," she gleefully misquoted as she sat down before the vanity-table mirror to pull the pins from her hair.

She'd taken on the Windom children of her own free will, holding out in the face of all Brent's and even the children's opposition. Yet even so, she had wondered at about one o'clock this morning how she was going to open and run a restaurant while at the same time being a surrogate parent.

Of course, Mrs. Manning was the solution. She should have thought of it herself.

She had little hope Brent would prove to be helpful. In a few days, weeks at the most, he'd get tired of the responsibility and drift back into his devil-may-care attitude. She had few illusions about this man; she even hoped her absurd attraction for him would last only as long as he remained at Marmion House. No doubt this silly infatuation would fade quickly enough.

She stopped to look at herself in the mirror. With her hair mantling her shoulders, her cheeks pink, she wondered if this was the way Brent had seen her last night, just before he'd kissed her so passionately. Try as she might, she couldn't fool herself any longer. What she felt for him was as overwhelming as a tidal wave.

Though she wouldn't call it love—that name being reserved for the holy tie of matrimony—the wild tempest he could arouse in her with no more than a look must have some name. But all the ones she could think of were harsh and ugly—lust, concupiscence, incontinence—words thundered from pulpits and whispered in private.

She could almost wish she were married, so she could stop feeling this way about him. That reminded Bethany that a letter to Gerrald was long overdue.

She'd reached the final "d" in his name and was chewing on the end of her pen trying to think of what else to say when someone knocked abruptly at the door. Glad of an excuse to put down her stubbornly silent pen, Bethany called out permission to enter and turned to face the door.

Brent took a deep breath before he went in. It had been the right thing to do. In his eyes, Bethany was so beautiful he hardly remembered to breathe when he looked at her.

Her rich brown hair, interlaced with hints of copper, coffee, and even gold, flowed in deep ripples over her shoulders. It had looked just like that last night when he'd been bold enough to run his hands over the silky waves. He could still feel the way the strands had seemed to respond to his touch like a living creature.

"I'm off to work," he said, and reflected with a smile how perfectly husbandlike he sounded. This fresh pink room could be his bedroom, his and hers. She could be his wife, newly risen from their shared bed, getting ready for another day. He wished it were so. Then he'd have the right to delay her by taking her back to bed.

Brent was dismayed, not so much by the idea of such a companionable arrangement, but by how little it frightened him. He wondered if she would let him kiss her good-bye.

"Then I will see you this evening," she said. "Is Jerry going with you?"

"He's working for you now, remember? Unless you don't want him to."

"No, that's all right, I can still find a use for him."

"Then I'll be going."

"Wait, Brent."

It still amazed him that the sound of his name on her lips could set his heart to pounding. Sometimes she irritated him unspeakably; but when she said his name, he found himself once again lost in love for her.

She walked across the room toward him and firmly closed the door that he'd left open out of respect for her reputation. "We have to talk."

"About last night?" he asked. Her cheeks flared pink agaɪ.. as she nodded silently. He wondered if she'd spent as much time last night asking questions of the ceiling as he had.

Looking down at her empty hands, Bethany said, "I want your word of honor that nothing like that will happen again."

"Why? Didn't you like it?"

He reached out and put his hand over both of hers. He couldn't be mistaken in her reaction to his touch. She had been utterly honest last night when she'd confessed to wanting him. That confession had buoyed up not only his heart but his self-conceit. He'd been very proud of himself until the thought occurred that it wasn't just her passion that he wanted. Passion alone was too cheap; he wanted her love.

"Whether or not I liked it is irrelevant," she said, stepping back, her posture tight. Her eyes were somber when she lifted them to meet his.

"That's about the only thing that is relevant," he said. "Bethany, there's so much I . . ."

"We have to think of the children," she interrupted. "What if one of them had seen us? It could have upset them. What if my grandfather had come down? You wouldn't be allowed to stay here and *that* would have upset them because you'd be breaking your word."

"Maybe you're right," he said.

"I know I am."

"All right. I won't kiss you when there's a chance the children might see us." He took a step forward. She retreated.

"That . . . that's not good enough."

"For instance, they can't see us now." He loved to watch the sparks come up in her eyes like the Fourth of July.

"But Faye might walk in." She backed up another step.

"True. So you don't want me to kiss you under your grandfather's roof, is that it?"

"That's right. Or anywhere else, for that matter."

"Never?" He let his fingers flow over the roundness of her shoulders. She couldn't back up any more; Dory's cradle was behind her.

"N-never."

Brent could feel her will melting. "Are you sure you can trust my word? The temptation to break it is huge," he said in a whisper calculated to set her quivering. He could almost taste the softness of her lips. She'd stand out against him for a moment and then . . .

"I know I can rely on your word, Brent." He looked down into the depths of her eyes and was taken aback by the trust that he saw there. "I can rely on it, because it means something to you. You wouldn't give your word and then renege."

"No," he said, letting her go. "I wouldn't."

"Is it . . . is it because you're a gambler? I've heard that gentlemen who play cards for money pride themselves on keeping their word no matter what."

"I'm no gentleman," he said, a little more crisply than he'd meant to. He was angry at himself for being such a fool. Damn it, he hadn't come in here to have a chat! "I'm just what I am. A rum seller and a gambler. And you're a good girl. An Upper Grove girl."

"Where are you from, Brent?"

"You don't want to hear the story of my life, sweetheart. It's not a story for pretty ears like yours."

He'd forgotten her strength and tenacity. When he put his hand on the doorknob, she was there, leaning her back against the door. "I've already guessed most of it," she said. "You're not that complicated, Mr. Houston."

She'd never flirted with him before. It intrigued him. Brent decided to let her talk. "All right. Let's have it. What wild and romantic past have you saddled me with?"

"Well . . . for one thing, you don't talk like a man who is uneducated, so I think you must have gone to school in the East."

"That's right. Harvard."

"Oh, don't joke! Then I think you must be an orphan."

"Why?" How shocked she would be to learn that he only *wished* he were an orphan. He had disappointed them, angered them, and finally hurt them to the point that he knew there could be no going home. Better to have come from nothing rather than to have such painful memories.

"Because you were so kind to the children. Only someone who knows what it's like to lose his parents could have been so compassionate."

"You're an orphan, aren't you, Bethany?"

Her long lashes swept down onto her cheeks. "Yes. They

both died in that typhoid epidemic five years ago. The town lost a lot of people that month."

"I know. That's how I come to the Golden Lady."

"Oh?" she said, making it a question.

He shook his head. "Nope. You're telling the story of my life. Not me."

"Where was I?"

"Orphans."

"Oh, yes. Well, I don't know if you were in an orphanage or not—I think maybe you were since you don't want the children to go to one. But I think you must have been apprenticed to someone and they were cruel to you. So you ran away. Then you were very wild and became . . ." She indicated his present circumstances with a graceful gesture.

He clapped his hands together in ironic applause three times. "To be honest, you got one thing right."

"What?"

"I was wild, very wild. But I was educated in California. My parents are still alive—so far as I know. And I didn't run away, I was asked to leave town by the combined voices of my teacher's husband, the sheriff, and the town council. My sole apprenticeship was on the medicine show circuit with a brief stint in the gambling halls of England. The only person who was ever cruel to me was my wife. Which was just as well, because she left me. And the Golden Lady was willed to me by the former owner under circumstances so scandalous, even I don't care to remember the details."

With a careful but strong hand, he put her aside and opened the door. Bethany's eye were dazed as though she'd taken one too many jolts in the boxing ring. But he'd no sooner started down the long hall than she called after him, "Brent?"

Though he didn't care to answer questions, he still couldn't resist the sound of his name in her sweetly husky voice. He didn't turn, but he did stop. "What?"

"You've been to England?"

He laughed. He couldn't help it, or stop it. That question,

after what he'd admitted, collected all the reasons he loved her into four succinct words. Peal after peal of his ringing laughter echoed through the halls of Marmion House, bringing out all the inhabitants in only slightly more complete attire than the last time.

Fourteen

As Bethany welcomed her first guests into The Isabella Café, her head hurt from an equal mix of excitement and fear. Her smile, she was sure, revealed nothing but the certainty of success, showing nothing of the sick feelings in her stomach.

Looking around, she congratulated herself on the achievement of her vision. The orange muslin had indeed turned red and made admirable curtains. The candles, surrounded by wreaths of flowers, lent just the air of mystery and elegance she had pictured. Already all but three of her tables were full, she told herself, and just as quickly reminded herself that it wasn't full seats that indicated success. It was whether they would fill up again tomorrow night.

Mayor and Mrs. Tubbs were looking at tonight's menu with the clerk of the court and his wife. Miss Ivey sat there too, peering over the menu at the other people in the room.

Constable Richardson had escorted Miss Hart the milliner through the door, confirming rumors about their friendship.

Mr. Curtis, the musical schoolmaster, had come alone and was even now tying a napkin around his neck in anticipation.

A party of six travelers from the Station Hotel had just asked to be seated and as Bethany indicated their table with a gracious gesture, she blessed Mrs. Manning's friends who worked there for sending them over.

Bethany waved her fingertips to her grandfather, seated nearby and grinning hugely at everyone he saw. When

Virgil Emmett appeared in the doorway, his hair still showing the tracks where his comb had been dragged through it, Mr. Ames waved the younger man over.

"Couldn't miss this," Virgil said to Bethany as he sat down. She handed him a menu, her smile warmer than for a stranger.

"Thank you for coming. I'll tell Charlene you're here."

She hurried into the kitchen. Pots bubbled and steamed. A shimmering heat filled the air above the stove while rich fragrances hinted at enchantments to come whenever someone opened or closed the kitchen door.

"Charlene, half the town's out there."

"Really?"

"Well, fifteen people anyway."

"That's good. How much longer before I can use the oven?" she asked, hovering protectively above her desserts.

"Ten minutes. I'd better serve the soup. Thank goodness the bread's already out there."

"Let me do that," Charlene said, wiping her floury hands on a towel. "You still have to garnish those plates."

In answer to her sister's doubtful glance, Charlene laughed. "And no, it's not too heavy. I'm feeling very strong these days. It must be the Missouri fresh air."

Though Bethany had her doubts about the medicinal qualities of mere air, she stood back to let Charlene pick up the tray. "Start with Grandfather's table and work your way around to Constable Richardson's. He's so busy gazing into Miss Hart's eyes, he probably won't notice the difference between old shoe leather and filet mignon."

Charlene's eyes brightened. Even in the midst of her distractions, both emotional and professional, she could be interested in this piece of news. "No! Then it's true about them? And with Miss Ivey sitting right across the way!"

"I don't think the constable ever gave her any real encouragement, do you? I think their romance was a political ploy engineered by Mrs. Tubbs. I certainly hope that soup's not too hot. And . . . Virgil's out there, sitting with Grandfather."

"Don't worry," Charlene said. "I won't dawdle."

"I didn't . . ." But her sister had gone out, carrying a tray crowded with the first dozen bowls of Potage Royale. They'd made enough for twenty-four people, never thinking there'd be that many customers this first night. But with fifteen already seated, there was always a thrilling possibility they'd run out.

Looking at the trays of salad already made up and ready, only sixteen bowlfuls, Bethany prayed that Jerry was able to find more lettuce. She told him not to come back without it, even if he had to raid someone's garden as furtively as a rabbit.

Bethany took the pork tenderloins from the oven. They were brown and crisp and perfect. As she moved the pan to the top of the stove, she congratulated herself on this small success.

On the whole, the last few days had been a series of triumphs, large and small. Dory remained as delightful a baby on long acquaintance as on first meeting her. Jerry and Mr. Ames were getting on like a pair of schoolboys who'd declared themselves to be best friends. Mrs. Manning was still speaking to Mr. Ames, though somewhat tartly, and Faye followed her about like Mary's lamb.

New clothes, store-bought, had seemed to soothe the little girl's anxieties, though she still would not say her prayers. Yet as Bethany's preparations for the café became more hectic, she found herself looking forward to those quiet moments when she knelt beside Faye's small white bed. Faye had echoed "Amen" last night, which went down on the ledger as a large triumph.

Charlene came back in for the second tray. "So far so good," she said breathlessly and lifted the second tray. "Virgil . . . I mean, Grandfather liked the soup."

"That's nice. Tell Virgil . . . I mean, Grandfather that I'm glad." Bethany sighed when Charlene went out with the second tray. Virgil, discouraged by Charlene's sudden coolness, had not repeated his proposal of marriage. But he still came around to the house almost every evening, and had been instrumental in getting the wallpaper up in the dining room here at the café.

Though Charlene did her very best to be no more than friendly, Bethany could see the strain showing on her sister's face. She sympathized more than Charlene knew. Some of that strain had begun to appear on her own.

If only Brent . . . Bethany pushed him out of her thoughts, taking up her pastry bag full of mashed potatoes. As she piped a decorative trim around each pork tenderloin with a steady hand, she hoped again all her hard work would be appreciated.

Jerry appeared, a bag slung over his shoulder. He sniffed the air and ran his tongue around his lips. "Smells right good. What's that you're doing to it?"

"Just a little extra touch. Did you get the lettuce?"

"Sure thing. Two heads, like you said."

"All right. Start washing it."

"Me?" The boy looked at the tub of water she pointed to as though he suspected alligators to be lurking in the depths.

"Yes. You're going to make up eight bowls of salad just like those on the tray. And you have until this course is served to finish them all."

"But I don't know anything about cooking, Miss Bethany."

"Then it's time you learned."

"But . . . but . . ." He stammered, choked, and then said, "That's women's work. I'm a feller! Fellers don't . . ."

"Yes, they do," she said firmly. "Nearly all of the world's great chefs are men. It's a very respectable career. But you have to start at the bottom. In this case, at the bottom of the salad bowl."

Though there were really only a few years between them, Jerry seemed convinced that Bethany was more to be respected than the oldest grandmother. Under her guidance, he approached the bowls with somewhat less trepidation, though without any great enthusiasm. Soon he was washing and drying lettuce, his shirtsleeves rolled up. Next, he learned how to "fatigue" a lettuce leaf. He tossed them with the oil with clumsy energy.

"I saw Mr. Brent while I was buying this stuff," he said.

Bethany's hand jumped and she laid an extra squiggle of potato on a tenderloin. "That's nice," she said, determined not to ask any questions.

"He wanted to know how it was going over here. I couldn't really tell him, but it looks good, huh?"

"Very good. That's enough oil, Jerry. Now divide the lettuce up on the plates and add the green beans and cauliflower. The last thing is the pomegranate seeds, but not too many."

He shrugged. "Okay, if you say so."

Brent had no intention of coming tonight, for all the reasons he'd mentioned before. Bethany had a vision of Mrs. Tubbs stalking from the café in snobbish silence if Brent appeared in the doorway. Despite that, Bethany couldn't help wishing that he could be there. If the café was a success, it would be due in large part to him.

But really, she had to concentrate on her work, not daydream about Brent Houston. The tenderloins still looked a little plain, despite the cornucopia of vegetable vegetation that decorated the plates.

As she carved a few extra rosettes from radishes, she cast a fond look at the large stove, shiny in locomotive black with steel accents, standing against the wall. Just when she'd begun to despair of ever getting the other stove to maintain something like an even temperature, this new stove had arrived. Absolutely the latest model, it was designed and built to put more heat into the food and less into the kitchen. One of the more major triumphs of the week had been the ease with which Bethany and Charlene had mastered the new range.

The Garden brothers, sweating despite the refreshing autumn breeze, had lugged the gleaming sheet-steel stove through the front door to her and Charlene's excited surprise.

At first, Bethany had rushed to thank her grandfather for the magnificent gift, determined to refuse it because she was certain he couldn't really afford it. But he denied all knowledge of it with a sly grin. Only when Charlene gave a giggle did it dawn on Bethany who had contributed it.

"Some men give diamonds," Mr. Ames said, looking at the ceiling with an innocent air.

Charlene added, "But a stove is so much more romantic. Just think, Bethany. You can look at the thermometer and imagine it's Mr. Houston's heart."

Keeping her pride up with an effort, Bethany responded with, "In that case, it's sure to read zero."

"Like that?" Jerry held out his first completed salad for her inspection. The pomegranate seeds, translucent and ruby red, were piled in the center, which actually looked better than having them scattered around.

"Excellent," she said, giving praise where it was due. "But you mustn't make them one at a time, you know. Put all the lettuce out, then add the other ingredients to each bowl before moving on to the next ingredient. You see?"

"Sure. That makes sense."

Not much else did, Bethany reflected as she returned to her work. At about the same time she'd received the stove, she'd gotten at least another of her wishes. She hardly saw Brent at all. He was gone before she woke up, and never returned until late. When they did speak, it was about the children. He shied away from any other subject in a manner as marked as it was hurtful.

Charlene hadn't returned yet. Wondering if everyone had finished their soup, Bethany arranged the radish roses and carrot curls. Placing quenelles of ground salmon on smaller plates, she sprinkled them with dill and mushroom sauce. She'd serve these and the pork while Charlene took care of the last-minute baking.

Wiping her hands on her apron, she peeked out the

swinging door. Charlene stood by their grandfather's table, laughing at something Virgil Emmett had said. Bethany signaled to her sister. Charlene either didn't see her, or didn't choose to see her. Even besotted Constable Richardson noticed Bethany before Charlene or Virgil saw her. He said in a loud voice, "I think your sister wants you."

Bethany served the entrees while Charlene, a little sheepishly, retired to the kitchen to finish her baking. She had decided to offer a choice of desserts, including chocolate-almond torte, blackberry vacherin with meringue layers but without the cassis liqueur in deference to the anti-alcohol mood in Cedar Groves, and finally Dutch Apple Pie. She chose this last to prove that she could bake something simple as well as something complicated.

Bethany served Mayor and Mrs. Tubbs their entrees. "I hope you're enjoying your meal," she said politely.

"Looks okay," Mr. Tubbs said dubiously, poking the fish dumpling doubtfully with his fork. He reached out for the salt shaker before he'd even done that much to his pork. Bethany tried hard not to grimace as he sprinkled the salt liberally and indiscriminately over her carefully seasoned meal.

"The soup was . . . interesting," Mrs. Tubbs said. "So different."

"I first had that soup at a gala dinner for Mrs. Commodore Vanderbilt." Bethany couldn't resist dropping a little reminder that she'd been places and met people that Mrs. Tubbs could only read about in *Harper's Bazaar*. Miss Ivey at least looked at her with revived respect.

"Well," Mrs. Tubbs said with a short, unconvincingly laugh, "we haven't the refinements of New York society here, but I hope to see your sister and yourself at our little meeting tomorrow afternoon. Charlene is such a dear girl; I'm sure she'll be an ornament to Spiritual Cleanliness."

"I don't know if we'll have time to attend . . ."

"Oh, you must. We altered the time of the meeting so

you'd be able to. Three o'clock in the afternoon, at my house."

"In that case, Mrs. Tubbs . . ."

Mayor Tubbs gave a snort and leaned back. "Not bad," he said, patting his mounded stomach through his striped waistcoat.

Bethany shot a disbelieving glance at his plate. He'd eaten everything but the design in only the few minutes she'd been speaking with Mrs. Tubbs.

She noticed that two more people, a man and a woman, had entered and were looking about as though trying to choose a table. As Bethany showed them to seats, she was thinking with relief of the extra salads being prepared in the back room. They were up to seventeen people already. Just as she thought that, the Zimmerman family came in, all eight unfailingly cheerful members from the grandmother to the baby. What with moving two tables together and counting on her fingers, Bethany forgot the faint instinctive warning she'd felt when she heard Mrs. Tubb's invitation.

Hours later, her hands stinging from washing soda and hot water, Bethany stood on the stoop to lock the front door. Tired, she inhaled deeply of the cool evening air, hoping to refresh herself. Despite having spent the last day moving through a constant sea of food, she hadn't eaten anything since breakfast and felt a little shaky. Tomorrow, she'd be more sensible. At the moment, she longed only for bed.

A golden moon sailed among the fleeing clouds. Something in the air hinted at rain to come. Bethany was glad of her smooth luster coat, stout shoes, and the wool fascinator she'd draped over her head. She made a mental note to be certain the children all had rubberized coats for rain.

Deep in her own thoughts, she paid little attention to the footsteps behind her. Obviously someone else was hurrying home after a long day, perhaps a bookkeeper or a clerk kept late counting over the inventory. Yet despite her carefully reasoned conclusions, Bethany felt compelled to hurry her steps. The bag clutched under her arm held today's receipts, a far greater sum than she'd imagined. The footsteps behind her started to run, coming closer and closer.

Then a hand clutched at her shoulder and she froze, a strangled cry breaking from her lips.

"Bethany! It's me," Brent exclaimed, folding his arms around her. He cradled her against his broad chest while at the same time trying to peer into her averted face.

She clung to him limply, trying to drag air into her empty lungs. His hands were strong as they moved on her back, his heart thrummed beneath her ear. She could have stayed like that forever, taking strength from him. But slowly she straightened up and put distance between their bodies.

"Brent!" she said, letting her breath out. "My word, you scared me to death!" Anger replaced relief. "What are you doing, sneaking up on me that way? You scared me out of a year's growth!"

"I'm sorry. I didn't . . ."

Light suddenly flooded over them as someone in an apartment above them opened a window. A gruff voice called, "What in tarnation's a-going on down there?"

"Nothing, Mr. Roach," Brent called, keeping his eyes on Bethany. She studied the square caps of her shoes, embarrassed by her lack of self-control. "Everything's fine."

"Zat you, Mr. Houston?"

"That's right."

"Got a leak in my roof. Ain't coming through yet, but the plaster's not lookin' so good."

"I'll send Mr. O'Dell to look at it tomorrow."

"S'all right. Night. Night, miss."

"Good night," Bethany said civilly to the unseen man and walked on.

Brent took her arm when he caught up to her. Petulantly, Bethany shrugged free. She didn't need to see his face to know he was grinning at her. He said, "I've heard you had quite a success tonight."

"Oh, Brent," she said, turning toward him impulsively,

her indignation forgotten. "We had twenty-nine people! I had to send Jerry out for more lettuce twice!"

"That's wonderful."

"Wonderful! I can't believe it. Everyone loved the food and they all thought the café was just beautiful. It's all such a relief."

"Don't tell me you had doubts?"

Bethany glanced at him. Was he teasing? "Of course I had doubts. You'll think I'm dreadfully silly, but I actually had mental images of people walking out after one bite."

"That will never happen. You're much too good a cook. I only wish I could have been there."

"Me too," she said softly. "It didn't seem real without you."

He went on, without seeming to have heard her quiet admission. "So tonight's receipts are satisfactory?"

Bethany looked down at the ground. Ruefully, she said, "I don't know if I'll ever get used to taking money. I did what Grandfather suggested—just put the bill on the table—but making change flustered me."

"I didn't think anything could do that," he said, his voice warm.

Bethany wanted to avoid that tender note in his tone, for she knew too well what it did to her. She asked brightly, "How did you hear about our success?"

"Constable Richardson came in to my place after he took Miss Hart home."

"I thought the constable was a teetotaler."

"He is, but sometimes a man wants a drink. Sometimes to drown his sorrows; sometimes to celebrate his happiness. Tonight, he was happy."

They were out on the road now, walking up the slight grade that made all the difference between Upper Grove and Lower Grove. The road had a silvery gleam under the moonlight, as though they were walking on a river.

"Don't you want to know why he was happy?" Brent asked. He didn't wait for her to answer. "He said it was the happiest day of his life, so far. He figures the happiest one of all will be in about three months. Seems Miss Hart has her heart set on a New Year's Day wedding."

Bethany stopped and smiled up at Brent, excited. "You mean, they're engaged?"

"He seems to think so. Does that please you?"

"Did he propose at dinner? Oh, never mind. He may have proposed after dinner, but it doesn't matter."

"What's dinner got to do with it?"

"Don't you see? Every girl in town will be dragging their beaus along to our café in the hopes of working the same miracle."

"Why is it a miracle?" he asked, amused.

"They've only been going around together for years. But after one of *my* dinners, he proposed." She hugged herself in delight. "That sounds like a miracle to me."

She turned to go on up the hill. Once again, Brent had to catch up to her to take her arm. Then he slowed her down, step by step, until they were strolling arm in arm. "Nice night," he said.

"Yes, isn't it," she said, sighting up at the drifting clouds, black against the silvery moonlight.

He wasn't wearing gloves. His warm hand slid into hers so he was no longer holding her arm as a gentleman should, but holding her hand like a lover. His touch reminded her of all the desires she'd tried to forget.

As they walked along, in peaceful concord, Bethany realized her right elbow kept bumping into something at his side. Her brows drawing together, she shot a clandestine glance at his chest. A slight bulge showed under the left side of his coat at the level of his ribs. Her eyes widened as she realized what it was. Did Brent always carry a gun?

"Bethany," he said as though starting a new subject, "will you tell me how your fiancé proposed to you?"

"Why?"

He shrugged. "I'm thinking of making a study out of it. Now Constable Richardson, whether under the influence of

The Isabella Café or not, says he just swept Miss Hart off her feet. He says the way to do it is to not give the girl a chance to say no. Now Mr. Milner—he was there tonight too—he says, he let his wife propose to him. That way he wasn't responsible for supplying any of what he calls 'mush.' By which I think he meant poetry and love words."

Bethany found herself asking a question before she'd known she was thinking anything of the kind. "How did you propose to your wife?"

He stopped in his track. "I've been waiting for this," he said. "Call me a coward again if you like, but I've been avoiding you for just this reason."

He took her gently but firmly by the shoulders and turned her to face him. The moon came out from a cloud and he could see her smiling. In the insubstantial light, which washed all color away, he could have sworn he saw in her eyes nothing but affection for him, even love. Under that gaze, he could be totally forthright.

Brent said, "Yes, I was married. For a few brief months in the summer of '72. We were both kids who thought we'd found the lasting kind of love. We were wrong. She left me for someone with more money, who offered her a world of excitement and thrills. She broke my heart and I thought I'd never get over her. But I did."

"How old were you?"

"Nineteen. We were both nineteen."

"*I'm* nineteen," Bethany said.

"And I'm thirty-three." His face showed such tenderness that she caught her breath. "But you're very different from Min. She was—" Suddenly he grinned as though at some memory. "She was flighty, to say the least. Full of fun but with no more brains than a gnat. A breeze could change her mind and she almost never arrived at the place she said she was going, and certainly *never* on time."

"She sounds charming."

"Yes, she was. Very charming. I wasn't the only one who thought so."

"What became of her?"

"Last I heard, and this was a long time after, she was living in a palace in St. Petersburg with a Russian prince. I don't know if it's true or not, but I wouldn't be surprised."

"And what happened? You know, with your marriage?" Had she been kissing and weaving fantasies around a married man?

"I'm divorced, Bethany."

"Divorced?" she said. For a moment it was as if she hadn't any idea what the word meant. In her head it sounded like the tolling of a great bell. She knew what knell it sounded. She was in love with him. Terribly, desperately in love. And he was divorced.

"Does it matter?"

"Matter?" Her hand fell away from his.

He went on talking, faster now. "You've understood so much. My business, my desire to be free, my feelings for you. Don't let this little piece of my past come between us. It's over and done with, forever. I'm a free man."

"But . . . divorced?"

Fifteen

It rained for four days straight, heavy, soaking rain that made the unpaved streets run with mud. Even the Spiritual Cleanliness meeting was put off until the following week. When the weather finally broke, October had rolled in, bringing with it mellow morning mists and cool evenings. One crisply bright day, Bethany and Charlene took little Dory out to the gazebo in the back garden to take advantage of the sunshine.

They spread their wet hair, rinsed in the rain barrel to add softness, over towels on their shoulders to let the warming air help dry it. Relaxing, they talked over the slow business of the evening before, and made a few last-minute adjustments to tonight's menu, while the snugly dressed baby lay on a blanket on the wooden slats of the floor.

"One day," Bethany said dreamily, "I'd like to offer a variety of dishes, instead of a French-style menu."

"Everyone who was there enjoyed the choice last night," Charlene said, bending from her chair to pick up the baby's rag doll that had slid beyond Dory's limited reach.

"Yes, but what if we lose a customer because they don't like trout and that's what we're serving."

"There seemed to be enough last night that even if they hadn't liked the Salmon Wellington they wouldn't have gone hungry. Even Mr. Clyde walked away full last night, and I was beginning to think that was impossible!"

"He's turning out to be a regular customer. I hope our prices aren't too high for him. A dollar a meal *is* high."

Charlene shrugged. "He did say it was an extravagance but that it was worth it. Frankly, I think he just wants something tasty. He'd boarding at Mrs. Woolcott's. That woman feeds her children on nothing but skimmed milk and porridge. I can't imagine she feeds the schoolmaster any more luxuriously."

"Well, with a little brown sugar . . ." Bethany said. She smiled down at the baby, who had maneuvered over on her stomach, to investigate Bethany's glossy brown boots. "She's turned out to be such a pretty baby," she said, scooping Dory up.

Charlene reached out to stroke the baby's narrow back. "And she's plumping up nicely. But she still has a way to go. I saw Mrs. Naylor's baby yesterday. He looked like a little bear cub, he was so roly-poly."

Bethany could tell Charlene was eager to hold Dory, so she handed her over, albeit with reluctance. When she looked into those eager, curious blue eyes, she felt as if she were observing the world the same way as Dory did. Everything seemed so new and fascinating, even the play of the feeble sunlight through the pierced railings of the gazebo. When she gave her up, the world seemed a little flatter, a little less bright. To be able to constantly revive that luster would almost reconcile one to having lots of babies.

She found herself tracing over and over again the sinuous vines that decorated the arm of the cast-iron chair she sat in. Her thoughts had gone around and around the same way for half the night. Now she sighed, tired, wretched, and confused.

Bethany glanced over at Charlene, bouncing the baby on her knee, and envied the discipline of her mind. Charlene had made a firm decision that she wasn't going to marry Virgil or even show him affection. So far as Bethany could tell, her sister suffered no second thoughts. She didn't lie awake till all hours wondering if she'd done the right thing or not.

Charlene sang softly, "This is the way the ladies ride,

ladies ride, ladies ride. This is the way the ladies ride all on a Sunday morning!" Dory laughed, waving baby fists.

Charlene said, "I hope Grandfather can talk Judge Carr around. It would be just terrible if we had to give the children up! Faye's settling in so nicely, and Dory . . ." She kissed the baby's soft cheek.

"At least they were old school friends. I'm sure Grandfather still has influence with the judge, if he ever comes back. It's a scandal, a grown man shirking his duties because he's afraid of his niece!"

"I'm afraid of Mrs. Tubbs too."

"Don't worry. Nobody in their right mind would send children to an orphanage if there's someone willing to care for them. I'm sure it will be all right."

"I hope and pray it will be. For your sake. I know you feel just as though they were your own already."

"One day, you will have your own," Bethany said lightly, insinuating a forefinger into Dory's ribs. When the baby giggled and looked around, Bethany wiggled her finger and said, "I'm gonna get you!"

A few moments later Bethany realized Charlene was crying.

"My dear!" she said in shocked surprise. She took the baby from Charlene's trembling hand and put her down on the blanket, placing the rag doll where Dory could reach it.

She laid a comforting hand on Charlene's forearm and said, "What is it, dear? What's wrong?"

"N-n-nothing," Charlene sniffled as she dug in her pocket for her handkerchief.

"Do you feel ill? It was staying up so late last night after all this hard work. You came into the house and . . ." Bethany stood up.

"No, no. I'm . . . it's not my heart . . ." Charlene caught her hand and motioned for her to sit again. "Well, it *is* my heart, only not the working part. It's just that . . . I never will have any children of my own, Bethany. Not when V-Virgil's going so far away."

"You never did tell me where it is he's going." Bethany spoke softly, aghast that her offhand prophecy had brought such unhappiness.

"I don't know if you remember his brother, Lionel? He was already out of school by the time we went in. He went west, to Oregon. He's got a fine orchard now—he grows cherries. He wants Virgil to come out and be his partner."

"Oregon?" Bethany said, feeling it might as well be the moon. If there had been a trip calculated to kill Charlene, a trip to Oregon would be the most effective. "But that must be at least a thousand miles. Doesn't Virgil realize that you would never . . ."

"He doesn't know how sick I was. I . . . I haven't had the courage to tell him." She blew her nose with a defeated snort. "He never treats me like I'm sick. With Virgil, I can forget all about it."

Now it was Charlene's turn to give the reassuring pat. "Don't worry, Bethany. I will never abandon you and Grandfather. And now you've brought these beautiful children into my life, a blessing from God. You all need me much more than Virgil does. I'm happy with my choice . . . quite happy."

So much for the discipline of Charlene's mind. Bethany leaned over and kissed her sister's rose-petal cheek. Then she sat down. "Never lie to me, Charlene. I've known you all my life and I can tell."

Charlene couldn't meet Bethany's eyes. "Let me lie," she said in a low, passionate tone. "I need to believe it myself."

Bethany knew about lies told to oneself. She'd done everything she could as she lay awake night after night, trying to block out her feelings toward Brent. To her shame, the fact that he was a divorced man didn't make any difference to her feelings. She still loved him with a passion that shook her whole body whenever she thought of him.

She knew, however, that his divorce should make a difference. In the eyes of many people, even people she loved and respected, no decree would free a person from a marriage constituted by God. So long as Brent's former wife lived, he would be married to her. Any other tie would be bigamy.

Though Bethany told herself *she* was too sophisticated to believe that, one of her earliest memories had been of her mother and grandmother whispering about another woman, a divorced woman who remarried. The very word "divorce" had an ugly, sinful sound like the hiss of the first Serpent.

If Brent had marriage to her in mind—how high her heart leaped at the notion!—could she ever really feel secure in that marriage? Or would the knowledge of that other wife eat away at her, making her peevish and unlovable? Brent had extricated himself from one marriage. Would that make him more likely to want to escape from another?

Bethany shook her head. She was conjuring dragons out of thin air. Though Brent obviously found her attractive and sympathetic, he'd never said one word about marriage. It was unutterably foolish to sit here making herself miserable over something that would never happen.

Charlene too seemed to shake off the thoughts that oppressed her. She bent down to pull a corner of blanket over Dory who had gone to sleep with the blissful unconcern of the very young or very old. "What about you?" she asked.

"Me? There's nothing wrong with me."

"What about Brent?"

"Brent?" Bethany asked, as if trying to place the name.

Charlene gave her a look in which affection mingled with exasperation. "He's obviously wildly in love with you. . . ."

"No, I don't think so."

"That's not the impression I got the other evening. You remember . . . when you were kissing him in the library?" A laugh rippled from her at her sister's startled expression. "I saw the firelight and peeked in to see if anyone was there. What I saw . . . well, you'd walked in on Virgil and me but we weren't doing *anything* compared with you two."

Bethany ran her hand over her hot cheek. "That wasn't planned, Charlene. It just happened. I have his word it won't happen again."

Charlene looked wise. "Didn't he walk you home last night?"

"Yes, but nothing happened."

"It will. He's showing every sign of interest."

"And you know so much about that!"

"Well, I do, as a matter of fact. I've always flirted more than you, Bethany. Virgil isn't the first man I've ever kissed, any more than Ronald was. Ronald wasn't the first man to propose to me even."

"He wasn't?" That came as news to Bethany.

"No. My first proposal was from Earl Becker. We were only six or seven, but he said he wanted to marry me. And then Lucius Cullen, and Marcus Daniels . . . and those were just the ones here in town. Did I tell you I saw Lucius the other day with his wife?"

"No, you didn't mention it. I suppose Joshua Lowell proposed too. He was very attentive last year as I remember."

"Yes, he asked me. But he's so wild. Aunt Poste warned me against him and she was right. He got so angry when I refused him that I was actually frightened of him." She dropped her eyes. "There were some others too, Bethany."

"So why did you accept Ronald Diccers, for goodness' sake? He's the dullest man we know."

"No, Gerrald Stowe's much more boring. Which is why I turned him down too."

Bethany stared. For a moment she'd been confused by the parade of men who'd found her sister entrancing. The mention of her own fiancé amid all the others almost passed unnoticed. Then she said, "Gerrald? *My* Gerrald?" Charlene nodded silently, her face filled with shame. "Why didn't you tell me?"

"Aunt told me not to. She didn't want to ruin your chances when he started paying attention to you. She thought you'd be too proud to accept him if you knew he'd asked me first."

"She was right," Bethany said in a low voice.

Charlene hurried to say, "It wasn't as if I even knew he felt that way about me. He just asked me during a dance. I said 'No, thank you,' and he didn't seem to take his refusal very hard. He only bowed. I couldn't believe he'd been serious. The next thing I knew, he was dancing with you. I never gave it another thought."

Bethany looked at her sister's face, mirroring her own concern and pain. "It's not even as though we are identical," she said wonderingly. "Our coloring is the same and our height, but no one has ever mistaken you for me. Or me for you, for that matter."

"It couldn't have been a mistake," Charlene said slowly. "He called me by name, you see."

"No, I don't mean that he proposed to you thinking you were me. I mean . . . he must have asked me to marry him because I'm so much like you. If he couldn't have the original, I suppose he decided to take a copy, however poorly executed."

She thought of the short, painfully stiff note she'd written to Gerrald last. She might as well have been writing a duty letter to a maiden aunt instead of to the man she ostensibly loved. She knew what love was now. It swept her past all her moorings into a new country where everything was both strange and wonderful. Small wonder she was so frightened. She was lost and alone, with no landmarks to guide her back to familiar country. If only she could be certain Brent was in love too. Then she wouldn't be alone.

She ran her fingers through the long waves of her hair. "Mine's about dry," she said, standing. "I'd better start assembling the quail. I'm going to have them all wrapped in bacon and puff paste before taking them down to the café. That way, all I have to do is cook them when someone comes in."

"Bethany," Charlene said, bending to scoop up the baby, blanket and all. "Don't let this . . ."

"It's all right," Bethany said reassuringly. "I'm not angry. I'll just write Gerrald a note, telling him I've changed my mind. And don't feel bad. I actually changed my mind before we left New York, when he was so unreasonable about this trip. I decided then and there that I really couldn't marry a domestic tyrant."

At three o'clock, wishing it would start to rain again, Bethany and Charlene skewered their best afternoon hats to their elaborately dressed hair and set off toward Mrs. Tubbs's house for the postponed meeting. Mrs. Manning, Dory in one arm and Faye behind her skirt, said, "Don't forget to watch your backs," as the girls left.

"What does that mean?" Charlene whispered as they reached the end of Marmion House's walkway.

"I don't think she likes Mrs. Tubbs very much."

"I can't say I blame her. She has cold eyes, like a fish."

Certainly there was something fishy about Mrs. Tubbs's effusive welcome. The small paisley print of her very tight jersey and skirt made her seem as though she were outfitted in scales, adding to the illusion. The white sash of her league bisected her impressive torso on the diagonal.

She took their coats and hats, tut-tutting when she saw their dresses. "But you're not wearing your sashes! We mustn't have that! You're part of the membership and we must stand together. Fortunately, I have plenty more."

Mrs. Tubbs left them standing in the hall while she hurried away. Bethany could hear the murmur of ladylike voices in another room of Mrs. Tubbs's grand white mansion. Though festooned with gingerbread and carved trim, it always seemed more like an iceberg than a wedding cake. Perhaps it gave that impression because the paint was so blindingly white. Or perhaps the inflexible will of the woman who lived there colored Bethany's perception.

"Let's go in," Bethany murmured to her sister. "There's a draft here."

"But I'm sure Mrs. Tubbs wanted us to wait."

"That's too bad for her." Bethany took Charlene's arm and impelled her forward.

The parlor began opposite the bottom of the stairs. As the two sisters appeared in the doorway to the left, a silence, as blighting as a sudden frost, fell over the guests. Some blushed, as though caught in a bad deed. Others paused, cake halfway to their mouths. There were about a dozen women, all from Upper Grove, all wearing the white satin sashes. The sole exception was also the only male, a dark man in a black coat.

For a moment, before he turned, Bethany felt exactly as though she saw some friend of hers in the lion's pit. Everything in the room, everything within her, seemed paralyzed. What was Brent doing here, of all places?

Then someone laughed, a high nervous sound like a whinny, and the spell was broken. People moved, talked, and ate as naturally as can be.

The man turned, and she wondered at herself. Of course, this wasn't Brent. Brent had no potbelly for one thing, nor did his shoulders stoop. Though both men's hair was black, Brent's wasn't flecked with dandruff or greasy. Nor did he wear a clerical collar.

This man should have been the ugliest thing imaginable, but when he smiled, Bethany sensed a certain shy charm. Judging by the way the relentlessly youthful Miss Yardley hung on his every word, she'd obviously come to the conclusion that all he needed was a good woman to make him presentable. She looked like a most eager volunteer.

When he excused himself to greet Bethany and Charlene, Miss Yardley stared after him with an expression reminiscent of a baffled cat staring after a flown bird. Bethany could almost see her tail lash.

"You must be Miss Forsythe. *Both* Miss Forsythes." He smiled at Charlene while he shook Bethany's hand, and vice versa. "I'm Thomas Vance. Of the First Church," he added as though afraid they wouldn't understand why he wore no tie unless this was explained at once.

"How do you do, Mr. Vance. I've heard many nice things about you," Bethany said. Though she hadn't meant to sound condescending, something about the Reverend Mr. Vance made her want to pat him on the head as though he were a stray dog. Charlene looked at him with that starry-eyed attentiveness that Bethany knew masked a real impulse to laugh.

Mr. Vance wriggled at this mild praise. "No, not really. I do try to reach my flock but sometimes it's very difficult. I hope we'll see more of you at services?"

"Oh," Mrs. Tubbs fluted from the rear. "They're so busy, dear Mr. Vance. Working girls, you know." With a toothy grin, Mrs. Tubbs handed Bethany and Charlene the white sashes she'd gone to find.

"Slip them over your heads. Then you'll look just like us. Only much, much smarter. I was saying just the other day, wasn't I, Agnes, that the Forsythe girls have come back from New York with all the smartness of that very smart city."

"Yes, indeed, Mrs. Tubbs. Your very words." Miss Ivey swallowed a bit of cake and came hurrying over to fulfill her role of echo. She hastily shook hands with the two girls. Bethany had never before noticed what small feet and hands Miss Ivey had.

"I hope you're well, Miss Ivey," Bethany said.

The small lady opened her mouth to answer only to have her words snatched by Mrs. Tubbs. "Oh, dear Agnes is never ill. I couldn't get along without her for a whole day, you know."

"That's right. I'm never ill. *Never.*"

"One of the hardest workers for the church," Mr. Vance put in. "I'm afraid many people 'slack off' as it were— please pardon the idiom. If it weren't for the Miss Iveys of this world, the spiritual end would never be able to function."

Irreverently, Bethany wondered what a "spiritual end" looked like, envisioning a hall closet jammed with old souls and worn-out righteousness. She further wondered if it were "spiritually clean" to have such things around collecting spiritual dust.

The subject drifted, as subjects will, into a discussion of Sunday School and the shortage of good molders of the church's youngest members. Bethany paid little attention, happy to indulge her imagination. Then she glanced idly at Miss Ivey and felt a thrill of shock.

A sparkle of humor flashed and danced in Miss Ivey's mild eyes. Her pert face had a glow that made her look, if not pretty, at least like someone worth knowing. But she wasn't smiling *at* anyone. It was as if she found her thoughts to be a source of entertainment as rich as did Bethany.

As if she'd spoken her thought aloud, Miss Ivey met her eyes. For a moment they seemed to share a secret. Then Miss Ivey's face became as dull and uninteresting as before. But Bethany was left with the unsettling feeling that she'd pigeonholed Miss Ivey improperly years ago, to her own misfortune.

There was something else different about Miss Ivey today that Bethany couldn't quite place. Her hair was the same neat bun, drawn low on her neck, and her blouse was spotted with crumbs as usual. Bethany resolved to ask Charlene, who was asking interested questions of the reverend, what she really thought of Miss Ivey.

"Well, Mrs. Tubbs said lightly. "Though this is fascinating, we must call the meeting to order. Time and tide, you know . . ."

She clapped her hands ringingly. "Attention, everyone. If you'll just take your seats, we'll get started." The women in the room made a concerted movement toward some rows of chairs that Bethany hadn't noticed before.

"Flossie, Rose," Mrs. Tubbs said, shaking a playful forefinger at two young women hovering by the tea tray. "No more chitchat. Important business today."

At that moment Bethany realized Mrs. Tubbs loved power. Her cheeks glowed with it and she seemed ten years younger as she made every woman there do her bidding. Bethany glanced down at her white sash. When had she put this thing on? Had it been of her own free will?

"Come now, Reverend," Mrs. Tubbs said, still in that arch and artificial voice. "Let's have a really rousing prayer, hum? Get things off to the right start."

She said to Bethany and Charlene, "Plenty of room, girls. I'm sure you'll enjoy yourselves. We have a busy agenda, you know, lots to do."

"What agenda?"

Once again that admonished forefinger waved. "Spiritual Cleanliness, of course. There's so much dirtiness in the world, don't you think? And it's a woman's place to clean, to scour the secret corners, to brighten and refresh even the worst sinner. But listen to me! Scolding everyone for talking and here I am chattering away like a monkey. Have a seat, girls. Mustn't hold everyone else up."

"I'll show them," Miss Ivey volunteered. "There's three empty chairs together at the back."

Sixteen

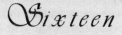

"I just can't believe it!" Bethany stormed. She stood right there—backed up by that tame reverend of hers—and told me right to my face! If Charlene hadn't laid her hand on my arm, I swear I would have torn off her false front!"

Brent and Mr. Ames exchanged one of those looks that said *"Women!"*

"But, Bethany," her grandfather said. "You haven't told us . . ."

"But even pulling off her hair would have been too little! Nobody cared about these children when they were living on their own. They could have starved like dogs or burned down the house and nobody would have noticed. But we take them in and suddenly they're in terrible danger!"

Brent took a deep breath, caught up to her as she turned in her pacing, and took her by the arms. Fully aware of Mr. Ames's eyes on his back, Brent pulled Bethany into a deep, lingering kiss.

She had the softest lips in the world. Her scent was white violets and lilies. He had to concentrate hard to keep from losing his head. Only by exerting all his will when she softened and relaxed against him, emerging from her first shock, could he let her go.

"Now, what did Mrs. Tubbs say?"

Bethany blinked her long lashes and said wonderingly, "Didn't I tell you?"

"No."

She smoothed her hair and shook out her skirts. He

noticed she couldn't quite bring herself to look at her grandfather. When she looked at him, however, he saw the spark of anger in her eyes about to be drowned by tears.

"She's going to send the children to the orphanage at Rixford."

"Impossible!" Mr. Ames said. "I haven't spoken to Grover Carr as yet, but Brent . . ."

"You're too late, Grandfather. *She* talked to him this morning. I forgot, or never knew, that she was his niece."

"That's right." Mr. Ames stroked his mustache meditatively. "And the daughter of his older sister at that. You didn't know Druscilla Carr, did you, Bethany? A hard woman. Nearly had me, you know. Good thing your grandmother came along or I wouldn't have been able to call my soul my own. Poor old Grover lived completely under Druscilla's thumb from the time they were children. I believe she used to give him castor oil."

"Well, now Mrs. Tubbs wants the children to get their castor oil at the Rixford orphanage. She says this house isn't suitable for children. Not suitable! Why, I was a child here for years."

Brent saw the quick glance she gave him. He'd become so adept at reading her that he could tell she was holding something back, something about him.

"Is it the house that isn't suitable? Or the people?" He took her hand and made her look at him. "What did she say about me, Bethany?"

"I wouldn't have minded so much," she said softly, "if she hadn't made that spineless reverend pray about it. He went on and on. 'Weaker vessels,' bad companions, girls led astray, and how women are so much more prone to temptation than men. And all the while Mrs. Tubbs sat there staring at us, and nodding her head, until I thought I would scream."

"I've heard about the Reverend Mr. Vance," Grandfather said in a grim tone. "Very popular with the ladies. Contributions are way up."

Bethany continued, indignation sending her voice high and hardening her eyes, "After the meeting was over, she came up to me. She said that she was sure it would be much healthier for the children at the orphanage, that they'd be happier there. She was so smug! She said she was sure someone would adopt the baby right away, though she thought Faye had a sullen face."

"Has she come up with a plan for Jerry?" Brent asked.

"Oh, she felt certain he could find an apprenticeship somewhere. And when I said the children had decided they didn't want to be separated, she became very snide about Mrs. Windom."

Brent wondered if Bethany believed what Mrs. Tubbs had said. He knew that the news of his past had shocked and frightened her. Though her response to the kiss he'd just given her meant he still had hope, he understood that she was struggling with inbred conventions that she hardly realized she believed. "What did she say?"

Bethany bowed her head. "Nothing important. Besides, it couldn't be true."

"What if it was true, Bethany?" he asked in a low voice. "Would it make a difference?" He held his breath while she hesitated.

"No," she said and he sighed. "No, of course not. It doesn't matter what their mother did or how many different fathers they have. They think of themselves as a family, and they're going to stay a family."

"Did you tell Mrs. Tubbs that?"

"I told her she should be ashamed of herself, speaking ill of the dead, and Charlene and I walked out. First, though, I took off my Spiritual Cleanliness banner and dropped it on the floor. That whole idea's nothing but an excuse for Mrs. Tubbs and her ilk to meddle in other people's business!"

Brent and Mr. Ames exchanged another look, a worried one. They'd had a long talk yesterday about just this problem. Mr. Ames didn't want either of his granddaughters completely cut off from the society of Cedar Groves. As women, they needed the support and friendship of other women. Yet here was Bethany burning not only her boats, but her bridges.

"Perhaps you shouldn't have done that," Mr. Ames ventured to say. "After all, they do excellent work. Why, their efforts built the steeple when the old one fell into the vestry. Donations were slow so they held bake sales and auctioned off a quilt. They raised the needed money in no time"—he coughed modestly—"with a little help from me."

"And they've put quite a dent in my business. I don't thank them for it; however, I can admire their tenacity."

"And you have to think of the café," Mr. Ames added. "If you alienate so many of your clients . . ."

Bethany stared at him in disbelief. "You're worried because of that? Didn't you hear what I said? Mrs. Tubbs wants to take the children and separate them. Stick them in a soulless orphanage, for goodness sake. Faye's only just starting to feel comfortable here and Dory . . . do you want that sweet little baby to go to strangers?"

A series of knocks at the front door interrupted whatever answer the men meant to give.

Mr. Ames stood up. "I'll see who that is. Mrs. Manning wanted the afternoon off. She had her best bonnet on too."

Bethany sat in the red brocade chair her grandfather had vacated. She rested her chin on her fist, her eyes hooded as she plotted a way to defeat Mrs. Tubbs.

Looking at her, Brent marveled at his good taste. When they'd first met, he'd fallen in love with a pair of blue eyes, a trim figure, and an air of defiance. Now he loved her for her spirit. She never admitted defeat, never asked for a favor or surrendered an ideal. Yet at the same time, she could be so lovingly tender, a woman of compassion as well as passion. Though he'd chosen with his eyes the first time, he now knew he would choose Bethany with his heart over the fairest woman in the world.

Yet, the very things that made her admirable made it

impossible that she should ever be his. So, though he despised himself for it, he decided to use her best qualities against her. Let her be his in name, and she would soon be his in love.

Brent tugged at his suddenly too-tight tie. "Bethany," he began. He wondered if he should go down on one knee onto the rich red carpet.

"If only Virgil weren't going to Oregon," she said. "Then Charlene could marry him, and they could adopt the children. But he's off to grow cherries and I'm very much afraid Charlene will weaken and go with him."

"Weaken?"

Bethany glanced up at him as though surprised to still find him here. "Yes, she's so much in love with him that it's making her miserable."

"Love makes you miserable?" He hoped she wasn't looking for an argument. "I thought it was supposed to make you happy—like the verse on a Valentine."

"I think it could be like that," she said, her eyes becoming soft and dreamy. "Love must be wonderful when everything is just right. I've seen many very happy couples."

Brent stroked the back of her hand where it lay loose on the arm of the chair. "People have to take risks sometimes. Maybe even when everything isn't perfect. If we all waited to marry when there are no problems, the human race would be a handful of old people in Egypt or somewhere, just waiting to die out."

"Of course, you're right." She drew her hand away, curling it into a fist and covering it with the other. "Even if Grandfather could marry Mrs. Manning . . . or would a judge think he's too old to adopt children?"

"No one could think your grandfather is old. But that's a big responsibility to ask anyone to take on. Believe me, I have experience now as a semifather."

"A semifather?"

"I've been giving fatherly advice, so that makes . . ."

"Fatherhood is more than advice," she said, her eyes

starting to laugh. They reminded him of a blue sea with sunlight striking sparks from the water.

"Okay. Well, I paid for the kids' new shoes, which is something a father's supposed to do." He dropped his voice to a whisper. "Don't tell the boys at the Golden Lady but . . ." He glanced around the room furtively.

Bethany leaned closer. "Yes?"

"I even changed Dory's diaper. Once. She squirmed like a polliwog." He held his forefinger to his lips. "Shh. No one must ever know."

On a ripple of laughter, she said, "I'll carry your secret to the grave."

"I know I can rely on you." He saw the fine color flow into her cheeks in response to the sincerity that wiped the humor from his voice. He took her hand, running his thumb over her knuckles. "Bethany?"

Once again, she couldn't meet his eyes. Softly, shyly, she said, "Yes, Brent?"

Grandfather Ames cleared his throat in the doorway. "Someone to see you, Bethany."

Saying, "Oh, my dear girl, I felt so sorry for you," Agnes Ivey came fluttering in. Bethany was reminded of nothing so much as a trapped sparrow trying to find her way out of a room. Miss Ivey blundered into a low table, tripped over the rug's fringe, and was only saved herself from buttering herself all over the floor by Brent's last-minute grab.

She threw him a "thank you" over her shoulder as she rushed forward to embrace Bethany impulsively. As she threw her arms wide, her bag on a long strap struck a vase. Brent fielded it, setting it upright again. If there had been anything in it, he would have been drenched.

Bethany pressed Miss Ivey firmly into a chair and returned to her own. Miss Ivey kept talking as though all the bottled-up words inside her had to come pouring out. After years of feeding on the bland crumbs of Mrs. Tubbs's utterances, echoing them faithfully, Miss Ivey seemed determined to sup on the spicy banquet of saying what she meant.

"I just turned scarlet for you, I really did. And I wasn't the only one, you know. So many ladies came up to me afterward and confided that they simply hadn't known which way to look. I mean, it's one thing to attack an establishment—oh, how do you do, Mr. Houston? *So* nice to see you again—but quite another to publicly humiliate one of our own."

Bethany glanced up at her grandfather, hovering around the sideboard as he said, "A glass of sherry, Miss Ivey? It's not too early for a little taste of something."

"Oh, well, since it's so close to sundown, I don't mind if I do." She grasped the delicate stem of the crystal glass and sipped a little of the straw-colored liquid.

Taking a deep breath, she said, "To be completely honest, I really don't know what's gotten into Mrs. Tubbs, though I shouldn't name names. But lately she's been just a little . . ." She tasted another sip of sherry to assist thought. "Yes, I think it's safe to say she's been a little dictatorial of late. And that's simply not what Spiritual Cleanliness should be about."

"I told my granddaughter about the church spire," Mr. Ames put in.

Miss Ivey nodded. When she spoke again, some of the foolishness had left her voice. "That's what I mean, Mr. Ames. Good works, encouraging noble thoughts and high ideals. Not pointing the finger at those who have strayed from the fold. I'm sure they couldn't help themselves." She shot a look at Mr. Houston from under her slightly heavy brows.

Bethany didn't dare look up at Brent. "That's very kind of you to say, Miss Ivey. I never knew you felt this way."

A little color came into Miss Ivey's ivory face. "I never knew I did either. But if Mrs. Tubbs will humiliate you that way, Miss Forsythe, who's to say who she'll turn on next?"

"That's true," Brent said. "It might even be a friend."

Miss Ivey put her glass on the marble-topped table at her

elbow, clinking it accidentally with Bethany's. Though it didn't topple over, it teetered. Brent stepped forward and stilled the rocking glass. "Part of my occupation," he said when Miss Ivey thanked him.

Miss Ivey rose to her tiny feet. "I didn't mean to stay but a moment, Miss Forsythe. I just wanted you to know *some* of us have sympathy for you."

"Thank you, Miss Ivey," Bethany said, touched. It had taken a considerable effort, she felt certain, for Miss Ivey to step out of the shadow of her idol.

Mr. Ames offered Miss Ivey his arm. "I admire your courage," he said. "If you'll allow me to get my coat, I should call it an honor to escort you home."

Miss Ivey's confusion was pretty to see. It was difficult to judge her age. Her face lay claim to forty, but her manner when facing a man was that of a nervous sixteen.

Remembering the wink she'd given at the meeting, Bethany wondered if even now she saw the true Miss Ivey. Perhaps the laughing girl she'd glimpsed for a mere moment today remained concealed somewhere behind the meek, mild spinster she showed the outside world.

Bethany spoke her thought to Brent after Mr. Ames and Miss Ivey had left the house. He said, "A lot of people hide themselves away out of fear."

"Fear of what?"

He lifted a shoulder in a careless shrug. "Disapproval, or a fear of not fitting in. You've done it; we all have."

"No, I haven't. I'm always the same."

He smiled, and her heart lifted. "No, you're not. Sometimes you're a ravaging hellcat. . . ."

"Never!"

"And sometimes you're a sweet little kitten by the fire, just waiting to be patted into purring."

Her nose wrinkled. "What a revolting image."

"Sometimes you're as proud as a queen, and then again I've seen you as mild as May."

"You paint a picture of a very confused woman," she said,

trying to keep the conversation light. But a gleam had come into his wild eyes and Bethany felt feminine awareness blooming into life within her. He got that look whenever he was about to take her into his embrace.

She'd risen when her guest had left but had remained by the Queen Anne armchair, her hand lying casually along the wood-trimmed arched back. Now he laid his hand over hers. "Bethany, about the children . . ."

"Yes, I should have asked Miss Ivey if she knew any way to stymie Mrs. Tubbs. There has to be some way."

"There is."

"There is? What?"

"You might not care for it, that's all."

Bethany looked at him, her eyes alight with hope. "I'm sure whatever it is I'd be more than willing to do it."

"Maybe not this. It means quite a sacrifice."

She turned toward him, her brows twitching together. "Anything's better than seeing Faye, Dory, and Jerry in an orphanage. Why, they might never see each other again and that would break their hearts."

"All right," he said, nodding as if he decided to take her at her word. "I went to see Judge Carr a couple of hours ago. I wanted to talk to him about some other matter but turns out I got to his house about half an hour after Mrs. Tubbs had left. I didn't need your grandfather along to tell me the judge was henpecked. He looked pretty low."

"And he told you what she had in mind."

"That's right."

"Why didn't you come to warn me at once?" Bethany asked, hurt. "If I had warning, I would have known how to face her when she came up with her suggestion."

"I'm sorry," Brent said. "I had some business to take care of first."

"Business? What business could be more important than the children's happiness?" She'd never understand men, if she lived forever.

"Well," he said, rubbing the back of his neck and smiling

as if at a joke she couldn't see. "There are certain formalities involved. People to see, permission to obtain . . ."

"I would have thought saloon business could wait," she said haughtily. "At least until you had the chance to tell me how to help the children."

"Oh, are you *going* to let me tell you?" he wondered.

Bethany saw the justice of his comment. She looked down and smiled at herself. "You're right. I apologize. Please tell me what you have in mind, Brent."

He shook his head, not in refusal, but in amazement. "This isn't the way I planned this at all. I thought it would be . . . I guess I'm a romantic at heart."

"A . . . a romantic?"

Bethany felt that strange, half-painful constriction of her breathing that struck her whenever Brent's eyes took on the intense look he only turned on her. What would be a sacrifice? What would she not like? What did it have to do with romance?

"A man imagines certain things happening in a certain way. I mean, when I sit down to buy a building I don't expect the conversation to be about alligators. When I give the drummer an order for whiskey I don't expect him to offer me sixteen pairs of children's parasols instead, though with the way the liquor business is going that may happen soon."

"How did you expect this conversation to go?" she asked.

Once again, he reached out to take her hand in his. "Oh, this one I've been over and over in my head. I thought I'd start by saying that you're one of the finest women I've ever met. Then I'd say that what Dory and Faye really need is a mother, and Jerry needs a father. Then, I'd kind of lead up to the next point on my list."

"The next point . . ." She gave in to the slight urging of his hand, stepping closer to his side. Looking up into his eyes, she felt as though the color had changed since she'd first met him. They were as young and fresh as the newest leaves in spring with the sunlight dancing down through the green.

He put his hand to her cheek and she knew with deep trembling that in one more instant he'd kiss her. Then he'd know the answer to his question without ever having to ask it.

The front door slammed, setting the ornaments in the room to jingling and swaying. "Bethany!" Charlene called on a note of sharp excitement.

Brent said, "Damnation!"

Letting go of her, he stalked away to stand in the half-circle of the wide bay window, glaring out into the afternoon.

"In the drawing room." Bethany stared after Brent, as frustrated as he was.

Charlene came in, her cheeks rosy red and her hat askew. "Bethany," she gasped, holding her hand to her side.

Instantly alarmed, Bethany went to her. "Charlene, are you all right? Come, sit down. Brent, a glass of brandy, quickly!"

Waving her gloved hand, Charlene turned down the brandy. "No, I'm . . . I'm all right. It's just . . . I ran . . . all the way. Stitch in my side."

With tender hands, Bethany unpinned her sister's hat. "Where are the children?" she asked.

"Mrs. Manning's got 'em at the Station Hotel. I took them there so this daughter of a friend of hers . . . whew." She leaned back in the chair and fanned herself with her hand. "My goodness, I remember when I could run up that hill and never have to catch my breath once."

"You've been ill," Bethany said gently. "And you're not used to running."

"That's a relief. I thought I was just getting old." She straightened up. "How do you do, Mr. Houston?"

"Miss Charlene," he said with a half bow.

She looked at him and then slowly she turned her head to

look at Bethany. Without knowing quite why, Bethany found herself blushing again.

"What did you want to tell me?" she asked.

"Oh, my goodness, yes. It's Mrs. Manning. You just won't believe what I saw." She took a deep breath and said it all at once. "Mr. O'Dell and she were sitting there together in the downstairs lounge and I swear he was holding her hand and if he hadn't just put a new garnet ring onto her finger you can call me a Dutchman!"

"Next time," Brent muttered, "I'll try a public place."

Seventeen

❦

"Are you certain?" Bethany gasped, sinking into her chair.

"You know Manny," Charlene said, pulling off her gloves by the fingers. "She doesn't give much away. But Mr. O'Dell was grinning all over his face and I swear he was about to tell me when she stopped him."

"But it's impossible. They only just met."

Charlene glanced down at her own ringless hands. "Sometimes it doesn't take very long," she said with a mysterious smile.

"I don't believe in love at first sight," Bethany said. A choked noise from Brent made her glance at him.

"A crumb," he explained, coughing stagily.

"Besides," Bethany went on. "She's in love with Grandfather. She's been in love with him forever."

Her sister only shrugged, still with a dreamy expression. Brent said, "People change, Bethany. Sometimes they don't realize it for a while."

"But not for five *years*?" She shook her head. "I'll talk to Manny and find out what really happened."

"When?" Brent asked reasonably. "You've got to be at the café in forty-five minutes."

She twisted around to see the cherry mantel clock ticking away, its burnished brass pendulum waving away the minutes. "Goodness, is it five o'clock already? And my *coquettes de macaroni* not done. Well, I'll have to make them at the café."

She bolted from her chair only to be stopped by Charlene. "If I'm right, then this may be a blessing in disguise. I mean, we may lose Manny as our housekeeper but it will answer Mrs. Tubb's complaint about the children."

"How?"

"I'm sure Mrs. Manning would be happy to have them. Mr. O'Dell's children are nearly all grown-up and it's not as if . . . you know . . . there will be any more." She colored at having to make such an indelicate reference in front of a man.

"That's true," Bethany said, successfully avoiding Brent's gaze. She was less successful at quelling the disappointment in her heart. He had no reason to ask her his question, if the children were adopted by Mrs. Manning and Mr. O'Dell.

Though it was wrong of her to use the children for her own ends, she knew she could make a good home for them. With Brent at her side, she could do anything. Not to mention the fact that if it should turn out that she was wrong in thinking he felt more for her than passion, raising three children together would give him plenty of opportunity to fall in love with her.

Bethany hurried to put the quail and all the other ingredients into her basket. Brent followed her but, disappointingly, made no effort to continue their previous conversation. He said only, "When you close tonight, wait for me. I'll see you home."

A week ago she would have protested violently that she was perfectly capable of walking alone, thank you. Today, she simply said, "Thank you."

By the time she was ready to go, Charlene had changed her skirt and shirtwaist for a clean dress. She had only to take her basket from the pantry.

"What have you made for tonight, Miss Charlene?"

She smiled at him. "Orange and lemon pudding pie, an open apple tart, and two Rich Cakes."

Bethany asked, "Those are so simple, Charlene. Didn't

you say you were going to make something really special for tonight?"

"I was going to . . . but Virgil stopped by and I . . . I thought I'd make something he'd like. He's fond of simple desserts. Besides, everyone seemed to prefer my apple pie last night to either of the other two desserts. I think your dinners were so wonderful that they didn't want anything too rich or fancy to follow. And also . . ."

"Yes?"

"I'm trying, Bethany, but I just can't think of enough recipes that don't call for alcohol. No Tipsy cakes, no babas au rhum, no *Schwarzwalderkirschtorte* . . ."

Brent looked like he didn't know whether to bless her for sneezing or run for the door. Bethany explained in a quick aside, "Black Forest Cherry Cake. It's wonderful!"

"But what good is it without the kirsch?" Charlene asked. "I can't use rum, or framboise liqueur, or crème de cacao. . . . Most of the best recipes I know call for alcohol in one form or another. Even trifle calls for brandy or wine."

"You could leave it out," Brent suggested. The looks Charlene and Bethany turned on him told him bluntly that he might as well suggest that they leave out the beef from roast or the sponge from sponge cake.

Bethany gave her sister a sympathetic hug around the shoulders. "I know," she said. "I'm in the same situation. No wine sauces."

"And after you made all that mushroom wine sauce and shipped it out here! I'd forgotten about that."

Shrugging, Bethany said, "We'll just have to think of temperance as a challenge to our creativity."

Her sister nodded determinedly. "And think how we'll astound everyone when this temperance business blows over."

"If it ever does," Bethany said pessimistically.

"One day it will," Brent said. "But in the meantime, there's a café waiting to open."

"You don't have to remind us," Bethany said. "I wish

Grandfather had kept the horse and buggy. These baskets get heavy."

"But . . ." Brent said, then studied the ceiling.

Charlene looked at her sister, then looked at Brent. A tiny smile set her lips to quivering. Bethany narrowed her eyes and gave her sister a reassuring nod. "I forgot—um—something," Charlene said. "Upstairs—ah. Don't start without me, Bethany."

"I won't."

Brent said, "And I thought *you* were a terrible liar."

"Don't change the subject. What do you know?"

"Me? About what?"

Bethany advanced on him, her basket banging her knee with every step. "Talk, Brent. I know Grandfather's keeping secrets around here. I can put two and two together."

"Yes. The only problem is you come up with twenty-two, more often than not."

She put her hand against his chest and shoved. It was like trying to move the house. Brent caught her hand and pressed it to his heart. Keeping his eyes fixed on hers as though he'd drink her soul, he lifted her hand to his lips. He strew tiny, warm kisses on the tender inside of her wrist.

It was as if the whole world telescoped to this moment, this place, and the touch of Brent's lips teasing her skin. Her head began to swim and her eyes to close. She knew what he was doing, distracting her this way, but it didn't matter. Bethany couldn't summon the will to resist as he lifted her hand higher still to drape around his neck.

Then he was kissing her mouth, encouraging her ever so gently to open to him. This was no ferocious overthrow of her good sense; this was the slow, insidious treachery of her own body working against her. He nipped and nibbled, licked and tasted until she was all but completely usurped.

Bethany only remembered faintly why it was important she not drop the basket to throw both arms around her lover's neck. Yet she still tried to press more closely against him. The hard ridge of something under his coat pressed into her side. It was uncomfortable, but not as uncomfortable as the sudden recollection of what that thing was.

"Brent," she said dreamily as he kissed the side of her throat. He hummed an answer. "Brent, move your gun. It's . . . it's . . ."

"Move my what?" He nuzzled her ear, only barely closing his teeth on the delicate lobe.

"Your . . . your gun. That is a gun, isn't it?"

"Depends . . ." He coughed and straightened up. "Um, sorry. Forgot I had it on."

"You haven't always worn that, have you? I never noticed it before last night."

"I used to wear it all the time. When the cowboys came through, every now and then there'd be somebody who only understood one kind of argument."

"Have you ever . . ."

"I've never had to kill anyone, Bethany. I hope I never will. But when you're in my game, sometimes bullets are part of the business."

"May I see it?"

"Why?"

"Curiosity."

He opened his coat cautiously, and strangely, holding the right side tight across his body while opening the left. Hanging on top of his vest—white with navy-blue stripes— was a tan leather holster, the wooden butt of a pistol protruding.

"I've never seen a holster like that before," she said, thinking that a gun had to be the ugliest thing man has ever invented.

"I don't like to seem to be armed, Bethany. It makes people nervous. On the other hand, I don't carry a pocket derringer. If I'm going to show someone my gun, I want it to look like a weapon, not a toy."

"It doesn't look like a toy." Bethany was aware that Brent watched her face with more than ordinary attention. She asked, "Why have you taken to wearing it again, Brent?"

She saw him make up his mind to be honest, and was amazed at how open he was with her now.

"There's been a couple of lowlifes hanging around the Golden Lady lately. Nolan doesn't like the look of them, and he can sniff trouble a mile away. He and my night barkeep, Paxton, have been staying there full-time. I'm hoping hard there won't be any trouble."

"And you wish you were there too, don't you?"

He chuckled, but not as though anything were funny. "You were right, Bethany. I can't evade responsibility. Now I'm trapped. There's my responsibility to the children balanced against my responsibility toward the men who work for me. I don't know what to do."

"Neither do I," Bethany admitted.

He walked the girls to the café. Bethany felt safe and protected while he walked beside her, and amazingly bereft when he left. Maybe her practice in prayer at Faye's bedside paid off, for she certainly had one sent to heaven for Brent's protection before he'd turned the corner.

After closing, Bethany and Charlene sat at a stripped table, in the yellow light of a kerosene lamp, counting out their money. The café's ledger lay open on the table beside them, so new that the pages wouldn't stay flat. On one side ran a list of their expenses. On the other, the total of their income. Bethany wrote down a number and turned the book so Charlene could see.

"Not very much," Charlene said.

"I knew it would take a long time to make any real money," Bethany said, "but I have to confess I had dreams about dollars rolling in like a tidal wave."

"I believe in dreams," Charlene said. "I had one last night about me and . . ."

"And who?"

Charlene shook her head. "It's too silly to mention."

"Was it about the café?"

"No. About Oregon. Like I said, it wasn't important." She busied herself in scraping the coins off the table and into a bag. "My, I'm tired. I had no idea being a waitress was so hard on one's feet!"

Bethany wanted to say that she wouldn't be able to run the café without Charlene. But she bit her tongue to keep the words back because they might be true, but they wouldn't be fair. Instead she said, "I'm thinking that Jerry might help to serve the dishes. Get him a nice white shirt and add a black vest, like those very smart waiters at . . ."

"Oh, yes! Only I don't think he's ready to grow a handlebar mustache, do you? And I never like to see a boy with his hair parted down the middle."

"No. It's not very attractive. You know, I was thinking that Jerry might even become a chef. He's already learned to make salads more quickly than I can."

Charlene put her elbows on the table and gave her sister a very straight look. "Bethany," she said, "do you really mean you're going to take care of these children forever? They're very nice children, but they're not yours."

"I know they're not mine," she answered, gazing past Charlene's shoulder. "It's just . . . I remember so well when Momma and Daddy died. Not just Manny coming to tell us at the Cranstons' farm, but how she looked and how it felt."

"It's funny," Charlene said. "I hardly remember at all. Everything else, yes, but not that. I'd even forgotten about the farm, except for the piglets. I remember the piglets."

"Yes, you loved them. You cried at leaving them when we came home after the epidemic was over."

"Did I cry when Manny told us about . . . Momma and Daddy?"

"Oh, yes. I didn't. I just felt sick and empty, as though someone had scooped out my insides and thrown them away. I knew, you see, that we were going to be alone forever, that there would be no one who would care about us the way our parents did. It was the most horrifying moment of my life. Even when Mrs. Manning hugged us, I felt alone."

Bethany smiled then, and patted Charlene's hand that had crept across the tabletop to grip her own sympathetically. "But I wasn't alone. I had you, my twin."

"Yes," Charlene said, a single tear sliding down her cheek. "Yes, we'll always be together."

"No matter how far away we are, we'll always have something special between us. Because we've been more than sisters; we've been friends."

Charlene frowned at her. "Bethany, are you saying . . . ?"

Bethany chuckled. "Do you remember how upset Aunt Poste was when we arrived in New York and saw we weren't identical? She should have known better, she'd seen us before. Somehow though she'd managed to persuade herself that we were practically indistinguishable from each other. And all those school dresses made precisely the same. I thought we'd *never* wear them out."

"That sickly blue flannel," Charlene said, shivering. "And those boater hats with the gray ribbons!"

"I wish we had them now," Bethany said. "Faye will need more things than she has at present when she starts school. I'm thinking of sending her in a few weeks, before the school year gets too old. I hated walking into a new classroom halfway through the year; all those eyes watching you! I hope to spare Faye that experience."

Bethany put away the neat piles of dollar bills. "I know," she said, "there I go talking like a mother again. But really, Charlene, who is going to care for them if not me? I hate the thought of an orphanage, no matter how kindly run."

"I'm sure it wouldn't be so bad. After all, many fine and upstanding citizens have come from orphanages."

"No doubt. But there are no guarantees the children wouldn't wind up being sent to different homes. I know that is what Jerry fears most of all. Think what it would have been like for you to be sent to Aunt Poste's and me staying here. We might have been separated for life."

"That would never happen," Charlene said, her voice unconvinced.

"It's happened before and will probably happen again. Dory wouldn't remember ever having a sister or brother. Even Faye might forget. But it would be Jerry I'd feel most sorrow for. He'd remember them; having them taken away would just about kill him. There's no way he'd be able to stop the court from acting."

"So what will you do?"

"I don't know," Bethany said with a smile and a shrug. "Brent said he talked to the judge today, but I never heard what the judge said. I kept getting interrupted."

"One interruption was me, wasn't it?" Bethany nodded, her eyes full of humorous exasperation. "All right. When he comes tonight, I'll just melt into the background. You won't even know I'm there. You'll think I'm a mouse."

"A mouse with a six-foot shadow," Bethany said. "Didn't you ask Mr. Emmett to escort you home tonight?" Her sister's blush was answer enough.

"You've asked me what I'm going to do with the children. I want to know what you're going to do with Mr. Emmett."

"I . . . I've told him I can't go to Oregon with him. I also told him that I'd been ill and that it wasn't wise to talk about traveling so far."

"And he said?"

"That I'd come most of the distance already, as measured from New York, and he wasn't sure but he thought I wasn't dead yet."

"He said *that*?"

"Virgil can be blunt. He also said I was the healthiest and hardest-working dead person he'd ever seen."

"When did he tell you that?"

"Right after I got off his knee. I mean . . . a few nights ago. I was saying good-bye."

"Good-bye? Or good night?"

"I always tell him good-bye, but I don't think he listens."

"Never marry a man who doesn't listen," Bethany admonished playfully.

"Oh, he listens to me. He thinks my idea of setting up a

bakery near to the cherry orchards is a good one. We're trying to think of a way to make cakes and pies to ship to San Francisco inexpensively. We think there's a market there for fresh fruit desserts as well as the fruit itself."

"That is a good idea!"

"Yes, it's a pity I won't be able to do the baking myself. I've promised to write down the recipe for my pastry for Virgil."

"I didn't think you followed a recipe."

"I don't, but I came up with one for Virgil. I only hope it turns out to be edible."

"So you're an asset to his work. That's good. Work brings men and women closer." How could she ever spend her evenings talking about saloon keeping? With anyone but Brent, it would be impossible. But she had a feeling he could make anything sound interesting and even dramatic.

Charlene stood up, and bent and twisted her back, trying to ease the kinks. "Why does staying up late working make me so much more tired than staying up late dancing?"

"I've wondered that myself. And my feet hurt more too, which when you consider the thin slippers we used to wear to balls is surprising."

"Do you miss all that gaiety?" Charlene asked.

"Not too much. Everyone always talked about the same things; who was courting who, what Mrs. What-is-it is wearing, and how much money everyone had. And it wasn't as if Gerrald was ever much in the way of entertainment."

"Have you written to him?"

"Not recently. You?"

Charlene shook her head. "I don't want to hurt Ronald, but I don't want to marry him either."

Bethany stood up and slipped her arm about her sister's waist. Giving her a little hug, she said, "Marry Virgil, Charlene."

"Oh, if you knew how I want to!"

"Then do it."

"If only he'd stay here in Cedar Groves. Then you and I could go on running the café and Virgil and I could make a good home for the children. Nobody could object to that. Everything would be perfect. . . ." With her sigh, she laid her head on Bethany's shoulder.

"He won't change his mind?" Bethany took the weight of her sister's trouble as easily as she supported her body. But perhaps it was time for Charlene to test her strength.

"He can't. He's already sold his farm. The only reason he hasn't left town yet is me."

"Are you afraid to go so far?"

There was silence. "A little," she said at last. "The doctors might have been right, you know."

"Yes, I know."

Charlene slipped free of Bethany's encircling arm. Restlessly, she began to pace back and forth. Bethany watched, her heart aching for Charlene's choice, yet knowing that there was nothing she could do to make the decision easier.

"It comes to this," Charlene said with that streak of rationality her lightness of heart hid so well. "I either stay here in Cedar Groves and live a long life—very long without Virgil in it. Or I head out into the West with Virgil and perhaps die on the way or soon after I get to Oregon."

"Or perhaps not."

"It's a long way to go on a 'perhaps,' Bethany."

"That's true."

"Then there are children. A farmer needs children. What if I can't? Or what if I die in childbed, the way Lucy McCoy did last year?"

"That's a nightmare all women face. Yet we go on getting married."

Charlene smiled at that. "Just shows you what fools women are. I swear, sometimes I think what I ought to do is flip a coin. Heads, I stay here; tails, Oregon."

"All right." Bethany slipped her hand inside the money bag and brought out a silver dollar.

"I didn't mean . . ."

But the coin was already spinning in the air. Bethany caught it with a style Brent couldn't have bettered. She slapped it down on the back of her hand. Slowly she peeked at the coin.

Charlene said, "This is silly. What does it say?"

"Are .you sure you want to know?"

"It's so silly. Of course I'm not going to let some soulless coin decide my future. What does it say?" She came over to lift Bethany's hand. "Heads. Oh."

"Cedar Groves?"

"Flip it again. Two out of three."

After the third flip, Charlene said, "Three out of five?"

"As many times as you like."

This time, Charlene caught the coin in midair. "That's enough. I have an answer. If I really wanted to stay here, I wouldn't keep flipping it in hopes of a different answer."

"Seems that way." Bethany tried to smile. She feared, however, it was a lamentable failure. They'd always been so close, more than sisters—friends.

Charlene kissed her cheek. "How will you manage the café without me?"

Sniffing, for she must be catching a cold, Bethany said, "If you can write out a recipe for Virgil, you can certainly write one out for me. I'll be able to use it, which is more than he would."

With her delightful giggle, Charlene said, "I'll tell him tonight. I wish he'd hurry." She fluttered to the door to try to peer out, but the lamp had turned the glass into a mirror.

Bethany realized that anyone on the street could see in, while they were blind. Thinking of Brent's distrust of the two strange men in his saloon, Bethany wondered if there were any thieves watching them count their money. Being a businesswoman had more dangers than she had ever dreamed.

But the sight of Virgil Emmett, so stalwart, so tall and about four feet wide to her anxious eyes, relieved some of her fears. If strength was enough to keep death at bay, Charlene's future husband would see to it that she'd live forever. The way his gaze went straight to Charlene's face and left it only with the utmost difficulty reassured Bethany that for her sister at least there would be no doubts of her husband's love.

"Virgil," Bethany asked. "Would you mind taking this money up to the house with you? I don't know how long I might have to wait for Brent, and I feel strange having it."

"Be glad to," Virgil said, taking the bag. "How did it go tonight?" he asked Charlene.

"You wouldn't believe it! Bethany and I all but fainted when we saw Grandfather walk in the door escorting . . . you'll never guess!"

"I might if you gave me enough time, but I'd hate to see you burst. Tell me," Virgil said.

"Miss Agnes Ivey!"

"Is that unusual?"

Charlene rolled her eyes at his density. "Unusual? she hasn't taken a step outside Mrs. Tubb's orbit in years! Yet there she was, looking very pretty I thought, though I'd love to have five minutes alone with her hat. And Grandfather! You would have thought he was sixteen. Well, forty, anyhow."

Bethany nodded in confirmation. "He seemed in the highest of high spirits, that's for certain. They seemed to have plenty to say to one another too, Charlene, did you notice?"

"I suppose it would be safe to reckon that this Miss Ivey's not the sort of gal your grandfather goes for?"

"She always seemed like the oldest and primmest of old maids," Charlene said. "But I wonder what she really thinks about anything."

Bethany rubbed her forehead with a crooked finger. "To tell you the truth, I'm beginning to wonder if I know anything about anybody. I had so many ideas when we came back to Cedar Groves and I don't believe one of them is unchanged. It's exhausting. I'm wondering if I even know anything about myself."

Virgil said, "I know that it's late and I know I have to get up early tomorrow. Are you ready to go, Charlene?"

"Let me get my mantle from the kitchen." As she passed Bethany, Charlene crunched up one side of her pretty face in what she called a wink.

Virgil stepped forward as soon as the door closed behind Charlene. "Bethany, I want you to know something."

"Yes?" she asked, wondering what was keeping Brent.

"I'd do my best for Charlene, no matter where we were. You see, I've always been in love with her, from the time we were kids. There's never been anybody else, and there never will be. I just . . . thought you should know."

He must have been taken aback by her reaction. She smiled wistfully and patted him on the forearm. "That's good. However, don't waste your eloquence on me. Tell Charlene."

"I . . ."

But the object of his affection had returned. She handed him her mantle to wrap around her shoulders. It fell heavily over her simple dress, the long back that was intended to drape over a bustle dragging it down. They went out, calling their good-byes. Bethany wondered at what point Charlene would gently, elegantly, let her lover know that her attitude had changed. No doubt she'd choose somewhere entirely appropriate and perfectly beautiful, like the point where the road rose up, giving passersby an unrivaled view of the town.

She could imagine it so clearly. Above the lovers, the swirling endlessness of the stars. Below them, the warm lights of hearth and home shining in the windows of beloved friends and relations. There he'd take her hand and stuttered broken words of love. In a moment, she'd shyly assent. All doubts and fears at an end, he'd enfold her in a gently masterful embrace.

Bethany sighed, her sniffles growing worse. Proposals were an absurd affair. Ancestors had the right idea. Marry people off when they were too young to complain—saved a world of trouble later. A straightforward matter of business, that's what marriage should be.

Despite these hardheaded thoughts, or because of them, Bethany sat down and gave herself up to tears. Fumbling for a handkerchief, she remembered using it to protect her hand from a hot pot. Suddenly the kitchen seemed too far to go. She let the tears fall unchecked.

"Bethany?" She looked up to find Brent in the doorway. His dark hat shaded his eyes, making him look like a stranger.

"Hello," she said with a limp wave.

"Are you all right?" He came into the café and she noticed there were raindrops soaking into the stuff of his long brown coat. He took off his hat and shook it, the drops spraying off.

"Is it raining? I hadn't noticed."

"Small wonder." He caught one of her tears on his finger. "How can you see the rain when you're raining yourself? Do you want a handkerchief?" He reached inside his coat. "Silk or cotton?"

"Cotton, please. Silk's too slippery."

"That's my girl. Practical if it kills her," he said, giving her the white square.

"I'm not practical," she said, mopping her face. "I'm probably the least practical person alive."

"Oh?" He sat on the edge of the table and let her talk.

"I think I know what to do, you see, and then things change so I make another plan and another, and none of them ever work out the way I thought they would."

"For instance?"

"For instance this place. I came here full of notions about starting a good restaurant in Cedar Groves."

"Didn't you have a good night?"

"No, it was fine, but what was I thinking? Charlene's right. They like simple food. If I made rabbit stew and biscuits they'd like it better than all the fancy dishes I know. Cedar Groves isn't New York; they're not interested in New York cooking. Plus, how long do you think the folks in this town are going to be able to shell out cash money for dinner? As you've told me about a hundred times since we've met, the cattle drives aren't coming through here anymore."

"It's not so bad as all that, Bethany. Milner's business is starting to boom. He'll be hiring some more men, and there's talk of building a factory. . . ."

"What kind of factory?"

"I don't know yet," he said, frankly grinning. "And you say *you're* not practical! All I know is that I've taken a lot from Cedar Groves and it's about time I started putting something back. After all, I've got to prove I'm a solid citizen if I'm to win Judge Carr's approval."

His handkerchief lay crushed and forgotten in her hand. "You never did tell me what the judge said."

She saw him take a deep breath. "He told me that he would have no choice but to turn the children over to the state orphanage unless I could prove my ability to provide a good home, not only financially but morally. He had some suggestions on how to do that."

"Like what?"

"Like . . . give up my business. Like . . . buy a home. Like . . . find a nice girl and get married right away. I told him I thought I could manage to do that. What do you say, Bethany? Will you marry me?"

She'd known it was coming. There was no starlit sky. No fragrant breezes. No stammering lover daring all in stumbling words of passion. He hadn't even stood up from his easy pose on the table, let alone get down on one knee. It behooved her, therefore, to match his businesslike attitude with her own.

She gave her eyes a final rub with the handkerchief. Her face must be red and her nose shiny. But one didn't need to look one's best for a mere prosaic matter of business.

"Yes, I will. It's the best way to keep the children out of the orphanage."

He ran the backs of his fingers down her cheek. "By all means, let's think of the children."

Eighteen

Bethany tried to ignore the effect his touch always had on her. "I think it's best," she said, none too evenly, "if we spell everything out, just as when we made our arrangements with this building."

"All right," he said, crossing his arms. "This is another partnership, after all."

"Exactly." She hesitated, wanting to choose her words with care. "Am I right in assuming that you are not suggesting a mere marriage of convenience?"

"It depends on how you mean that term."

She realized he wasn't going to give her any help. "I mean, marriage in name only. You live your life; I live mine."

"You'll go on running the café?"

"I'll try. It may be hard without Charlene. She's marrying Mr. Emmett and moving to Oregon."

"Is she? Interesting. But let's not stray from our negotiations." Brent's eyes had hardened into sea ice. She knew she was seeing him the way men must see him when they gambled across the table from him. Ruthless, controlled, looking for every chance to exploit a weakness. "How else do you see our marriage?"

"I think we should agree that this is for the children's sake. Emotions will only cloud the issues at hand."

"Which emotions, Bethany?"

With a gulp she said, "Any emotions."

"You think we can live under one roof and never quarrel

or laugh or . . . anything. Nothing between us. Just cold, hard common sense."

"I . . . I suppose so." Though she had confessed to feeling more for him than mere liking, that evening when he'd kissed her in the library, she wasn't about to fulfill all the duties of married life for the sake of the children. What she wanted was his word that he wouldn't command those duties from her, but she had no idea how to ask delicately for what she wanted. Of course, delicacy had always been rather wasted on Brent.

Her eyes sought his face. Trying to keep her voice from shaking, she said, "And of course, we'll stay apart at night too."

"I don't understand."

She flashed him a look of impatience. He wasn't usually dense. But she simply couldn't put it any plainer, though she wanted the terms of this part of their relationship to be the clearest of all.

Brent stood up. "If you mean you'll go on sleeping in the same bed as now, I have no objections, for a while." Bethany nodded. She could manage that. Then he continued, "If, however, you mean *I* continue sleeping where I'm sleeping now, that's not acceptable."

"Not . . . not acceptable?"

"Absolutely not acceptable."

"Where will you sleep, then?"

"With you." As her eyes widened in shock, he gripped her wrist where it lay on the table. He reached for her other hand where it rested on her lap. Exerting firm control, he brought her to her feet. Just before his mouth came down on hers, he repeated, "With you."

The knowledge that he could make her want him was like a drug in his system. He craved more. Moving her hands to his waist, he let go. Cupping her face between his palms, he made love to her mouth, imitating there the things he wanted most of all.

Her arms tightened around him, bringing their bodies into

contact. He felt the sweet flowering of her breasts against his chest and stifled a groan. Though her passion was innocent, she was ripe and grew more so with every embrace.

What really drove him mad, though, was the memory of each time he'd kissed her before, laid over the present. He could remember the first time, and the time after. He could remember the feel of her hands on his naked skin, which only made him hungrier for her touch again. What would it be like to have a thousand such memories, making each new embrace richer and more fulfilling? Brent figured that at some point—maybe after the ten thousandth time—he'd probably die, though with a permanent smile on his face.

While he tasted the velvet smooth skin at the side of her throat, he felt one of her hands slide up to clasp his neck. The delicate, inhibited graze of her fingers over the sensitive nape forced that stifled groan to break out. Instantly her fingers stilled. "Did I . . . hurt you?"

"Oh, God, Bethany," he said, slanting his mouth over hers again. He wanted her so badly, he ached, but to tell her so might give her the wrong impression. Already his mind was racing, with thoughts of tabletops, of floors, and even walls; anywhere looked good right now.

He kissed her deeply, lingeringly, feeling her confidence return. When she essayed a dainty thrust of her own, he could have laughed with delight, except he was afraid it would come out more like a primitive howl of possession.

Unconsciously, she moved closer still to his body, wriggling a little. Brent wanted to run his hands down her back, to persuade her hips into close contact with his, but didn't dare frighten her. He tried to think of icebergs, frigid seas, and British bedrooms. The mental images did him about as much good as they would have done in Equatorial Africa.

"Brent?" she sighed.

"I'm right here, honey. I'm right here."

The hardest thing he'd ever had to do was tear his lips

from hers. He pressed her head against his shoulder and held her tightly. She sighed and snuggled closer.

"I like kissing you," she sighed, muffled against his collar.

"That's good. I like kissing you." He could have kicked himself for lying. "Liking" didn't begin to cover it.

"If we're married, will we kiss all the time?"

"No. Not all the time."

She gave a little gurgle of laughter. "I guess not. I still have to cook, especially if you're giving up the saloon. You can't kiss me while I'm cooking."

"No." It didn't matter that they weren't kissing. Her warmth so close to his body had the same effect.

"But you'll kiss me sometimes?"

"Whenever you want. But, Bethany . . ."

"Hmmm?"

"I'm not a boy. Kissing you is wonderful fun, but it's not enough."

He felt her slowly growing rigid, until she no longer nestled against him. It was as if he embraced a mere image.

She pushed away from him. With eyes cast down and her face averted, she said, "I understand. If that's how you want it to be, I can find that acceptable."

"Acceptable!" He gripped her shoulders and gave her just enough of a shake to emphasize his point. "Do you know what you're agreeing to? Do you have any idea of what I'm asking you to do?"

"I know what most girls know."

"Oh, good. That means you're completely ignorant."

Her eyes flashed at that. "Not completely. You're not the first man I've been engaged to, remember."

"Maybe not. But I'm the only one you're going to marry."

She'd be his, his for life. The elation that flooded him at the thought almost made Brent lose his head. But his pride rejected a bride who gave herself solely out of an unselfish desire to help three orphans. Brent wanted Bethany's desires to be totally selfish when it came to the two of them. He wanted her to take and take, everything he had to give.

"Yes," she said again. "I will marry you. When?"

He wanted to say "tonight." Somehow, though, neither his apartment above the Golden Lady nor her virginal room at Marmion House were the right settings for their first night together. He knew where the right place was, but at the moment it was sheeted in dustcovers and perfumed with damp.

"How long do you need?" he asked.

"I'd like to wait until after Charlene is married. That won't be long; Mr. Emmett has to leave soon."

"You're going to miss her."

"Very much," she said shortly. "Do you have any brothers or sisters?"

"I have a brother, or at least, I used to. Knowing Cliff, he probably still lives in Darien."

"Darien, Connecticut?"

"No. Darien, California. A town even smaller than Cedar Groves."

"That's hard to believe," she said with a brief, mechanical smile. She walked away from him, picking up her wrap, hat, and basket.

Brent noticed that she never faced him all the way, keeping her profile toward him. As much as he enjoyed the classic lines, he knew he could only guess her real feelings by the look of her fine eyes. Nonetheless, he began to wonder if she were somehow disappointed in him. Should he have insisted on an immediate marriage?

"Who do you want to have marry us?" he asked, taking the wrap from her arm.

"I suppose it might as well be Mr. Vance."

"Him?" He draped the cloth over her shoulders, his hands lingering there a moment.

"Why not?"

"You weren't very impressed with him, I thought."

"No. But he's the pastor of my church and I've always

wanted to be married there. Of course, I also wanted a spring wedding. There's this rosebush with silver . . ."

"I don't think we can wait till spring."

"No, Judge Carr wouldn't . . ."

"I mean, I can't wait till spring." He tilted up her chin and kissed her over her shoulder. Her lips didn't relax under his. He could have persuaded her to relax but he backed off, realizing she needed a little time to adjust to the new ideas he'd put into her head.

With a smile he released her. Picking up his hat, he put it on and adjusted the brim. "Ready to go?" With a hand cupped around the glass chimney of the lamp, he blew out the flame.

They came home to a celebration. Mr. Ames had brought up champagne cold from the cellar. The pale gold liquid fizzed and bubbled in the thin crystal glasses. Bethany had hardly walked in the door before her grandfather thrust a stem between her fingers. "We've been waiting for you," he cried. "Come on, Brent. Pour another glass for yourself."

Charlene stood before the open fireplace, her Virgil's arm about her waist. Her eyes sparkled, but Bethany didn't think it was from the champagne. Above her, Virgil grinned broadly at everyone and everything.

When Charlene saw Bethany, she stepped away from her lover and dashed to her sister. "Oh, Bethany, it was such a surprise," she exclaimed with a wink of her right eye. "He proposed on the way home."

"That's wonderful. You'll have to tell me all about it," Bethany said, kissing Charlene's cheek. Together, they went up to Virgil. Bethany had to stand on tiptoe to kiss her bashful brother-in-law-to-be. "I'm so glad for both of you."

"I'll take good care of her, Bethany. I swear."

"I know." She patted him reassuringly on the arm. "I have faith in you."

He cleared his throat, embarrassed, and took a swig from his glass. "I've never had champagne before. It's funny stuff. Tastes harmless, but I feel like I'm a balloon."

Bethany said, "Keep drinking it and you'll feel like a hero. How many glasses have you had?"

"Just the one."

"Yes," Charlene said, "but Grandfather keeps filling it up."

They smiled into one another's eyes and suddenly Bethany felt like an outsider. She sipped her own champagne and looked around the room.

Jerry sat on the settee with Faye, giving her stolen sips of his champagne. Dory rested on Manny's hip, up past her bedtime but full of smiles. Then she saw Bethany and let out a yip of excitement, reaching out her arms.

Leaving her sister, Bethany put down her glass and took the baby from Mrs. Manning. "There you are, lovely," she said, brushing the pale gold hair back from Dory's smooth forehead. "Bethany missed you."

Dory gurgled her answer, grabbing for the fringe that draped Bethany's bosom. So different from the ragged infant who had first stolen her heart, Dory now wore a neat flannel wrapper, tied with a blue silk ribbon under her throat. A lace-trimmed bib caught the inevitable drool.

"She's gotten fatter," Mrs. Manning said. "I weighed her at the grocer's and she's put on another half pound. So has that one." She pointed at Faye. Her left hand shone with a bright stone.

"Did Mr. O'Dell give that to you?"

At once, Manny dropped her hand, trying to conceal it behind her skirt. She grumbled, "Don't see why you young things should have all the romance. Most likely, you don't even know what to do with it."

"Are you going to marry him?" Bethany looked at Mrs. Manning in wonder. Her face seemed softer and younger, especially with the pink tinge coming up in her cheeks.

"I'm not thinkin' that far ahead. He's a good man. I could be mighty fond of him."

"But what about . . ." Bethany looked at Grandfather, who was urging Brent to have a glass of champagne. Brent smiled but shook his head, pointing at the clock on the mantel.

Mrs. Manning tossed her head like a young girl. "Hmmph! I'm tired of waiting for that ol' stick in the mud. I've wasted the best years of my life . . . well, I don't regret it."

Bethany met Brent's eyes across the room. He raised his glass to her and took a sip. Somehow, she could tell exactly what he was thinking. He was remembering, as she was too, those passionate moments in this room that night, the first time she realized what power he had over her. She was grateful for his restraint but with a feminine thrill wondered what it would be like when that control was gone.

Bethany asked Manny, "Would you ever marry a divorced man?"

Mrs. Manning frowned at her, the same expression she'd used when the girls were young and building walls of "nothing" in answer to questions about their day. "That's a funny question."

"I want to know. I need to know."

Mrs. Manning's gaze shifted to Brent, now submitting to having his glass refilled. "Oh, well," she said abruptly. "If the man loved me enough, I'd marry him like a shot. Provided of course everything in his past was legal and aboveboard."

Bethany nodded and suddenly said, "Ow!" She glanced down to find that Dory had worked the knuckle of her hand in between her lips and was now gumming it with a will. "I think she's starting to teethe."

"Is she? I'll get her a nice hunk of polished maple to soothe 'em."

The two women huddled over the baby, trying to see into her little mouth. "I see something . . ." Bethany said. "Is that a tooth?"

"I can't hardly believe it is, considerin' how little she fusses. She's the happiest youngster I ever seen," Manny said. "I don't think I've heard her give more than a yelp since . . ."

A sudden tinkle like the shivering of a glass bell called their attention to Mr. Ames. "If everyone's glass is charged, I'd like to propose a toast to the health and happiness of the engaged couple. Brent, my boy, Bethany's glass is empty. Would you mind . . . ?"

"Certainly not." He brought the white-swathed bottle across the room and tipped some pale gold champagne into the glass. A little slopped onto the tabletop. "Oops," he said.

His eyes were strangely bright. As Bethany balanced the baby on one arm to lift the glass with the other, she shot a confused glance at him. Did he sway, ever so slightly, on his feet? He grinned at her, not his usual smile of masculine superiority, but a silly, lopsided grin that made her frown.

"There!" Mr. Ames said. "My dear Charlene, we are losing you too soon from our happy family circle. But I have no doubt that your life to come will be an example of happiness to future generations of Emmetts. To the future!"

"To the future!" they all said and put their glasses to their lips. Brent drained his at a gulp and then put his arm around Bethany and the baby for everyone to see.

"Got an announcement," he said loudly. "They're not the only ones who are that way about each other."

"Brent!" she muttered. "We were going to wait!"

"Why? Your congratulations, everyone. Bethany has agreed to be my wife." The effect of his announcement was spoiled for Bethany by the hiccup he gave. But as everyone else was crowding around her exclaiming, she was the only one who heard it. Faye hung on her skirt, her small face puzzled.

"Yes. Yes, it's true," she said in answer to Charlene's excited question. Her sister hugged her, baby and all. Dory frowned and kicked. Bethany put her against her shoulder, patting her back, and glared at Brent past the baby's head.

"Well, well. Congratulations, my dear boy," Mr. Ames said, shaking Brent's hand with painful enthusiasm. "This calls for more champagne." He turned to Jerry. "Would you mind bringing the other bottle out from the kitchen?"

"Sure, sir."

Charlene said, "I better make some cheese straws or something, or we'll all be fogged from drinking without eating." Wherever Charlene went, Virgil was sure to follow. Brent stood by Mr. Ames, talking to him in a low voice.

Faye tugged on Bethany's skirt. Sitting down on the armchair, the baby still against her shoulder, Bethany asked, "What is it, dear?"

"Where will you live?"

"I'm sorry; I don't understand. Where will I live?"

"You know. Charlene's going to Organ . . ."

"Oregon, Faye. It's a state in the Pacific Northwest." Bethany looked up at Mrs. Manning who shook her head and shrugged.

"That's right," Faye said. "Oregon to grow cherries. An' Mrs. Manning's goin' to marry Mr. O'Dell and he's got lots of children already. I guess you'll go live at the Golden Lady."

"I don't know where we'll live, Faye, but it won't be the Golden Lady. Why can't I just live here?"

Faye's eyes, too mature for her face, scoffed at this naive question. "You can't live in the same house after you're married as before. Everybody knows that!"

"Oh. Well, we'll leave that up to Mr. Houston, shall we?"

Faye nodded, but didn't seem reassured. Jerry had come back with the second bottle of champagne, emerald-green and gold-crowned. The "pop" like that of a small cannon made everyone jump and laugh. Faye brightened. "Can I have some more of that fancy lemonade?"

"No, you may not!" Both Bethany and Mrs. Manning spoke at once.

Bethany turned her attention to Brent. He leaned against the wall, his head hanging. Noticing her look, he gave her that absurd smile again. Then he said, "Gotta sit down."

"I'm going to put the baby down," she said to Manny. "I'll be right back."

Brushing by Charlene and Virgil, who'd come back to announce that the hors d'oeuvres would be ready in a few minutes, she hurried out.

While she dressed Dory in one of her little nightgowns, tickling her tummy and reciting the "Cat and the Fiddle," she wondered what had gotten into Brent. If she didn't know better she could have sworn he was tiddly, but that was impossible. Who ever heard of a grown man—and a saloon keeper to boot—getting drunk on two little glasses of champagne?

She laid the baby down in the crib Charlene had had Virgil set up in the nursery. There were no knobs on this one for Dory to pull off and swallow. The baby's big blue eyes watched her as she lowered the lamplight to a gentle gleam. Turning on the threshold, she smiled and said, "Good night, Dory. I love you."

She'd hardly gone three steps into the hall when she remembered that she'd wanted to change out of her spotted and stained shirtwaist. Earlier in the evening an accident with sauce had splattered her, half landing on her apron, the other half on her sleeve. In the wardrobe closet that connected with the nursery, she was choosing another white blouse when she heard a noise. "Charlene?"

With her blouse over her arm, she came out, buttoning the front of her fresh corset cover. "Brent!"

"Your bed is much more comfortable than mine," he said. Then he slowly turned over to face her, propping his cheek on his hand. His green eyes were somnolent, but a spark awoke in them when he saw how she was dressed or, rather, undressed.

"Get out of here," she demanded.

"Why?"

"Why? What if my grandfather came in? He'd shoot you."

"Is he likely to come in? Besides, he might go for a gun, but it would be a shotgun."

"That would suit me fine," she said viciously.

"I don't know," he said. "A shotgun wedding has its drawbacks." Lifting his head off his hand, he patted the bedclothes. "Come here."

"No." She peered at him. "You *are* drunk!"

"Yes, I am. Somewhat."

"On two glasses of champagne?"

His mysterious smile was interrupted by a hiccup. "On a glass of anything. I'll tell you my deepest, darkest secret, Bethany. If you'll come here."

She took two cautious, careful steps closer to the bed. She still felt confident of being able to make a sudden leap backward out of range if he tried anything. Especially as he couldn't possibly be his usual quick-handed self. "What secret?"

He sat up and leaned forward. "I can't drink." He shook his head at her look of disbelief. "Word of honor. I have no stomach for the stuff. One sip of whiskey is enough to put me under the table."

"But I've seen you drink at your apartment. The decanter on the sideboard."

He whispered a word so softly that she stepped closer to hear him repeat it. She exclaimed, "Tea?"

He nodded and seemed for a moment to forget how to stop. "Tea. That's all. I've been bribing bartenders to give me tea instead of whiskey since my first game."

"And now you own your own place?"

"What better way to be sure I go on getting tea and nothing but tea?"

"That's logical."

"Now will you come here?"

"Why?"

"Don't be so suspicious," he said, leaning back on his elbows. "I can't do anything to you. Haven't you ever heard that in drunken men desire oft outruns performance?"

"No. Is that from the Bible?"

"Shakespeare. It means I'm harmless at the moment."

That might be the truth, Bethany thought, with narrowed eyes. However, Brent never seemed less than dangerous to her. Yet as he lay there, she thought that he did *look* like a man who wouldn't contemplate an attack of a weak-willed woman's virtue.

Her fingertips skimmed his coat, still warm where it was flung over the end of her bed, and leaped away from the tan leather of his shoulder holster hanging on the bedpost. Then she walked around to stand at the side. Looking down at him, she supposed she should have felt disgust. After all, a man sunk in alcohol was one of the more pitiful sights. Yet the sight of Brent sprawled across her bed far from repelled her.

"Should I make you some coffee or something?"

Reaching out, he idly brushed the lace flounce at her hip. "That's pretty. What a shame you girls hide your nicest clothes under all those dresses."

"Coffee, Brent? It'll help sober you up."

"I'm growing more sober all the time."

He sat up and insinuated his arm around her waist. For a moment he rested his forehead against the cool cambric at her hip. "If you want the real truth," he said, "I've been three-parts drunk since the day I met you."

"Have you?" she asked, running her fingers through the living silk of his hair.

"That feels good."

"To me too." She went on ruffling it. "Why did you kiss me that day?"

"Which day?"

"The first day I met you."

"I don't know. You were glaring at me and I just wanted to kiss you. And now I'm going to marry you. Maybe I got hit by the train that day and everything since then has been part of an interesting afterlife."

"I don't think so," she said, laughing at his nonsense.

"Could be," he insisted. "'Cause I'm in heaven now."

Bethany found herself kneeling on the bed, facing him. He ran his hands up into the masses of her hair, kissing her with light fluttering touches. Though it was pleasurable, she yearned for the deep, drugging kisses he could give her. Bethany reached out and wrapped her arms around him.

Nineteen

Bethany had never felt so alive before. Though there was some shame being here like this, a man and a woman together alone and actually on a bed, there was far more joy.

The desire in his eyes when he raised his head seemed to burn away her embarrassment. She tilted her chin, inviting him to return to her mouth. When he didn't instantly comply, she said, "Brent, do I have to ask?"

His hands were tight on her upper arms. For a moment she feared he'd push himself away from her. She knew how strong his self-control was—hadn't she reason to feel grateful for it?—but now she realized a rebuff born of even the highest principles would crush her.

There was nothing light or fleeting about the kiss they shared. It was as if they were exchanging some part of their individual souls. She could have cried, if it weren't for the heat that flared through her. She wanted to be closer to him.

"Bethany . . ."

She wanted things she couldn't begin to name. Remembering his touch, she reached for his hand and raised it to her shoulder. His fingers caressed the smooth skin, but it wasn't enough. She made a slight noise of frustration deep in her throat and rolled her shoulder back, letting his hand drop. When the heel of it rested against her breast, she sighed with contentment.

"Bethany, are you sure . . . ?"

She raised heavy eyelids. "If you don't, I think I'll die." Then she kissed him, leaning full into him, letting his solid body take her weight. She tried to kiss him, the way he kissed her. Bethany felt him take flame. His hand stayed where she'd put it and moved of its own accord. It didn't feel as good as she recalled.

"What have you got on?" he asked. "Armor?"

"Look and see," she said, blushing to hear such provocative language from her own lips.

Over Brent's shoulder, she caught sight of herself in her vanity mirror. She looked utterly wanton, her hair coming down in long twists, her lips swollen, her eyes dark and enigmatic in the rosy light of her ruby-glass lamp. With Brent's white shirt blocking her view of the rest of her, she couldn't be sure whether all of her looked as abandoned as her face.

She felt the touch of his fingers at her front and closed her eyes, becoming that scandalous woman she saw in the mirror.

"I shouldn't be doing this," Brent muttered as he undid the buttons down the front of her corset cover. Alcohol made his head light but his fingers retained their nimbleness.

"What are you saying?" she asked, reaching out to pull his shirt out from his waistband.

He felt the cooler air against his heated skin, instantly followed by her hands slipping under his shirt. Brent wanted her skin against him in a way that alarmed him with its violence. He jerked apart the embroidered lace. Frowning with surprise, he demanded, "What's that?"

Bethany tossed her hair aside to look down at herself. "My corset, of course."

"But it's red!"

"Yes. It's a very fashionable color . . ."

Her smooth white skin looked whiter still against the cardinal red of the corset. It had no shoulder straps so the rounded contours of her shoulders were revealed above the double row of red lace that ran around under her arms. A satin bow tied off the lacing that ran up the front. Her petticoats buttoned on the bottom edge, giving her that perfect nipped-in figure that every woman longed for and the fashions demanded.

But what made his eyes grow hard was the way the apparatus pushed down and flattened out the most beautiful part of her young body. He remembered the brief glimpse that he'd stolen on a previous occasion before his sanity had returned. They had been so exquisite that not even his dreams had been able to improve on them. Now they were squeezed and minimized.

He tugged at the ribbon. "Do you always wear this thing?"

"Of course. I'm too big on top and it makes my clothes fit better. Don't you like it?"

"I hate it."

"I guess it is in the way," she said, smiling in a way he recognized as both ancient and powerful.

"It's not that, or at least . . ." Between the rows of embroidery, the lacing pulled free with a slight ripping sound. He heard her take an involuntary deep breath and saw her rib cage rise and fall.

Looking into her eyes, he ran his hands firmly up from her waist, feeling the reddened ridges that the corset bones had dug into her body. "Don't wear them ever again, Bethany. I don't care if your clothes fit like sacks."

"But, Brent . . .

"And you're not too big. Believe me." He bent his head to kiss the scented valley and Bethany caught her breath. She didn't know why he'd looked so formidable or why her corset seemed to trouble him so. Everyone wore them. The department stores were full of them. Two corsets apiece had been the first things Aunt Poste had purchased for her and Charlene on arriving in New York. She'd feel naked without it.

As Brent moved his mouth on her skin, as his hand brushed over her breast, Bethany decided being naked had its advantages. He peeled back the stiffly boned contraption, freeing the buttons that connected it to her petticoats. Then he dropped it over the side of the bed.

When she wore nothing above her waist, he moved away from her and lay down on his side. Bethany continued kneeling, suddenly unsure of herself. His gaze traced over her, giving nothing away. She shivered and crossed her arms in front of herself.

"Cold?"

"A . . . little."

"Then come here." He held out his hand. Bethany looked at him, still hesitating. He said, "Second thoughts?"

"No. It's just . . ."

Some of the humor she'd missed came back into his eyes. "If it's any consolation, I think you're the most beautiful woman I've ever seen in my life. I've been going crazy imagining you like this. The reality is better still."

Slowly, she let her arms drop and slipped her fingers into his. She realized she'd been waiting for words of reassurance, words to tell her that she didn't repel him. "I've imagined you too," she admitted.

"Tell me." He pulled on her hand and she found it was easy to lie down beside him.

"I . . . never touched a man's chest before. Not a naked chest."

Keeping his gaze on her face, Brent tugged his tie free of his collar and tossed it over his shoulder to fall where it might. His collar followed and he pushed the buttons on his shirt free with his forefinger and thumb. "Be my guest," he invited.

She ran her hands through the swirling patterns and discovered his nipples. They puckered at her touch. Her look of surprise made him chuckle, very softly and suggestively. "Yours do that too," he said.

"But I'm not cold now."

He encouraged her to lie back against the pillows. Bethany watched him, not wanting to miss anything. She didn't know what would happen next, yet the one thing she didn't feel was afraid. Eager, embarrassed, and enraptured, yes.

He smiled as he leaned down to press his warm, moist mouth to her shoulder. No sooner had she adjusted to that sensation than he moved only a few inches over and down. She felt the stirring of his breath there at that sensitive point and then the heat of his mouth.

Instantly she cried out, her hands seeking blindly across his back. Brent felt the light scraping of her nails through his shirt as she sought for something to hold on to. Though the champagne still glazed his brain, he realized just what this moment must mean for her.

Since her return to Cedar Groves, the foundations of her neat and polite world had shivered more than once. Now they were cracking and falling under the pressure of his mouth on her soft, pink nipple. As he concentrated on pleasing her, he vowed to make her first time right. If it took all night to prepare her, then it would take all night. He only prayed he wouldn't be a crazy man by then.

She'd drawn one knee up, her white slipper resting flat on the bed. Brent ran his hand over the silken stocking that showed black against the foaming white fall of her petticoat. He found the edge of her garter, sunk into the flesh above her knee, and the lace on her drawers tickled his fingers. But now he couldn't be distracted by the intricacies of a lady's underclothing. He longed to brush the untouched softness of her thighs, knowing he was the first, the only, and the last man to explore her.

"Bethany," he said hoarsely. "I want . . . won't you take off the rest?"

"Everything?" He saw, with delight, how the shock in her eyes was quickly overlaid with excitement.

"Every stitch. I want to see you. All of you."

She drew her lower lip between her teeth and flicked her gaze over his body. "I will if you will," she dared.

He chuckled and was surprised to find that laughing in bed with Bethany felt as natural as kissing her. To prove it, he once more sank down next to her, tasting and exploring her mouth. He let his hand stay at the edge of her drawers, feeling the heat there, longing for the paradise that lay a very few inches away.

Slowly, giving her time to adjust, he lay the heaviness of his palm over the meeting place of her legs. He went on kissing her, once again showing her without words what he wanted them to do together. She responded by opening for him like a parched flower to the rain from heaven.

He increased the pressure of his hand ever so slightly. She whispered his name on a note of astonishment. "What are you doing to me?" Her head tossed restlessly. He'd never seen her so beautiful. Her cheeks were pink and her half-closed eyes held a wild glitter.

"It's all right," he said on a growling note. "I won't do anything you don't like. Do you like this?" He began to rotate his hand from the wrist.

"I don't . . ." she said suddenly. "Just don't stop."

He obeyed, willingly. Ignoring his own body's increasingly clamorous demands, he focused all his attention on her. Even through the full cotton garment that separated him from his goal, he could feel just how close she was to finding fulfillment. Her soft cries, the wracking shudders of her awakening body, the way she grabbed his shoulders as though he were the only solid thing in the universe all combined into a triumphant sense of completion.

He gathered her into his arms while the vibrations still flooded her. The emotions between them ran close to the surface. There was no more need to hold back. His pride had been swept away with her innocence. "Bethany, I love . . ."

"Bethany, dear. May I come in?" A delicate tapping at the bedroom door broke the fragile bond between Brent and Bethany.

"Damn!" he said. Never had a man meant a curse more. "You've got too many relatives, honey."

Her eyes flew open. She thrust herself back out of his

embrace. In a hoarse whisper, she cried, "Oh, my God! You've got to . . . quick, the closet. You can slip out through the nursery."

"Bethany, are you asleep?" Charlene rattled the knob.

"It's all right," Brent said quickly under his breath. "I locked it when I came in. I wasn't *that* drunk." He was entirely himself now, except for a rush of frustration. He could even smile and say with more humor, "Too gosh-darn many relatives!"

"Bethany?"

"You'd better answer her," he said, sliding off the bed. He grabbed up his shoes and his coat. The holster snagged on the bedpost and he swore under his breath as he jerked it free.

"Yes? Just a moment, Charlene. I . . . I'm not decent."

Not decent? She was depraved! Bethany didn't bother to watch Brent leave. She only thrust out her hand in the direction of the wardrobe closet and snatched up her robe, mistaking the right arm for the left, battling the bedeviled thing.

"Bethany?" Charlene called again. "Why is the door locked?"

As she hastened across the floor, Bethany tugged the remaining pins from her hair, giving the long mass a shake, rather than having it look as though her lover had been running his hands through it.

She turned the key and opened the door. "What is it?"

Charlene was taken aback by her vehemence. "I thought you'd like to talk. Did you fall asleep?"

"Yes, I . . . laid down for a few minutes and must have dozed off." She faked a yawn. With her hectic cheeks and swollen mouth, she must look like a delirious fever patient, not a girl who'd been wooing Morpheus.

Bethany realized Brent couldn't escape from the nursery without Charlene seeing him as the two were in the same line of sight. "Let's go to your room," she said. "Mine is such a mess."

"Oh, that's all right." Charlene stepped forward. Bethany gave way.

As she closed the door, she saw her lover step into the hall. He still carried his coat and shoes, though the holster was now once more in place. He had his watch in his hand. He mouthed the words "Half an hour."

Bethany shook her head with a feeling of panic. Unable to meet his eyes, she shut the door.

Charlene had seated herself at the vanity and was gazing at her reflection in the mirror. "Virgil says I remind him of spring. I don't see it myself."

"I had no idea Mr. Emmett was a poet." The coverlet on the bed was a relief map of wrinkles. The only way one person could have made so many would be to twist and turn like a whirling dervish. Bethany hurried forward to smooth it out.

With the toe of her crocheted slipper she kicked something white that skittered across the floor to bounce onto the hand-hooked rug. Bethany peered at it. With a thrill of horror, she realized it was Brent's patent collar!

"Oh, Virgil has a lot more to say than you might think. He never lets a day go by without reading the newspaper back to front. Of course, he's a Republican while the newspaper's Democratic but he says it's a wise man who knows what the opposition is up to."

She studied her face more closely, pulling at the side of her cheek to smooth out the skin and to see the curve of her jaw. "I hope I'm not getting a spot. That would be horrible. Almost as bad as getting one on your wedding day!"

"Yes," Bethany replied absently. With a horrible feeling of impending doom, she remembered Brent flinging away his collar with a gesture both expansive and devil-may-care. What if Charlene had seen the incriminating item?

Trying to be inconspicuous, Bethany sidled over to the rug. She picked up the slack of her petticoat and dropped it lightly over the glaring whiteness of Brent's collar.

"Do you think I should cut my hair quite short?" Charlene asked. "It would be easier to care for in Oregon."

"You're not going to a wilderness, I hope." Her knees felt quite shaky. Bethany closed her eyes and seemed to feel again the incredibly arousing sensation Brent called into life with just a touch of his hand.

"You *are* sleepy!" Charlene exclaimed. "I think you're asleep on your feet!"

"I'm not used to . . . working so hard."

"That must be it. Me, I feel so very wide awake. I think getting engaged is good for me."

"What are you going to do about Ronald?"

Charlene toyed with an ivory-backed hairbrush. "I'll write him a letter before I go to bed. Do I really have to return my pretty ring?"

"Would you ever want to wear it again? What would Virgil say?"

"He *is* jealous, silly boy. I've told him over and over again that I never cared a nickel for Ronald, but he says he wouldn't be surprised if Ronald came all the way out to Oregon to get me back."

"What a horrible thought!" Bethany resolved to write to Gerrald first thing in the morning to tell him to cancel any plans he was making for a wedding.

"Isn't it? That's why I'm glad we're getting married so soon. Do you think next Wednesday is too soon? Of course, I won't be able to have a really fancy wedding but I thought we could wear those dresses we had for Mrs. Finster's lawn party that was rained out. I remember at the time we said the lace skirts were pretty enough for a wedding."

"We can't wear those. We'd freeze! It's going to be October in three days."

Charlene lifted her shoulders in a careless shrug. "I suppose. Seems a shame not to get some wear out of them."

"You can dazzle Virgil in the spring. When does he want to leave?"

"Wednesday."

"The same Wednesday?"

"Yes. I thought we could be married in the morning and leave by the three o'clock train."

"Then you'd better wear your traveling clothes."

"Oh, no. I won't be married in black cashmere! People might mistake my wedding for my funeral."

Impulsively, Bethany started forward. Only at the last instant did she remember to shuffle, so the incriminating collar would be dragged along under her petticoat.

She put her hands on Charlene's shoulders and leaned down to look at their similar faces in the mirror. "Don't talk like that. You can be married in a feed sack or your best silk ball gown and no one will say anything but what a lovely bride!"

Charlene patted Bethany's cheek with her small hand. "What about you? What are you going to wear when you marry Brent?"

"I haven't thought about it. Anyway, the clothes don't matter. Only the ceremony."

"That's true, though Aunt Poste would simply die to hear you say so." Charlene sighed. "I wish you would get married on Wednesday too. I'd hate to go away without seeing you married. And if we had a double ceremony, then we'd only have to cook for one reception!"

"How practical." She kissed her sister's temple where the wayward curls began. "How will I ever manage without you?"

"Without me? Oh, you don't need me."

"Yes, I do." She spoke a little too seriously and saw a little shade of regret come in Charlene's forehead. Smiling, she set about chasing that shade away. "But not as much as Virgil does. For heaven's sake, Charlene, be sure he has his hair cut before the ceremony. He looks like a bear!"

"One thing at a time," Charlene said. "I'm trying to get him to try a different kind of tie."

Bethany swallowed hard. "Tie?"

"It's like I told him yesterday. Wide ties are for schoolboys. Now what I'd like to see him wear is one of those string ties. I think they're so dashing and yet tidy. You know, Bethany, the kind of thing Brent wears. Would you ask him where he buys them? I might get Virgil one on Monday."

Bethany remembered Brent pulling his tie loose and flinging it away, just before he'd opened his shirt. Trying to be nonchalant, she turned her head to rake with her eyes the rag rug beside her bed.

"Poor thing," Charlene said, starting up from the low stool. "Here, sit down. You got a stiff neck while you were sleeping, didn't you? Do you want me to rub it?"

"No, thank you. I haven't a stiff neck, I was just thinking about something I forgot to do."

"I must say I envy you a little, Bethany. Virgil's the most wonderful man in the world and I wouldn't trade him for the President of the United States, but your Brent has something special."

Bethany liked the sound of that "your Brent." That was how she felt about him. As though somehow they'd come to belong to one another. "He's turned out to be a surprisingly nice man."

"And you're wild about him. Oh, don't look at me like that! I can tell."

Bethany couldn't quite meet Charlene's bright gaze. "He's not the sort of man I ever pictured myself marrying. But Judge Carr said that if Brent married a respectable girl, he wouldn't take the children away. Whatever else I may be, I am respectable." Though not nearly as respectable as she'd been an hour ago.

"My," Charlene said with a sigh, "there certainly have been a lot of changes in our lives since we got off the train just a few short weeks ago."

Bethany half laughed, half sighed. "Lately it's been like a switchback road zigzagging down a mountain. And me in a runaway stagecoach!" She shook her head in wonder. "I feel as though I haven't taken a calm breath since we left New York!"

"There's nothing more to worry about now," Charlene said, nodding confidently. "It will all be clear sailing from here on in. After all, what could possibly go wrong?"

Bethany felt a cold chill on her spine. "I wish I could share that sentiment. I just wonder what disaster will strike tomorrow."

"That sounds awfully pessimistic. Maybe you're just suffering from a little touch of liver. I think I saw some of Manny's spring tonic in the pantry if you want a spoonful."

"It's not spring."

"It is in my heart," Charlene said, then laughed at herself. "Listen to me! Besides, you don't have to take it just at one season of the year. Sulfur and molasses puts spring into your step year round."

Bethany made a face. "How can a woman who creates the most wonderful Raspberry Cream Dacquoise in the world even bear the thought of sulfur and molasses?"

"Well, I don't intend to raise my children on Raspberry Cream Dacquoise, and sulfur and molasses, or a black draught and blue pill, never did *us* any harm." Charlene yawned, as prettily as she did everything else. "My, it's getting late. And I want to get up early tomorrow."

"Why? We don't have to work tomorrow. Just church."

"Yes, but there's a picnic afterward. Miss Ivey mentioned it. I was hoping you might make your Chicken Maryland."

"All right," Bethany said after a quick mental review of the pantry supplies.

"And I'm going to make a butter cake. Virgil says that's what his mother used to make, though I doubt it will be as good as hers. Have you ever noticed that nothing a woman does is ever as good as a man's mother can do it?"

"Now who's pessimistic?"

Charlene laughed and Bethany joined in, thinking all the while that a half an hour must have already passed. Maybe the champagne caught up with Brent. Yet a deep inner certainty told her that he was watching a clock somewhere down the hall, counting off each ticking moment with impatience. Bethany wondered if she would have the nerve to open her bedroom door for him, knowing what he wanted.

Then Charlene said, "You know what I'd like?"

"What, dear?"

"I'd like to sleep in here tonight. Like in New York, when we'd sneak into each other's rooms to giggle and gossip after everyone had gone to sleep. What silly secrets we used to share! Who danced with whom and how many times, and what all the other girls were wearing. They seem so unimportant now."

"Yes, I remember." Bethany thought again about Brent. Though she had to admit he excited her with his wild and wicked ways, the powerful effect he had on her was frightening. Part of her wanted to hold on to her girlhood for a little precious while longer, though the woman in her longed to share the ultimate embrace with him.

Then, too, Charlene would soon be beyond sisterly confidences, except through the medium of a letter. Bethany smiled at her sister. "Run and get your things."

"Wonderful!" She capered over to the door. Then Charlene looked sly and stole her hand into her pocket. She brought out a fancy black silk cravat. "And while I'm gone, I'll give this to Mr. Houston! He mustn't trifle with *my* sister's affections!"

Twenty

Sunday was a faultless fall day. Above the church steeple, the sky seemed as richly blue as a tournament tent at some medieval festival. The grass still held summer's emerald tint through the cooling nights had brought out flourishing color in all the trees. They glittered with red-gold and green-gold, intensifying at times into hot scarlet and deep maroon.

While waiting for Mr. Ames to finish talking to the pastor, Bethany stood on the church steps with other young women, most of whom were *not* members of the League of Spiritual Cleanliness. Some she'd known in school; others were newcomers to Cedar Groves. With a few exceptions, they all jounced or swayed, comforting the babies in their arms. Those without children gave every sign of soon having at least one.

Holding Dory lightly to her shoulder, Bethany listened to advice from Annie Wagonner, once the weepiest girl in school, now a laughing, competent wife and mother. Her dark auburn hair had been passed onto little Avery, sleeping with his mouth open. "Now my older one, he scooted around on his rear for the first years of his life. I swan, he wore out more pairs of little flannel drawers . . ."

"When did he start to walk?" Bethany had seen the older boy, now three, tearing around playing Indian with the others.

"First time he wanted something that was out of reach. He just stood up, grabbed that cookie, and walked away fast before I could nab it back. You could have pushed me over with a feather!"

"Seems they just up and walk when they're ready," Mae Belford, another old classmate, said, leaning over them from the step above. Her plump daughter, just out of babyhood, sat beside her, playing with fallen leaves. "That's a pretty baby," Mae said, holding out her arms to Dory invitingly.

With a sense of jealous reluctance, Bethany let Dory go. Mae held her in the crook of her arm with practiced ease, tickling Dory under the chin to see her smile. "Makes me want another one. How 'bout that, Lisa Jane? Wouldn't you like a baby brother or sister?"

The little girl glanced up from her leaves. "No," she said clearly.

The women laughed. Bethany, unable to take her eyes off Dory, saw with real pleasure how quickly the baby looked around for her and moved one hand in her direction. "I wonder where *your* sister is, Dory?" she asked, slipping the baby away from Mae.

"We all think it's real nice of you to take on those kids," Annie said.

Mae nodded. "It's a big job, raising somebody else's young'uns. It's more'n enough trouble raising your own."

Ida Parks turned to listen. "It's not so bad," she said, balancing her toddler on her hip and indicating with a gesture her husband's two oldest children. The other two were playing tag with Faye and some other kids of about the same age. "As long as you've got someone they'll mind. 'Sides, you marry a man for better 'n' worse even if he comes with a wagonload of children."

"Yes, it helps to have a man around," Annie agreed.

For just an instant, everyone looked at Bethany. She could feel the questions in their eyes. Either Judge Carr, not famed for his discretion, or Mrs. Tubbs, who had none at all, had let the cat out of the bag regarding Brent and Bethany.

One of the pregnant women put her hand on the place

where her waist used to be. "I don't know. Sometimes a man's more trouble that a whole houseful of kids."

"When are you due, Lila?"

"Not for another month. I liked to have died this summer."

"Did your feet swell much?" Mae asked.

"Much! I busted out two pairs of shoes till I got smart enough to go barefoot. That's why I wasn't in church for most of the last two months. Can't come to church barefoot."

"I must say, though," Ida put in, "those plates you've been painting are just beautiful."

"Well, I had to be doin' something with my time. Nobody ever told me how boring it is to be expecting."

The other girl, not so far along, put her fist against her back and twisted it. "It's my aching back that's making my life a misery. Seems like it doesn't matter what I do, it bothers me. And I sleep on a feather bed!"

"Put a switch of red alder under your mattress. That'll help," Annie volunteered.

An older woman with an infant in her arms and a two-year-old hanging on her skirt, whining, said, "And after you have the baby, keep that switch atop the mattress and you won't have another till you want one."

"Why not?" Bethany asked.

"'Cause your man comes near you, you whack him with it!"

Once again, laughter broke out. Bethany hid her blush by rubbing noses with Dory. "Silly, silly," she whispered. Dory chuckled with glee.

After a while, the group on the stairs broke up, some to see if their children had fallen into the pond, some to separate squalling siblings, others to chase their husband's hands out of the dinner baskets.

Singing a little lullaby, Bethany walked back to the patch of grass Manny had chosen for their picnic. Annie had shown her how to use her large shawl as a baby sling, to give her arms a rest, but she liked to have one arm around Dory. She was such a tiny thing that Bethany felt somehow that she ensured her safety with some magic created by her touch.

When Brent got into step beside her, Bethany broke off her song, self-consciously. He put back the fold of shawl that shaded Dory's face from the sun and smiled at the baby, sleepy-eyed from so much fresh air.

"Is it my imagination, or is this baby on the quiet side?"

"She's very happy—that makes her quiet."

"But you're sure she's all right?"

"We had the doctor look her over. He said Faye did a good job caring for her. Dory's a little thin but otherwise she's absolutely perfect."

Brent shook his head. "If he says so. But it's been my experience that babies cry a lot and there's hardly ever a peep out of this one."

"Your experience?" Bethany gave him a leery sideways glance. Was this some new part of his past?

"Well, every time I've traveled on a train where there's a baby in any one of forty-seven cars, you could hear it cry from the locomotive to the caboose. But I've been living in the same house with Dory for well over a week and I don't think I've heard her cry yet."

"Marmion House is very well built. The walls are thick. You probably just can't hear her cry sleeping at the other end of the house."

Brent touched her on the elbow, making her stop and look up at him. "I don't sleep at the other end of the house by choice, Bethany."

She'd known it was coming. She had considered herself fortunate that he hadn't brought the subject up at breakfast or on the walk to the brick-fronted church set among the trees. Her grandfather, always discreet, had walked on ahead, letting Brent and Bethany have time alone.

Charlene and Virgil had dawdled behind them. Sometimes by a trick of the wind, Bethany could hear what they were talking about. The future, their hopes, how much they loved each other. Brent had discussed ideas for a new business, asking her opinion and, Bethany was afraid, exposing her ignorance.

Now, as he looked at her with those eyes that reminded her of the first buds of spring, she said, "It's not my choice, either."

"Bethany!" There was no mistaking his happiness for shock. Yet she felt as though she'd betrayed herself.

"I couldn't throw Charlene out last night, you know. We only have a few more days together. She'll get married on Wednesday and then, for all I know, I'll never see her again."

"We'll visit them anytime you want to. Oregon isn't that far off in these days of trains. It isn't as though we'll have to take a Conestoga wagon over the mountains."

The sound of that "we," so intimate and yet so natural, made Bethany's heart constrict with a painful kind of bliss. "All the same, it's a long journey."

"Bethany . . ." A thinking frown drew his dark brows together. "You're worried about Charlene on this trip, aren't you? I mean, more than just worried about her going to live so far away."

She admitted it. Then she told him, in simple words, about Charlene's illness, about the long hours of nursing, the terrible moments when death hovered so close that Bethany had felt the brush of wings against her cheek as she knelt at the bedside. She gave him the joy of her sister's recovery and the fears of a permanently weakened heart.

Brent put his arm around her and listened in silence. Bethany leaped against him, feeling for the first time the comfort of a stronger arm. "I don't know what will happen," she said. "Maybe Virgil will have enough care and consideration for her. Maybe she will make it there and thrive. I don't know."

"You're afraid."

"Terribly," she said, turning her face against his smooth wool coat.

"Do you know why I want to marry you, Bethany?"

"Yes."

"Do you really?"

He put his crooked forefinger under her chin and raised her face. Something in his gaze told her that her first answer would be the wrong one.

"The children . . ."

He shook his head, slowly.

"Re-respectability?" she said, her mouth strangely dry.

"Not even close."

"Why, then?"

His mouth twisted into a wry smile. "It's because you're such a good mother."

She tossed her head free. "What is that supposed to mean?"

"You mother everyone. Even Mrs. Manning. You watch out for them and care for them. Smooth their paths and scold them into the right behavior. It's remarkable."

"And I suppose *you're* looking for a mother too? If that's your idea, Mr. Houston . . ."

He smoothed his hands over her shoulders, then tightened his grasp. He bent, careful not to crush Dory. His kiss was quick and light but enough to silence her. "Don't be ridiculous," he said. "*I* don't want a mother for me. But I want a very good one for my children, both those present and those to come."

Bethany supposed that was reasonable but she still felt a little angry and more than angry, a little wounded. "It's just that . . ."

"What?"

"Nothing. It's foolish. Of course, you want a woman who can care for children. Any reasonable man would make that a consideration when looking for a wife."

"Of course, the fact that one sight of you can send me spinning might have something to do with my choice too."

"It does? I mean, I do?"

"You do," he said seriously, but with a light in his eyes like sunlight dancing on water.

"Oh, well, that's all right then."

"Mind you, none of that would matter," he continued, "if you weren't a darn good cook into the bargain."

Bethany gave him a playful shove and he laughed. She looked up at him, standing tall against the sun, and thought how much she loved him. If only she dared to trust her intuition. It told her that Brent loved her, had loved her from the first.

Yet she could imagine so plainly his look of consternation if she told him she had fallen in love with him. He would try not to hurt her, but that glint of pity in his eyes would give away the fact that he was looking for a bedmate, a mother for his children, a hostess, and nothing more. Better to keep her love locked in her heart, though it might gnaw like a caged lion, than to risk hearing the truth.

She only hoped she'd be strong enough, when he came to her on their wedding night, to keep silent. It had been a near-run thing last night, when her emotions had run so hot, to keep a still tongue in her head.

Like a plump black starling, Mr. Vance scurried across the green grass, calling to them. His round face red and shiny, he stopped, pulling out a handkerchief to mop his face. "It really isn't possible . . ." he panted.

"What isn't?" Brent asked.

Bethany looked at the church. Her grandfather stood on the steps, his arms crossed on his chest. Though he was some distance away, she could tell by the way he huffed through his mustache that his chat with the reverend had not gone well. Maybe Brent had been right this morning, when he had volunteered to talk to Mr. Vance about their being married here.

Mr. Vance caught his breath. "You see, I have an obligation to the congregation. To allow outsiders to be married here—well, what next?"

"An outsider?" Bethany protested. "Why, Charlene and I were baptized here as was our mother. Virgil's been going here since he was in swaddling clothes and as for Brent, when he marries me, he'll be part of this congregation too. You can't . . ."

Recognizing that his volatile Bethany had gone past seethe into full boil, Brent gripped her arm. "Bethany, why don't you go along and help Mrs. Manning. The reverend and I need to discuss this, man to man."

As he turned her away from the nodding reverend, she glared into his face, showing plainly how much she resented his patronizing tone. He closed one eye in a lightning-fast wink. Puzzled, she walked away more leisurely than she'd first intended.

"Now, Reverend," Brent said, watching her go. He turned on his most charming, we're-all-men-together smile. If the reverend had been smarter, he reflected, he'd be putting his hand on his wallet about now. For Brent was determined to scheme, hustle, and con his way into getting married here, if that was what Bethany wanted.

Used to sizing men up at a glance, Brent saw that there was no real harm in this portly man. His burden was merely a whopping sense of self-importance combined with a role in society that fostered a good opinion of oneself. No doubt he was anxious to retain both that position and his good opinion.

"I'm sorry, Mr. Houston, but I can't see my way to it. Your mode of life, the irregularity of your living arrangements at the present moment . . ."

"Even though the girl's grandfather lives there too?"

"Mr. Ames himself is no reference. True, he is a regular churchgoer. Yet he has never been asked to be a member of the council, and why? Because he lives openly with a woman not his wife!"

"If you mean Mrs. Manning, she's his housekeeper."

"Yes, that's her name. And those two young ladies being sent off to a city of sin and wickedness when they were no more than girls. One's imagination boggles at the scenes of depravity they must have witnessed there. Cotillion balls and licentious goings-on in the gilded palaces of the rich!"

Brent eased the fit of his hat. He wondered what kind of novels Mr. Vance had been reading. "Is that so? Bethany hadn't mentioned anything like that. Why, the girl's been holding out on me."

"Mr. Houston!" The pastor's voice had risen. "Are you wearing a gun?"

Brent realized when he'd lifted his hand to his hat that his coat had parted. "Yes, for purely defensive reasons."

"This passes all bounds. Guns in the house of the Lord. No, this only confirms my . . ." His eyes went big. "Don't draw that . . ."

With a snap of his wrist, Brent showed him that all the chambers were empty. "I didn't say it was loaded." He grinned at the ashen pastor. "You know what, Vance? I like you. You've got grit."

"I . . . I do?" Mr. Vance said, lowering his hands.

"You really think I'm the biggest sinner unhung and yet you told me to my face that you wouldn't marry Bethany and me. That took pluck. But you're all wrong about me."

"I don't think so."

"Well, you're sure as blue blazes wrong about Bethany. She's the dearest girl in the world. Do you really think someone depraved would take on three orphaned kids and an ex-saloon owner? My Lord, man, if she were Catholic, they'd be telegraphing the Pope for a quick canonization."

"Oh, my goodness, you're Catholic?"

Brent tried again. "Now it doesn't take a genius to figure out where you're getting your facts from. Mrs. Tubbs doesn't much care for Bethany. I don't know why. Maybe Bethany's a little too sharp when it comes to people telling her what to do for Mrs. Tubbs's taste. Maybe it's just one of those women things we men can't ever quite figure out. But you can take my word for it that Bethany's one hundred percent solid gold."

The sun glinted off Mr. Vance's bald spot as he shook his head regretfully. "You must understand, Mr. Houston. When it comes to choosing between a fine upstanding woman like Mrs. Tubbs—the wife of the mayor!—and yourself, I must . . . Did you say, 'ex-saloon owner'?"

"I promised Bethany I'd sell the business. But I'm willing to make you a better offer."

Fifteen minutes later they shook hands. "If you ever decide to take up gambling, Reverend, be sure to stay away from my table. I don't care to lose my back collar stud."

Mr. Vance chuckled. "I still think you may be getting the better end of the deal."

Brent looked off to where Bethany sat on the grass, her skirt a swirl around her, the baby asleep on her lap while she read a story to Faye. "You may be right," he said.

He'd given Mr. Vance a serious problem and Brent could almost feel sorry for the reverend as he walked away. Explaining to Mrs. Tubbs why he was going against her wishes wouldn't be easy. But considering what the reverend had received, Brent managed to reserve his sympathy.

He'd gone from being a prosperous businessman to a freeloader in his fiancée's house. He'd just promised a substantial sum for a new roof for a church of which he was not at present a member. Moreover, he'd sworn not to sell his business but to close it down, which made it a dead loss. It would drain his resources until he could come up with a use for it, not to mention the fact that he would have to continue to pay Nolan and Paxton, the dealers, and the piano player until he could find them new jobs.

Then Bethany smiled at him and Brent wondered if he'd really come out a loser or not.

He sat down beside her.

"Everything okay?" she asked, turning the page.

"Yes. You'll be married here whenever you like."

"Thank you." Her smile softened and he felt more than ever that he had won. Then she glanced down at Faye, resting against her side and said, "Shall I go on? Or are you hungry?"

"No, I'm not," the girl said, twisting around to look up at her. "Jo's not going to go all mushy over this Laurie-boy, is she? I hate mushy stories."

During dinner, Brent found himself sitting next to Virgil. Though they were about to marry sisters, which made them almost relations, Brent had never really talked much to the farmer. "So, Oregon's the place to be," he said, trying to start a conversation.

"Seems to be. Mind passing the gravy?"

"Sure. Here. What made your brother decide to haul up stakes and go there?"

Virgil shrugged and waited until he swallowed to answer. "Lionel's always been the restless one in the family. He liked being a farmer but hated the plowing. I guess now he doesn't have to."

"What's wrong with plowing?"

"You ever do any?" Virgil glanced pointedly at Brent's shiny shoes and white shirt.

"More than a little. My father had a small farm in California. He liked the sunshine, but not the work."

"Sounds like Lionel. But I bet the soil in California's dirt, not half clay that breaks the point of your triple-forged steel plow clean off!"

"Clay? Really? I hadn't heard that was much of a problem in these parts."

Virgil's gray eyes showed just a hint of contempt. "Don't imagine you've paid much attention."

Brent nodded. Though he could remember hearing farmers complaining in his place about the hardships of the life, he'd usually been too busy playing cards to listen. Besides, his general feeling was that farmers were always complaining about something. Too little rain, too much, poor prospects for the next year, and no hope for this one. When he did listen, it was only to express silent thanks to God for getting him out of California before he'd become a farmer in earnest.

"No, I haven't paid much attention," Brent admitted. "But I may have to start."

Charlene said, "Oh, don't let's talk about farming! I'm going to hear nothing but cherries, cherries, cherries from now on."

"There's apples too, don't forget," Virgil said, grinning.

Brent frowned at the roll in his hand. Bethany leaped over toward him and whispered, "What's wrong?"

But Brent only fixed his eyes on Virgil. "What kind of clay?"

"I don't know. Clay."

"Brown or white?"

The farmer only lifted his broad shoulders and looked blank.

Bethany asked, "What different does it make? Virgil said you can't plow through it."

Brent leaned back on his elbows and squinted at the sky. It was too good to be true. There had to be a catch. Glancing at Bethany, he realized that it was possible his luck was still holding. "You remember when I told you I went to England once?"

"Certainly."

"You did?" Charlene squealed. "Oh, how I'd love to go there. What was it like, Brent?"

Passing over her questions, he said, "I didn't mention the fact that my father was British, did I?"

"No, you must have skipped that part." Even though her voice stayed calm and level, Brent saw her eyes taking fire from his excitement.

Charlene whispered loudly to Virgil, "I bet he turns out to be the long-lost heir of an earl or somebody."

"Not even close," Brent said. "He was from a smallish city in the heart of England. It has only four claims to fame. A cathedral. A river. A famous battle there, after which Charles the Second had to go hide in a hollow oak tree."

Bethany supplied the name. "Worcester?"

"You know your history. But do you know what else Worcester is famous for?"

Three faces looked at him blankly, four if he counted Dory. He let the suspense build a moment and then said one word. "China."

The faces looked no more enlightened. "Porcelain. Pottery. Worcester has one of the biggest, oldest, and most famous potteries in the world. And my father was one of their top men until he ran into a little trouble with a woman."

"Like father, like son," Bethany murmured with a fond light in her eye.

"He came over to work in a New Jersey pottery where he met my mother. Then they decided that California would be better for father's health . . ."

"What had he done this time?"

He laughed. "I was only two, so don't blame me. The point is that Father taught me about it. I didn't like it, any more than I liked being a farmer. It will be a strange and wonderful coincidence if I wind up in the pottery business after all."

Bethany said, "Aren't you going to go find out if it is the right kind of clay?"

"As soon as Virgil finishes his dinner."

Charlene reached out a pretty and languid hand. Snatching the plate from beneath Virgil's descending fork, she said sweetly, "He's finished."

Virgil sighed, shook his head, and grinned sideways at Brent. "I guess I'm finished."

The girls walked with them to Virgil's wagon. "Now I'm no expert," Brent said, "but I have a good feeling about this. If it's the right kind of clay, we could start a pottery. Of course, we'd need machinery and then we'd have to train folks in the techniques. I wonder if . . ."

"You wonder what?"

He knew her well enough by now to know that she wasn't likely to let him slide out of telling her with an "I don't know." "I wonder if my father is still alive."

"Do you think he'd come out and help us, if he is?"

Brent shrugged. "Depends on whether he's still alive or not, doesn't it?"

"How old would he be?"

"I don't know. Early sixties?"

She took his arm and asked, "What if this isn't the right kind of clay?"

"I'm not expecting high quality kaolin, Bethany. I'd be happy to find refractory clay—that's the kind that can withstand high temperatures. Then we could start a brick-yard or make tiles."

She gave a little skip, as high-hearted as a girl. "I can't wait until you come back."

"Me, either." Stopping, he let Virgil and Charlene get a little ahead. Then he swooped down and captured her lips under his. She didn't resist at all, instantly melting against him, giving him her heart as well as her kiss. Brent felt a surge of tenderness well up inside him. He was breathlessly in love with her and longed to tell her so.

"By God," he said more than a little fiercely. "I'll make you love me yet!"

"But, Brent, I . . ."

"Trouble brewing!" Virgil called, pointing back the way they'd come.

"Is that Jerry?" Bethany asked as they looked back.

Brent squinted against the sun, dazzling through the trees. He'd hardly had time to see the two boys, their bodies tight with anger, standing face-to-face before one shoved the other. In an instant, they were punching away at each other with all their infinite energy.

Bethany clutched his arm as a smaller figure in a skirt launched herself at the legs of the boy who wasn't Jerry. His yelp of agony carried to them clearly as she bit him.

"That's Faye!" Bethany called. "Come on!"

She hitched up her skirt behind her and ran, her high brown boots seeming to skim over the earth in a foam of white lace. Brent followed her. If it weren't for the little girl, he would have held Bethany back. It was best to let boys fight things out for themselves, but girls tended to get hurt in those kinds of battles. Bethany herself might get injured.

When she broke through the circle of boys, the two boys were on the ground, wrestling and trying to land what blows they could. As soon as she arrived, some of the boys who'd been cheering the fight caught back the combatants. Brent stepped onto the contested ground immediately after Bethany.

She went at once to Faye, lying shaken on the ground. "Are you all right, dear?"

"Let me at him!" the little girl panted. "I'll teach him."

Brent put himself between the boys, Jerry still glaring, the other one trying to reach the sore place on his leg. "That's enough. Let 'em go."

"She bit me!"

"Whatsamatter, Harris? Can't take it?" Jerry jeered.

Bethany had helped Faye to her feet. She smoothed the tousled hair, adjusting the round comb that held it back. Her pinafore had a long grass stain down the side and the lace frill was torn. The little girl began to cry, more tears of rage than pain or sorrow. "He shouldn't of said it!"

"Said what?" Bethany asked, tugging free the handkerchief tucked in her waist. She licked it absently and began to wipe the dust from Faye's cheeks.

There was a short silence. The crowd of boys and young men began to drift away in groups of twos and threes. The boy Harris looked as though he'd rather be somewhere else as well.

Jerry stepped forward. In a voice that seemed to have dropped an octave in the last few minutes, he growled, "You better watch yourself. I hear any more talk like that and I'll push your teeth in."

"Yeah?"

"Yeah."

"Don't hit him again, Jerry," Charlene said. She'd only just arrived, showing more exasperation at Virgil for not letting her run than consternation over the fight. "He's had enough." She turned her clear blue eyes on the other boy. "You're William Harris's boy, aren't you?"

"Yes'm," he said, digging his toe into the ground. He shot Jerry a hate-filled look but didn't seem to be able to meet any of the adults' eyes.

"My, it seems like only yesterday that your father was fighting Mitch Carson up Main Street and down for asking your mother to the Fourth of July dance. Do you remember, Bethany? Father had to help break it up. You remember . . . that day we all went downtown because they'd just finished the new depot."

"Oh, yes."

"I guess men have to fight. 'Specially over girls."

"Are you done, my chatterbox?" Virgil asked. Charlene flirted with her eyes at him. Brent admitted that Bethany's twin had a certain charm all her own, though it wasn't the sort to appeal to him, not anymore. He glanced at Bethany, still trying to clean up Faye, and saw that she was troubled. She kept giving Jerry sorrowful glances that were making the boy abashed and uncomfortable.

"All right," he said, clapping his hands together once decisively. "You boys shake hands and apologize. It's Sunday, for God's sake, and you shouldn't be fighting."

"Or taking the Lord's name in vain," Bethany said softly.

"What? Oh, right. Come on, you two. Shake."

Grimy fingertips brushed in reluctant obedience to the letter, if not the spirit, of his command.

"Now beat it," Brent said to the Harris boy. The boy's hostility showed in his eyes but he complied, walking away with his shod feet dragging in the dust. He turned once to give them all a corrosive glance.

"Charlene," Bethany said. "Will you take Faye to Manny? I think she said she was about ready to go home and give Dory a nap. You'd like a nice bath, wouldn't you, Faye?"

"I'm okay," she said, wiping her nose with her sleeve. "'Sides, I ain't had any ice cream yet. The cranker done give out 'cause his lumbago was acting up again."

Bethany nodded. "No more fighting, though."

"Try crying, instead," Charlene counseled. "That works on boys much better than biting them." She saw the glance her sister gave her. "What?"

"Come on, Charlene," Virgil said, putting his hand under her elbow. "Show us where this ice cream is, Faye. Did I ever mention that I'm a champion cranker?"

Brent and Bethany faced a mutinous Jerry. He began brushing the dust from his once-white shirt and beating the thighs of his long pants. "Give it up, son," Brent said. "You won't ever look like new."

"Jerry," Bethany said. "Was it about a girl?"

Seasoned bluffer though he was, Brent knew how hard it was to lie when she fixed that thoughtful, intent gaze upon him. Jerry, with so much less experience, gave up without a struggle.

"No, ma'am. Leastways, it was about Momma."

"Your mother?"

"Don't know how that Harris knew about it, but I guess maybe the whole town's talkin' now."

Brent answered the appeal in Jerry's glance. It would be torture for the boy to tell her, but she had to know. Brent could spare him that much.

"Get along for that ice cream," he said to Jerry. "But don't knock anybody else down until I show you how."

"I know how."

"Not so you win with the first punch, you don't. A good fight never lasts long enough for the other fellow to lay a finger on you. Remember that."

Jerry nodded, but his lively grin did not return. He squared his thin shoulders and walked off as though marching away to face his firing squad. Brent knew that bullets must seem easier to face than the ridicule and whispers of a small town.

He turned to face Bethany, her hands on her hips and determination compressing her full-lipped mouth. "All right," she said. "What's going on?"

"You already know part of it. Mrs. Tubbs told you that day she said she'd see the kids in the orphanage." She still looked blank. "Remember how she talked about Mrs. Windom."

"She said . . . she said the children all had different fathers. So? Many women marry more than once. I've known a few who had two husbands before they were twenty-five."

"But Mrs. Windom *didn't* marry more than once. Jerry's father was the only one she ever married."

"Oh!" Bethany said on an intake of breath. "I see."

He watched her closely. If she was the girl he thought she was . . .

"That does make a difference," she said thoughtfully and for a moment his heart dropped with a sickening sensation of disappointment.

"It does?"

"Of course, it does. I shall have to have a long talk with the schoolmaster and Mr. Vance. We mustn't have Faye or Dory teased. I don't know what to do about Jerry. He can't fight the whole world to protect his sisters."

"I'll handle Jerry. But what about you?"

"Me? Oh, when they're old enough, I'll explain to the girls . . . maybe I should explain to Faye now that women aren't always wise in matters of the heart. Sometimes they make poor decisions. I'll have to remind her that her mother's errors in judgment don't mean there's anything wrong with *her*. After all, she can't fight the whole world either."

Brent realized it was a waste of time to doubt Bethany. She would never let him or anyone else down. "Come along, Miss Forsythe. I'm going to buy you a dish of ice cream."

Twenty-one

◈

In the end, Charlene was married in her pale blue satin. She and Bethany had decorated the drawing room with all the last of the roses, interspersed with shaggy mums and branches of red-berried, red-leaved dogwood. Mr. Vance, his finger holding his place in a black book, waited in the curve of the big bay window.

Mr. O'Dell's oldest son played the violin. Charlene walked down the aisle on her grandfather's arm to a simple haunting tune of Clarence's own making. As the quavering strings reached their highest point, Virgil stepped out to claim his bride and face the minister. "And he gave her such a look," Mrs. Manning told Bethany later, "that my knees just 'bout turned to jelly! And I'm no young thing to have my head turned either."

For Bethany hadn't been there. At the last moment, as she followed Charlene, she'd turned back into the hall. She leaned against the wall, one hand flat to support her, and listened to the achingly sweet strain of the violin. She'd heard the pastor's first words and fled.

Brent found her in the little gazebo at the bottom of the garden. He didn't say anything, just sat down beside her and put an arm around her shoulders. Together they listened to the soft sighing of the wind in the brilliant trees.

"Is it over?" Bethany asked.

"Yes. Right now everyone's raving about those little crunchy things you made."

She shrugged. "We didn't go to very much trouble."

He looked at the soaring simplicity of the rear of Marmion House, so different from the Italianate gorgeousness of the front. "I used to think this house must be a cold and soulless place to live. But now I like it."

Bethany was grateful to him for introducing a less emotionally loaded topic. "I've always been fond of it."

"Do you want to live here for always?"

"I've thought about it. It has plenty of bedrooms and Grandfather will be lonely now that Mrs. Manning is going to marry Mr. O'Dell."

"Is she?"

"I think so. She's been in a perfect swivet ever since he asked her. Besides, she told me that the Station Hotel wants to hire her to supervise the maids. It would be a perfect position for her. She couldn't do that job and still be Grandfather's housekeeper. That wouldn't work out."

"No. Does Mr. O'Dell have any objection to his wife working?"

Bethany shook her head. "Do you?"

"If running the café makes you happy, Bethany, how can I object to it? Of course, it's going to be difficult without Charlene, but you can find somebody else to bake your cakes."

"It isn't the loss of her cakes that has me upset."

His arm tightened around her. "I know. But you are going to need someone to help you . . . and even to replace you temporarily at times."

"Why?" She stared for a moment as his slow grin spread across his face. Then she blushed. "Oh. Babies."

He brushed his knuckles along the curve of her cheek. "I've seen you with Dory. I can't wait till we have one of our own."

"I'll throw away my alder switch."

"Alder switch?"

"Never mind. You really want children, Brent? A wild, irresponsible bachelor like yourself?"

"I won't be a bachelor come Sunday. Come Sunday night,

I hope to be well on my way to fatherhood." He chuckled and kissed her cheek. "Have I ever told you I love to watch you blush?"

She moved away from the comforting circle of his arm to sit, with a prim spine and proper expression, a suitable distance away. "What unusually clement weather we're having!"

"I find it a little too warm, frankly."

"Odd, when I'm doing my best to chill you."

He came a little closer and insinuated his arm around her waist. "That's very difficult," he said in her ear. "I'm naturally hot-blooded."

"So I can tell," she said softly and lifted her face for his kiss. They'd hardly had a chance to speak since Sunday, between the regular work of operating the café every day but the day of rest and preparing the trays and trays of food for Charlene's wedding reception. Though the actual number of wedding guests was small—merely Charlene's best friends from school, their husbands and children, and the most important of Mr. Ames's former business friends—the number of reception guests had exploded.

Only by exercising eternal vigilance and the most refined cunning had Bethany kept Mr. Ames from dosing the punch bowl with more alcohol than existed in most home remedies. Bethany herself had begun to wonder if a course of Lydia Pinkham's Vegetable Compound wouldn't work a miracle with her increasingly middle-aged blood.

Then she looked at Brent and didn't feel a day older than she was. Nineteen had always been such an in-between age, neither woman nor girl. Being with him, feeling his lips on hers, his arms holding her tightly against his body, she felt all woman. She lifted her hand to his head and ruffled her fingers through the soft strands of his hair.

"I can't wait for Sunday," he murmured, moving to nip her throat.

"Neither can I." She tugged on his hand, moving it from her back to the curve of her waist. Somehow his touch made her feel better, more alive. With a quiver of anticipation, she wondered how touching him everywhere would make her feel.

He kissed her lips again. Bethany parted them for his gentle invasion. After a moment or two of paradise, she felt his hands on her shoulders. He pushed her away. She could feel the reluctance in his hands.

"Four more days," he said. His lips smiled but his eyes were intense. "Thank God for cold baths."

"Does that help?"

"No. But it takes my mind off you for as long as it takes me to get into the tub. Once I'm in, though, you come right back."

Looking down, she reached out to toy with a highly incised button on his blue and gold striped waistcoat. "Maybe one day we could take a bath together . . ."

"Together?" He pressed her hand against his body. "That did it! Now I won't even be able to escape the thought of you there. I'll be imagining the door opening and you coming in . . ."

She glanced up at him when he broke off. His eyes had a faraway, rather glazed look and his breath was coming fast. She gloried in the notion that she–Bethany Forsythe—had the power to make him go wild. Then his attention returned to her and she realized anew that power worked both ways.

She said, "I wish it didn't have to be four days. . . ."

He patted her hand. "I know. Me too."

"I could visit you . . . tonight." She hadn't meant to say it, though she'd been thinking of it for days, but she didn't mean to go back on it.

"What are you saying, Bethany?" He tried to see her face.

She turned away, looking at anything, the deflowered bushes, the gazebo railing, the floor, rather than let him look into her eyes and see how completely and shamelessly she wanted him. Before he could say another word, she hurried to say, "I mean, now that Charlene is going away, I'm going to be very lonely. And you are at the other end of the house so no one will hear me if I come to you, and we *are* getting married in a few days anyway, and I haven't seen you lately, and . . ."

He kissed her. She tightened up all over, then relaxed, giving herself into his hands. Whatever he decided would be all right with her.

With a soothing touch, he smoothed back the hair from her temples. "No," he said. "We'll wait."

"Why? Oh, it's because . . ."

"Don't get any funny ideas, sweetheart. I'm not saying no because I don't want you anymore or because I've changed my mind about marrying you."

"Then why won't you . . . let me?"

"Because I want your first time to be perfect. I haven't always been a good man, Bethany. Let me do one thing the right way, the good way."

"Thank you," she said, her eyes moist. Brent had turned out to be a better man than she'd dreamed he could be. "It can't be easy for you."

"You have no idea," he all but groaned in reply.

"I mean, all these changes. Suddenly you're a father-to-be, the founder of a new business . . ."

"We'll see about that . . ."

"Oh, I have every confidence in you."

"I appreciate it, but if this clay isn't Kaolin, your confidence may be the only thing I've got left."

"You'll still have these," she said, lightly touching the backs of his hands.

"As if you'd let me take up gambling again."

"As if I could stop you." She stood up. "I suppose we should be going back to the house. Everyone will wonder where we are."

"Do you mind them gossiping?"

"I can't stop them, either."

"Hey," he said, twitching her hand. "Can I show you a card trick?"

"Now?"

"Watch." Leaning to one side, he brought out a new pack of cards from his coat pocket. He held it up, encouraging her to break the paper band that sealed it. "Are you watching closely?"

"Yes," she said warily.

Almost too quickly for her to see, he separated the cards into two stacks and just as rapidly shuffled them together again. "One more time." They came together again with a rippling noise. "Now cut."

Using her fingers as delicately as though she picked a flower's petal, she lifted half the deck off the other. He reassembled them into a pile and held them almost negligently in his left hand. "Okay, now do you believe there's no way I can tell which cards are on top?"

"Yes," she said, slowly, her eyes narrowed.

"Say abracadabra."

"Abracadabra."

"Now watch!" As quickly as snapping fingers, he peeled cards off the top, calling them off before he glanced at them. "Jack of hearts, king of spades, ace of clubs, queen of diamonds."

"That's not a diamond," she said, looking at the un-doubted eight of hearts.

"No? Are you sure?"

"Look for yourself."

He glanced at the card. "It looks like a diamond to me. Are you sure you know one when you see it?"

"Brent, that's a silly question. If you didn't do the trick right . . ."

He let the blue-backed cards cascade to the ground. The sunlight commanded a glitter from a ring cupped in his left palm. His heart-stealing grin slipping onto his lips at the expression on her face, he asked again, "Are you sure you know a diamond when you see one?"

Bethany supposed she was gawking like a rube getting her first glimpse of the big city. She glanced at the ring in his hand and then at his face, which wore a grin big enough to light a city block. "Oh, Brent," she sighed.

"Try it on. It won't fit anything on me but my little finger and it doesn't look right with hairy knuckles." She straightened the fingers on her left hand and let him slip it on. "Hum, a little loose," he said, turning it.

"No, it's perfect."

"You haven't even looked at it."

"I wasn't talking about the ring."

He took her into his arms. They shared a kiss that did not plumb the depths of passion or involve any kind of gentle battle. Bethany felt as though she'd given her heart into his keeping for all time. The words that would be spoken over the two of them by Mr. Vance later in the week would only reconfirm the promises of this moment.

"We should go in," she said after an eternity passed with her head on his shoulder.

"Hmmm? I suppose so." He made no move to release her, resting his cheek on her hair.

"They'll be thinking about going to the station, and Charlene will need my help to change. And you are the best man."

"Oh, I made my toast. Joy and prosperity. Everybody drained their glasses."

"I hope they weren't drinking from the punch bowl. Grandfather added something to it."

"Spiked? I wondered why Mrs. Tubbs was smiling."

"Was she there? The nerve!" But she didn't lift her head from his shoulder.

"Your grandfather's been an important man in these parts. If our manufactory gets going, he'll be important again. Mayor Tubbs isn't going to risk insulting him." He dropped a kiss on her head and smoothed his hand down her back.

Something about his last words troubled Bethany. But with his hands moving sensuously over the satin of her dress and the scent of his male body filling her thoughts, she couldn't figure out why.

He said in her ear, "I'm so glad you've given up your corset, Bethany. I kind of like knowing it's just you under there."

"Why . . . ?"

"Lots of reasons," he said, his voice dropping to a murmur.

"And you've stopped wearing your gun, haven't you?"

"Now that the saloon's closed, there's no need for me to wear it."

"Good." She enjoyed the sensations he aroused with his gently cupping hands and the tantalizing heat of his kisses. But a nagging thought still troubled her. "Why will Grandfather be important again?"

He raised his head. "He told me he'd be happy to invest in our new factory, if the clay turns out to be workable. Major investor equals importance. But I really don't want to talk about your relatives, Bethany."

"I don't understand." Bethany moved back, her hands still clasped loosely about his waist, but their bodies no longer touching.

"Grandfather told us he'd lost all his money, but he never would say how. Everyone seems to know he's poor and yet he goes on living in the same style. The butcher never once complained about giving us credit for our meat or the grocer about our supplies. The only thing different is that the horses are gone, but you can't tell me he's been living on what they'd bring in. And now he's offering you money?"

"Why don't you ask him about it?"

"I've tried. He's too slippery. But something is not quite right. I can feel it."

Brent cleared his throat. "Maybe he's living on savings. For all you know, he's got a thousand dollars under his bed in a lead-lined box and that's what he's going to use to buy into the business." Once again, he tried to reach for her.

Bethany eased herself out of his arms. "I just can't believe he'd tell us he was destitute if he wasn't."

"Are you sure that's what he said?"

"Of course I am. I could show you the letter. Charlene saw it too. He told us that he'd had many 'reverses' and that his financial situation was grim. 'So much so that I doubt I shall be able to command the necessities of life ever again.'" In answer to his inquiring look, she said, "We read it so often trying to find a clue to what had happened that I all but memorized it."

"You must have written for details."

"Well, yes, my Uncle Poste did so. But Grandfather's answers remained very vague. When I came out here, I thought I'd be able to talk to him, as we did before we went away. We used to be able to discuss anything with Grandfather. He'd tell us about the bank, and we'd tell him about school. . . ."

"That's odd," he said, stepping away from her.

"What is?" She looked over his arm into his face.

"The bank. Your grandfather was president, wasn't he?"

"That's right. His father founded it and Grandfather ran it. If Father had lived, he would have gone on working there, as well."

"It's just strange that Mr. Ames claims to be completely pauperized and yet the bank is just as strong as ever." In answer to her look, he said, "Usually a bank president and his bank sink or swim together. I've never heard of one failing and one thriving. Unless the president's a crook . . ."

"You're not calling my grandfather a crook, Brent Houston?"

"Put down your cudgels, Bethany. If he were a crook, the *bank* would have failed and he'd be in Mexico by now, living it up with the iguanas." He rubbed his hands together thoughtfully.

"The way I see it, we have two choices," he said. "One, I can ask around town, find out what he's been doing, who he's been talking to, find out if he's sold anything valuable."

"That sounds good."

"Problem is we'd set the whole town talking about him.

Sooner or later, he'll hear about it and then we'd have to explain what we thought we were doing."

"And the other way?"

"We march in and ask him."

As they walked up the verandah steps, Brent said, "You know, if things had been a little different I probably would have kissed you right here. Do you remember that night, after you'd bearded me in my den at the saloon, and I wound up accepting your grandfather's invitation?"

"Yes, I do." She remembered something else about it too. "I had the funniest feeling that night . . . as though everyone were laughing at me. I was probably just nervous, serving my first big dinner in Cedar Groves."

"Probably."

But something in his tone or expression gave him away. She followed him into the kitchen, saying, "Brent? You mean you really were laughing at me? Why?"

"Let's find your grandfather."

"Not until you tell me what was so blamedly funny."

"How 'bout if I tell you Sunday night?"

"Why not now?"

His laughing eyes were full of light. "If you trust me, you'll wait."

"That's a low thing to say." She paused. "All right. But only because I trust you."

He laid his hand very softly against her cheek, caressing the curve of it. "You don't know how much that means to me. Let's find your grandfather."

It wasn't difficult to cut him out of the crowd. Bethany waited in the doorway, accepting the japes of friends who were counting the minutes it seemed until she and Brent were married. She kept an eye on him, seeing him interpose a word or two into the chat Mr. Ames was having with a few other businessmen.

In a moment Brent was part of the conversation. After that, he somehow maneuvered Mr. Ames, both through a word in his ear and a hand under his elbow, over toward the door. Yet something he said made the older man stop and shake his head in a definite refusal.

Bethany started forward, only to find Mrs. Manning in her way. "Charlene's getting ready to go. She doesn't want nobody else but you."

"I'll go up in a minute."

"You better go now. That smile of hers don't fool me a mite. She's scared to death."

"She is? But I thought . . ."

"If you don't know her any better than that by now, girl, you just haven't been paying attention. Are you going up, or not?"

"I . . ." Over the heads of the others, Brent glanced at her. His expression was oddly stern, a deep gouge carving itself between his brows. The strength of her desire to smooth all such frowns away shook her with its power. She remembered what he'd said about her being a mother to all the world. But she hadn't the slightest wish to mother Brent. Her desire was to take him into a private room and kiss him until he forgot how to scowl.

Then he smiled and for no other reason than to answer, she smiled at him. He made a high sign, telling her to go with Mrs. Manning. Bethany raised her eyebrows and he nodded vigorously, shooing her off with a gesture.

Her curiosity still gnawing at her, she went upstairs to the modest little room at the rear of the house. She paused before entering the short lobby between the hall and Charlene's room. This would be the last time she could expect to hear her sister's cheery greeting, the last time they'd share a quiet word. She didn't know how to keep from crying.

"Oh, thank heavens it's you! I was afraid it was Virgil! Bethany, what am I going to do?" Charlene was literally shaking so hard her flowered and feathered hat kept slipping off her hair. She snatched it off and tossed it onto the bed.

"What's wrong?"

"Wrong? Oh, mercy!" Charlene sank onto the edge of the

pretty flowered armchair she'd saved from the attic long ago and covered with a pale chintz. She put trembling fingertips to her eyes as though trying to regain her calm.

Bethany looked around. Charlene's trunk, hardly unpacked from their trip home, stood bound and corded in the corner. A wide-mouthed valise stood on the bed, gaping and disgorging a variety of disordered garments. Charlene herself wore her neat traveling suit with the broad belt that made her look ethereally pale and slim. Looking closer, Bethany realized it was not the black cloth alone that made her pale.

"You're shaking with fright, poor thing!"

"I must be insane," Charlene said. "I don't know Virgil at all. For all I know, he'll beat me. And I don't think he really loves me, you know. I think I've just fascinated him."

"What about you? You love him, don't you?" Bethany sank onto her knees beside Charlene's chair and took her hands down from her eyes. "You do love him?"

"I don't know what love is! I always thought it was being swept away, forgetting the dull world in his arms, living only for the other person . . . I don't feel like that at all!" She sounded as disappointed as a child getting brussels sprouts instead of cake on her birthday.

"How do you feel?"

"Wretched." She said rapidly, "I see all his faults, you know. He's a messy dresser, he likes to drink beer, he always forgets to hold the door for me . . ."

"He is a man," Bethany said, and reflected that she sounded like a woman with a hundred years of experience.

"Yes, he is, but that's no excuse. He says 'I seen,' and 'lookee there,' and he . . ." She dropped her voice to a murmur. Even as close as Bethany sat, she couldn't hear.

"What does he do?"

"Oh, Bethany! He snorts when he laughs!"

Bethany tried hard but this was too much for her self-control. She began to laugh.

"Oh, don't! It's awful . . . he sounds just like a pig in clover!"

Fearing that was how she'd sound herself in another minute, Bethany buried her face against the cushion, her shoulders shaking. After a moment she heard Charlene's giggle break out, a trifle guiltily.

"No, really," she said. "It's impossible. I can't go through my whole life with a man who snorts. I . . . I should go mad. Stark mad."

Lifting her head, Bethany wiped a tear from her cheek. "You should have thought of that before . . . you're married now."

"I know, I know. But I didn't think it through. I was thinking about what to wear and how the drawing room should look. I wasn't thinking about actually spending the rest of my life with Virgil. And then there's the *other* part of marriage. Oh, I can't do it!"

"What other part?" She couldn't be afraid of the cooking.

"You know. The night part."

"Oh. Well, so far, Brent and I have . . ."

"You've done it with Brent! Bethany, I can't believe it. That's the most outrageous . . . Was it nice, or as horrible as the old women say?"

"Wait a minute. I haven't done anything with Brent . . . or at any rate, not anything to speak of. But to tell the truth, I'm really almost looking forward to it."

"I'm not. But then you get to be with Brent and I get to be with Virgil. Oh, you're got to help me."

Bethany looked into her sister's terrified face. She knew Charlene's moods well, but fear definitely seemed to have her in its grip. Whether it was fear of the nights to come or the days, Bethany couldn't be sure. But as always, she would do her best to see Charlene happy.

"Very well. What do you want me to do?"

"Tell Virgil that . . . that I'm sick. That's it. Tell him I'm sick. The excitement, lack of sleep, anything. Then tell

Grandfather the truth. He'll have to talk to the judge and Mr. Vance. There has to be a way . . ."

"Charlene, honey, may I come in?"

Bethany was looking into Charlene's face when Virgil called to her from outside the door. It was as if she stood at the bedside when the prince kissed the Sleeping Beauty. Charlene's eyelids fluttered and she caught her breath on a gentle "oh!" Then a warm glow mounted into her cheeks while her eyes awakened, sparkling into full realization as life returned.

"Yes, dear. I'm almost ready. Would you close that bag for me, Bethany?"

"But . . ."

Charlene only smiled as she went into her husband's arms.

Half an hour later, as the white and blue decorated buggy waited on the street, Charlene and Virgil said their last good-byes. The last long hugs were over and an awkward silence fell, broken only by the women's sniffles.

Brent cleared his throat and they all looked at him. "This might be a good time for Mr. Ames to tell you all something. Mr. Ames . . ."

"Oh, yes! Ah, my dears, I'm happy to be able to tell you that the report I gave you regarding my financial crisis is, ah, largely a fictitious one."

"He means he lied," Brent interrupted. "He's not broke, there's plenty of money to keep the house going, you're not penniless after all."

"It was a ruse," Mr. Ames said as his granddaughters advanced on him. He held out his hands pleadingly, his mustache twitching in agitation. "If you'll listen to my reasons, I'm sure you'll applaud them."

"What reasons?" Bethany demanded.

"Over the past few months I began to realize from your letters that the young men you were going to marry were not the right sort. Namby-pamby rich men's sons. That's not what I wanted for you and this aunt of yours knew it. It was as if she went out and selected the worst possible mates for my girls, instead of the best."

Charlene said, hurt, "I can't believe you lied to us."

"I *had* to. You wouldn't have been happy with them. And what if something happened and they lost all their money? How would they manage to support you? Now these two fine young men . . ." he said, glancing between Brent and Virgil, with something of his desperation in his eyes. Charlene gave her new husband a glance and stopped glaring at her grandfather.

"I can't be too angry, Bethany. If he hadn't lied, I wouldn't have met Virgil again. I would have had to marry Ronald."

"All the same, he could have just *asked* us to come back here."

"But I never expected you to work so hard, Bethany. I thought you'd look around a little, find someone more wholesome, and write a note, sending your fiancé his marching orders. But it didn't work out that way . . ."

"No, it didn't. Grandfather, how could you?"

Brent tucked his arm around Bethany's waist from the rear and held her back. He said in a deliberately audible whisper, "Don't shred him to bits, Bethany. We still need him to invest in our pottery."

With his touch, half her feeling of outrage faded. She still didn't care to be manipulated as her grandfather had done, but she couldn't argue with his results. Besides, she told Brent earlier that if all he had was his nimble fingers and faster brain, she'd still stay with him.

Virgil glanced into the library. "We're going to miss our train if we don't hurry, Charlene."

"Where's Faye?" she asked. "She wanted to ride with us to the station. She said she'd never seen such a pretty buggy and she reckoned it would be a good few years before one was garnished for her."

Brent said, "I'm glad to hear she has no immediate plans

to be married. I don't think I'm ready for that part of fatherhood."

"You're never ready," Mr. Ames said.

"Maybe she's lying down," Bethany said. "It has been a long day. She got up at six to help us decorate."

"I'll go," Mrs. Manning volunteered. She'd been wiping her eyes with the edge of her apron ever since the wedding ceremony had begun. Now she walked up the stairs, leaving a group of people below who hardly knew what to say to each other.

Charlene and Bethany drifted together for one final good-bye in the doorway, their arms about each other's waists. "I hear Oregon is beautiful," Bethany said.

"You will come and visit?" Charlene glanced at Virgil, who was peering into the library to see the time. She said to the air, "We've never been separated before, you know."

A sudden thud from upstairs shook the brass swag lamp above their heads and made everyone look up. "Mrs. Manning?" Brent called. "Are you all right?"

There was no answer. Bethany disengaged from Charlene and hurried to the foot of the stairs. "Manny?"

Brent was at her shoulder as she started up. She hadn't gone a dozen steps before she realized she was taking them two at a time. "Manny?" she called again when she reached the landing.

Bethany ran to the nursery door. Mrs. Manning lay on the floor next to the crib, her face ashen. One thing Bethany had learned in New York was how to deal with a faint.

"Open a window," she said to Brent as she pulled Mrs. Manning into a sitting position. Then she pushed the older woman's head toward her knees.

Charlene, Grandfather Ames, and Virgil all came into the room. The men paused, at a loss. Already Mrs. Manning was starting to rouse, muttering and trying to sit upright. "I've never known her to faint before," Mr. Ames said.

As Brent sent a window rattling upward, letting the crisp

air roll in, Charlene walked over to the crib. "My goodness, can this baby sleep through everything? Come say good-bye to Auntie Charlene, sweetie bunnikins. Upsa . . . She's gone!"

Twenty-two

All three children were gone.

The adults met in the kitchen after searching the house and grounds. Mrs. Manning had Mr. O'Dell in tow, his bright blue eyes hooded with worry.

"There's a few things missing from Faye's and Jerry's rooms," Charlene reported. "A change of clothes and that doll you gave her, Brent."

"And I found some of Miss Charlene's clothes tossed under the bed," Mrs. Manning added. "No sign of the valise."

"They must have been plannin' this right along," Mr. O'Dell said, shaking his head.

Bethany said, "Half a dozen diapers are gone too, as well as two of the feeding bottles and all the cans of lactated food. We have to assume they left of their own free will."

"What had you thought?" Brent asked. "That Mrs. Tubbs had had them kidnapped?"

"Don't laugh at me," she said sadly, resting her forehead in the heel of her hand. "I can't . . ." She sniffled, feeling the wetness come stinging to her eyes "I can't believe they'd run away."

His hand, warm and heavy, rested on her shoulder for a moment. "I'm not laughing," he said. "Believe me, I'm not laughing. There has to be some reasonable explanation for their behavior. Now everybody think. Did either Jerry or Faye seem unusual in any way?"

Everyone shook their heads after a moment's thought.

Mr. Ames said, "The boy was cheerful, I'll swear to it. We've been talking about a career for him. He's bright enough to go to college, though his education's been neglected. I was going to help him."

"What about the girl?"

"Happy as a lark," Mrs. Manning said. "Her new dress tickled her no end. She was twirling around to see the skirt fly up."

"When did someone see them last?"

"It must have been about noon," Bethany said. "That's when I took the baby up for her nap. Faye was . . ."

"She'd helped me get dressed," Charlene added. "That was about twelve."

Grandfather Ames pulled at his mustache. "And the boy was with me all morning, then I lost sight of him just after the wedding."

"I seen him," Virgil put in. "He was bringing up some bottles from the cellar. I told him to get cleaned up 'cause he had dust all down his front."

"And it's almost three o'clock now," Brent said. "They can't have gotten very far. We'll find them."

Virgil glanced at the kitchen clock. "I better go downtown and telegraph my brother that we won't be coming in for a couple more days."

"Has the train gone already?" Charlene asked, checking the clock too. The hands stood at ten of three.

"No, but we'll never make it now. And I know you. You'll stay until those kids are found."

"You don't mind?"

His eyes softened. "Of course I don't."

Brent said, "There's enough of us to search every road. Mr. Ames, you go get your horses from Wendleman's farm. Head out toward Buckeysville. Virgil, can you take your wagon down toward New Columbus after you send your telegram?"

The men nodded and instantly dispersed. Charlene went with Virgil. Mrs. Manning said, "I'm going to wait here, in case they come back. But Mr. O'Dell and his sons can cover the east and west roads."

"Sure as you know," Mr. O'Dell said. "We'd be pleased."

Alone with Brent, Bethany wiped her eyes. This was no time to be emotional. Her fear seemed to lend her energy. "What about us?" she said, looking up at him.

His fingertips brushed her cheek. "That's my girl. You and I will search the town."

"You don't think they went back to that dreadful house?"

"They might have. It was their home. We'll look, but I doubt they'd be foolish enough to go to the one place we'd be sure to look."

"You should have said something before. We could have ridden in with Charlene and Virgil."

"It's better if we walk. We might see something that we'd miss from the back of a wagon."

As they walked to town, Brent had to keep slowing her down. "There's no point in exhausting yourself. Faye has had plenty of experience in caring for Dory. They'll be all right until we find them."

"Does that thought make *you* feel any better?" she asked, pressing on.

"Not really. I can't imagine why they'd run away. Unless they were concerned about our marriage."

"I think Faye was worried about it," Bethany said. "She asked me some very strange questions yesterday."

"What questions?"

"Things like . . . do mothers with a lot of babies love one better than another? She wanted to know if mothers ever forgot their children after the children move away."

"What did you tell her?"

"I tried to say the right things but I'm not a mother, no matter what some people think. It may be different when you have children of your own." She stopped in the middle of the dusty road to say, "You don't think *I* made them run away, do you?"

She saw the struggle on his face as he was torn between

telling her the truth or a comforting lie. "Oh, my God," she said, turning to march on. "How could I be so stupid!"

"Bethany, you couldn't have known they were planning this! Don't go blaming yourself!"

Taking strides as long and as fast as her hampering skirts would allow, she said, "We have to find those children and tell them that it doesn't make any difference to us. And if Faye doesn't want us to get married because she's afraid of losing my love, then I'll find another way to keep them with me."

"No!" Brent all but shouted. He caught her arm and forced her to stop. "No, we're getting married no matter what. We'll convince Faye and Jerry, and Dory too if we have to, that there's enough love in our hearts for a hundred kids. But don't promise not to marry me to make them happy."

"What difference does it make?" she asked, looking into his eyes. He'd come out without his hat. The cool October breeze stirred his hair, moving the hank that had fallen across his brow, giving him a formidable look.

"What difference . . . ?"

"You're only marrying me to keep them out of the orphanage and because . . . because there's this . . . this awareness between us."

"Oh, yes. There is. And if I wasn't in such a hurry, I'd show you just how strong that 'awareness' is. It's so strong we could even call it love."

"Don't." She put up her hands to stop him. He bluffed too well; she might find herself believing him.

"Don't what? Don't tell you I love you? I do, and I expect your relatives to jump out from behind that bush in a body and stop me before I can say another word but the devil with it! I love you."

"You don't have to tell me that. I'm going to marry you for several good and sufficient reasons. We don't need to pretty it up with a lot of words we don't mean."

"Damn it, I've been trying to tell you I love you for days!"

A little fountain of joy began to bubble through the swamp of worry and fear that engulfed her. He wouldn't be so rude unless he meant it. "Word of honor?" she asked shyly.

"Damn it, I'll prove it. . . ." Throwing out his hands to grab her to him, he looked black when she skipped back out of reach.

"I want your word of honor that you love me. Otherwise, how will I know you're telling the truth?"

"You're just going to have to trust me on this one."

As his arms slid about her, Bethany said, shivering, "Brent, we don't have time . . ."

"Haven't you noticed? Time stands still when we kiss."

Bethany learned then that words didn't matter. Whether he ever said it again or not, she'd always know that he loved her. But she hoped, as her arms stole around his neck, that he would say it and often.

When they moved apart, they stared giddily into each other's eyes. "See," he said, "time did stand still. Nothing's changed."

"Everything's changed."

He acknowledged that truth with an inclination of his head. "Bethany, aren't you forgetting something?"

"The children!" She started forward again, but he caught her skirt and pulled her back.

Taking her hand, he said, "No. Now I want you to say it to me. I've been waiting a long time to hear it."

Suddenly shy, Bethany looked down at their linked hands. "Brent, I . . ."

"Mr. Houston! Oh, Mr. Houston!" The faint, sharp cry carried to them clearly.

He swore vehemently. Bethany couldn't agree with his methods but she was in perfect accord with his feelings. She finished her sentence but her words were lost in the repetition of that piercing call. "Oh, Mr. Houston!"

"Who is that? A crazy woman?"

The figure flourished a scarf in the air, hurrying forward, sometimes tripping over her long skirt. "It's Miss Ivey, I think," Bethany answered. "Maybe she's seen the children!"

Bethany straightened her back as she let the knocker of Mrs. Tubb's front door fall. Even knowing that Brent waited around the corner of the large wraparound porch didn't make her feel less nervous. After a moment she knocked again, hearing the noise echoing off the polished surfaces inside.

She turned her back to the white-painted door and said loudly, "Nobody home!"

The door opened. "Bethany, what are you doing?"

"Oh, Mrs. Tubbs! I . . ." Her heart pounded from surprise. She grasped at the tail end of the speech she'd prepared. "I . . . I've come to apologize."

"Apologize?"

For the first time that Bethany could remember, Mrs. Tubbs did not present a picture of her usual pristine self. Wisps of hair sprang loose from her restrained knot and her simple waist and skirt were skewed. Her dark eyes squinted as though she had a thundering headache too.

"Yes," Bethany said. "It's been bothering me that I was so rude to you. I had no right and I'm sorry."

Mrs. Tubbs blinked, perhaps taken aback by the abject humility with which Bethany apologized. "That's all right," she said. "Everyone makes a mistake sometime."

"I'm hoping you'll allow me to rejoin your Spiritual Cleanliness movement."

"I'm sorry. That's impossible."

Bethany allowed her face to fall. "Oh, please. I'm going to be so lonely now that Charlene's gone. If I could join a really worthwhile group—give myself something important to work toward like Spiritual Cleanliness . . ."

"Charlene was a sweet girl. Did she catch her train? I didn't see Mr. Emmett's wagon pass by."

"Yes, they made it but with only moments to spare. Why can't I join?"

"Really, Bethany, a nice girl wouldn't ask for an explanation."

Bethany didn't know how long she could stand being condescended to. She wondered if Brent had managed to find an open window by now. Once again, she dropped her gaze meekly. "If I knew why, I could work to correct my faults."

"Well, if you must know . . . I could never allow someone who is tangled up with a man like Brent Houston to pollute our league."

"Oh, you don't have to worry about that. We're all through."

"Through?"

"Completely! You were right about him."

Magic words! There are no words more flattering than "you were right." The average person could listen for days to that theme being developed.

"I was?" Mrs. Tubbs said, stepping back.

Bethany took instant advantage, entering the house, though her instructions were to keep Mrs. Tubbs talking at the front door while Brent searched the large white mansion. But Bethany reasoned it would be harder for Mrs. Tubbs to close the door in her face if she was on the right side of it.

"Yes, absolutely right," she said. "He's nothing but a rum seller, interesting only in ruining men's bodies and souls to line his pockets. I could never marry a man so irresponsible."

"No good could come of it," Mrs. Tubbs agreed. "A woman needs a quiet, steady man, someone she can mold, guide, and direct."

"Exactly my feeling. And of course, I really don't know about Mr. Houston. What his background is, for instance. Who knows what sort of people his parents might have been."

"As I always say, if the race is to thrive, we must stop

marrying questionable men. The quality of America is to be found in her women."

"Exactly. You're very wise. And if a woman goes astray, you are right to rebuke her. I'm glad you opened my eyes. I'd hate to bring shame on Cedar Groves by marrying badly." Bethany saw that this was the right way to talk to Mrs. Tubbs. The other woman became expansive under these ladles of cream.

"Tell me," Bethany said. "Is Spiritual Cleanliness a national organization, like the Women's Christian Temperance Movement?"

"Not yet," Mrs. Tubbs confessed. "But Dr. T. Elliot Farrar founded the movement in Cleveland. He's a doctor *and* a minister, you know."

"Fancy!" Bethany exclaimed. Where was Brent?

"He's begun a small community there, drawing highly intelligent young men and women from all over the country. He screens them for past defects and decides whether each person should marry. Then he chooses their mates for their complementary qualities. He writes to me. We are spiritually linked, you know. Would you like some pamphlets?"

"Oh, please." Very eagerly, Bethany said, "Please tell me more about Dr. . . . Dr. Farrar . . . How did he . . . ?" But not all her assumed interest could cover up the sound of a baby crying, a cry she instantly recognized.

"Excuse me," she said politely to Mrs. Tubbs. She walked past her and put her foot on the first step of the curving staircase that came down into the hall.

"Bethany Forsythe, don't you dare go up there without asking permission!" Mrs. Tubb's shoes rattled over the hardwood floor of her mansion. "I've never seen anything so rude! Your mother would be ashamed of you!"

"I doubt it." Bethany hurried up the stairs, leaving Mrs. Tubbs looking about her in frustration. As she reached the landing, she glanced back to see Mayor Tubbs, arrived at last, brought by Miss Ivey.

"Brent?" Bethany called. She began to work her way down the hall, following Dory's cry.

"It's all right. They're here."

He came out of a doorway, Dory in his arms. Bethany flew down the hall to see for herself. "Is she all right?" she said loudly.

"Fine and dandy. She started to cry when I woke her up. Faye's here too. I think she's drunk something. She seems sleepy."

Bethany went in. Mrs. Tubb's own room, obviously, overwhelmed by grand furniture. She would have guessed it by the air of cold severity, even without the sternly gray pamphlets scattered with open pages through the room, revealing lurid representations of drunkard's brains, broken homes, and downward paths to moral turpitude.

Bethany put her hand on Faye's smooth forehead. "She feels warm. Wake up, Faye, wake up." She shook her gently. Turning to Brent she said, "Where's Jerry?"

"I haven't found him yet. But the things that are missing from Marmion House are here. She must have packed the bag for them."

"Bethany?" said a tiny voice.

Bethany helped Faye to sit up. "You're all right now."

"I feel sick. The room's going 'round and 'round."

"Perfectly natural. Close your eyes and you'll feel better." She let the girl lean against her side, keeping an arm around her. Looking at Brent, who joggled the baby trying to comfort her, Bethany said, "Find a glass of water, please."

Miss Ivey came into the room and took the baby from Brent. "There, there, little one. There, there." She smiled up at him as the baby quieted. "I've always had a knack with children. There's a water bottle in that cabinet, Mr. Houston."

"What's going on downstairs?" Bethany wanted to know.

"Mayor Tubbs is storming and Eugenia is crying. I'm afraid she's always been a sadly disappointed woman."

With a word of thanks for Brent, Bethany helped Faye sip

some water. "Just rest, dearest. We'll take you home in a few minutes." To Brent she said, "Hold her hand. I'm going downstairs a moment."

"What for?"

"To ask Mrs. Tubbs what she has done with our son." In answer to his grin, she said defensively, "Well, he is, isn't he? More or less?"

With nervously working hands, Mrs. Tubbs pleaded her case. "But, Tommy, I only wanted things to be different! With Spiritual Cleanliness as our watchword who knows how far we could go?"

"Go? I don't want to go anywhere!" Mr. Tubbs paced, his gaitered feet looking strangely small beneath the vast width of his waistcoat.

"But with the women behind you, you could be governor. That's what you wanted."

"When I was a boy, Eugenia. When I was a boy, I had big dreams. Now I'm happy being mayor, but I can't be that anymore once this gets out. Kidnapping kids to send 'em to an orphanage! I'll be lucky if *I* vote for me come November! I won't even be able to run."

"Oh, no," his wife said, her voice rising in real fear. "You won't take that away from me, Tommy. You couldn't take that away from me."

"It won't be me, Eugenia. It'll be the voters."

"Excuse me," Bethany said, finding a chance at least to break in.

Just as if his wife weren't sobbing her heart out on her red plush settee, Mr. Tubbs switched on a smile. He came over, his large hands, their backs covered with reddish hair, outstretched. "Miss Bethany . . . I've hardly had a minute to see you, what with the press of town business. I do hope you won't let this little unpleasantness . . ."

Bethany managed to avoid having her hands clasped. "Mayor Tubbs, I simply want to know where Jerry Windom is."

"Certainly, certainly. Tell her, Eugenia."

"I don't know," Mrs. Tubbs said wearily. "I don't know."

"Eugenia." Mr. Tubb's voice came heavy with warning.

"I don't know," she repeated, more stridently. "I only managed to find the two littlest ones. I gave the girl a little tonic in a glass of water. It made her sleepy and I carried her here. The baby was easy."

"Why did you take clothes for them?"

"They would need things at the orphanage. The state can't provide *everything*. They haven't got the budget."

"What about Jerry?"

"He is too big to drug and carry. I was going to get him to come to the house by telling him his sisters were here. But I couldn't find him."

Bethany told Brent Mrs. Tubb's story. "And I believe her."

"But that still leaves us with the problem of where Jerry's got to."

"I know," Faye said, struggling weakly to sit up. "He went to the saloon. Mr. Ames didn't have any more whiskey for the punch bowl when Aunt Charlene brought out a new batch."

"Grandfather didn't say . . ."

"Jerry wanted to surprise him."

"But why hasn't he come back yet? He's had time to walk between the Golden Lady and home half a dozen times." Bethany surprised Brent looking oddly grim. "What is it?" she asked in an undertone.

"Let's get these girls home, Bethany. Then I'm going to the Golden Lady."

Half an hour later Bethany and Brent stood in the gathering dusk behind the saloon, softly arguing. "I'll give you your own way on anything in the world. You can paint our bedroom in mint-green stripes or shave my head, but you are not going in there with me."

"Yes, I am." She'd been saying it for the past half hour. Brent had been getting more and more eloquent as his frustration mounted.

"You might get hurt."

"We're wasting time."

"No, *you're* wasting it," he said angrily. "I could have been in there already."

"You're right," she said, having learned the power of that phrase. While he blinked, dazzled by her seeming submission, she said, "So let's go."

She started forward. He caught her back and hissed violently, "At least stay behind me, for God's sake."

Just then, above their heads, a window smashed, a glass globe flying out. Fragments of glass spangled the air. Bethany hid her eyes against the arm of Brent's coat as a shrill shout broke in the air as thoroughly as had the paperweight. "Help! Help! Please, somebody . . ."

The voice cut off abruptly. Bethany couldn't be sure if she'd heard a groan or not.

Bethany knew Brent didn't spare her a second thought as he charged in the rear door of his saloon. Someone had already broken the lock.

He hurried through the storage rooms. Bethany, less familiar with the layout, moved more slowly. A small window behind her would have let in more light if someone hadn't papered it over. She knocked over some empty bottles in the narrow passageway. They rattled and clinked with the soulless chatter of their kind.

Instinctively, Bethany shushed them. She left them and stumbled on, barking her shin on something knobby and almost tripping over something that seemed to skitter under her feet. "Brent?" she called softly. "Where are you?"

She groped her way to the wall and began to feel around for a door. She knocked something off a shelf. By the echoing sound of it when it hit the bottles, it had been a tin pot.

At last, just when panic was being to wash over her, she found the door. It swung on its hinges and Bethany pushed through. It was lighter here. Light enough to see the gun a very ugly man held in his fist, pointed at her heart.

"Ah thought there was a herd o'buffler in there," he said. He looked entirely ordinary, the sort of man who might go anywhere and pass unnoticed. The only thing slightly remarkable about him were the high-laced boots he wore with his pant legs tucked into the top. "Who you?"

"I . . . uh . . . work for Mr. Houston."

"A fancy piece, huh? My, you're a purty little thang."

"Thank you. Would you mind pointing that somewhere else, Mr. . . . Mr. . . . ?"

"Jist cawl me Sugar, girlie. 'Swhat all the girls call me."

"Mr. Sugar. That gun is making me very nervous."

"Don't see ya shakin'. 'Sall right, though. Soon as my partner's done up there . . . hey, what's keepin' ya, Slim?"

"Slim's met with an accident," Brent said from the stairs. "Bethany, *why* couldn't you have stayed outside?"

"How's Jerry?"

"He's had a bang on the head, but he's otherwise fine. He was sincerely disappointed to learn that the 'whiskey' in my decanter is nothing of the sort."

"Grandfather would have been a lot more disappointed. It would have spoiled all his fun." She started toward the stairs, to see to Jerry, when a drawling voice called her back.

"Uh-uh. Not so fast, girlie."

From above their heads, Brent's voice lashed down. "Touch her and I'll shoot you now."

Bethany turned. The man with the gun stood with one arm reached out toward her, as though he wanted to take her around the neck.

"You ain't fast enough," the man said.

"Yes, I am," Brent answered. "I can shoot the pips out of a playing card flipped in the air. I can whip the eye out of an Indian-head penny as it spins. I can shoot that gun out of your hand and drill you through the heart before your finger can close on the trigger."

"Yer bluffin'."

"Maybe," Brent allowed. "Put down the gun."

Bethany felt like the last leaf on a tree branch, clinging by the merest thread to safety. The lightest breeze could bring her fluttering to the earth. She held on to the strong, confident sound of Brent's voice, though she was unable to take her eyes from the tiny black hole pointed at her head.

Brent said, "I'm going to count to five. Put the gun down or I'll shoot it out of your hand."

"That ud be mighty fancy shootin'." But the outlaw's voice had begun to quaver. He had to clear it before he could force out the bravado. Spitting, he missed the cuspidor by a good three feet.

"Now, you realize, of course," Brent said with even more assurance, "that there's a chance I'll miss the gun and hit your hand instead. The angle's a little off from up here. Have you ever been shot in the hand? They say there's no pain more severe. All the nerves are there in your palm. Once you sever them, there's no way to put them back. You'll lose the use of that hand."

The tiny black hole began to shake before Bethany's eyes.

"That would be a pity." Brent clicked his tongue against the roof of his mouth. "And you're right-handed too. Oh, well. One . . . two . . . put the gun down . . . three . . . four . . ."

Twenty-three

❦

This was supposed to have been his wedding night, Brent reflected as he sat in the deep armchair in the drawing room at Marmion House. By now, he should have made his beloved his own, clasping her in her arms. But no, here he sat alone by the fire.

Jerry and Mr. Ames, who might have rallied 'round at this moment, had decided to go off on a fishing trip, to catch the last of the good weather. Mayor Tubbs, full of apologies and sincerities, had come and gone, hinting at a seat on the town council anytime Brent wanted it. Mrs. Tubbs was visiting relatives in St. Louis for what was described as "a long-planned trip." Even Virgil had taken his wife to spend the night at his old farm, the future site, perhaps, for the Autumn Fires Pottery Company.

Listening to the silence, for Marmion House was so solidly built that the noises from upstairs couldn't penetrate this sanctum, Brent resolved to get himself a dog. At least, he'd have some companionship.

The door opened. Brent didn't even bother to raise his eyes.

Mrs. Manning said, "Oh, you're here. Have you seen the sewing I was doing? A shirt for the boy."

"No, I haven't."

She peered at him. "You look a little down in the mouth. Something wrong?"

He just glanced at her, speakingly.

"You might as well get used to it," she said heartily. "With any luck, you'll be living like this for years!"

He sighed. "That's hardly possible, unless circumstances alter."

She chuckled as she tidied the room. "Go on, it can't last forever. Sooner or later, Dory will go to sleep and then you won't have anything to worry about."

Brent asked, "Are you going to marry Mr. O'Dell?"

"I haven't decided," she said proudly. "Maybe I will; maybe I won't. I'll tell you one thing though, I won't be here when the next bride comes through that door."

"You mean after Bethany . . . ?"

"Of course I don't. I mean that there Miss Ivey. Oh, she's a sly one!"

"Miss Ivey?" Brent scratched his head. "Why would she ever come as a bride to this house?"

"Didn't you see her in church today? Making eyes at him as though he weren't old enough to be her father!"

He hadn't noticed much in church. He'd been too busy thinking that this was where he was getting married today to notice anyone else. But he grasped at a vague memory of Mr. Ames and Miss Ivey standing together talking for some time after the service.

"Oh, she's sly," Mrs. Manning said again. "If she wants him, she'll have him, mark my words. And then she'll be livin' it up as the mayor's wife, which is what she wanted all 'long if I'm any kind of judge."

"But the election's next month. There's not enough time . . ."

"We have elections every four years. Do you think she can't wrangle enough votes his way in four years? She's been Mrs. Tubb's right hand since the Deluge, and she knows every woman with any 'fluence in this town. He'll be mayor before he's sixty-five and you can pay me five dollars cash when it happens."

"It's a bet," he said.

"Here it is!" She pulled out a shirt from behind a cushion

on the settee. "I forgot I shoved it there when Hiz Honor called. I'm going to make a pot of tea; you want any?"

"No, thank you."

"Well, suit yourself. I sure hate to see a grown man moping around like a lost hound dog."

"Look . . ."

"I know, I know. You reckon you got cause. But there's ways and means if you know what I mean. I'll be in the kitchen if anybody needs me."

After she left, Brent walked to the first landing of the staircase. He could still hear a lullaby, a little off-key now at this the thirty-second time through. As he hesitated, not sure if going up to volunteer to take over was a good idea or not, Mr. O'Dell slipped into the hall. "Psst!" he said, making Brent look down.

Mr. O'Dell sketched a salute. "It's all done we are now," he said in a low voice like a conspirator. "My gals have glossed the place till it looks fit for a queen."

"Thanks, Tully."

"Er, and speaking o'queens, where . . . ?"

"She's in the kitchen, making tea."

"Tea!" He licked his lips. "Good night, Brent, and—er—all the best of fortune shine on you."

The softly buzzing lullaby had ceased. He had time to draw three breaths as the gaslight in the nursery was slowly, slowly turned down to a dim glow. A woman in a white wrapper came out, closing the door behind her with endlessly painstaking care. She listened, her ear pressed to the panel. Then her shoulders slumped in relief.

"Is she asleep?" Brent hissed.

Bethany startled, jumping around and only just keeping back the exclamation that rose in her throat. Glaring at him, she hurried along the passage, the train of her bridal peignoir floating behind her. "Yes." She nodded. Putting her finger to her lips, her eyes told him in horrid detail what would happen to him if he woke the baby.

He put his hand over hers where it lay on the banister rail. "Come on," he said on a breath.

She didn't speak, just opened her eyes wide.

Swinging wide his arm, he pointed down the stairs.

She drew back, shaking her head. Touching the lace-encrusted yoke of her new robe, she mimed the impossibility of leaving the second floor so inadequately dressed.

"Don't argue," he growled.

With a glance over her shoulder at the closed nursery door, she followed him, knowing that a voice raised to even a whisper might be enough to wake Dory.

On reaching the hall, she said, still in a low tone, "I never knew teething could make such a difference to a baby. I thought she was going to scream herself blue."

"But you think she'll sleep on, now?"

"She's exhausted, poor little mite. Me too." She looked at her new husband, at his grim expression, his strong forearms revealed by his turned-up sleeves, and above all at the silver striped waistcoat he'd worn to their wedding. "I'm sorry," she started to say.

His head jerked. "I'm sorry . . . what did you say?"

"It's just this isn't much of a wedding night."

"Not yet."

She drew back a little. "But . . ."

"Are you thinking about the . . . accommodations?"

"Accommodations?"

"The beds, Bethany," he said with an edge to his tone.

"Well, yes, I am." Bethany felt a slow wave of heat washing into her cheeks. Perhaps she was revealing too much knowledge or, worse still, eagerness. But it was hard to pretend to be totally ignorant.

"You have a point," he said. "The bed I've been using isn't big enough for two, and Faye's in yours tonight because of the baby. But there are other rooms. Charlene's . . ."

"I couldn't . . ."

"Your grandfather's or Jerry's . . ." At each suggestion,

her expression betrayed her feelings. He nodded as though at some decision taken. "Okay," he said.

She sighed in relief. The sad truth was, that now she came to it, she was frightened. It seemed like such a very strange thing to do. Try as she might to keep busy during the last few days, pictures of the night to come kept filling her head. She could imagine being in the same room with Brent, even kissing him and enjoying the pleasures they'd known up till now. But when it came to turning down the gas and taking off her clothes, her imagination closed down.

She felt a slight breeze stirring the fine muslin of her nightclothes. Looking around, she saw that the big front door stood slightly ajar.

"Okay," he said again. "I agree. We can't be together here."

"No," she said, walking to the door.

Before she could close it, he bent and swept her off her feet. As he tossed her lightly up to settle her more securely, she clasped her arms around his neck. "Brent!"

"Hush. Don't wake the baby."

He carried her outside, pushing the door farther open with his foot. "Where are you taking me?" she demanded. "I'm not dressed!"

"You are a noisy little thing tonight. It must be catching."

"Brent, this is outrageous!"

She heard the firm snick of the front door shutting behind them as he carried her down the walk. Looking back, she saw Manny waving out of the sidelight window. "At least the children won't be alone," she said.

"I'm an excellent strategist," Brent bragged.

"Not really. You have to put me down sometime."

"True. But I hope to persuade you to stick around."

He kissed her. Holding her securely under the knees and around the back, he couldn't move his hands but nevertheless when he went on walking, she rested somewhat more tractably against his shoulder.

When he passed the gate, however, she said, "Brent, you

can't go into the street! I'm in my nightie for goodness' sake!"

"Don't worry. If there's a town ordinance against it, I'll pay your fine."

He carried her half a block before she asked on a ripple of laughter, "Aren't I getting heavy?"

"Light as a feather . . ."

"No, I'm not. And you're beginning to blow like a whale."

"I am not!" he said, hefting her up. "Besides, a groom is supposed to carry his bride over the threshold."

"But few thresholds are a block wide. Where are we going, anyway?"

"Our house," he said, balancing her awkwardly in order to fumble with the latch of a white-picket fence.

Bethany looked at the house, gleaming white under the rising moon. The steeply sloped roof, the funny little hooded balcony that stood out from the attic level, the triple window over the front porch, were all familiar to her, but as though she remembered them from a dream. Whole glass reflected the moon's glow and the roof lacked not a single shingle.

"But this is the Trumbull place!" she exclaimed as he swept up the front steps and thrust open one side of the double door.

"No, it isn't. It's the Houston place."

"The . . . ?"

He carried her over the threshold and set her down, making some production out of wiping his brow. Yet she wasn't fooled. The big smile crinkling his eyes gave him away.

"Nobody's lived her for years," she said, inhaling the fragrance of new paint as if it were incense. "It's not grand enough for Upper Grove anymore but I've always loved it. Did Charlene tell you I always dreamed of living here?"

"No. I bought it three years ago," he said solemnly. "I thought if I ever got married and wanted to settle down respectably, this would be the house I'd want to bring a bride to. It sounds kind of foolish and sentimental, I guess, but the first time I saw it, I thought I could be happy here. With the right someone."

He tilted her face toward him, gazing at her in the insubstantial light that flooded every room. "I thought the first time I saw you that you were the one for me, Bethany. I couldn't live here with anyone else."

She reached out her arms to him, feeling magic pulsing in her fingers. They kissed for a long time, standing in the hall, the dreams they'd created for themselves alone merging into a shared whole.

Brent whispered, "I think I'm drunk on your kisses."

"I'm pretty light-headed my . . . ooh!"

She opened her eyes as he nibbled his way down her neck, her body beginning to shake with pleasure. There was a faint glow coming from the top of the stairs. She said softly, "You must have been working like dogs the last few days to get this place ready."

"Mr. O'Dell and his sons are invaluable. But never mind that . . ."

Bethany gripped his shoulders as his hands began to weave spells on the surface of her gown. She began to wonder if they were going to spend the whole night in the foyer, but didn't know how to suggest they move elsewhere.

"Your lace tickles my nose," he said, chuckling deep in his chest. He treasured the sound of her sighs, sealing each one away in his memory book for the long hours he'd be forced to spend away from her by work and outside responsibilities.

"Brent?" He'd found the small buttons on the lace front of her nightrobe, but hadn't yet begun to unfasten them. She could feel the heat of his hands through the fabric and longed to feel them on her skin. "Brent? Did you finish any rooms besides this one?"

A flight of steps later, he opened the door to the bedroom

on the second floor with a proud sweep of his arm. "My lady's boudoir," he said.

Bethany stepped in. The October chill could not compete with the fire in the hearth. Around the bed, the whole room was shimmering with the light of a dozen candles. The flickering light caught the golden gleam of the intricate brass bed and made the brilliant red of the silken coverlet glow.

"I recognize this," she said, letting her fingers drift over the cool material. "It's from your apartment."

Brent leaned against the door, letting her accustom herself to this room. "Do you mind?" he asked tenderly. "That it's from the Golden Lady? You see, I've imagined you on it so many times when I'd lie in bed unable to sleep from wanting you. I can throw it on the floor if it bothers you."

"No," she said softly. "It doesn't bother me." Her gaze met his for a moment, then flicked away. "Don't look at me like that," Bethany pleaded, suddenly shy.

The idea of him lying awake with thoughts of her in his head, hot, wild thoughts, started an answering heat bubbling inside of her. If he looked at her with that raw hunger, he might see that the feeling was in her as well. What would he think of her then?

"How should I look at you? I've told you before you're the most beautiful woman I've ever seen. You'll have to forgive me if I stare."

"I'm not . . ." she said, instinctively deflecting the compliment.

"I'll be the judge of that." His shoulders came off the door in a kind of a lunge, but at the last moment he controlled himself. Give her time, he counseled his hot blood. His wisdom let him take her hand without going insane, though the turbulent longing in his soul demanded her heart.

Exerting all his self-control, he said, "We don't have to . . ."

"I'm scared," she whispered. "Will you hold me?"

"Of course, you're scared. New things are frightening. But I won't let any harm come to you. You're the most precious thing in my life."

"I am?" He felt the warmth of her breath against the sensitive skin of his neck and started counting silently to a hundred.

"Yes," he said, and had to clear his throat. "Listen, do you remember the first day we met?"

"You . . . kissed me."

"Yes. I couldn't help it. You were so defiant and so dear. I fell like a sack of potatoes from the back of a truck wagon."

"You fell? I didn't see . . ."

"I fell in love with you, Bethany. At first sight."

"Oh!"

He loved that tiny intake of breath she gave whenever some new thought illuminated her mind. He'd heard it often, but it never failed to tickle his heart.

Wrapping his arms around her securely, he embraced her without pushing to make any flame start within her. "We don't have to do another thing but this, Bethany."

Brent felt the pressure of her small strong hands against his chest, slowly trying to put some distance between them. For a moment his arms tightened as if of their own free will. Brent quickly realized however that this was not the way to assuage her fears.

Bethany stepped toward the highly carved oak vanity in the corner of the room. A celluloid toilet set lay there, all fitted up in a plush velvet case, complete from hairbrush to salve box. "You've thought of everything."

"Manny's gift," he said, never taking his eyes off her.

She sat on the padded bench and lifted her hands to her hair, still in a neatly plaited mass of curls at the back of her head. One by one, she began to remove the pins that held her wedding-day hairdressing together.

The long strands of her hair fell to surround her shoulders. She reached out and picked up the brush and began to drag it through the silken weight. All the time, she kept darting glances at him in the mirror.

"Bethany," he all but groaned. "Do you have any idea what you're doing to me?"

Her full lips took on a new fascinating curve. "Oh, yes," she said, surprising him. "Oh, yes."

She stood up, still moving with that easy, languid grace as though she wanted to infinitely extend each moment. Tilting up her chin, she shook her head slightly, setting the brown and copper glory of her long hair swinging with a hushing rustle over her back. Brent's mouth went dry. He hadn't any idea she could be so sensual. He'd seen it in her innocently, but now he saw she possessed a woman's full awareness.

One by one, her eyes still holding his, Bethany slipped the buttons free on her robe. The thin muslin slid friction-lessly to the ground. Underneath, she wore another gown, also of muslin, also lace-embellished. But this one left her arms bare, golden in the candlelight. Her beautiful neck and shoulders rose above the deep inset of lace that dipped down into her cleavage.

She laughed delightedly at the look on his face. "Charlene said you'd probably like this one best."

"You discussed this with Charlene?"

"Why not? You obviously have been planning with Manny and Mr. O'Dell. Besides, Charlene and I always promised each other that whoever got married first would tell the other all about it." She looked at him with her sparkling eyes. "You're not angry?"

"No. So you know all about it?"

She nodded. "It sounds awfully odd. But Charlene looked . . . I don't know . . . not different exactly, but older?"

"What else did Charlene say?"

She blushed and once again failed to meet his eyes. "That the first time wasn't easy."

Walking the few steps to take her into his arms, Brent

sought in his mind for something to say to ease her maidenly fears. "I'd never hurt you willingly."

"I know. That's why I'm here. If I didn't trust you . . ." She raised her arms to lie loosely about his neck and tried to smile. "After all, I trusted you with my life. I'll never forget the way you bluffed that man into dropping his gun."

"Bluff? I'll have you know I'm every bit as good a shot as I said I was. If you like, I'll prove it."

She gnawed the edge of her lip. Then she said, "You have other things to prove tonight."

The red silk was cool under her body, but it took fire from her skin. In a moment he joined her there, his nakedness gloriously male. He'd left her nightgown on, but had kept nothing to conceal himself. Bethany let her eyes wander and couldn't keep her hands from following. The effect her touch had on him left her breathlessly amazed.

Brent groaned and rubbed his face against her hair. "Don't worry," he panted. "I won't break."

"I don't want to hurt you."

"I can stand it," he said through his teeth. But after a minute of sweet torture, he snatched her hand away and held it against his thundering heart. He kissed her almost ruthlessly and rejoiced when she met his ardor with her own.

Soon she was moving underneath him, mindlessly. Lifting away from her mouth, he said quietly, "Bethany, do you remember when I was in your room that night we celebrated Charlene's engagement? Do you remember my touching you, and how it felt?"

She nodded silently, her eyes tightly shut. "If that's what you want," she said. Brent was disappointed by the martyr-like quality of the words. But then she moved his hand from her shoulder to her hip and opened her eyes, smiling eagerly.

When the pressure inside her had spent itself, leaving her washed-up on some new shore and making him silent with awe, Bethany said, "Charlene didn't mention *that*."

Brent leaned his forehead against hers and chuckled silently, not sure if he was delirious or just unconscionably happy. "Let's not mention Charlene, Bethany. I've had enough of your friends and relatives for the time being."

"Me too. Brent . . . is it time?"

"You tell me." He lay over her, searching her face. She ran her hands down the strong columns of his back, either side of his spine. Lifting up, all the splendor of her body rising like a wave under him, she whispered one word.

"Just trust me, Bethany."

Perhaps there was a moment of pain but she couldn't feel it in the overwhelming joy that flooded her body and soul. The wonder of their joining went far deeper than mere pain or pleasure. Too caught up in the wonder of the moment to do more than clutch Brent tightly, Bethany seemed to catch a glimpse of something beyond the physical. She saw the pattern of her own private universe and knew she'd found the heart of it in Brent's arms. Then the physical reality caught up with them and whirled them both away.

Some time later, when the candles had burned down more than a few inches in their holders, Bethany awoke to Brent nuzzling her cheek. She lay inside the curve of his body, feeling his strength like a bulwark behind her.

Wriggling, she sighed softly to let him know she was awake. When his hand moved up from her stomach to brush lightly across her sensitized breasts, she moved more restlessly and her sigh was much more than a sigh.

"Do you still want to know why we were laughing at you that first evening?"

"Of course I do." But she wasn't really paying any attention, not with his warm fingers giving her so much delight.

"It's because I'd just asked your grandfather if it would be all right if I married you."

"What?" She lifted heavy eyelids to gaze at him, his face so close to her own. He nodded and lifted his eyebrows.

"Then they all knew all along. . . . Why didn't somebody tell me?"

"Are you mad?"

She thought about it. "No. I had to find you on my own. Love isn't something you can be helped into, like a carriage."

"I do love you, Mrs. Houston."

"I like the sound of that."

"Which part? The 'I love you' or the 'Mrs. Houston.'"

"All of it." She giggled but her breath caught. "Really, you have the most *talented* hands."

"Bethany," he said, his voice unwontedly serious. "I know it's a terrible risk to take. I mean, right now it's just you and me, but there must be a relative or a friend or the President waiting to spring out at us from a closet or somewhere. Nevertheless, I'm prepared to take a chance on it to hear . . ."

Carefully, she sat up and pushed her hair back, planning to tease him a little. The anxiety she saw on his face humbled her. Did he really have any doubt? Meeting his eyes, she said, "I agree the risk is terrible, but I'm a gambler now too, I suppose, if only by marriage. But just to be on the safe side, I'll whisper it."

Her breath tickled his ear. "I love you."

They lay in each other's arms for a long moment, listening hard. In their new house, silence echoed, broken only by the wind and the beating of two joined hearts.

"No relatives," Brent said at last. "Hallelujah."

Epilogue

Brent paced back and forth on the depot platform like a tiger longing to run away from a menagerie. Bethany watched him until she got tired. "Sit down, Brent. You won't make the train come any faster by walking every mile with it."

He came and sat beside her. But his fingers kept tapping on his thighs and his foot swung like a nervous pendulum. "It's late, isn't it?" he asked for the fourth time.

"No. We're early." She laid down her knitting in her lap and put her hand over his to still it. "It's going to be all right," she said with groundless optimism.

The rapturous beauty of a morning in mid May had no power to move them. In vain, the boughs of white dogwood and pink red-bud threw out their branching arms to embrace the blue sky. The two on the platform were fascinated only by the twin curves of steel rail disappearing around the bend to the west.

Bethany took up her knitting again, determinedly shaking out the knots that had magically appeared during the few seconds it lay on her lap. When Agnes Ivey had married Mr. Ames, one of the first tasks she'd undertaken, besides remodeling all the bathrooms in Marmion House, was teaching Bethany how to knit. It still remained for Bethany to manage on her own.

Though little Mitchell had come through his first winter without any things knitted by his mother, many other willing and skilled hands keeping him clothed, Bethany was committed to giving her son a sweater for his first birthday, one week before Christmas. At the rate she was going, Christmas would be here indeed before it was done. She didn't know what she had done with all her free time before she was married.

"Was that a train whistle?"

"I didn't hear anything," she said.

There'd been no answer to Brent's first telegram, or to the letters he'd written once he'd learned his parents were still living at the same address in their small California town. It wasn't until last December when he'd written again at Bethany's urging to tell of the birth of their son that he'd heard a word.

He said, "Are you sure you wouldn't rather wait inside?"

"I'd rather be with you." She smiled at him, loving him with all her heart. "And you're too restless to sit in there with me."

Lifting her hand, he kissed it. "What did I ever do to deserve you?"

"Whatever it was, don't do it again. I don't think you could handle two of me."

"Hmmm, handling two sounds pretty good to me." He glanced back to be sure the station manager's window blind was down. Then he stole his nimble hand to the placket of her blouse.

"Behave," she said in a low voice. But her severe tone was spoiled by a sigh. Bethany had been in such a swivet all week, preparing for this big day, plus Agnes had taken it into her head that *her* old house needed spring cleaning, that there'd been no time to indulge their passion for married pleasures.

"You know I'm good at being sneaky and underhanded," Brent said.

"I know." Most of their moments together were stolen. Adding another child to the family had cut even further into their precious free moments, especially as Mitchell had been weak in his first few months.

Now, of course, he was making up for lost time. Bethany claimed that his weight gain was due to all the spoiling the baby got from parents, grandparents, assorted friends, and Faye. The girl had confessed that while she loved Dory, what she'd wanted most of all was a baby brother. She was an extra pair of hands to Bethany but complained that there were too many people eager to help out when she wanted to take the responsibility herself.

"I should stop by the café before we go home," Bethany said. "Manny is going to attempt to roast a leg of lamb and I promised I'd be there to help."

"Tully O'Dell's a brave man. I never would have the courage to tell my new bride the day after I got married, 'Darling girl, you just can't cook.'"

"Aren't you glad you don't have to?" She sparkled at him. Then she said, "She cried when he told her that, you know. Then she came to me."

"And now she's roasting legs of lamb. And they say the age of miracles is past. Should we go there for dinner tonight?"

"Maybe not. She's made amazing progress. Business at the café hasn't fallen off at all, but I don't think we should. She might get flustered over such an important occasion."

Brent had calmed down during this chat. But now his eyes drifted again to the track and he juggled his foot up and down more vigorously than before. Maybe she shouldn't have been so discouraging when Agnes had suggested having the band there to greet the train. At least then Brent would have been keeping time to music.

Everyone had wanted to be there, from Grandfather Ames, longing to show off *his* bride, to Mayor Tubbs, eager to greet a potential voter.

But Bethany hadn't even brought along little Mitchell, feeling that this first meeting between Brent and his parents in almost twenty years would go more smoothly without distraction. Now she was beginning to wonder if she'd been wise. She had never seen Brent so discomposed since the day he'd saved her from "Mr. Sugar." She still recalled how Brent had wept with relief once he realized she was safe.

Putting down her knitting with care, Bethany let her mind drift over all the changes that had happened since that afternoon. Faye was growing up into a proper young lady, top of her class in math. Jerry had taken a sudden interest in architecture as the "Houston Place" was altered to accommodate a bigger family. He would be apprenticed to a firm in Sedalia, run by an old friend of Judge Carr's, next year to learn draftsmanship before going on to college. And Dory called her Mama and Brent Papa, filling them with delight as keen as though she were theirs by blood.

Mrs. Tubbs had come back from St. Louis with a planchette under one arm and books on spiritualism under the other. The spirits she raised satisfied her, if no one else. She still went to church, however, always mindful of her husband's position.

Under Agnes Ames's powerful leadership, Spiritual Cleanliness had raised enough money in three months to buy a church bell, specially cast just for Mr. Vance's steeple. Now the ladies were turning their attention to beautifying the town. Bethany herself was commissioned to head the committee to decide what kind of bulbs would look best in front of the jail. A war was already shaping up over daffodils versus tulips.

"That was a whistle! Don't you hear it?"

"No, I . . . wait." It was faint and far off, like the call of a bird high in the sky. "Yes, I think you're right."

The stationmaster's blind flew up with a spinning rattle. "That'll be her a-coming now, Mr. Houston."

"Thanks, Sam." Brent stood up, shaking out the legs of his trousers. Bethany ran her gaze over him as he took off his hat to comb his hair with his fingers. How could she still be so crazy in love with him? Some people said it was a scandal for a woman to worship her husband so obviously, saying ill-natured things like "Thou shall have no other gods before me." But Bethany figured that her love for Brent was God's gift to her and therefore He couldn't very well object.

Leaning forward, she gave a little tug to his coat. He glanced down, his thoughts on the train, but still sparing a smile for her. She said, "I love you, you know."

His smile grew wider, less absent. "How many times have we come to the station in the last few years? Seeing people off, receiving the machinery for the factory, sending off our first shipment . . ."

"Many, many times."

"Every time I come down here, I think about a blue-eyed girl scolding me for not taking better care of my pregnant 'wife.'"

"Did I tell you I had another letter from her? They've just had their second . . ."

"I remember the way you felt in my arms and how much I wanted to snatch you back aboard that train and carry you to the ends of the world."

"Sssh," Bethany said, aware of the open window blind.

But Brent took her hand and pulled her to her feet. "Haven't you noticed that every time I come home from the depot, I take you to bed?"

She glanced toward the window. Reassured that the stationmaster wasn't listening, she whispered, "Why do you think I send you down here so often?"

Locked in each other's arms, they didn't even notice the black and red locomotive glide into the station. Not until a great gout of steam smelling of hot iron was released from the brakes did they come back to a sense of where they were. Very aware of the stationmaster's grin as he appeared on the platform, Bethany turned to take up her knitting and stuff it into her bag.

"There they are," Brent said, taking her arm and turning her toward the cars.

She saw a little, thin woman with a veil to her hat stepping down, taking the porter's hand but talking vivaciously to the man who stood with his back to them. Then she looked past him and saw her son. Her sudden silence and the glow on her face must have alerted the man but he didn't turn until she was safe on the ground and the porter's tip was in his hand.

By then, Brent and Bethany were standing only a few feet away. His mother extended black-mittened hands to him, her pale brown eyes already overflowing. Then she glanced up into her husband's face and curled her hands in against her chest.

Bethany glanced between Brent and his father. They stood like a couple of monuments but with living eyes. Mr. Houston, though some inches shorter than his son, had broad shoulders and burly arms that his tweed suit could scarcely conceal. His hair was that pale blond that never seems to age until it turns white. In his face, a map of wrinkles and seams, two green eyes glowed against his farmer's tan.

"So," he said, crossing his arms on his chest. "You've decided to follow in my footsteps after all. What kind of luck are you having?"

"Some," Brent said laconically.

Bethany caught her mother-in-law's eye. In it, she saw the same laughter at the dear blockheads that she knew sparked in her own. Though it wasn't spoken aloud, the word "Men!" seemed to hover in the air.

Then Brent elaborated. "We've been asked by the state to send samples to the Paris Exposition next year."

"You'll be competing with my old firm, then. Know what you're sending yet?" His voice was deeper than Brent's, with a slight rasp from smoking. He'd never lost the liquid syllables of his native accent that were merely a hint in his son's words.

Brent glanced at Bethany who nodded encouragingly. "No, I don't know what we'll send. I was hoping you'd give me some advice."

Mr. Houston's lips twitched. Then, as if against his will, he smiled. At his elbow, his wife raised her eyes to heaven as though giving thanks. "I'll do better than that. I'll help you make it. And so can the others."

"Others?" Brent asked.

"You didn't think we'd come all this way alone?" His father took him by the arm and turned him around.

Bethany and Brent found themselves confronted by what looked like a sea of smiling faces. All three of his brothers were there, with wives and children. Both his sisters with nieces, nephews, and brothers-in-law he'd never met. Everyone held still for a moment and then, like a wave breaking on shore, there were laughter and tears, and embraces that included not only Brent and Bethany but the stationmaster until it was all straightened out.

Some stayed at the Marmion House, by prior arrangement between the elder Houstons and Mr. and Mrs. Ames. Others stayed at the home of the former Miss Ivey, so that Bethany understood why it had needed to be aired and cleaned. Bethany and Mrs. Houston were old friends by the time sundown came, the way smoothed by her mother-in-law's instant understanding that Mitchell was the most perfect baby under the sky.

In the cool green of the evening, when most of the children were asleep, Bethany sat in a circle of women, discussing everything from bean soup to whether a nude could ever be called "art." She found out that Brent's sister Louise could play the banjo and that his brother, Cliff, had his photography praised in a prestigious journal. Cooking seemed like small talent indeed beside this, until Mrs. Houston started sharing recipes.

Bethany had to wait a long time in bed before her husband appeared in the hall. Then she heard him go on talking to the older of his brothers, Vince, until the hands on their bedroom clock had moved on another fifteen minutes.

When the door opened, she was muffling a very fake yawn. "My goodness, I didn't think you were *ever* coming."

"I thought you'd be asleep by now."

Would she ever grow tired of the sight of him taking off his shirt? The soft gaslight modeled the muscles of his chest and back, even more highly sculpted now, thanks to his hard work. More than once in the past eighteen months had Brent himself picked up a shovel at the clay pit, more than once had he himself lifted machinery or lugged a tray of washed clay from one end of the factory to the other.

"Was your father impressed by the factory?" she asked, taking her hairbrush off the bedclothes. Lifting up the ends of her hair where it flowed over her left shoulder, she began to brush.

"You know, I think he was. Of course, he doesn't give much away."

"Your mother says he's happy."

"Then he must be." He yawned too, nothing feigned about it. "I can't believe they all came out. I never expected it. I swear I've talked more today than in a year!"

"You're tired?"

"Exhausted."

Bethany glanced down at herself. Her hair hid everything. Perhaps too much. As though she wasn't thinking about it at all, she flipped away the side of her hair that was brushed.

But Brent had turned aside to reach in the top drawer of the bureau. He frowned and pulled the drawer out farther. She said, somewhat breathlessly, "You know, I've been so busy the last couple of days that I think we don't have a clean nightshirt between us."

"That's okay," he said, taking a last look in the drawer.

It wasn't like Bethany to forget anything. All his brothers and brothers-in-law had commented, speaking out loud, or with a glance, on her looks; all his sisters and sisters-in-law had said something complimentary about the beauty of their home.

"Brent . . ."

He couldn't hide his grin any more when he turned around. Nor could he hide anything else. "Gee, I sure am tired," he said, then ducked as she shied a pillow at him.

After long slow kisses turned hot and wild, he said, "Do you really think you can be naked in our bed and me not notice the second I walk in the door? I don't care how long your hair is."

"What gave it away?"

"This," he said, kissing one pink tip. "And this," he added, tasting the other.

He heard the softly swelling cry break from her lips and instantly covered her mouth with his, drinking the sound. "Sssh," he whispered. "The walls have ears."

She nodded and tried to be silent. But when she pushed him back among the pillows and began to drive him slowly out of his mind, it was she who had to warn him about restraint.

It was useless. As the storm mounted in their souls, driving their bodies before it, silence was the last thing to be considered.

Bethany came back to herself with their cries still echoing in the air. The only thing that made her feel better was knowing Brent blushed just as hard as she did. Then they laughed. "God," he said, "we probably woke up the whole house. And it wouldn't be so bad . . . but my parents are right next door!"

"You know what your problem is, Brent?"

"What?"

Her smile held all the love in the world as she leaned over him to whisper, "You've got too many relatives."

Our Town

...where love is always right around the corner!

__*Take Heart* by Lisa Higdon

0-515-11898-2/$5.99

In Wilder, Wyoming...a penniless socialite learns a lesson in frontier life—and love.

__*Harbor Lights* by Linda Kreisel

0-515-11899-0/$5.99

On Maryland's Silchester Island...the perfect summer holiday sparks a perfect summer fling.

__*Humble Pie* by Deborah Lawrence

0-515-11900-8/$5.99

In Moose Gulch, Montana...a waitress with a secret meets a stranger with a heart.

If you enjoyed this book, take advantage of this special offer. Subscribe now and get a

FREE
Historical Romance

No Obligation (a $4.50 value)

Each month the editors of True Value select the four *very best* novels from America's leading publishers of romantic fiction. Preview them in your home *Free* for 10 days. With the first four books you receive, we'll send you a FREE book as our introductory gift. No Obligation!

If for any reason you decide not to keep them, just return them and owe nothing. If you like them as much as we think you will, you'll pay just $4.00 each and save at *least* $.50 each off the cover price. (Your savings are *guaranteed* to be at least $2.00 each month.) There is NO postage and handling – or other hidden charges. There are no minimum number of books to buy and you may cancel at any time.

Send in the Coupon Below

To get your FREE historical romance fill out the coupon below and mail it today. As soon as we receive it we'll send you your FREE Book along with your first month's selections.
